Philip Caveney, born ....
a two-year spell at ...., Manchester,
writing and presenting a weekly film review programme. He is a professional and freelance journalist,
and his previous novels include *The Sins of Rachel
Ellis*, *Tiger Tiger*, *The Tarantula Stone*, *Speak No
Evil* and *Black Wolf.* He lives with his wife and child
in Heaton Mersey.

Strip Jack Naked

Philip Caveney

First published in 1994
by HEADLINE BOOK PUBLISHING

First published in paperback in 1994
by HEADLINE BOOK PUBLISHING

A HEADLINE FEATURE paperback

10 9 8 7 6 5 4 3 2

ISBN 0 7472 4215 1

Printed and bound in Great Britain by
Cox & Wyman Ltd, Reading, Berks

HEADLINE BOOK PUBLISHING
A division of Hodder Headline PLC
338 Euston Road
London NW1 3BH

For Grace

'I was afraid, because I was naked; and I hid myself.'
Genesis 3:10

'As I was going to St Ives,
I met a man with seven wives,
Every wife had seven sacks,
Every sack had seven cats,
Every cat had seven kits:
Kits, cats, sacks, and wives,
How many were going to St Ives?'
Traditional

Prologue

It is always the same dream, exact in every detail.

The young woman strolls around the department store. She takes her time because she has the whole afternoon ahead of her. It is only a few weeks before Christmas and everything is lit up with garish neon colours. Lavish decorations hang from the ceiling, streamers and tinsel in shiny metallic shades, huge round balloons printed with smiling Santa Claus faces and every so often, a tall fir tree heavy with baubles and tissue-wrapped make-believe presents. Carols play from an unseen hi-fi system, the voices of choirboys, impossibly sweet and angelic as they work through all the popular tunes. The store is, of course, crowded with shoppers, many of them eager-faced children being shepherded about by their harassed parents.

The young woman is in her mid-twenties. Her name is Catherine and she has dark, shoulder-length hair, turquoise eyes and a full, nicely-shaped mouth. Many young men have kissed that mouth and told her she is beautiful but now, as far as she is concerned, there is only *one*

young man in her life. Catherine has lived with him for
over two years and she has come here today to buy him
a Christmas gift. He wants her to set a date for their
wedding, and she is thinking seriously about whether she
really wants to become Mrs Jack Doyle. She suspects
that, deep down, maybe she does.

Making her way to the aftershave counter, she
squeezes into a gap and selects a tester for a cologne
called *Tycoon*. She smiles, imagining Jack's face if she
were to present him with something with a name like
that. She sprays a little of the fragrance on to her wrist
and raises it to her nose, but she grimaces, shakes her
head. No, that one won't do at all, she doesn't want to
be enveloped by a smell like that when she's cuddled up
to Jack. Somehow it smells like it sounds – pompous,
over-bearing and shot full of testosterone. Now she tries
another cologne – this one's in an apple-shaped bottle
and it's called *Adam*. She sprays some on to her other
wrist and . . . yes, that's much more the kind of thing she
had in mind. It has a fresh, citrusy aroma that she thinks
Jack will like. Her mind is quickly made up, she's not
one to spend hours over a simple decision like this . . .

In his sleep, Jack urges Catherine to take more time,
to try some of the other fragrances. He wants to detain
her, keep her there safe in the crowded womb of the
department store, because he knows that a bad thing is
going to happen out on the street. But as he watches, a
helpless observer in the dream, she attracts the attention
of the sales assistant and makes her purchase. The
cologne is handed to her in a stylish little carrier bag

and she prepares to leave the store . . .

Jack cries out in his sleep and, miraculously, she seems to hear him, lifting her head to glance around, a look of surprise on her pretty face, the face that Jack sees so clearly in dreams but which he is unable to conjure up in the cold light of day. The music swells as the stereophonic choirboys hit the crescendo of *Ding Dong Merrily on High*. Catherine smiles, shakes her head. She is mistaken. She thought for a moment that somebody was calling her name. Turning from the counter she moves through the crowd to the exit. Jack watches her in mounting dread . . .

She is out on the street now. It is already dark and all the shop windows are a blaze of light. The air has a cold snap in it and her warm breath clouds as it leaves her mouth. She lifts the collar of her cashmere coat, pulls the belt a little tighter around her. By the store's entrance there's a busker, a dishevelled old man in a donkey-jacket and bobble hat. He's coaxing a discordant tune out of a wheezy accordion. His fingertips are blue and there's a dewdrop hanging from his nose. Catherine moves over to him and tosses a couple of coins into his accordion case, which lies open at his feet. They exchange smiles and Jack wants her to linger there a while, talk to the man, request a favourite tune, *anything*. If he can just disrupt the pattern of events for one moment, she will be safe and things will all be different.

But no, she turns away and moves on, along the busy pavement. And now there is the bus shelter. She sees it and steps into the glass and metal structure, gaining relief from the cutting edge of the wind. Behind Catherine, Jack can see one of the windows of the department store. It depicts a tableau from *Snow White and the Seven Dwarfs*, the scene where the heroine is discovered asleep in the dwarfs' cottage. The model dwarfs move their heads and arms mechanically, in a crude attempt to fill them with life, but their eyes remain blank and staring. Groups of entranced children are gathered at the window with their parents, enjoying the presentation. In the bus shelter, other people are arriving. Catherine reaches into her carrier bag and takes out the cologne, begins to read the writing on the box.

She does not see the bus coming into view on the other side of the road. Jack watches from his lair of dreams, knowing that there is nothing he can do. The bus is already out of control, the driver crumpled in his seat as he suffers a major coronary, the steering-wheel sliding through his twitching hands, his foot stamping involuntarily on the accelerator. The bus veers sharply to the right, crosses the road and heads towards the bus-stop, its headlights dazzling. Some of the people in the shelter see it coming and they begin to scatter. Catherine is still reading, her head down. It is only when she realizes that a powerful light is illuminating the small print that she senses something is wrong. She glances up in surprise, lifting one hand to shield her eyes from the glare.

Jack sees it happen in sickening slow-motion.

The bus mounts the pavement and strikes the shelter head on, tearing the flimsy structure out of the ground

4

and shattering the glass panes into a million flying fragments. For an instant, Catherine is like a figure in one of those glass domes with a blizzard of snow-like particles whirling around her. The front of the bus strikes her and she is lifted clear of the ground. She is carried across the pavement and smashed clear through the window of the department store, shards of heavy plate glass ripping into her clothing, her flesh. As Jack watches, sobbing, her body begins to come apart, arms tearing out of their sockets, legs bending at impossible angles, intricate patterns of blood hanging in the air like hideous decorations.

Of course, she is not alone. Other bodies come crashing headlong into Snow White's fantasy world. Shoppers and children are pulped to bloody rags of flesh by the grinding wheels of the bus; but they are merely moving shapes on the periphery of Jack's vision. He has eyes only for Catherine, *his* Catherine, the woman he has lived with and loved for more than two years, tearing like a rag doll, her precious blood splashing across the floor of the ruined fairy-tale cottage. Reality has intruded into the world of make-believe and the last shards of glass are still falling like alien snow as the bus finally comes to a halt, a great red beast gorged on human life, now gone torpid.

A terrible stillness falls over the scene. Somewhere there is screaming, somewhere alarms are clamouring but they seem so very distant. Jack can see Catherine's face in close-up, her eyes wide in shock. She is surprised to be dead, she has not planned her shopping trip to end this way, she expected to return to Jack that night, to share his bed and hold him in the warm, slumbering darkness. Death is a different quality of sleep and one for which she is not prepared.

Now, as Jack watches, he sees Catherine's lips quiver. She is looking at him, trying to frame them around a word. One arm is rising, her hand still clutching the box of cologne as though trying to pass it to him across an interval of more than one long year. He wills her to try harder, to shape the word with her mouth. It will be something to remember, something to cherish. But as in all the other times Jack has had this dream, she cannot complete the task. All that emerges is a last, slow exhalation and he sees her eyes are glazing over. She is gone, her spirit has fled its shattered body.

Catherine's arm falls to lie beside her, still clutching the cologne, the ambulancemen will have to prise it from her cold fingers.

Jack is sobbing in his sleep now because he knows that this is where the dream ends, but this is the point where he must emerge into a reality that is worse than his awful dream, because in the dream, at least, Catherine is back, even if only for a short time. He can see her as real as life, can almost touch her . . . if he can only learn to reach across the barrier that separates them.

The sound of a siren fills his head and a flashing blue light veils the carnage. It is time to go . . . and yet he tries to cling tenaciously to sleep, sinking his fingernails into the mist of the fading dream. He can't hold on to it, as it curls through his fingers like smoke. He is impelled to return, kicking and struggling to a life that has lost all meaning.

He wakes, alone.

PART ONE

STRIP JACK NAKED

Chapter One

Jack Doyle lay in his narrow bed, gazing blankly up at the cracked, water-stained ceiling. He was toying with the idea of getting up, but hadn't yet decided if he could face another day. The dream had rattled him. He thought he'd finally shaken it off, that the eighteen months that had elapsed since Catherine's death were enough to heal all the old wounds. But no, once again, the dream had risen from the dark pool of his subconscious, as vivid and meticulous as ever.

With a sigh, he yanked aside the duvet and rolled into the chilly no-man's-land of the outside world. It was after midday. Rain hammered against the window and it was as cold as ice inside the flat. It was early April, but it felt more like November. Not for the first time, he thought about getting out of this godforsaken country, heading for somewhere warm and distant where nobody knew him . . .

He moved across to the ramshackle wardrobe where his suits waited patiently for him. He ran his fingers lovingly across the tops of the hangers. His clothes were about the only decent possessions he had left. Everything else of value had been sold, or pawned or lost on the turn of a card. But his clothes were different, he could never part with them. He slipped a hand into the inside pocket of a charcoal-grey jacket and took out his wallet. He glanced at the contents. A few pieces of out-of-date plastic; a collection of business cards from people who would no longer give him the time of day; and thirty-five pounds in well-used notes. He fingered the money nervously. It was all he had left.

He slipped the wallet back into the jacket. There had been bad times before, he reminded himself, but then there had always been avenues of escape on the horizon. Lately, there had been the discomfort of watching those avenues close down, one by one.

Jack dressed quickly, slipping on a pin-striped cotton shirt, a pair of silk boxers, grey socks. He knotted a Paisley tie around his neck and secured it with a solid silver antique pin. Then he put on the Armani suit and polished brogues. Closing the wardrobe door he studied his reflection critically in the mottled full-length mirror. He moved across to the chipped washbasin and splashed a little *Roger & Gallet* on to his unshaven face, a token gesture that was the extent of his morning ablutions. Glancing at the bottle he saw there was less than a quarter of an inch left. Soon he'd be smelling of nothing but his own fear. He thought again about his dream, the fictional cologne spray called *Adam*, a detail so consistent that at one point he had actually started believing in its existence and had spent weeks trekking around the shops asking for it.

He thought wistfully about the time when he breakfasted at the Dorchester. He'd been doing better for himself then, and that was a reward for when he'd pulled off another astute business deal. He closed his eyes and could almost taste it. But that of course, was in the days when it seemed like he just couldn't put a foot wrong. Jack sighed, settled for a cup of black coffee and a cigarette.

Jack Doyle had set up the software company, Vectorcom, on a wing and a prayer as soon as he'd left college. He'd created an easy-to-use database and spreadsheet on which the company's reputation was quickly founded. Vectorcom flourished. By the age of twenty-eight, Jack had a luxury penthouse in Mayfair, an E-Type Jaguar and more importantly, he was planning to marry the girl of his dreams.

And then Catherine had died, and suddenly nothing seemed to matter any more. After the shock had receded, Jack had sunk into lethargy. He missed important appointments, avoided paperwork, failed to do essential research. Instead, he embarked on a six-month binge of drinking and gambling, leaving his disgruntled partners to carry the company on his behalf. Without him to lead it, Vectorcom soon became a sinking ship and it was a case of jumping off or going down with all hands. Jack chose the former course of action, signing over the rights to his software creations to his partners. But he still found himself saddled with massive debts when the company finally went under. By the time he'd cleared them, his personal resources were looking alarmingly slender.

The six months that followed were the most sobering period of his young life. He was King Midas in reverse. First to go had been his prized E-Type. He took to walking about Mayfair and told friends it was part of a fitness programme. 'Been putting on a bit of weight,' he would say, patting his non-existent stomach.

'Right,' they said; but their cold eyes and mirthless smiles told him they knew the real story and were secretly delighted. After years of watching Jack Doyle succeed, they were eager to watch him fail. Soon, he could no longer afford his apartment. After some searching, he found the seedy boarding house, tucked away in Ladysmith Road, Soho, and managed to scrape together enough for the deposit. Gazing around his grubby bedsit he realized he'd fallen about as far as he could. From here on it was the reality of day-to-day survival, of scrambling to make ends meet.

With increasing desperation, he'd been obliged to look for freelance work around Soho. He'd recently managed to get a few weeks of it, installing software for Leo King, a guy he had originally met in a card game. King owned a string of Soho sex shops and was having trouble keeping stock of his varied range of products. So, the Vectorcom database, once used to check company assets and VAT invoices, now listed the dubious merits of whips, chains and inflatable sex dolls. Officially, Jack was breaking the law installing the pirated database on to King's system. He no longer owned any rights to his own creation. The installation and subsequent training of King's employees had kept the wolf from the door for a few weeks but now that source of income had dried up he was faced with the inevitable question: How much longer could he struggle on for?

This morning he'd woken to the realization that he'd finally hit rock bottom. Thirty-five pounds wouldn't see him through one more day in this city, wouldn't even make an impression on the back rent he owed. He would have to find himself a stake, an opportunity to start over again. He could think of only one person in London who owed him a favour – and it was to Leo King that he planned to make his pitch.

Opening the front door to his bedsit, his spirits sank as he came face-to-face with his landlord, Leonard Riggs – a man who somehow contrived to look every bit as unappealing as his name: a big, gangling fellow with a square, heavy-jowled face, thick with grey stubble. He grinned at Jack, displaying brown stumps of teeth that clearly had never known the tender ministrations of a dentist.

'Oh, Mr Doyle,' he said gleefully. 'Looks like I just caught you.' He had a slow, resonant voice, which was capable of making the most innocuous remark seem smug and patronizing.

'I was going out,' said Jack, an unnecessary statement under the circumstances. 'Business,' he added, defensively.

'Such a busy man,' observed Riggs, stepping into the room, just the same. He stood there, gazing around with naked curiosity in his eyes. He jangled loose change in the pockets of his brown hopsack trousers in a clanking rhythm, a habit that seemed designed purely to get on Jack's nerves. 'Busy, yes. That's the trouble these days. Everybody rushing about, trying to make a quick buck. It didn't used to be like that.'

Jack eyed his landlord warily, aware of the reason for his visit. 'I'm sorry, Mr Riggs,' he said. 'But I really do have to go out.'

Riggs turned his head and smiled at Jack.

'A minute, you can't spare? In such a rush? What I have to say won't take long, Mr Doyle. I've been trying to pin you down for a week now. Always, you are just about to go out. Busy, you say. Well . . .' He sucked on his teeth for a moment and recommenced the business with the coins.

Jack waited hopefully, holding the door ajar but it was quite plain that Riggs had no intention of leaving the room until his mission was accomplished. Jack sighed and closed the door.

'So what's on your mind?' he asked, hoping he'd get a quick reply, but knowing somehow, that he'd get the guided tour.

'On my mind, Mr Doyle? Nothing really. Nothing I can put my finger on. But a man in my line of work, he prides himself on being a good judge of character. I like to think I can weigh a fellow up, do you see? But you now, Mr Doyle, you're a mystery to me. A closed book.'

Jack looked towards the ceiling. 'Mr Riggs, if you could just get to the point . . .'

'Again with the impatience! Just why, I ask myself, should you be so brusque with me? Most people in this house . . . most of my guests . . . I get the measure of them pretty quick. They go out at eight-thirty, they come in at five-thirty. Down there in my basement rooms, I hear their feet on the stairs. I'm a happy man. It brings a little order into my life. I like order, Mr Doyle. Those people, they work normal hours, they pay their rent on the dot . . .'

'Yes, well, I can explain that . . .'

'But you, Mr Doyle. An enigma you are! Yes, I think that's the right word. An enigma.' Riggs rolled the word slowly around on his tongue as though enjoying the taste of it. 'You go out, maybe, twelve-thirty . . . you come in, maybe, five o'clock in the morning. It's unsettling. I get to wondering, what line of work is he in, my Mr Doyle?' He moved over to the fridge and peered inside, observing a loaf of mouldy bread which he prodded with his index finger, leaving a round indentation in its purple and green surface. Then he grinned, crookedly. 'A scientist, perhaps?' he mused. 'Conducting research into alternatives to penicillin? Or are you just trying to start a mouse farm?' He snickered at his own joke.

'That *was* careless of me,' admitted Jack, hurrying over to the fridge and sweeping the loaf into a pedal bin. Jack turned back to Riggs. 'I keep meaning to clean up,' he said, lamely.

'I hope so, Mr Doyle. I know this house isn't Buckingham Palace, but it's home to me and my guests and I dare say it beats sleeping on the streets.' He turned to gaze out of the window, as though estimating the possibilities of sleeping in such a downpour.

'Look, I'm sorry about the rent,' said Jack. 'That's what you've come about, isn't it? I'll have it for you tomorrow.'

Riggs shrugged indifferently.

'Mr Doyle, I hope you don't think I came up to talk about money.'

'It did cross my mind.'

'Understand me, Mr Doyle. I enjoy being a landlord. It's my vocation. But the money side, now, that's my least favourite aspect. Haggling, I don't like. I simply won't do it. If somebody owes me money, say ... well, let's take you for example, Mr Doyle. Say a man like you who owes me, what, around one hundred and sixty pounds? Do you think I would ever mention it? No, I would rather bite off my own tongue! I'm a shy man, Mr Doyle, mentioning a matter of one hundred and sixty pounds and threatening to call in the police, well, that's simply not my style.' He sauntered over to the wardrobe and gently prised it open. 'What I would more likely do is wait till you were out. I'd come up here with my master key and I'd take all these fancy clothes here ... you have very nice clothes, Mr Doyle, I notice things like that. Yes, I'd take them to a fellow I know who deals in these things and I'd say, "the whole lot, one hundred and sixty pounds!" I'm sure they're worth a great deal more but I wouldn't be looking for a penny over, you understand? And that way, I would have my money and you would have paid your rent and everybody would be happy!' He turned back and smiled at Jack benignly. 'Yes, that's most likely what I'd do,' he concluded.

Jack ran a hand nervously through his hair.

'Well now, Mr Riggs, there's really no need to do anything as rash as that, I can assure you.'

Riggs looked affronted.

'We were talking *theoretical*, Mr Doyle! I hope you don't think that I—'

'Just promise me you won't touch the clothes till tomorrow, because I'm going to be paying you, cash on the nail! You see, I couldn't work without my clothes and if anything ever happened to them ... tomorrow, Mr Riggs, you can depend on it. And now, I really do have to go out.'

He began to usher Riggs towards the door.

'Take as long as you like,' Riggs said, as Jack bundled him out on to the landing. 'I don't want you thinking that I'm the pushy sort. Why, never in my life have I haggled with a guest, never!'

Jack nodded. He locked the door securely behind him and headed for the stairs with a fresh sense of urgency. Riggs padded behind him, calling down after him. 'Always so busy, Mr Doyle! You've got to learn to take things steady! No good for the heart, such agitation, no good at all ...'

Jack went down the stairs two at a time and out through the front door, leaving Riggs' moaning voice behind him. He stood in the rain for a moment, tilting his head back to allow the falling drops to cool his face. He had a brief and horribly vivid vision of Leonard Riggs gleefully unhooking his suits out of the wardrobe.

Panicked, Jack turned and almost sprinted in the general direction of Soho.

Chapter Two

Jack turned right on to Berwick Street and wandered down as far as the Hot Sensations Theatre, a building with a garish plastic facade that could be illuminated after nightfall. The name of the theatre was picked out in tall red letters, flanked by ancient, mottled pictures of big breasted women. It was a little after two P.M. and there was scant business to be had at the moment, but just inside the entrance a blonde woman in a red satin mini-skirt was sitting cross-legged on a high stool. Jack paused and glanced in. She waggled her tongue at him in lewd invitation, then relaxed as she realized she knew who he was. She grinned and went back to chewing her gum. There was an irony there, Jack thought. Prostitutes were only overly familiar with complete strangers. To their friends, they showed more reserve.

'Hello, Ruby,' he said, stepping closer. He had got to know Ruby and the other girls when he had worked at the adjoining sex shop installing the computer system for Leo King.

'Hello, Jack. Haven't seen yer for ages! What you been up to?'

Jack shrugged. 'Oh, this and that,' he said.

She reached down a plump hand and gave his balls a playful squeeze. 'Too much of this and not enough of that!' she snickered. 'What brings you round here, then? You slumming it today?'

'Yeah, something like that.' He nodded his head towards the entrance. 'Leo in?' he asked.

She nodded cautiously. 'Yeah. Dunno if he wants to see anyone though.'

'He'll see me.' Jack assured her. 'For old time's sake.'

He pushed aside the beaded curtain and went through the opening. Ruby turned and called after him. 'You come and see *me* for old time's sake. I'll put the lead back in yer pencil!'

Jack grinned. She would too, he thought. He strolled along a narrow corridor, wrinkling his nose at the stale, spermy stink of the place. Ahead of him, to his left, a door opened and a solitary old man came out of one of the peep-show cubicles. He wore a flat cap and a tweed overcoat and looked like everybody's favourite grandad. There was barely room for them to pass and the old man caught Jack's eye, glanced away nervously, his face reddening. He flattened himself against the wall to allow Jack to pass and then scuttled away towards the entrance.

Jack shook his head. Poor old bastard, what a pathetic way to end up. He wondered glumly if his own prospects were any better. He continued along the corridor, turned right and paused at the open doorway of a small cubicle-cum-office. King was sitting at a desk with his back turned, his thin body enveloped in a black overcoat. He was using a personal computer. Jack cleared his throat and King looked back over his shoulder.

Leo King was a half-caste, the son of a West Indian street trader and a Liverpudlian mother, from whom he had acquired a broad Scouse accent. Now, in his late-twenties, he was doing very nicely for himself in the skin trade. His stubby fingers glittered with gold rings and he had a miniature ingot on a chain around his neck, the collar of his white shirt left open to display the overt symbol of his success. His dark eyes studied Jack thoughtfully for a moment, as if deciding whether to greet him or tell him to fuck off. Then a white grin split his face.

'Jack mate, how yer doin'? Come in, come in, haven't seen yer fer a while!'

Jack pushed his way past a tower of magazines and into the office, and glanced around for another seat. There wasn't one so he perched himself on the edge of Leo's desk beside the computer. 'Sorry about the mess. Gorra big consignment of Danish porn and nowhere to store it. Couldn't pass it up at the price. 'Ere, gerra load of this!' He fished a magazine from a pile beside him and opened it to the centre spread. He held it out for Jack's inspection. 'She's earnin' her money, wouldn't you say?'

Jack nodded. 'That a donkey or a Shetland pony?' he asked.

Leo shrugged. 'Who do I look like, David fuckin'

Attenborough? Take it, if you want to.'

'That's all right, thanks. I prefer to see people riding horses, rather than the other way around.'

Leo chuckled. He tossed the magazine away, opened the drawer of his desk and took out a bottle of Glenfiddich. He poured two stiff shots and handed one to Jack with a sly wink. The two men drank and Jack grimaced as the fiery liquid went down.

'That's good,' he said. 'You always like a shot of the hard stuff in the afternoon, Leo.' He nodded towards the computer screen. 'Any problems with the database?'

'No, it's *sound*. Dead simple to use. A kid could 'andle it.' He paused. There was a brief, uncomfortable silence. 'So er ... what brings you round, Jack? Anything special?'

Jack studied his glass for a moment. 'I'm looking for a favour,' he said, quietly.

Leo's grin slipped for a fraction of a second and a wary look came into his eyes. 'A favour?' he echoed. 'What kind of favour?'

'I'm looking for a stake, Leo.'

'Yeah? Try the Bernie Inn down the road.'

Jack didn't react to the joke and Leo frowned.

'Must be losin' me touch,' he complained.

'I'm afraid this is serious,' said Jack. 'I'm in a fix, Leo, or I wouldn't ask. I was thinking around two grand ...'

'Jesus, I'll say it's serious!' Leo was shaking his head. 'I don't know, Jacko, that's a lorra wedge.'

Jack bridled. He didn't much care for being called 'Jacko'. He thought it lacked respect. 'Leo, you know I wouldn't ask if I wasn't desperate. I'm looking to make a new start and I just need a little capital.'

'Make a new start at what?'

'Well, the software business. It's what I know best. I mean, you said yourself that my system is a doddle to use.'

'But you told me it wasn't *your* system any more. You said that you'd let the rights go to somebody else when your business was in trouble.'

'Yes . . . well, sure, so I'll create another one, won't I? A *better* one. I just—'

But again Leo was shaking his head.

'Maybe you haven't heard, Jacko, but there's this little thing called "the recession".'

'Oh yes? And it's knocked the bottom right out of the vibrator market, has it?'

'You'd be surprised.' Leo waved a hand at Jack to calm him a little. 'The truth is, mate, if you want to borrow money around here, there's plenty of places you can go to. I could put you in touch with somebody who'd give you two thousand quid, just like that, no questions asked.'

'Really?' Jack brightened a little.

'Mind you, I'd only recommend it as a last resort.'

'Why's that then?'

''Cos the geezer I'm thinkin' of is a right villain. Oh, he'll lend you as much as you like, but his interest rates would be a lot steeper than "The Bank That Likes To Say Yes". He's called "The Armenian".'

Jack grimaced. 'What kind of a name is that?' he asked.

'Only one he answers to. And I've yet to meet a

man stupid enough to ask him about it. He employs a stoneface, big Scottish lad called Tam McGiver. A right fuckin' animal, sort of bloke who'd pull your nuts off and eat 'em raw if you crossed him.'

Jack shrugged. 'You got a phone number for these people?'

'Jesus, you really *are* serious, aren't you?'

'Like I told you, Leo, I'm desperate. And if *you* won't help me out—'

'Not so much won't, as *can't*. Tell you the truth, I'm in the process of opening up a Spanish connection to the business. I'm backwards and forwards to Marbella every other day and my cash flow isn't the best.' He flipped open an address book and copied a phone number on to the back of one of his business cards. He handed it to Jack and watched as he slipped it into the breast pocket of his jacket. 'Think very carefully before you get into this, Jacko. I wouldn't want it on me conscience that I dropped you in it with a gorilla like McGiver.'

'Beggars can't be choosers,' observed Jack.

'No, I suppose not . . .' Leo looked suddenly thoughtful. 'Tell you what,' he said, 'I may have something for you, just short-term, like. You used to be a fairly 'andy poker player, didn't you?'

'Still am,' Jack assured him.

'Hmm. It's just that I've got a game organized for tonight and somebody's dropped out at the last minute.'

'A game for money?'

'Of *course* for money! I could get you in if you'd be interested . . . only—'

'Only what?'

'Well, it might be out of your league, Jacko.'

'What do you mean, out of my fucking league?'

Leo held up a glittering hand to calm him.

'Don't get me wrong, mate. No slur intended, like. It's just—'

'Just what?'

'This is a serious game and there's some unpleasant people playing.'

'So? I can handle that,' snapped Jack.

Leo frowned, topped up their glasses.

'A bloke called Lou Winters is a regular. Ever heard of him?'

Jack shook his head. 'Another villain?' he asked.

'Yeah. Big operator these days, spreads his net very wide. Dope, girls, protection . . . you name it. Uses a respectable business operation as a front. He goes everywhere with a hired hand called Eddie Mulryan. Another animal but a different species to Tam McGiver. First time I met Mulryan, I thought he was the nicest bloke I'd ever met. Then I dropped a couple of grand to Lou in a poker game. Didn't have the readies to pay up. Lou gave me two days to sort it out. I figured it could wait longer. Lou sent Eddie round . . . and he left with the money in his pocket.'

Jack gazed inquiringly at Leo but clearly he wasn't going to get any more of an explanation than this. 'He put the frighteners on, did he?' prompted Jack.

'Let's just say that Mr Mulryan has a very persuasive manner,' said Leo, grimly. 'And I'm never going to get in that position again. When I play with Lou, I make sure I stay within the limits of what I can afford to lose, there and then. Otherwise, I fold and sit there watching the big boys. So all I'm saying is, be aware of what you might be getting into.'

'No sweat. You'll get me in the game then?'

Leo shrugged. 'Dunno. 'Ow much yer got to play with?'

Jack sighed.

'Thirty-five quid,' he said.

'You are joking I hope!' Leo studied Jack for a moment and realized that he was being deadly serious. 'Christ, you *are* in a bad way, aren't you?' He shrugged. 'They won't even let you sit at the table with that. Rules of the house. They expect you to put down a minimum three hundred quid just to get dealt in.'

'What's all this "they" business? I thought it was *your* game.'

Leo laughed hollowly. 'Yeah, it used to be. Now I just organize it, provide the venue, the cards and the booze. And I wouldn't dare miss a session. Mr Winters wouldn't like it.'

Jack considered this. 'OK, how's about you loan me the three hundred?'

'Oh, I dunno Jack! It's like I said, this Spanish thing—'

'Come on, that's chicken feed to you. That's only . . .' he waved at the pile of magazines beside him, '. . . a dozen of those things. I'll pay you back, with interest if you like. You know, I've done you a few favours in the past, Leo. Remember how all your staff used to rip you off before I got the database installed? I've probably saved you thousands over the past few months.'

'Yeah, yeah, tell me about it!' Leo sighed. He still looked worried. 'All right, I'll stake you for that, no problem. But be careful, Jacko. Lou isn't the greatest poker player, I've seen him drop five grand on a bad night. But he's a jammy sonofabitch and he's got the clout to take it all the way. You lose the three hundred and you drop out, all right?'

'Don't worry about me. I know what I'm doing.'

'I hope so, pal.' Leo opened another drawer and took out a metal cash box. He counted out a slim pile of tens and handed them to Jack. 'The game's upstairs above me private cinema in Wardour Street. You know the place?'

Jack nodded. 'What time?'

'We sit down to play at eight o'clock. Be there for ten to eight. If yer late, yer don't gerr'in. It goes without saying you don't tell anybody else about this.'

Jack feigned a look of astonishment. 'Golly! You don't mean to tell me this is *illegal*! Listen, Leo, stop acting like my mother, for Christ's sake. A year ago, I was running my own company and pulling down a salary of forty grand a year. And I drove an E-Type Jag when you were still dreaming about opening your first wank palace.'

Leo smirked but his eyes were without humour.

'Oh yeah, you were the man of the match at one time, Jacko. Really big news. But yer lost yer luck, mate. I've seen it happen to a good few people and mostly, it never comes back again. Never.'

Jack drained the rest of his whisky, folded the money and slipped it into his wallet. 'Thanks for the advice, Leo.' He got up from the desk and made for the door. 'See you tonight.'

Jack walked with determination back along the corridor. He felt his old confidence returning, coursing through his veins like a drug. 'This time,' he whispered, 'I'm coming back. I feel it. I really do.'

He walked past Ruby, who was busily sweet-talking a guy old enough to be her father. He stepped out into the wet and cold of the street, aware of the wallet in his breast pocket, heavy against his heart.

Chapter Three

Jack timed his arrival carefully. The last thing he wanted was to get there early, with his desperation steaming out from every pore. No, better to act casual, breeze into the place just before they locked the doors as though it was the most natural thing in the world. So he took a seat in a café opposite Leo's private cinema, where he nursed a cup of lukewarm coffee and smoked a few cigarettes. When the minute hand on his watch was grazing five-to-eight, he strolled across to the cinema.

He went in through the modest entrance and stood for a moment in a twilight of red plush and blue neon. The bored looking girl at the box-office directed him up a flight of stairs and he was met at the top by a hefty goon in a hand-me-down tuxedo, who frisked Jack rather clumsily and then led him along a corridor.

The goon knocked on a door and waited for a moment, his jaws working rhythmically around a wad of chewing gum. After a short interval, the door swung open and Leo peered out. He nodded at Jack, gave the goon a dismissive twitch of his head. The man grunted, strolled away and Leo took Jack's arm, pulling him towards the doorway.

'I was beginnin' to think you'd bottled out,' he said, under his breath. He stepped back and Jack followed him into a small, smoke-filled room. Leo bolted the door behind them and Jack quickly took stock of his surroundings. The room was shabby and bare of furniture save for the round, baize-covered table, a collection of wooden chairs and a well stocked drinks cabinet. There was a powerful light suspended low over the table and it illuminated the faces of the four men sitting around it. Leo turned back from the doorway and put a hand on Jack's shoulder.

'Gentlemen, this is Jack Doyle,' announced Leo. 'Jack, this is Lou Winters.'

Jack nodded to Winters, a thin, runty looking guy dressed in a grey suit. Winters was sipping at a glass of whisky, his long face expressionless. It was the face of a mortician, Jack decided, or maybe even one of his clients. Dark hollows beneath the eyes and cheeks, thin lips that probably never smiled. An expensive cigar jutted from his clenched teeth and a plume of white smoke coiled upwards beneath the spotlight. The whole effect was topped by an unmistakable toupee, jet black in colour. Lou studied Jack perfunctorily for a moment, as though he had no interest whatsoever in the newcomer. He nodded curtly and then his grey eyes flicked away to peer at a girlie calendar fixed to the wall.

Sitting behind and slightly to the right of Winters was a big, solidly-built man with a rumpled, potato-like face.

Inexplicably, despite the heat in the room, he was wearing a heavy, grey overcoat. Leo didn't bother to introduce him, but Jack deduced that this was Eddie Mulryan, Winters' minder. Mulryan stared at Jack and his wide face broke into a lop-sided grin. He had large white teeth that were too perfect to be his own and he gave Jack a playful wink, as though the two of them were sharing a private joke. Jack was caught off-guard by this unexpected show of *bonhomie* – Leo had led him to believe that Mulryan was some kind of monster.

Leo had already moved on to the next man. 'This is Alf Buckley,' he said, indicating a bearded man with a ruddy face and a mop of curly red hair that seemed at odds with the sober pin-stripes he was wearing.

'At last, some new blood!' said Alf, heartily. 'Hope you're a good loser, Mr Doyle, I'm feeling lucky tonight!' Jack immediately pegged this bloke as the game's no-hoper. Anybody who felt the need to advertise themselves in this way could usually be relied upon to stink at poker. Jack noticed, too, how Buckley was fidgeting nervously with a gin and tonic and how his watery eyes kept flicking restlessly to the unopened pack of cards on the table, as though anxious to begin playing.

'And last but not least, Mr Walter Tipton.' Here was a little man in his late-sixties with grey hair, a prominent nose and small black eyes, peering out of thick bifocals. Tipton was the only player dressed in casual clothes, a golf shirt and chino slacks, giving the impression he'd just wandered in off the eighteenth green. He had a glass of milk in front of him.

33

'A godamned duodenal ulcer!' growled Tipton. 'Doctor says I can't drink alcohol anymore! I ask you, what's life worth if you can't have the occasional mother-fucking drink?' He had a strange voice, shrill like a woman's, yet somehow, course and gravelly. He turned to Leo. 'You going to make introductions all night or are we going to play?'

Leo waved a hand dismissively at the old man.

'Calm down Wally, or you'll give yourself another ulcer,' he muttered. He pointed Jack to a vacant chair, moved over to the drinks cabinet and poured him a Glenfiddich. Then he stepped back to the table, handed Jack the glass and slipped into the remaining seat. 'Well gents,' he said, 'I think we all know the rules of the game, but for Mr Doyle's benefit I'll reiterate. It's basic five-card stud, Jack. Aces are high. Three hundred quid on the table to start. Ten quid minimum bet with no limits. You 'appy with that?'

Jack nodded.

'Right then. Let's play poker, shall we?' Leo broke the seal on the pack, shuffled the cards expertly and set them down on the table to be cut. Alf Buckley drew an Ace and was the first to deal. Wallets came out of breast pockets and everybody put down their money. Jack noticed that Lou Winters' wallet looked reassuringly fat and that there was clearly a lot more where his first three hundred came from.

Buckley dealt everybody a hole card, face down, and the game began. Jack spent the first few hands playing cautiously, appraising his opponents. His suspicions about Buckley had been well founded. He might have been a nice bloke to enjoy a pint and a chat with, but he had no business whatsoever sitting down at a poker table. The man was simply hopeless, his cherubic face signalling every decent hand he was dealt. When it was a poor one, which was most of the time, he was totally unable to control the glum expression that accompanied it, yet time after time, he tried to bluff his way through a round, forcing the bets up recklessly in the doomed hope the others would fold and give him the pot.

It was obvious to Jack that Buckley had been invited along simply because he was an easy mark and didn't have the good sense to recognize the fact. Within an hour, his three hundred notes had been apportioned out to the other players – but this didn't seem to deter him. He kept dipping into his wallet with a pained expression on his face, vainly trying to mask his desperation with an oafish quip. It was almost a shame to take the money off him. Almost. But there was no room for conscience in a game like this and Jack was taking too much of Buckley's money to feel anything for the man but contempt.

Walter Tipton was a better player by far but too cautious for his own good, squandering the good hands he got by calling too early. He won several times but rarely took more than a hundred. He grumbled all through the game, whether he won or lost. Nothing was right for him. The room was too hot and smoky, his milk wasn't chilled and he thought he was coming down with sinusitis. Jack figured the whole thing was a ploy to distract the others from sussing out his playing patterns and to some degree it was effective, but after an hour of the old man's continual grousing, Jack could have reached across the table and cheerfully throttled him.

Leo was an accomplished player but the cards just weren't going his way tonight. After an hour and a half, he was over five hundred pounds down. The bulk of the winnings were split between Jack and Lou Winters and for another half an hour the luck of the game twisted backwards and forwards between them.

Winters was no slouch at the game. He had perfected the proverbial 'poker face' a look of complete boredom that never varied from hand to hand. He seemed to follow no regular patterns, simply playing his hunches and bringing off what Jack suspected were some outrageous bluffs in the process. He was the only player offering Jack any real competition. Having established this fact, Jack started to put on the pressure and suddenly the game was going all his way. He won two big hands in a row and found himself with two thousand pounds. He'd won the stake he had been looking for and though he could hardly drop out of the game this early, a policy of cautious play from here on would ensure that he still had plenty left when the game reached its conclusion; except that suddenly, he didn't feel like being cautious. The cards kept falling right for him and his instincts told him to go with the flow. He continued to win and by midnight he had three thousand five hundred pounds in his corner.

It was around then that Buckley decided to call a halt

and threw in his final hand. He had drunk the best part of a bottle of gin and his face was beginning to show the effects, his cheeks mottled with red. 'Not my night,' he muttered. 'Someone up there . . .' He gestured vaguely at the ceiling. 'Somebody up there's got it in for me. You fellers will have to give me a chance to get my own back sometime.'

'Of course,' Leo assured him. 'Next week. I'll get in touch when I know the details.' He stood up and escorted Buckley to the door. The man was shaking his head.

'Four thousand down,' he said, to nobody in particular. 'Not my night. Jus' not my night.' He paused in the doorway, then composed his face into a feeble grin. 'You fellers better watch out next week,' he said. 'I'll be gunning for ya!' He stumbled out and Leo closed the door.

'Arsehole,' he said, as he returned to his seat. 'I wish we could find a few more like him.'

Jack got up to help himself to another drink.

'What does he do for a living?' he asked.

'He's a fookin' bank manager!' said Leo. 'No honestly, he is! He's a . . . a banker.'

'A total banker,' observed Winters, drily.

Leo chuckled and even Tipton managed a snigger.

'What say we raise the stakes?' asked Jack.

Winters gazed at him for a moment, then shrugged. 'Suits me,' he said indifferently. 'Fifteen quid minimum?'

'How about twenty?' Jack glanced at the other two. 'What do you say?'

Leo nodded. 'Why not? Wally?'

Tipton scowled. He clearly didn't relish the notion but

he was out-voted. 'Nearly my bedtime,' he observed. 'Maybe just a couple more hands.'

Jack resumed his seat. It was Leo's turn to deal. He gave the pack a thorough shuffle, then dealt out the hole cards and one face up. Jack glanced at his hole card. The Jack of Hearts. A good omen, he thought. His upcard was the King of Hearts. He glanced around at the other upcards. Winters had the Queen of Spades, Tipton, the Seven of Clubs and Leo, the Ace of Diamonds. Aces were high so it was up to Leo to open the betting. He slid two tens into the pot. Jack did the same and Winters and Tipton went along. There was eighty pounds in the pot. Now Leo dealt the next round of upcards.

Jack had the King of Clubs, Winters, the King of Spades, Tipton, the Two of Diamonds, Leo, the Ace of Hearts. Once again it was up to Leo to start the betting.

'I'll go a ton,' he said quietly. He counted out tens and dropped them into the pot. Jack considered this move. There were two possibilities. Either Leo had a third Ace in the hole or he was trying to bluff the others that he did. Going by Leo's usual style, the former was the more likely of the two; but then again he could just be going for shit or bust. If that was the case, he'd have to be bullied out of the game. Winters had the King and Queen of Spades – a very good start towards a Royal Flush. Who could say what he had in the hole? Jack quickly computed his chances of bringing that off in five cards. One chance in something like six hundred and fifty thousand, if he remembered his tables correctly. He didn't think he should sweat it out on that score. Tipton, he was sure, had nothing at all.

'I'll match your hundred . . .' said Jack, quietly, '. . . and I'll raise you another hundred.' He counted out the notes and then glanced at Winters who simply grunted and pushed two hundred pounds more into the pot.

Everybody looked at Tipton, who seemed far from happy. He made a big show of glancing at his hole card again, then muttered something beneath his breath. 'I'm still in,' he said defiantly and added his two hundred to the pot, which now held seven hundred and eighty pounds.

Leo paused to take a gulp of whisky, then dealt the next round of cards. Jack drew another namesake, the Jack of Diamonds; one more like it would give him a Full House. Logic told him he had something like one chance in seven hundred of getting it. He could feel confidence jolting through his system like an electric current.

Winters had been dealt one of the two remaining Jacks, the Jack of Spades. For him, too, the cards were falling brilliantly. All Spades, Jack noticed. He only needed the Ten to make up an apparently perfect Royal Flush . . . but did he have that Ace in the hole? Jack didn't think so. Leo had two Aces for certain and a possible three if Jack's hunch was right. Tipton had just picked up the Two of Clubs and Leo . . . Jesus, Leo had another Ace! Clubs this time . . .

Now Jack had to fight hard to keep the look of irritation off his face. Four Aces would shit all over his Full

House from a great height. What to do? Drop out this round and wait for another chance? Not when he felt so certain about that next turn of cards. No, best to try and frighten Leo out of the game, bump the betting up till he got the jitters and folded out of sheer panic. If he didn't have that fourth Ace tucked away, he'd soon buckle under . . .

Leo was opening the betting yet again.

'Two hundred,' he said. He sounded confident; a mite too confident, Jack thought.

'Two hundred,' agreed Jack. He looked Leo straight in the eye. 'And I'll raise you another three hundred,' he said. Leo flinched a little and Jack nearly grinned. *You don't have that other Ace, do you son?* he thought. *And provided you don't draw it on your last hand . . .* He computed the chances of that happening. About one chance in four thousand. Not the best of odds, but a doddle compared with what Winters would have to pull out of the hat to attain his Royal Flush. Jack counted the five hundred into the pot and glanced at Winters inquiringly.

'Five hundred,' said Winters, his voice expressionless. He put in his bet.

'I'm out,' said Tipton, quickly. He dropped his cards into the discard pile as though they were red hot. 'Worst hand I've had all night,' he complained.

There was now one thousand, nine hundred and eighty pounds in the pot. It was suddenly very quiet in the room. Jack felt a tenseness in him as he waited for the last turn of cards. Leo dealt them almost in slow-motion. Jack felt his heart thump as he was handed the Jack of Clubs. He could have leaned forward across the table and kissed it. He now had his Full House. He turned his head and followed the line of Leo's arm as it dealt to Winters. The Ten of Spades! For an instant, Jack was assailed by a terrible doubt. If Winters had that Ace in the hole . . .

Instantly, Jack shrugged off the idea. The odds were totally against it and Winters' luck hadn't been in that league all evening. No, he was bluffing. Had to be . . .

Now Leo was dealing himself his final card and everything in Jack's body seemed to tense up. *Don't let it be the Ace*, he thought, offering up a silent prayer to the gods of the table. The card turned in Leo's hands and it was . . . the Six of Spades! No use to anyone. No use at all. Jack relaxed, persuaded himself not to let out a sigh of relief. Leo was as good as out of the running, though it was still his turn to open the betting. He sat there for a moment, studying the other players' cards, as though debating whether he might try and bluff it out. Then he gave a grunt of disgust and threw his cards into the discard pile.

Jack checked out his remaining assets. He had two thousand, seven hundred and eighty pounds left. He thought it unlikely that Winters would stay with it any longer but he might try and pull something.

'I'll go a thousand,' said Jack and counted the money into the pot.

Now, you bald bastard, let's see what you make of that! Winters stared at him implacably across the table.

'I'll match you,' he said at last. 'And I'll raise you another . . . shall we say, ten thousand?'

Jack rocked back in his chair as though he'd been punched in the face. Ten thousand pounds! Sonofabitch was trying to stonewall him, scare him into folding his winning hand. He stared at Winters for a moment and then he noticed the tiny beads of sweat popping from his forehead.

Yeah, sweat it you shyster, you're bluffing and we both know it!

Jack turned his face to Leo.

'Can he bet that much?'

Leo's face was blank but his eyes were worried. 'Sure he can. There's no limits.'

Jack nodded, turned back to Winters. 'You carrying that much cash?' he inquired, matter of factly.

Leo shook his head.

'I'll write a personal IOU for the balance,' Winters said. 'That be good enough, Leo?'

'Of course.' Leo glanced briefly at Jack. His expression said, *'Well, nice try, kid'*. But Jack wasn't finished yet.

'Write the IOU,' he told Winters. 'I'll do the same.'

Winters sneered. 'Oh, well, I don't know about that, Mr Doyle . . .'

'Well, I do. If you can write one, so can I. We can't have one law for you and another for the rest, now can we?'

Winters frowned. 'But *I'm* good for it, Mr Doyle. I'm not so sure *you* are. If what I've heard about your finances is correct, you'd be very hard put to pay your debt. Why don't you just fold, it would be a lot less trouble for you . . .'

'For *you*, you mean!' Jack grabbed a notebook and pen and tossed it across the table. 'Write it, Mr Winters. Then we'll see whether you've got that Ace under there.'

Winters glared at Jack, his eyes hostile. Then he shrugged, uncapped the pen and carefully wrote out a chit for five thousand pounds. He put that, together with six thousand in cash into the pot. He handed the notebook and pen to Jack.

Jack put his remaining one thousand seven hundred and eighty pounds in and wrote out an IOU for nine thousand, two hundred and twenty. He signed his name with a flourish.

'I'm calling,' he said. 'Otherwise this could go on all night.'

Winters stared at him. Then he did something he hadn't done all night. He grinned. It was a horrible, mirthless grin, his thin face seeming to hinge across the middle to reveal prominent, yellow teeth. He reached down and turned over his card. It turned slowly in his hand. It was the Ace of Spades.

No, no, no! A voice in Jack's head moaning. He opened his mouth to say something but all that emerged was a low, guttural groan.

Then something hit him in the pit of the stomach and it was as though the skin of his belly ruptured and a big shard of ice plunged in through the hole, chilling him, freezing him to the marrow. He sat there and all he could see was that Ace, face up on the table. He tried to pick up his own cards, but his nerveless fingers fumbled them and they scattered across the floor at his feet. Tears must have welled in his eyes, because abruptly, the Ace blurred, became a fuzzy oblong with indistinct black smears on it.

'Well, you've got balls,' observed Winters. He reached out and pulled the pile of wealth towards him across the table. Jack had to fight an impulse to make a lunge for it. That was his last hope in the world being pulled away from him. He dashed the tears from his eyes and glanced at Leo, but he was studying his hands intently, as though he had never noticed them before.

'Wait,' gasped Jack. His tongue was warm lead in his mouth. 'You . . . you're surely going to give me a chance to get even?' He was horribly aware that he sounded just like Alf Buckley.

'Oh, I believe I've had enough for one night,' replied Winters calmly. 'And besides, Mr Doyle, what would you play with?'

'I'm . . . I'm sure Leo here would stake me a few hundred, just to get back in the game . . . isn't that right, Leo?'

Leo shook his head sadly. 'Forget it, kid,' he said quietly. 'You're finished.'

Jack stared desperately at Leo. It wasn't so much the indignation of having a younger man call him kid. It wasn't the dismissive scorn in his voice. It was more the awful finality of the statement. Jack was finished, clapped out, washed up. It was all over for him; except that there was still worse to come.

Winters had picked up the IOU. He was studying it intently as if searching for fine print.

'Nine thousand, two hundred and twenty pounds,' he observed. 'A tidy sum. When do you propose paying it?'

'I . . .' Jack swallowed hard, struggling to dredge up a pathetic ghost of a voice from somewhere deep inside. 'I'll need . . . a little time.'

Winters smiled sweetly. Now the game was over, he couldn't seem to stop smiling. 'Quite so,' he said, playing at being Mr Reasonable. 'Let's say three days, shall we? I'll send Eddie to pick it up on Friday.'

From his seat by the wall, Eddie favoured Jack with a grin and a sly wink. Under the circumstances it seemed positively surreal.

'Three days?' Jack blinked. He felt like a man abruptly woken from a deep sleep. He tried to focus his mind on the matter at hand but it was still smoke, coiled sleepily around that Ace on the table. 'Uh . . . I thought maybe . . . a couple of weeks.'

'Three days,' replied Winters. 'If you don't have it when Eddie calls, he'll be more than happy to go over the alternatives.'

Jack nodded. Suddenly, more than anything, he wanted to be out of this room, back in the sanctuary of his own place. He might be able to function there, he might be able to think.

'I, uh . . . guess I'll be . . . getting along then,' he announced, to nobody in particular. 'Thanks, uh . . . for—'

'A nice game?' asked Winters, making no attempt now

45

to conceal his scorn. 'Any time, Mr Doyle, any time. But perhaps you should stick to Strip Jack Naked – you seem to have a flair for it!'

Jack got to his feet with difficulty. He felt like he'd aged fifty years, was aware of every creak and click of his joints. He was aware of eyes watching him in sick fascination. Incredible, to see a man totally destroyed, yet leaving the scene of the accident under his own steam. He directed his footsteps towards the exit and began to fumble with the lock. He couldn't make his fingers work for him. Leo followed him over and opened the door. As Jack shuffled on to the landing he followed him outside, closing the door behind them. For an instant their eyes met and Leo's look of pity burned through Jack.

'You stupid twat,' he said quietly. 'You've screwed yourself this time.'

Jack nodded. He felt punch drunk.

'Leo, about your three hundred . . .'

'Jesus, forget about that!' snarled Leo. 'We'll write that one off to experience. Just think about Winters' money. Nine thousand quid! Jesus! And don't even think about not gerrin' it, Jacko. Mulryan, will chew you up and spit out the pieces.'

'I don't know where to start looking,' whispered Jack, desperately. 'Leo, I don't suppose . . .?'

'Jack, do me a favour. Go home and have a good stiff drink. And in future, keep away from me, all right? They say bad luck is catching.'

Leo went back into the room, slamming the door in Jack's face.

Jack stared at the closed door for a moment, feeling reality ripping into him with steel claws. He turned and went slowly down the stairs, willing his feet to place themselves one in front of the other.

He supposed he must have walked home; supposed because he didn't remember pacing the rain-spattered streets. He only knew that presently, he was fumbling at the lock of his front door and he was soaked to the skin, his teeth chattering. He went up the stairs to his room, still moving haltingly, like a drunkard. He got the door open, stepped into the room and switched on the lights. He stood there swaying, wondering if he had a bottle tucked away for an emergency. He turned his head and saw the open wardrobe, the dark empty place where his suits used to be. The darkness yawned at him.

'No,' he said quietly. 'Ah, no, no, Riggs, the bastard, he hasn't . . .'

He moved towards the wardrobe and then the tears came again in earnest, his shoulders shaking with the grief of it and this was the end, for sure, the last, terrible indignity and worst, oh, worst of all, was the feeling that he'd somehow brought it on himself.

He gazed blankly into the black open maw of the wardrobe and it was like looking into the belly of a beast that had come to devour him. How easy, he thought, to go into that blackness, to let it swallow him, obliterate him, remove him entirely from this harsh world in which he could no longer live.

But then an image came looming out of the blackness; a deserted stretch of beach under a clear blue sky, a row of date palms swaying in a gentle breeze. It occurred to him that the holiday he had been promising himself for years was long overdue. But holidays cost money and . . .

He slipped a hand into his jacket pocket and pulled out a crumpled business card – the one Leo had given him with a phone number scrawled on the back. In that instant, he knew exactly what he would do, knew at the same time that it was madness, but like a drowning man, he had to grasp at whatever wreckage drifted his way. Trouble was he didn't have much time. Just three days. He didn't know if he could ever hope to pull it off, only that he had to give it his best shot.

Chapter Four

Jack trudged purposefully along Portobello Road, dressed in his one remaining suit and horribly aware of time passing. It was a bleak grey Tuesday afternoon, but despite this the market was in full swing, its long rows of stalls packed with tourists swarming like hungry locusts, clicking their cameras at everything they saw.

Preoccupied, Jack took little notice of anyone else. His priority now was self-preservation and his frantic cogitations the previous evening had led him to one inescapable conclusion. If he wanted to emerge from this mess in one piece, he had no option but to get out of London, go as far away as possible. And that meant going overseas. A few hundred miles wasn't sufficient distance to shield him from the wrath of Lou Winters.

Jack noticed a crowd of people gathered around a small table on the pavement where a scruffy old man in a shapeless grey overcoat was performing the famous three cup trick. Jack hadn't seen this done for years and momentarily his worries were forgotten as he stopped to observe the old man's impressive sleight of hand.

'S'easy. Spot the ball n' winna tenner! One paahnd to 'ave a go . . .' he was saying. ''Oo's first? You sir! Right, keep yer eyes onna baawl . . .'

Jack grinned, shook his head and considered the old saying about a sucker being born every minute. If he'd had the gift of quick hands, he might have considered this scam for himself, though it would have taken a lot longer than three days to raise the kind of money he needed. He remembered that he had an urgent appoint- ment and forced himself to move on. The old man's cracked voice followed him for some distance along the street.

'Oh, bad luck, sir! Must've lost concentration there . . . again? Very well, sir. That'll be another paahnd! Right, keep yer eyes onna baawl! Back it comes and rahnd it goes, where it ends up, no one knows! That one, sir? You sure? Oh, bad luck, sir! Right, oo's next . . .?'

Jack frowned. He had woken at dawn, haunted by recurring dreams of the previous night's game. Looking back, he couldn't believe Lou Winters' luck in pulling that Royal Flush in five cards and had begun to wonder if he hadn't palmed the Ace. If he had cheated, he'd done a bloody good job of it and Jack had been too stunned to accuse him of anything at the time. Now of course, it was immaterial. If cheating was involved, you had to confront the bastard there and then, shake the spare cards out of his sleeve. Too late to think about it now. A debt was a debt and he wasn't going to worm his way out of this one.

When he'd finally dragged himself out of bed, he'd

gone down and hammered on Riggs' door, but if he was home, he was keeping very quiet in there and the door, of course, was locked. Once again, there was nothing Jack could do. If he'd had the hundred and sixty rent money on him, then maybe, just maybe, he could have rescued his suits. He had nothing but a handful of coins. Kicking the door down and trashing Riggs' room would have given him some kind of consolation but the next thing he knew, he'd have the police on his back and right now he could do without that kind of aggravation.

So he had done the only thing left to him. He had phoned the number on Leo's business card and had asked for an appointment with 'The Armenian'. He'd felt faintly ridiculous even saying the words, like a character in a James Bond movie but the man on the other end of the line didn't seem to find it odd at all. He'd given Jack an address off Portobello Road and told him to call there at eleven o'clock.

Jack traced the address to a paint-blistered doorway in a soot-blackened Victorian office building. He rang the bell and the door was opened by a decrepit looking old man in a tweed coat and a flat cap, who appeared to have been sitting all alone in the middle of a draughty hallway. The man had a mottled bluish-red complexion and a large dewdrop of snot hanging from one nostril. He smelled of ale. He gestured to a bare wooden staircase leading to the upper floors. Beside it, an ancient elevator had a makeshift OUT OF ORDER sign hanging from the door.

Jack looked at him uncertainly.

'I'm here to see . . .'

'The h'Armenian,' finished the old man. ' 'E's on the third floor.' Jack wasn't sure if this meant that The Armenian was the only person doing business in this dusty old warren or that the old man could guess his intentions simply by looking at him. He hoped to God it wasn't the latter. The last thing he needed was for his desperation to be written all over his face like a warning sign. He watched as the man went back to his chair and eased his ancient frame into a sitting position, then reached for a can of Special Brew standing on the floor beside him. Jack shrugged and turning away, climbed the creaking staircase to the third floor.

The lighting was poor up here and there was a musty smell of damp plaster and rotting wood. He stood for a moment on the landing, looking around and then noticed a faint glow of light coming through the frosted glass of an office door. He went to it and tapped politely with his knuckles.

'Come,' said a voice.

Jack opened the door and stepped inside.

A rush of warm, stale air washed over him. The one window in the office was closed and a large fan heater was blasting hot wind into the small room. There were two people in there. Behind an old teak desk sat a tubby little man with a round red face and small, delicate features. He had a tiny pencil moustache which gave him a vaguely Latin look and his dark brown hair had receded completely from the top of his skull, leaving just a few extravagant curls around his ears and at the back of his neck. Despite the heat in the room, he wore a thick woollen overcoat and a pair of expensive tan gloves. He was reading a magazine and didn't even glance up as Jack entered.

On the other side of the room a man was leaning against a filing cabinet, his feet crossed in a nonchalant pose. He looked like trouble. His hair was cropped close to his skull, leaving nothing more than a shadow of stubble. He had a lean, pock-marked face with chiselled features; a high forehead, a sharp Roman nose and well defined cheekbones. He was dressed in a loose fitting black suit over a plain white T-shirt and he had his thumbs hooked under a pair of elaborately embroidered braces. The long length, lace-up Doc Martens on his feet were an eloquent testimony to his origins. He *did* look at Jack, surveying him calmly with his cold, grey eyes. An arrogant grin shaped his wide mouth. This was undoubtedly Tam McGiver ... which meant, presumably, that the man behind the desk was his employer, The Armenian.

'Mr Doyle to see you,' announced McGiver in a gravelly Glaswegian accent. 'He phoned this morning.'

The Armenian lifted his gaze from the magazine, seemingly with the greatest reluctance. Jack noticed with a twinge of surprise that it was a copy of *House Beautiful*. The Armenian studied Jack for a moment as though able to ascertain a man's credit-worthiness simply by looking at him.

'Nice suit,' he said at last. 'Bespoke tailoring?'

Jack nodded.

'You can always tell. You can't buy suits like that off-the-peg, it isn't possible.' He had a softly spoken, almost lisping voice, shot through with the vestiges of some middle European accent. He returned his attention to the magazine for a moment, then flicked his gaze back to Jack. He crooked a finger, indicating that Jack should approach the desk. The Armenian pointed to a photograph in the magazine, showing a lounge interior. 'I don't know,' he said. 'The Laura Ashley print wallpaper against an apricot ceiling . . . and then a turquoise dado rail? To me it *clashes*. What do you think?'

Jack was nonplussed, to say the least. This was literally the last question he had expected.

'Umm . . .' He shrugged. 'I agree, it . . . it looks kind of odd.'

The Armenian nodded.

'If it was *your* lounge, what colour would you paint the dado?'

Jack frowned. 'Uh . . . I . . .' He glanced at Tam McGiver for a moment and the man was still staring at him, the ghost of a smirk on his lips, making him feel distinctly uncomfortable. He wished he could just get on with talking about the money, he would feel less out of his depth. Maybe this was some kind of bizarre test. At any rate, he'd have to take a stab at it. 'Peach?' he said hopefully.

'Peach.' The Armenian considered this for a moment. He nodded gravely, seemed vaguely impressed by the answer. He looked across the room at McGiver. 'Peach,' he said, with more conviction this time.

'Cerise,' growled McGiver. 'Peach is tonally too close to apricot.'

The Armenian stroked his chin reflectively. 'I see what you are getting at, Tam, but my fear is that the result could be just a little too *gaudy*. Peach might be the compromise I've been looking for . . .'

Jack had the distinct impression that he'd just stepped into an episode of *Monty Python*. Did all villains spend their lives sitting around discussing interior decorating?

'Look,' he said, 'I'm really no expert.'

The Armenian smiled, nodded. 'Quite,' he said. 'But it's always interesting to get a fresh opinion.' He closed the magazine with an air of finality. 'So, er . . . Mr . . .?'

'Doyle. Jack Doyle.'

'Mr Doyle. You want to borrow some money?'

After the last few minutes such directness was reassuring.

'Er . . . yes. Yes, I would.'

'And what figure did you have in mind?'

'Two thousand pounds,' said Jack; and thought, *Enough to get me out of this fucking country, mate.*

The Armenian shrugged.

'Well, this is an inconsequential amount of money, Mr Doyle. I'm sure something can be arranged.'

'It's to get my software business back on . . .'

The Armenian held up a plump, gloved hand.

'It's of no interest to me what the money is *for*, Mr Doyle. All that concerns me is that you agree to pay the outrageous amounts of interest that I will be charging you.'

'Which are . . .?'

'On two thousand pounds . . . I presume you are taking the loan for the standard twelve months . . .?'

'I guess so.'

'Then that would be twelve payments of five hundred pounds, due on the first of each month. If you miss a payment, the monthly sum doubles.'

'That's pretty steep,' observed Jack.

'Indeed it is. But then people only ever come to me when they are desperate. Under normal circumstances such a small amount could be obtained from a bank or finance company. Obviously you have decided that such institutions would turn you down flat. The fact that you choose to come to me suggests that you must be in desperate straits.'

'It's more a question of *time*,' Jack assured him. 'These things take time to process and I . . . I need a quick decision.'

'Oh, quick decisions are my speciality. Convince me that you appreciate the gravity of the undertaking and you'll be free to leave here with the cash.' The Armenian leaned back in his chair, reached into his inside breast pocket and took out a gold cigarette case. He offered it to Jack, who reached forward and took one. 'That, Mr Doyle, is the only time *I* shall give you something. If you agree the terms, from now on, every month, *you* will give to me.'

'I appreciate that.' Jack took out his Zippo and lit their cigarettes.

The Armenian blew out an ostentatious cloud of smoke.

'Ah, but do you? You see, I worry about these small amounts, more so than with the big ones. Sometimes, a client will think to himself, well, I didn't sign any forms, they have no real proof, he isn't going to make an issue over a few thousand pounds, now is he? But they're *wrong*, Mr Doyle. You see, with me it's a point of honour. If somebody owes me and tries to worm out of his commitment, I'm liable to treat him with the utmost severity . . . or rather, Mr McGiver here is. He's my debt collector you see and he's not a man to be trifled with.'

Jack glanced apprehensively at the big Scotsman.

'I'm sure he's not,' he agreed.

McGiver gave him a big, toothy smile, revealing wide gaps in between the ivories.

'One other question I always ask. Aside from the two thousand pounds that you obviously owe to *somebody*, do you have any other sizable debts at the moment?'

'None!' said Jack, perhaps a little too quickly.

The Armenian seemed not to take any heed of the reply.

'Obviously, if it transpired that you did owe large amounts to another source, I would naturally think twice before lending you a penny. A bad debt is a bad debt, after all. And if it should come to my attention that you were lying to me—'

'There's nothing else, really.'

The Armenian seemed satisfied. He inhaled on his cigarette, blew out another cloud of smoke. 'In that case, Mr Doyle, there's really nothing more to add. I'll hand you over to Mr McGiver, who will take care of all the details. I trust I'll never need to see you again. Good day,

Mr Doyle.' He returned to his magazine and continued reading from where he had left off. Jack was vaguely surprised that it had been so easy. He had anticipated lots of tricky questions. He turned and McGiver beckoned him with a quick movement of his bony skull. Jack followed him on to the landing and up the next flight of stairs.

'Where are we going?' asked Jack.

'Just up here aways. It's very providential, Mr Doyle. I had some business to take care of earlier, but then you phoned and I thought to myself, "Tam, this would be a good opportunity to show the new client how the process works." Let you know exactly what you're getting yourself into.'

Jack didn't like the sound of this at all.

'Well, look,' he said, 'I'm perfectly happy with the terms . . .'

'Happy?' McGiver seemed amused by this. 'You'd have to be an *arsehole* to be happy with them! Just in here,' said McGiver, indicating a doorway. 'It won't take a minute.'

They entered a dingy, empty room, the windows blacked out with sheets of cardboard. A forty-watt bulb barely illuminated the interior. A figure was slumped in a chair beneath the light. Jack stared in surprise. It was a naked man, hunched miserably in the wooden chair, his plump body held in place by lengths of tape that had been wound repeatedly around his chest and arms. More tape was pressed across his mouth and Jack could see tufts of dark brown beard sticking out from under it. It was going to hurt like hell when the tape was pulled off. The man raised his head as they approached and Jack was shocked by the pleading expression in his eyes. There were purple bruises about the man's face and a crust of congealed blood filled his nostrils.

McGiver strolled over to him and put a hand gently on his bare shoulder. Jack saw the man wince at McGiver's touch. The terrified eyes continued to stare imploringly at Jack.

'This gentleman owes us money,' announced McGiver cheerfully. 'He's been very stupid. Borrowed from The Armenian to pay off existing debts, then found he couldn't make the payments. He's had one previous warning but that failed to make a suitable impression on him. He's been sitting here for several hours now, reflecting on the error of his ways.'

Jack frowned, realizing that this could so easily be him, taped into the chair, awaiting punishment. He wished to God that there was some other way of getting the money he needed, but short of robbing a bank, he didn't see what else he was supposed to do.

'I've told him what's going to happen,' continued McGiver. 'Thinking about it is the worst thing of all. Much worse than the reality ... though I have to say, that's no bed of fucking roses either.' He left the man now and crossed the room to a small table set against the far wall. As Jack watched, McGiver removed his jacket and hung it on a peg. He picked up a workman's apron and hung it around his neck, tied it at the waist. Next he found a pair of canvas gloves and put them on.

Jack glanced nervously towards the door. He didn't want to be here in this room, but he knew he daren't leave without the money.

'It's a question of respect,' said McGiver. 'Most people who come to us for money know better than to abuse the situation. Others just don't seem to care what they do. With people like that, telling them isn't enough. They need to be *shown*.'

He picked up something heavy that was lying on the table. As he turned back to face the bound man, Jack saw that it was a heavy coal-hammer. McGiver walked towards his victim. The man started to make noises behind the gag, high-pitched squeaks, the kind of sound a pig might make in a slaughter-house. He struggled in the chair but to no avail. His eyes were very big and Jack could see the whites of them all around the tiny circles that were his pupils. He was staring at the coal-hammer, seeing nothing else but that.

'Jesus,' whispered Jack. 'You're not going to—'

'Kill him?' McGiver chuckled. 'Not this time. If he misses another payment, then maybe we'll write him off as a bad debt and then . . .' He shrugged. 'Ah, but he's not going to miss another one, are you, wee man?' He crouched down beside the chair and put a gloved hand on one of the man's legs, just above the knee. 'All he gets this time is a wee tap,' he said. 'That's usually all it takes.'

He raised the hammer up to head height, held it there a moment, then brought it down hard on to the man's left kneecap. The knee shattered with a dull crunching sound, bone and cartilage tearing through the pink flesh as the weight of the hammer destroyed it.

'Fuck!' said Jack and took an involuntary step backwards, but he couldn't look away. The man's body jolted with the shock and his eyes bulged grotesquely in their sockets. From behind the gag he made a hideous, bubbling groan of agony. Blood squirted out of the wound, splattering McGiver's apron. He stood up and moved quickly out of harm's way. The spattering of blood on to the lino mingled with the stream of urine running uncontrollably from the man's bladder. His head flopped forward on to his chest as he lost consciousness.

Jack stared at the still figure in the chair, aware of his heart pounding within him, a feeling of nausea rising in his stomach. He watched as McGiver strolled back across the room. The Scotsman threw the hammer carelessly on to the table, pulled off the gloves and untied his apron.

'He'll behave himself now,' he observed, with a satisfied tone in his voice. 'And he'll pay his debt, even if he has to borrow the money from somebody else.' He retrieved his jacket and put it on. He turned back to Jack and smiled. He reached into his pocket and took out a thick wad of notes. 'Now then, I believe it was two thousand you wanted?'

Jack nodded dumbly. He was afraid to open his mouth in case he was sick.

'And you're quite sure you want to go through with this?'

Again Jack nodded. The man in the chair gave a low groan as though the pain was bothering him even in his sleep.

'What happens to him now?' murmured Jack.

'Oh, don't worry about him. Somebody will drop him off at the hospital. Terrible accident that, but it could happen to anybody.'

'He won't tell?'

McGiver shrugged. 'What do you think? He might be lame now but it's preferable to being dead. Which he soon would be if he said the wrong thing. Once he's out of hospital, I'll pay him a wee visit, talk about his new repayment programme. I think he'll agree the terms. Now then . . .' He began to count fifties off the roll, until he had two thousand pounds. He folded it and stuffed it into Jack's breast pocket. 'We understand each other,' he said. It wasn't phrased as a question, more a statement of fact.

Jack nodded. He could only pray that he would find a place to hide where neither McGiver or Mulryan could locate him. McGiver slipped a beefy arm around Jack's shoulders and walked him to the door.

'I expect you'll be able to find your own way down,' he said. 'I'm kind of busy just now. I'll see you on the first of May.'

Not if I see you first, thought Jack grimly. 'Shall I come here?' he asked.

'No need. We know where you live.'

Jack stared at him.

'But how—?'

'Oh, that's not important. You phoned this morning, I had plenty of time to find out. Though of course, if you do change your address, you'll be sure and let me know, won't you?'

Jack smiled weakly. He went down the stairs three at a time. The doorman let him out into the fresh air and Jack gulped down several big breaths as he made his way back through the rows of market stalls on Portobello Road. The next task was to find himself a travel agent and book the first available flight out of here. At the moment, he wasn't particularly fussy where it was, so long as it was several thousand miles away. With luck, he'd get away, he thought. If he could just keep that one clear step ahead . . .

Chapter Five

Jack stood across the street from Sammi's flat, staring blankly at the shabby doorway. He wasn't sure what had brought him here. Mostly, he supposed, it was the thought of going back to his empty bedsit, the prospect of being alone another night. Sammi was a girlfriend, of sorts. At least, if asked, that was how he would have described her. Jack's girlfriend. His occasional sleeping partner. Every so often, when the loneliness got too hard to bear, he found himself creeping shamefaced to the big Victorian house in Finchley where she lived.

He lifted a hand to pat the slight bulge in his inside breast pocket, the envelope containing a one-way ticket to Malaga. He'd tried several travel agents, phoned around half a dozen more and the earliest flight he could find was for ten o'clock Friday morning, which anyway you looked at it was cutting things uncomfortably close. He hadn't chosen the destination, so much as it had chosen him; it was the first place offered to him that seemed a suitable distance away. Jack didn't know much about Spain, but Leo always spoke well of the place, he was often over there wheeling and dealing with his various business contacts on the Costa del Sol. Maybe Jack could use his connections with Leo to his advantage.

A fine drizzle was falling now and the street lights had clicked on as the afternoon lengthened into a chilly twilight. The wet surface of the road reflected the pools of light in oily shimmers. Jack told himself that he could either stand here until the rain soaked through his clothes or he could cross the street and ring Sammi's doorbell. He knew he had little choice in the matter. He'd first met Sammi at a party, some months after Catherine's death, the two of them nursing their individual sorrows, bumping into each other in a crowded hallway, falling into nervous conversation. Perhaps they'd recognized something in each other, a mutual sorrow, a kind of unspoken misery. At any rate, something must have clicked between them. He'd been seeing her sporadically ever since.

As he drew nearer to the house he could discern the faint glow of light behind the curtained window of Sammi's downstairs bedsit. There were four flats, all served by the communal front door. He scanned the display of buzzers carefully, as though he had never been here before. There were four little glass plates, three of them bearing the neatly typed surnames of the flats' current residents. Sammi's was different. There was just her first name, written in a childish scrawl and beneath it, the face of a clown, a pierrot, probably cut from a greetings card. The pierrot had a tear trickling down from the corner of one eye and the effect was somehow heightened by the fact that moisture had got behind the glass and Sammi's name had partially dissolved, trailing long smears of black ink across the pierrot's white face. It was ironic how the image fitted Sammi perfectly: the poor sad clown who everybody dumped on.

Jack frowned and jabbed at the buzzer. After what seemed ages, there was the sound of a latch being turned.

The door swung back to the limits of a safety-chain and a solitary eye peered at him, framed by thick black shutters of lashes that nature could never have provided. The pupil of the eye was a pretty emerald green. It dilated a little, then contracted. Jack felt, but didn't see, the look of suspicion that must have accompanied it.

'Oh, it's you,' said Sammi's voice, flatly. Like most people these days, she clearly wasn't overjoyed to see him, but neither did she slam the door in his face. *Her first mistake*, thought Jack sadly. *She always lets me back in. Maybe that's the trouble.*

'Hello, Sammi,' he said. 'How've you been?'

The eye blinked resentfully.

'Oh fine! Just fine. No better for wondering where you'd got to. I thought maybe you'd died or left the country.' It was, of course, meant to be cutting sarcasm, but in Sammi's doleful tones it came across as just plain glum.

Jack frowned.

'I meant to call you, Sammi, I really did. But the phone service over there is so awkward and—'

'Over there?' Again, the eye narrowed. 'Then . . . you have been away!'

67

'Yes, to Germany. Didn't I tell you I was going? I only got back last night...' The lie tripped easily off his tongue. He always lied to her, he wasn't exactly sure why. To Sammi, he was still the high-flying, free-wheeling businessman who had masterminded Vectorcom. He played the part to the hilt, created the most outrageous deceptions to back up his extravagant claims. Perhaps he still needed one person in the world who didn't see him as an abject failure. He pulled a paper-wrapped bottle from his raincoat pocket and held it up to the gap in the door. 'I brought champagne,' he told her. 'I thought we would celebrate together. Vectorcom is going international.' He paused, glanced behind him at the falling rain, then lifted the collar of his coat with his free hand. 'If I could just come in for a moment and explain...'

The eye flickered and there was an audible sigh from within. Then he heard the rattle of a chain and the door swung slowly back. Sammi stood there regarding him dubiously. Her pale, thin features and tied-back black hair reminded Jack of the doorbell pierrot. She pouted, drawing her red painted mouth into a disapproving circle and lifted her skinny arms to place her hands on her hips.

She was wearing a plain white blouse and a red mini-skirt from which her skinny legs emerged like an apology. Her feet were jammed almost vertically into a pair of patent leather stilettos. She had always been conscious of her height and had half crippled herself over the years in desperate attempts to increase the distance from the top of her head to the floor. Jack had never found her physically attractive, that wasn't really the point. It was just that sometimes he caught glimpses of a pathetic, frightened creature hiding behind the mask of foundation make-up and it was with this that he identified. Like him, she had been hurt badly somewhere back along the way and also like him, she had never really recovered from the wound. The pair of them had so much in common.

'You could have told me you were going away,' she chided him. 'How long were you in Germany?'

'A few weeks.' He gestured at the short stretch of hallway behind her. 'Look, is it OK if I . . .?'

Sammi shrugged, shook her head, but not to say 'no'. Her long suffering expression seemed to ask the world in general just how she could be so forgiving. She turned away and Jack crossed the threshold. He closed the door behind him and followed Sammi into her room.

It was just as he remembered it; a crowded bedsit, predominantly pink in colour and featuring a bewildering assortment of frilly cushions and tacky knick-knacks. Her pride and joy, a collection of cuddly toys fashioned in a hideous day-glo fabric, regarded Jack balefully from the direction of the single bed at the other end of the room. Cats, dogs, bears and other assorted quadrupeds were grouped around the headboard as though standing guard over their mistress' chastity. Jack thought them the most frightful things he had ever seen, but Sammi adored them. Each one had a name and an invented history. Jack realized that they were substitutes for human friends and this seemed profoundly sad to him.

He handed her the champagne and slipped off his raincoat.

'Ooh,' she said, peering at the label. 'Moët and Chandon! That's the best, isn't it?'

'Of course,' he told her. 'Would I bring anything less? Grab a couple of glasses.'

She thrust the bottle back at him.

'You'll have to open it,' she insisted. 'I can't stand the bang!' She turned and hurried into her tiny kitchenette. He heard her rummaging in a cupboard and then she emerged carrying a couple of wine glasses. 'They're not even the right sort,' she observed.

'They'll do fine,' he assured her. He pulled the foil from the neck of the bottle, found the twist of wire and began to unwind it. Sammi grimaced and turned her face away, as though convinced that the cork would wing its way unerringly at her.

'So what were you doing in Germany?' she muttered.

'Bit of business,' he said.

'Monkey business, you mean.'

'No, honestly. *Big* business. Came up at the last minute. Fell right into my lap, so to speak.'

She seemed to remember she was angry.

'And you couldn't have called me, just once, to let me know where you were?'

'I *wanted* to, sweetie, honest. But you've no idea how busy it's been. My business contact over there helped me translate the Vectorcom database into German. Of course, I had to stay on to check for any glitches, but now it's up and running like clockwork.'

The cork came out with an abrupt pop and deflected

off a light fitting overhead. The champagne effervesced over the neck of the bottle and Sammi got a glass to it just in time.

'Must have got shaken up on the way here,' observed Jack. He filled their glasses to the brim, then raised them in a toast. 'Cheers,' he said. 'To Vectorcom.'

'Bottoms up!' Sammi giggled and they both drank. 'Mmm! I could acquire a taste for this stuff!'

'Not bad,' said Jack. 'Could have done with being a couple of degrees cooler.'

'Oh no, it's delicious!' She indicated the nearby sofa. 'Why don't we sit down?' she suggested. He nodded, followed her across to it. They relaxed and Jack set the bottle down on the carpet. They sipped at their drinks in silence. Now that he was here he was at a loss to find something to say to her. Lies seemed to spill so easily from his tongue but the truth was somewhat harder to deal with.

'How's work?' he ventured.

'OK,' she told him. She worked as a secretary in some nameless office, for some nameless firm in the city. Something to do with home furnishings. She'd told him all about it when they had first got together but now he couldn't remember a blessed thing about it. It bothered him that he didn't remember. Now that he came to think about it, he didn't know very much about Sammi at all. Perhaps she was just another stick to beat himself with. He reached out impulsively and took one of her hands in his. He examined it carefully as though he was considering reading her fortune.

'I missed you,' he said; and even this was a lie. She

71

hadn't even crossed his mind until he'd thought about going back to his bedsit and she'd been a more agreeable alternative.

'I missed you too.' She gulped down her glass of champagne and proffered it for a refill. Jack picked up the bottle and poured. 'But, Jack, don't think I'm criticizing now, but . . . well, I never really know where I stand with you. You come around one night and then I don't see you for weeks. I *know* you're very busy with your business and everything, but . . .' She seemed to run out of steam. She sat there staring into her glass. 'A girl needs to *know*,' she concluded lamely.

Jack nodded.

'It's difficult,' he observed. 'The business takes up so much of my time. But hopefully, in a couple of years, I'll be able to hire others to run it for me. Then things will be different.'

She glanced at him dubiously.

'Will they, Jack. Will they really?'

'Sure. See, it's the future I'm working for. My idea is to graft like mad now, while I'm relatively young; then retire early and enjoy the fruits of my labour. You know, only suckers work past the age of forty. Make all the right moves and I won't have to lift a finger when I'm older. And it's not just me I'm working for.'

He put his right hand on her knee and let it rest there. He felt a dark pool of despair welling inside him. The dream was to blame, he told himself. It always got him like this, undermining his sense of purpose, reminding him that underneath it all, life was shitty, waiting to jump out and club you to the ground. When he felt this low, he instinctively grabbed for the life preserver. He did it now, slipping an arm around Sammi's slender waist. He hadn't meant to be in this much of a hurry, but now he sensed the image of the double-decker bus – *Catherine's bus* – looming out of the darkness behind his eyes and he wanted to blot it out, eradicate it, override the awful images that threatened to fill his head. He pulled Sammi to him, nuzzled his lips against her neck.

'Jack,' she whispered. 'Please, can't we just—?'

He put his fingertips to her lips, stilling her half-hearted protests.

'I want you,' he said quietly. He kissed her softly on the mouth and she remained rigid in his arms for only a moment. Then he felt the tenseness go from her body, as though someone had pulled a plug. She opened her mouth to admit his tongue. He took the glass from her and set it down on the floor, kissing her more urgently now.

But the bus was still advancing, its front wheels mounting the pavement as it bore down on the bus stop . . .

'Oh, Jack, I've missed you,' whispered Sammi.

He didn't say anything. He filled her mouth with his tongue and tasted, not champagne, but cheap white wine.

The headlights, coming out of the darkness at him.

She put an arm around him now, clinging tightly to him, clamping her mouth on his, making it difficult for him to breathe. He rocked back to his feet, lifting her and carrying her to the bed. There was an awkward moment while he used one arm to scatter her cuddly animals to the floor. Then he laid her down and disengaged his mouth in order to snatch a quick breath. He began to undo the buttons of her blouse, difficult because she wouldn't release the stranglehold she had around his neck. She was clinging to him like a drowning swimmer.

The light, filling his head now, the dark solid mass of the bus towering over him . . .

'I love you, Jack.'

Her voice seemed to come from a long way off, as he peeled her skirt down over her thighs, acting now out of pure instinct, wanting to erase the past in the savage frenzy of his love-making, wanting more than anything else to forget; but knowing that he could not escape the memories no matter how fast he ran.

Jack lay on his back in the narrow bed, staring at the ceiling. Sammi lay with her head on his chest. Her cheeks were streaked with mascara. Now that it was done, he was itching to get out of this unfamiliar bed, out of this room, out where the falling rain could at least give him the illusion of being clean again. As usual, as he approached orgasm, he had shut his eyes and had tried to picture Catherine's face beneath him; but for the first time, he had failed. He could no longer conjure her image in his head. Her features were blurred by time and distance. Now she could only be reached in his dreams.

'I suppose you'll be going,' said Sammi, forlornly.

He looked at her for a moment, feeling a stab of guilt and then slipped an arm over her shoulders.

'Not for a little while,' he assured her. 'You try and get some sleep.'

She nodded, nestled deeper into the crook of his arm. He reached across her and switched off the bedside lamp.

'I'm a lucky girl,' she said, to nobody in particular. 'To have someone like you, it . . . it means a lot. Will I see you tomorrow?'

He shook his head.

'Not for a while, sweetie. I've got some things to do. Then I have to take a little business trip.'

'What, back to Germany?'

He nodded. He didn't dare tell her where he was really going. Somebody might come around asking questions.

'How long will you be away?'

'I'm not sure. As long as it takes. Don't worry, I'll get in touch.'

She seemed satisfied with that. She cuddled down a little, got herself comfortable. There was a long silence before she spoke again, her voice drowsy, at the edge of sleep.

'Jack, say you love me.'

'Hmm?'

'Just say it, Jack. You don't have to mean it. Just say you love me.'

'You know I do.'

'Yes, but I want you to *say* it.'

He steeled himself, knowing he was about to lie to her again. He managed by couching the sentiment in a different language.

'*Je t'aime,*' he murmured.

She sighed. 'French. That's so romantic.'

She quietened down then. After fifteen minutes or so Jack's arm was numb, but Sammi's regular breathing told

75

him she was asleep. He slid from her bed and dressed quietly in the darkness. He glanced down at Sammi. She stirred in her sleep, her arms searching for something that was no longer there. He stooped, selected a large pink teddy bear and put it gently down beside her. Her arms tightened around it. The bear's glass eyes stared glumly up at Jack.

Turning away, he found his raincoat, feeling like a cheap thief making a getaway from the scene of the crime. He tried not to think about Sammi waking up to find him gone. That wasn't a pleasant image at all. But she'd be better off when he was far away from here. Maybe she would find someone who cared, who *really* cared about her. And maybe in a different country, Jack would finally forget about Catherine. Maybe he would learn how to start living again.

He took a final look at Sammi and closed her bedsit door gently behind him.

Chapter Six

It was Wednesday morning, and Jack was back in his own neighbourhood at a little after two A.M. As he approached the house, he was perturbed to see that his bedroom window was illuminated. He wasn't in the habit of leaving a light on at night. Unlocking the front door, he stood for a moment in the draughty hallway, listening intently. The house was quiet but he had a momentary sense of misgiving. On impulse, he took out his airline ticket and wallet and hid them behind a large potted plant on the hall table.

Then he went slowly up the stairs, holding himself ready to run if it should prove necessary. It occurred to him that Riggs might be in there, looking for more booty and he balled his hands into fists at the thought, telling himself that nothing would afford him greater pleasure than to give the thieving bastard a good thumping.

He tip-toed along the landing and saw that the door to his room was ajar. He moved closer, extended a hand and cautiously pushed it open.

'Ah, Mr Doyle,' said Eddie Mulryan. 'You know, I'd

just about given you up.' Mulryan was sitting in Jack's armchair. He was sipping a cup of tea and despite the fact that he had the electric fire on full blast, he was still wearing his heavy overcoat and hat.

Jack's first impulse was to run; but he told himself he had nowhere to go to yet and besides, Mulryan was early, he wasn't due to show till Friday – the day Jack planned to skip to Spain. Jack stepped into the room, closing the door behind him.

'How did you get in?' he demanded.

Eddie smiled shyly, made an apologetic gesture.

'Gosh, I'm sorry, Mr Doyle. I've got this credit card that gets me in just about anywhere ... anywhere with a Yale lock, that is.' He had a soft, charming voice with a pronounced West Country burr in it, it pegged him as a native of Cornwall. 'Your landlord told me you were out, so I waited till all the lights were off and then I sort of, let myself in. Bit of a liberty really, but the rain and everything ... and Mr Winters was most insistent that I see you tonight.'

'Tonight? I wasn't expecting you till Friday. Winters said three days.'

Mulryan nodded. 'I know, I know, I do feel awful about it. But Mr Winters calls the tune, I'm afraid. And he felt ...' He trailed off, his face suddenly glum.

'Felt what?' Jack prompted him. He took off his raincoat and walked over to hang it in the empty wardrobe.

'Well, that you might need a bit of a reminder, like.' He seemed to become aware of the cup in his hands. 'Here, look, I hope you don't mind! I got a bit chilled standing out there and I thought a cup of char would warm me up. It's odd without milk, though. Do you prefer it that way?'

Jack waved a hand in dismissal.

'OK, so you've reminded me,' he snapped. 'Now, if you'll excuse me, I'd like to get some sleep.'

Eddie was shaking his head. 'Not as simple as that, I'm afraid, lawks no! You see, Mr Winters has been talking to various colleagues of yours and I'm afraid he's come to the conclusion that you . . . well, no offence intended, I'm sure, but that you're not entirely trust-worthy. So he says to me, "Eddie," he says, "you go up to Mr Doyle's house tonight and get a part payment out of him. Something to show good faith".'

Jack frowned. 'Well, that's unfortunate,' he said. 'You see, with me not expecting you till Friday, I've nothing for you. You come back then and—'

But again, Mulryan was shaking his head. He looked worried.

'Oh dear. Oh dear, Mr Doyle, that *is* unfortunate, as you say. You see, Mr Winters was very insistent on this point. At least a few hundred, he said. To show good faith.'

Jack spread his hands in a gesture of exasperation.

'What can I tell you?' he asked. 'I've nothing here.'

'I know,' agreed Mulryan, glumly. 'I took the liberty of searching your room.'

'You what?'

'I was most careful not to disturb anything,' added Mulryan defensively. 'I put everything back where I

79

found it. I was rather banking on you having something with you.'

'Can't be done, I'm afraid. Fact is, I can't get the money till late Friday afternoon, then I'll be able to pay you in full.'

'Oh dear.' Now Mulryan looked positively mortified. 'It's most irregular, I'm afraid. Mr Winters is a real stickler where financial matters are concerned.' He carefully set down the cup and Jack noticed that he had long spatulate fingers, the hands of an artist. He got to his feet. It seemed to take him a very long time to get up out of the chair. It was the first time Jack had ever seen him standing up and he was struck by his size. He seemed to dwarf everything in the room, including Jack. 'You know,' he said, 'I hate this kind of thing. I really find it most unpleasant. Tell me, Mr Doyle, are you right or left handed?'

'Right handed,' muttered Jack, bewildered by the sudden change of subject. 'Why do you ask?'

'I just wondered,' replied Mulryan. He was moving closer now and Jack began to back towards the wall.

'Now listen,' he pleaded. 'I've already told you, you'll get your money Friday, in full. So there's not much else I can say, is there?'

'Nothing,' agreed Mulryan. He sighed. 'But it doesn't make this duty any less unpleasant. If you could just give me something to take to Mr Winters. A few pounds . . . tell you what, how much have you got in your pocket?'

Jack slid his right hand into the pocket of his trousers.

'There's nothing here but small cha—'

That was when Mulryan grabbed him, clamping a hand round Jack's left wrist, in a grip that would not have disgraced a tyre-fitter, and throwing the full weight of his huge body at him. Jack slammed against the wall with a grunt. He tried to get his right hand out of his pocket but it was pinned in place by Mulryan's hip. Jack opened his mouth to yell for help and Mulryan stuffed his handkerchief into it, pushing it in with his fingers until it was packed tight.

'It's a clean one, Mr Doyle,' he said apologetically. 'I always make sure to bring a clean hankie with me, you wouldn't want to be biting on to other people's germs, would you?'

He kept his considerable weight pressed against Jack, reached into his pocket and withdrew a knife. A long, thin blade flicked out inches from Jack's face. Jack felt his guts settle with an almost audible twang. His eyes bulged in their sockets and he tried to make protesting noises around the gag inside his mouth.

Mulryan gave Jack a good natured wink.

'My advice, Mr Doyle, is to just relax. This won't take a moment. It's not very pleasant of course, but if you can manage to relax your muscles, you'll find the pain won't be quite as bad.' He lifted Jack's left wrist, sliding it up the wall until it was pinioned a few inches to the left of his head. Jack stared at it in mute terror, aware of beads of sweat popping on his forehead.

Mulryan brought up the point of the knife until it rested against the palm of the hand. Jack's strength evaporated. He struggled again, but it was feeble, useless.

'I do wish you'd had something for me, Mr Doyle,' said Mulryan regretfully. He smiled and put his full weight on the handle of the knife, pushing the blade clean through Jack's hand and deep into the plaster of the wall. Jack saw it happen a full second before he registered the pain. It felt like a burning cigarette grinding into his palm. He closed his eyes and tried to scream around the gag and he must have blacked out for an instant, because when he opened his eyes, Mulryan had pulled back on the knife and Jack's hand was still impaled on it. A scarlet trickle was pulsing down his arm, staining the cuff of his shirt. Mulryan gathered him closer as though trying to waltz with him.

'That's the first bit over with,' he whispered, his face inches away from Jack. His breath smelled of peppermint. 'Now here comes the worst bit. I don't mind telling you, I *hate* this bit, but Mr Winters always insists on it. "A memory jogger", he calls it and by golly, it does seem to work. What I'm going to do, Mr Doyle, I'm going to give the knife a little twist. It might help if you put your mind on something else for a moment . . .'

Jack was shaking his head, spraying sweat at Mulryan, but he didn't seem to notice. He was intent on finishing the job. He gave the knife a slow twist, first to the left, then to the right. To Jack, it was as though somebody was pouring acid into the open wound. Blackness descended for an instant and then he seemed to drift, suspended in warm liquid. But the final agony of the blade jerking free from his flesh jolted him back to wakefulness. He collapsed into Mulryan's arms and the big man was carrying him over to the chair. Then he was searching Jack's pockets, quickly, expertly, ensuring that he had not been holding out on him.

At last, he seemed satisfied. 'There now,' he whispered soothingly. 'All over with . . . keep your arm out, we don't want to get blood on your suit, do we?' He reached up and pulled the handkerchief from Jack's mouth, like a conjurer pulled flags from a top hat. Jack let out a long exhalation and would have slumped forward if Mulryan hadn't put a hand on his chest. 'Careful! My God, you've gone as white as a sheet. Here now, I've got a bandage in my pocket.'

Jack stared at Mulryan as he took out a hospital dressing, unwrapped it and began to wind it expertly around the lacerated hand. 'You take it easy now. If you feel faint, just put your head between your knees and take deep breaths.' Mulryan glanced down at large crimson stains on the front of Jack's suit and tutted loudly. 'You want to try and wash them out before they take a hold,' he advised. 'They say milk is very good for bloodstains, but you haven't got any milk, have you?' He finished tying the dressing. 'Now I'll make you a nice hot cup of black tea,' he said. 'You'll be as right as rain.'

Jack tried to talk.

'Cig . . . hett,' he whispered.

'What's that? Cigarette? Oh, certainly.' Mulryan fished out a packet of Silk Cut. Extracting one, he popped it into Jack's mouth and lit it with a red plastic lighter. Jack inhaled smoke and his body began to tremble violently.

'That's shock,' observed Mulryan. 'It takes you like that. I'll get the tea and then we can discuss what we're going to do about this money.'

He went to the kitchenette and Jack sat there, shaking, taking pulls on the cigarette and puffing out smoke in clouds. His left hand throbbed rhythmically, as though imbued with a life of its own. Only now, as the shock began to recede, did he realize the enormity of what had just happened to him. He glanced down at his last decent suit, ruined with splashes of blood and it was that, more than anything else, that made him cry.

'Now then, now then,' said Mulryan, as he returned with a cup of tea. 'Drink some of this, you'll feel better.' He tilted the cup to Jack's lips with great care, making sure not to scald him. 'A terrible business,' he murmured, as Jack sipped dutifully. 'You wouldn't believe the times I've had to do that but it never gets any easier. It's bad when you don't enjoy your work, but there can't be many people in this world who can honestly say that they do.' He took the cup away and set it down next to his own. His expression became grim again. 'Now, tell me about the money,' he suggested.

Jack's words came out in a headlong tumble, so anxious was he to get the message across.

'Get it for you! Friday, no problems, promise! You call, for sure, definitely Friday night and ... have the works for you, friend coming over from the States, bail me out, cash on the nail, you'll see ... just got to hang on, and you'll have it, in full, promise ...'

Mulryan extended a finger to touch Jack's lips as he raved uncontrollably.

'I hope you're not lying to me,' he said firmly. 'If I was to find out you'd been stringing me along, well, that would reflect very badly on me as a professional, you understand. And if that happened, Mr Doyle, I'm afraid I'd have to . . . well, *kill* you. And I shouldn't enjoy that at all. No, not one bit.'

Jack glanced up at Mulryan and for the first time he felt a flash of pure anger well up within him.

'You do enjoy it,' he hissed through clenched teeth. 'Oh, you protest like fuck, but deep down, you *love* it.'

Mulryan made a dismissive gesture with one hand.

'Oh, go on with you! You're just feeling put out! Understandable, really.' He got up and went over to the wall, retrieved his fallen knife, wiped it carefully on the discarded handkerchief. 'Now don't you worry about that wound getting infected,' he said. 'I keep the blade nice and clean.'

He folded the knife, slipped it back into his pocket.

'You think on, Mr Doyle. Friday at noon, I'll come a calling. You have that money for me . . . all of it. Or I'll kill you. You know I'll do it, don't you?'

Jack glanced furtively at Mulryan, then looked away, nodded.

'Good. Just so's we understand each other.' He pointed to the cups at Jack's feet. 'Get some milk in for Friday,' he said amiably. 'Tea's nicer with a drop of milk.' He gave Jack a last wink and turning, he went to the door and let himself out.

Jack sat listening to the slow clump of footsteps going down the stairs. The front door opened, then slammed shut.

'Friday,' he murmured. 'You'll have to catch me first.' The cigarette butt dropped from his fingers and extinguished itself in half a cup of tea. It made a brief hiss, then died.

Chapter Seven

Friday morning. The black BMW nosed through the high street traffic at a sedate thirty miles per hour. From the back seat, Tam McGiver stared out at the busy press of humanity on the pavements with a sour expression on his pockmarked face. Beside him, The Armenian was engrossed in the latest issue of *Homes & Gardens*. He kept shaking his head, tutting loudly to himself, presumably in violent disagreement with some views expressed on the subject of interior decoration.

McGiver sneered out of the window, thinking back to a rough childhood spent in a housing estate in Strathclyde, where kids very quickly learned how to be hard-knocks and where a grown man who read *Homes & Gardens* was liable to be strung up from the nearest lamp-post. His old man had been an unemployed shopfitter with a powerful thirst for Scotch. His old woman preferred gin. She had a broken nose and a reputation as the local 'bike'. Tam and his older brother, Alex, had sought solace in being so hard that nobody ever dared rib them about it. By the time they'd reached their teens, they were running a gang of tearaways and had established a reputation as people you didn't argue with unless you fancied a ride on a stretcher. Alex had been dead three years now, and Tam's parents, so far as he knew or cared, might well have joined him. Tam was the last of the McGivers. A dose of mumps in his early-twenties had neatly put paid to any chance of him furthering the clan, but he didn't lose any sleep over it. Kids were noisy bastards anyway.

It was the death of his brother that had finally persuaded Tam it was time to get out of Glasgow. Over the years, the brothers had worked their gang up into a pretty 'respectable' organization. Protection, loan-sharking, prostitution and drugs – they'd had their nicotined fingers in them all and were doing very well out of it. Alex was the brains behind the outfit and Tam provided the necessary muscle. It was a good combination. But then the heroin business had suddenly mushroomed in the '80s and a new gang had started to push its way on to their patch. The new guys were Americans with a Family connection. After having an increasingly lean time of it in their homeland, they'd relocated to Glasgow, intending to claim it as their own.

The McGiver brothers found themselves out-gunned. Where they'd relied on baseball bats to establish *their* superiority, *these* heavies favoured pump-action shotguns. They'd started making overtures to the brothers, offering to cut them in for a small percentage if they stepped down, quietly. Alex had refused to even consider their offer, had returned all their messages with ill disguised contempt. Tam had serious misgivings about the whole thing but it had been useless to argue with his big brother.

'It's taken us years to build up our operation,' Alex had said. 'They'll take it from us over my dead body.'

Prophetic words as it turned out. A few days later, Alex was found lying under a railway bridge with most of his skull blown away. Tam was left with two choices: go out for vengeance or leave with his tail between his legs. There was never any real conflict on that one. He'd left Glasgow the very next day.

By comparison, the scene in London seemed positively *genteel*. Tam had worked at a succession of jobs; night-club bouncer, drug courier, hired muscle; before coming to work full time as The Armenian's enforcer about a year ago. He liked the job and stayed with it, not because he respected the man, or anything dumb like that, but simply because The Armenian was willing to pay the kind of money that Tam asked for ... and got. There were no ambitions to move in on his employer's territory either. He had seen enough to know that behind the prissy facade, The Armenian was ruthless, that he possessed a mind that was capable of the most extreme cruelty.

With his own eyes, Tam had seen his boss finger a man, just because he had failed to show him the necessary respect. That stuff about it being a matter of pride was no exaggeration. If someone tried to cheat The Armenian out of fifty pence, he'd be prepared to spend a thousand pounds to avenge himself. You couldn't argue with determination like that and Tam had learned from his brother's mistakes, that in the face of a superior power, the last thing you did was oppose it. Better by far to join forces with it, let it work *for* you, let it enclose you like a protective barrier. And all you had to do in return was be an evil bastard. It was a great system if you had a flair for it. Tam was good at being an evil bastard. He had a real talent in that direction.

He still carried a lot of bottled-up rage about the death of his brother. He hadn't been with Alex the night he was killed, he'd been with a tart. He had never quite rid himself of the belief that he should have died alongside Alex and that his weakness for women had constituted some kind of betrayal. So these days he treated women like shit and on those occasions when he was called upon to inflict pain on somebody, he did it by imagining that they had been the organizers of his brother's execution. And in this inventive frame of mind, he wielded a razor, a hammer or a blowtorch to great effect – and he never had anybody cross him a second time.

Take this morning for instance. The BMW was gliding to a halt outside a newsagent's shop, the property of an elderly Pakistani by the name of Mukherjee. The man had a regular commitment to pay money for protection, a hundred a month, nothing extravagant. He was usually reliable but the collector in this area had reported that Mr Mukherjee had been thirty pounds shy of the figure last month and had asked for more time to come up with this month's money. He'd given some shit about being ill with an ulcer and how he was going to have to pay for a private operation. Clearly it was time to remind him of his responsibilities.

'Just shake him up a little,' murmured The Armenian, without looking up from his magazine. 'You like the rust or the beige here?' He tapped the page of soft furnishings with a plump finger.

'The rust. Beige is too bland. You want me to put him in the hospital?'

'Not this time. Don't break any bones.' He pointed to a sofa, covered in a textured ivory fabric. 'This is nice, though.'

'It'd show the dirt in no time,' said Tam. He got out of the car and strolled across to the shop door. He let himself in, wrinkling his nose at the powerful odour of curry spices that permeated the place. He moved past the shop's central aisle which was stacked high with merchandise. *Coining it in*, thought McGiver. *And the cheeky bastard has the nerve to hold out on his protection payments!*

From behind a counter, heaped with confectionery, the tiny, plump figure of Mrs Mukherjee regarded McGiver apprehensively. She was wearing a bright orange sari and had a large silver ring through one nostril. He stepped up to the counter and grinned at her, relishing the way she flinched.

'Good morning, Mrs M! I've called to see your husband. A wee business matter.'

'Yes, please, you go through, please!' She waved a hand at a bead-curtained doorway behind her, leading to the shop's living quarters. McGiver knew immediately that something was wrong. Mr Mukherjee usually acted like this was the entrance to a holy mosque, never allowing a heathen money collector across the threshold.

What's the wee bastard up to? he wondered. He studied Mrs Mukherjee closely, noting how her eyes kept flicking away from him. She was more than just nervous. She was near shitting in her sari.

'On his own in there, is he?' he ventured.

Mrs Mukherjee waved frantically at the doorway.

'Yes, go through, go through!' she shrieked.

Still grinning, McGiver did as she suggested. The door gave on to a narrow hallway. He followed the sound of a television set, canned laughter and applause. He entered a small sitting room, the walls painted a bilious green, the ceiling a fierce shade of orange.

The Armenian would puke if he saw this, McGiver thought. *They just love their bright colours, don't they?*

Old Mr Mukherjee was sitting in a floral print armchair in front of the television set. A toddler, a boy maybe eighteen months old, was sitting in his lap. The old man looked pale and drawn. *Maybe he has been telling the truth about being ill*, thought McGiver. Not that it made any difference. There were two other men in the room, young Asian lads wearing leather jackets and jeans. They got to their feet as McGiver entered, squaring up to him and giving him stonefaced glares. McGiver could see that underneath they were as jumpy as a pair of cats.

He smiled, pleasantly.

'Well, well,' he said. 'This is a surprise, Mr Mukherjee. A reception committee.'

'These are my nephews,' announced Mukherjee, unhappily. 'They have something to say to you, Mr McGiver.'

'Is that a fact.' McGiver studied the youths thoughtfully. The eldest was probably in his mid-twenties, the younger no more than eighteen. They were doing their damnedest to look mean and tough, but their dark brown eyes had a soft look about them and he could tell they didn't have much experience of this sort of thing. The eldest did the talking. He had a south London accent.

'My uncle isn't well. He's suffering from an ulcer and all this worry of meeting payments is making his condition worse.'

McGiver tutted sympathetically.

'Well, that's why I'm here. To take the worry off his shoulders. To make sure nobody comes in off the street and gives him trouble.'

'No, I don't think so. My uncle doesn't need any help of that kind. If he does, *we'll* provide it. So I must ask you, politely, not to come here again, OK?'

McGiver raised his eyebrows. He turned his head to look at Mukherjee. 'This your idea, was it? You call these boys in to handle things?'

Mukherjee shook his head, made a dismissive gesture with one hand. 'It was *their* idea, Mr McGiver. They say I am being foolish to be giving in to your demands all the time. I am telling them, I only try not to make trouble.'

'Very wise.' McGiver eyed the older of the two youths

coolly. 'So. You think the two of you can handle trouble. Is that right?'

The youth nodded. 'If we have to.'

It had gone very quiet now, a silence punctuated only by a burst of canned laughter from the television.

'Well, I'm not convinced you can cut it,' said McGiver, keeping his gaze locked into the young man's eyes. 'There's some desperate customers about these days, you know. Society's breaking down. The police are nowhere when you need them. Nowhere. It only takes one head-banger to come in here and start throwing his weight about and you lads would be expected to escort him off the premises. That's a big responsibility for a pair of wee bairns like yourselves. I don't know if you'd be any good at it.'

'Like I said,' the youth told him. 'We'd do OK.'

'That right?' McGiver smiled. 'Tell you what, why don't we put it to the test? Hmm? Let's pretend that *I'm* the headbanger, right. Let's see if you can escort me off the premises, what do you say?'

'Please,' said Mr Mukherjee. 'No trouble. I don't want any trouble.'

The youth didn't even glance at his uncle.

'It's all right. Mr McGiver is just leaving.'

McGiver feigned a look of surprise. He glanced quickly around the room. 'Who said that?' he whispered. 'Was it you? Did you say that? Jesus Christ, I thought it was John Wayne for a moment!' He narrowed his eyes and the smile vanished. 'Listen sonny, I'm getting a little tired of this. What say you fuck off out of it and let your uncle and me get on with our business, eh?'

'That's enough!' snapped the youth. He stepped forward, raising his hands to grab McGiver's lapels. Then he froze, a look of shocked surprise on his face. His eyes bulged in their sockets and beads of sweat broke suddenly on his forehead. His mouth dropped and a sound escaped, a tiny little whimpering noise. He gesticulated with his hand, as though planning to tear at McGiver's face. McGiver simply tightened his grip on the youth's balls, feeling them crush like eggs. He wrenched them hard to one side and the youth's eyes rolled up in his head, revealing the whites. He dropped like a stone, crashing to the ground at McGiver's feet with no more than a grunted exhalation.

There was a moment of stunned silence. The younger boy stood there staring at his brother's inert body, unable to believe that something could happen so quickly. Then recovering his senses, he fumbled in his jacket pocket and came out with a cut-throat razor. McGiver smiled. It was good to see that some of these kids were keeping the old traditions alive. He stepped back from the fallen youth and gestured to the boy to come at him.

'Please,' protested Mukherjee. 'Stop it now, this is senseless.'

'Keep out of it, Uncle!' snarled his nephew, speaking for the first time, a little boy trying to sound bigger than he was. His blood was up now and cold rage was flickering in those dark eyes. He wanted to avenge his older brother, the very thing that McGiver had had the sense not to do all those years ago. The kid made a feint with the razor but McGiver knew that's all it was. He didn't move a muscle.

'I used to use one of those back in Glasgow,' he observed matter of factly. 'I'll give you a tip. The best thing about a razor is the element of surprise. You whip it out, you cut somebody and you're out of there before they even know what's happening. But showing it to me like that . . . big mistake. Whatever you try now, I can see it coming a mile off.'

'You've got a big mouth,' observed the youth, circling McGiver warily. 'Maybe I'll cut you a new one.'

McGiver laughed.

'Nice line,' he observed. 'But could you hurry it up, do you think? I'm parked on a double yellow.'

The youth lunged at McGiver's face, fast but not fast enough. McGiver grabbed his wrist, jerked him forward off balance. He dropped to one knee and twisted the youth's arm backwards across his other bent leg. Then he thrust down hard with both hands and the arm snapped across his knee like a dry stick. The razor dropped from the youth's twitching fingers and he opened his mouth to scream, but he didn't make it. McGiver knuckled him casually, almost tenderly across the right temple and he was out cold, the scream trailing away on his slack lips.

McGiver got back to his feet, picking up the fallen razor as he did so. He folded it and turned to face Mukherjee. The old man was slumped in his chair looking stunned and sicker than ever. The toddler on his lap was looking down at the fallen youths and giggling merrily.

'Happy little feller,' observed McGiver, stepping across the bodies. He reached out a hand to the child and stroked his black curly hair. 'This your grandson, Mr Mukherjee?'

The old man nodded wearily.

'There was no need for any of this,' he whispered. 'No need for violence. I told them . . . I pleaded with them . . .'

'Quite so.' McGiver reached down and lifted the toddler out of Mukherjee's lap, before he could react. He moved to a vacant chair and sat the child down on his knee; the same knee he had used to break the youth's arm. He bounced him playfully up and down. 'Now you just come and play with your Uncle Tam,' he suggested. 'While I have a wee chat with your grandad.'

Mukherjee seemed to register what had just happened. He eyed McGiver warily. 'You had best give him back to me,' he said. 'He . . . he's nervous with strangers.'

'Nonsense! He's quite happy with me, aren't you laddie? Let's see now, what have I got that you could play with?' He thought for a moment. 'I know,' he said. He opened the razor and held it out to the child. 'What's this then? Would baby like to play with it? Would you? Of course you would!' He put the razor's handle into the child's chubby little hand.

Mukherjee stared. He made a small groaning sound.

'Oh my god,' he whispered. 'Please, no, take it off him!'

'I will. Just as soon as we've settled this problem about the money.'

Mukherjee stared at his grandson. The boy was gazing

at the bright shiny razor with evident interest. He was still at that age where he tended to put everything into his mouth.

'I ... I'll p ... pay you,' stammered Mukherjee. 'I'll pay you now!'

'Good. A hundred and thirty pounds, I think it is.'

Grey faced, Mukherjee struggled out of his chair and hurried to the door. He was shouting orders to his wife and McGiver was pleased to hear the sum of one hundred and thirty pounds being mentioned. He watched the toddler with interest. The child was raising his arm now, lifting the razor to his mouth. Mukherjee stood in the doorway, his hands clasped in an attitude of prayer.

'Please!' he whispered. 'I said I'll pay you!'

'Yes, but I don't see any money. And besides, that isn't *my* razor. It belongs to one of your nephews, doesn't it? You shouldn't let those boys bring such dangerous objects into the house.'

The child opened his mouth on the flat of the blade, then closed it. He began to suck enthusiastically. A thin trickle of blood welled on his bottom lip and ran down his chin. McGiver watched impassively.

Mukherjee's wife appeared in the doorway clutching a thin wad of money. She saw the crumpled figures on the floor, then registered what was happening to her grandson. She made a tiny, plaintive sound at the back of her throat. Mukherjee snatched the money from her and waved it desperately at McGiver.

'Is it all there?' asked McGiver, quietly. Blood was

now dribbling on to the toddler's chest, staining into the fabric of his white jumpsuit.

'Yes, sir! All of it, I promise. Only please, *please* . . .'

McGiver nodded. He took hold of the toddler's wrist and gently but firmly slid the razor out of his mouth. The cut on the child's lip was no more than a nick. Tam closed the razor and dropped it into his pocket. Lifting the child as he stood up, he handed him to Mrs Mukherjee. Taking the money from the old man, he folded it neatly and put it into the breast pocket of his coat. Mukherjee looked spent now. He sagged back against the doorframe, one hand clutched to his stomach. There were bluish rings around his eyes. McGiver gestured to the unconscious youths on the floor.

'Let's not have any more of that nonsense,' he suggested. 'All you have to do is make your payments. It couldn't be easier, could it?'

Mr Mukherjee shook his head, weakly. Tam smiled at Mrs Mukherjee and patted the toddler gently on the head.

'Bonny wee lad you've got there,' he observed. 'You want to look after him.'

McGiver strolled out of the room, down the corridor and into the shop. There were a couple of kids helping themselves to chocolate at the unattended counter. 'Oy!' he shouted. 'Get out of it, you little bastards!' The kids bolted for the open door and scattered out into the street. Grinning, he followed them. He walked over to the BMW and climbed in the back. The Armenian was talking on his car-phone, his expression grave. McGiver closed the door behind him and reached forward to tap the driver on the shoulder. The car accelerated smoothly away from the curb.

'OK, Lou,' said The Armenian. 'Thanks for the information.' He put down the phone and sat there looking thoughtful. Then he glanced up at McGiver. 'You were a long time,' he observed. 'Thought maybe you were having trouble.'

McGiver shook his head.

'The old man tried to pull something,' he explained. 'Bastard won't try it again in a hurry.'

'Good. I just took a call from Lou Winters. He was boasting to me how he took an IOU for over nine thousand pounds in a card game the other night.'

McGiver looked impressed.

'Nice one,' he said.

'Not really. The name of the loser was Jack Doyle.'

'Doyle? Jesus, isn't he—?'

The Armenian nodded.

'Lou's got his minder keeping an eye on him. He's got a feeling he might try and er . . . skip his obligation to pay. Maybe even skip the country. Borrowing two grand from me might just have put him in the market for an airline ticket to someplace else.'

McGiver frowned.

'What do you want me to do?'

'Check with Lou's minder. Mulryan, I think his name is. You know him, don't you?'

'We've met once or twice. Odd character, that one. Not the full shilling, if you ask me.'

'Well, whatever. I told Lou we should work together on this. If Doyle is trying to con the pair of us, he needs to be made an example of. See to it, will you?'

McGiver shrugged. 'Pleasure,' he said.

The Armenian raised his copy of *Homes & Gardens*.

'And now,' he murmured. 'Curtains. What do you think? The William Morris print . . . or the Regency stripe?'

Chapter Eight

'Goin' somewhere nice?' asked the taxi-driver, as the cab pulled up at Gatwick's departure terminal.

'Yeah,' replied Jack, but didn't elaborate further. The less people who knew his destination the better. He collected the rucksack that constituted his only luggage and reached out with his bandaged hand to open the door. A jolt of pain flickered up the length of his arm, making him grit his teeth. He stifled a curse, got out and turned back to pay the driver.

He'd left his bedsit at first light, terrified that Mulryan might pay him another unexpected call. He hadn't told Riggs he was leaving, in case the old bastard pestered him for more money. Dressed in a pair of faded jeans and a sweatshirt, he felt like an entirely different person. He'd spent several hours wandering aimlessly around the shops, chewing aspirin to quell the throbbing pain in his hand. More than once, he'd glanced over his shoulder with the distinct impression that he was being followed. He told himself repeatedly that he was just being paranoid. Mulryan wasn't due to call until midday; but Jack soberly reminded himself that the man seemed to have a liking for early appointments.

Fighting a mounting panic, he had forced himself to sit in a café and eat some breakfast, but his stomach was rebellious and he barely got down more than a mouthful. With one eye on the mottled, fly-specked clock on the wall, he took stock of his resources. He had about fifteen-hundred pounds to his name and not the slightest idea of what he'd do once he got to Spain. Still, just now that was the least of his worries. He thought about Eddie Mulryan and Tam McGiver and his stomach threatened to reject what little food he had managed to swallow. God help him now if the door opened and one of those animals walked in ...

Unable to wait any longer, he'd left the café and hailed a cab. Now, pushing his way through the busy airport terminal, he felt a little better, imagining himself being absorbed into the crowd. He located his flight check-in desk and joined a long queue of tourists, most of whom looked ridiculous in shorts, shell-suits, garish Bermuda shirts and sun-hats.

Eventually, he reached the desk, collected his boarding pass. The pretty brunette barely raised an eyebrow at his lack of any serious luggage, offered him a smoking or non-smoking seat and wished him a pleasant flight. Turning gratefully away he began to walk towards passport control.

Then the bad thing happened. He halted abruptly as something took a firm hold on one of the straps of his rucksack.

'Hello, Mr Doyle,' said a familiar voice in his ear. Jack turned, locked in nightmare, to find Eddie Mulryan standing at his elbow, smiling good naturedly down at him.

'Eddie! I . . . I didn't expect to see you here!'

'No, I don't suppose you did.' Mulryan stepped closer, slipped a brotherly arm around Jack's shoulders. It felt like a lead weight lying there. 'You've no idea how disappointed I am by this, Mr Doyle. Trying to run out on me . . . and you making me those promises and all. It doesn't look very good, does it?'

Jack licked his lips nervously.

'It's not how it looks!' he gasped, fighting to keep the desperation out of his voice. 'I'm here to meet somebody. The . . . the guy who's bringing in my money . . . *your* money! He'll be coming through those gates at any moment.' Jack attempted to take another step in the direction of passport control but Mulryan's powerful arm restrained him. He was shaking his head.

'Lying only ever makes things worse,' he observed ruefully.

'I'm not lying! Listen to me!'

'I know, Mr Doyle, I know. You're waiting for a friend. Which is why you're carrying that rucksack. Which is why I just saw you checking in on a flight to Malaga.' He sighed. 'You know, I thought . . . I really thought that after our little talk the other night, you'd be ready to play straight with me. Now, I see you'll never play straight. You're a bad egg, Mr Doyle. Beyond redemption. Perhaps it's better this way. Come along now, we'll go and see Mr Winters, shall we?'

He began to draw Jack towards the exit. Jack glanced desperately around at the crowds of milling tourists.

'I won't go!' he hissed. 'You can't make me. What are you going to do, kill me in front of all these witnesses? You'd never get away with it!'

Mulryan chuckled. 'Oh, I wouldn't be so sure, Mr Doyle. I've put bigger fellers than you to sleep in a crowd. Shall I tell you something about crowds? They don't see anything, not ever. It's so easily done. I just take that long blade of mine and I slip it in here.' He caressed the back of Jack's neck with his index finger, as though feeling out the exact spot. 'Push it up hard, right into the brain. Lovely neat job it makes, hardly any blood to speak of. Then I say, "Here, this feller's fainted! Is there a doctor?" And I walk off looking for one. And by the time anybody knows any different, I'm far away. Now, if that's how you want it, it's all right by me.' He had slipped his right hand into his pocket and there was a sharp, metallic click.

Jack shook his head. He had the awful sensation that his testicles were shrinking, collapsing in on themselves until his scrotum was a dry, empty sack.

'No,' he whispered. 'We'll go see Mr Winters.' He forced himself to put one foot in front of the other and they approached the exit doors.

This can't happen, Jack told himself. *Not when I was so close. I was nearly clear* . . .

The glass doors slid open with a hiss and they stepped out into the morning sunlight. Mulryan inhaled the fresh air deeply through his nostrils.

'Lovely mornin', he observed. 'I think there's a touch of spring in the air, don't you? Come summer, I think I'll go down to St Ives and visit my mum. Grand old girl, she is. I think you'd like her, Mr Doyle. And you know what? I think she'd like you. She makes the finest apple pie you've ever tasted.'

Jack's brain reeled. His eyes flicked left and right seeking escape, hoping for the first time in his life for the sight of a policeman. No such luck. Just a press of passengers, loading and unloading baggage, intent only on their departures. Mulryan led the way across the pavement to where a black saloon waited. At the wheel, a runty little man with a half-grown moustache was smoking a cigarette. He glanced up and grinned at the newcomers, displaying a set of rat-like teeth.

'Didn't take long,' he observed. His little black eyes studied Jack curiously as though relishing the moment, looking as he imagined, at a dead man. Mulryan reached past Jack and opened the rear door. Jack stood there looking into the claustrophobic interior of the car, knowing that once inside it, he might as well give up all hope. He put his hands on the roof of the car and braced himself, making his body rigid.

'Get in, Mr Doyle,' said Mulryan quietly.

'Go fuck yourself,' said Jack.

'Oh dear,' muttered his captor. Then he punched Jack expertly, almost delicately in the kidneys, masking the blow from view with his massive frame. Jack crumpled, doubling over in a spasm of pain and then Mulryan bundled him easily into the back of the car. Jack sat there hunched, gasping for breath, still clinging to his rucksack as though it was a life preserver. Mulryan got in beside him and slammed the door.

'Sorry about that,' he said. 'Now you be a good lad and there'll be no need for that kind of rough stuff, will there?' He nodded to the driver and the car moved slowly away from the kerb. Jack glanced wildly back over his shoulder, seeing his sanctuary receding rapidly into the distance.

'How did you know I was here?' he asked, bitterly.

Mulryan beamed, pleased with himself. 'I had a feeling you might try something like this. So I got Vince here to keep an eye on your place. When you went out this morning, he followed you. One step behind, he was, all the way. And when you got into a taxi and headed to the airport, Vince radioed me.' Mulryan spread his hands in a gesture that said 'easy as pie'.

Jack massaged his aching side, glanced out of the window again. The air terminal was already dropping back out of sight. He computed the odds, knowing he had to take a chance, that he had nothing to lose. Meanwhile, he had to keep talking. Mulryan was relaxing, settling back into his seat.

'What's going to happen to me?' asked Jack.

Mulryan frowned. 'We discussed that, remember? Don't worry, I'll make it quick, you'll hardly know a thing about it. But I expect Mr Winters will want to see it done.'

Vince snickered unpleasantly.

'Shut your mouth, Vince!' snapped Eddie.

Jack told himself it was now or never. He turned to

Mulryan and slipped on an expression of humble contriteness.

'Mr Mulryan, I want you to know that I don't have anything against you personally. I guess you're just doing your job.'

Mulryan nodded. 'True enough,' he said.

'I wonder if I could ask one last favour? Have you got a cigarette, please?'

Mulryan smiled. 'The condemned man, eh?' he said, sounding genuinely sympathetic. 'Why not?' He reached his right hand into his coat pocket and then hesitated, perhaps catching the merest glimpse of something in Jack's expression, perhaps remembering that he had used a similar trick on Jack the other night. That was when Jack hit Mulryan with his clenched right fist, putting everything he had into it, driving the knuckles hard into his mouth. The big man rocked back against the window with a grunt of surprise and Jack followed up with his forehead, smashing it into Mulryan's nose. There was a satisfying crunch as the bone broke and the nose spread itself across Mulryan's face like a rotten vegetable. Blood squirted down his white shirt and he flopped back, his eyes flickering. Now Jack twisted sideways and lunged over the seat to clap a hand across Vince's mouth. He felt the sting of a cigarette beneath his palm as it crumpled against Vince's lips. Vince let go of the wheel with a strangled scream and the car veered hard to the left, towards a metal safety barrier. Jack let go of Vince and clung tightly to the seat.

The impact jolted through the car. Vince jerked

forward and his forehead struck the wheel with a dull thud. The horn blared, a long, protesting squeal of outrage. Then there was a second impact as the vehicle behind crunched into the rear bumper, flinging Jack back against the seat. Vince lurched backwards too, his head spraying blood and the horn stopped blaring. There was a moment of absolute silence while Jack sat there stunned, scarcely believing that he had done this thing. Then his sense of reality came flooding back and he grabbed the handle of the door, flung it open and began to scramble out of the car. He would have made it too if Mulryan's arm hadn't wrapped itself around his neck, pulling him back inside.

'Oh doh, by fred, I dobe thig so.' The voice hissing in Jack's ear, distorted by the flattened nose. 'Cub here sudshine . . .'

Jack yelled and drove his elbow backwards hard, felt it thud into Mulryan's chest, heard the tortured exhalation of air. The arm relaxed its grip and Jack scrambled free, got out of the car; then in the same instant, remembered his rucksack. His passport and money were in there, he couldn't leave without it. He cursed aloud, turned back and saw it lying on the floor. Desperately he leaned forward and made a grab at it. In the same instant, he saw Mulryan, slumped against the window, his nose and mouth streaming blood, his eyes dangerous with shock and pain. The right hand came out of his pocket holding the knife and his fingers seemed to sprout steel. Jack snatched at the strap of the rucksack, just as the big man lunged with the knife. There was a dull squeak as the blade buried itself deep into the rucksack. Mulryan's eyes widened in surprise. He grunted, began to pull at the knife and Jack wrenched hard upwards with all his strength, snagging the blade and jerking the handle clear of Mulryan's fingers.

Jack backed away from the car, thinking he was clear, but Mulryan lunged a second time and his hand closed on the rucksack's other strap. He pulled and Jack felt himself drawn towards the car.

'No!' he screamed. He dug in his heels, put both hands to the strap, oblivious to the pain in his bandaged palm. He put his entire weight into the struggle and Mulryan fell forwards across the seat, his outstretched arm reaching from the doorway. 'Let go!' demanded Jack. 'Let fucking go!' He lifted a foot and brought the heel of his shoe down on Mulryan's hand, trapping it against the sill of the car. The plump fingers burst like sausages. From within the car came a bellow of pain. Jack was free, the rucksack clutched to his chest like stolen treasure. Then he was off and running up the road, in and Jout of the stalled traffic, his heart hammering in his chest, praying that he could make it back to the airport before his flight departed.

A hundred yards up the road, his breath pounding in his throat, he turned and glanced back. Mulryan was coming after him. He was shambling up the road, weaving like a drunk, his face buried in a bloody handkerchief, his broken fingers jammed into the pocket of his overcoat. His forehead was ashen and glistening with sweat and he barely seemed human, more like an unwieldly automaton programmed to pursue Jack to the bitter end.

Jack shook his head, cursed. He ran on, lengthening his stride, reassured by the sight of the airport departure buildings coming into view as he moved around a curve in the road. He was going to make it. *He had to make it*.

By the time he reached the entrance he was dizzy with exhaustion. The glass doors parted and he shouldered his way through the crowds, fumbling for his passport in the pocket of the rucksack. It wouldn't come out. He stared at it dully and then realized that Mulryan's knife was still sticking out of the bag. The blade had gone clean through the passport, pinning it in place. He covered the handle with his open palm and moved to a vacant seat in the lounge. As surreptitiously as possible, he tugged at the knife, trying to pull it out, but the wretched thing wouldn't come free. He glanced nervously around, convinced that hundreds of pairs of eyes were watching him – but nobody seemed to be taking the least bit of notice. Reassured, he gritted his teeth, tried again. At last, the knife came free. Pushing it into a split in the seat beneath him he got back to his feet. The Tannoy above his head kicked into life, startling him.

'This is the third and final call for flight AE6104 for Malaga. Would any remaining passengers please make their way to Gate 16.'

Jack grunted, started to walk towards passport control. *OK*, he thought, *Try for Christ's sake to look normal!*

Then he hesitated, turned towards the entrance doors as they slid open. Mulryan came in, staggering now and people instinctively pulled aside to let him by. The handkerchief against his face was a crimson rag.

No, no, no! Move, man. Keep walking! Jack began to walk briskly towards passport control. *Don't run. You'll look suspicious if you run.*

He reached the desk and saw, with a sinking sensation, that there was a sizeable queue. He joined the tail of it, biting his lip, looking, but not wanting to look, at the huge figure making tortuous progress towards him across the intervening space.

The queue moved up one.

Come on for fuck's sake, move it!

He glanced towards Mulryan. Closer now. Too close. Jack could see his glazed eyes, staring from above the bloody mask of the handkerchief. There was more hate in those eyes than Jack had seen in his entire life. Just a few yards away now . . .

'Sir?' Jack glanced up in astonishment. The uniformed man was holding out his hand for the passport. The queue had miraculously gone through. Jack stepped forward and put the passport in the man's hand, waited in torment as the man scrutinized it. He was probably wondering why there was a narrow slit right through the middle of it. After what seemed an eternity, the man seemed satisfied. He smiled, handed back the passport. Jack began to walk through the barrier.

'Midder Doyle!' The distorted voice stopped him in his tracks. It was alien, unfamiliar, the nose clotted with blood and muffled by the sodden folds of the handkerchief. Jack flinched. He turned slowly to look back at Mulryan.

'Hab a good trib,' said Mulryan. His eyes blazed with feral malevolence. 'Oh yes, hab a preasant tibe in Maraga. I be oud to join you just as soon as I bedder.'

Jack nodded grimly. He stood there and watched as Mulryan turned carefully on his heel and lurched away. He stumbled, almost fell, had to support himself by leaning on the arm of a chair, his chest rising and falling as he struggled to cling to consciousness. Then he was off again, swaying towards the exit doors.

The passport officer stared at Jack inquisitively.

'He's not been at all well,' said Jack; and turning, he hurried in the direction of the departure lounge.

Chapter Nine

Jack settled into his window seat with a sigh of relief, but he couldn't relax entirely, not till the plane was up in the air. He imagined Mulryan racing home to get his passport, somehow blagging himself a ticket on this plane . . . unlikely, of course, but he'd be more than glad to see the ground dropping away beneath him.

At any rate, he knew he couldn't stay long in Malaga. Mulryan knew his destination and was probably mad enough to follow him. Jack had never been to Spain and didn't have a clue about where to head for, but he suspected Malaga wouldn't be big enough to hide him from the wrath of Eddie Mulryan. He guessed he'd just have to see what turned up.

At the last minute, just before the doors were locked there was some commotion down the front as a late arrival scrambled aboard. Jack's muscles tensed involuntarily. He pictured a policeman coming down the aisle, with awkward questions about a car crash and subsequent brawl a short distance away from the airport; but the figure that came stumbling into view wasn't wearing a uniform. It was a guy about Jack's age, lugging a couple of attaché cases and sweating profusely from his dash. He drew level with the vacant seat beside Jack and paused to glance at his boarding pass. He was thin and very pale. Jack thought he looked ill. He was gasping and wheezing, as though he'd run harder than was good for him and there were bluish sacks beneath his eyes. He removed his leather jacket, reached up to stow his cases in the overhead locker and Jack could see the dark circles of sweat under the arms of his blue chambray shirt. He secured the locker door and dropped into the seat, still gasping for breath. Immediately, the plane began to taxi.

'Jesus,' he said, glancing apologetically at Jack. 'Cut that . . . a bit fine . . . didn't I?'

Jack nodded. He turned to glance out of the window at the runway as it moved away behind him.

Goodbye, Eddie, he thought grimly.

Now the newcomer was groping in the pocket of his jeans. He brought out a small tin and extracting a tiny pill, he popped it under his tongue. He sat still for a moment, his eyes closed. Gradually, he got his breathing under control.

'You all right?' asked Jack.

The man nodded, opened his eyes, forced a weak smile.

'I'll be OK,' he croaked. 'I chose a great time to go down with a chest infection.' He buckled his seat belt, having to pull it several sizes tighter around his waist.

The plane reached the end of the runway and turned around. There was a long pause and then the engines revved, the power of them vibrating through the length of the fuselage. It began to move down the runway, picking up speed. Jack watched the landscape sliding past him, faster, faster. Just when it seemed the plane would never lift off, it did, rising at an almost impossible angle. The ground dropped away steeply, details quickly dwindling to miniature dimensions. Then they were in cloud and all Jack could see was a woolly greyness. He felt deliciously enveloped, cocooned from the real world far below. It was almost a disappointment when they left the cloud cover and emerged into the clear blue sky above.

Mulryan walked along the driveway to Lou Winters' palatial residence and let himself in at the front door, fumbling the key awkwardly in the lock with his left hand. He'd gone straight from the airport to the taxi rank and told the driver to take him to the casualty department of a hospital on the other side of town. As his cab passed the wreckage of Vince's car, he'd seen Vince being loaded into the back of an ambulance and had sunk well down in his seat for fear of being spotted by the police that were frantically trying to get the traffic moving again.

'Bloody hell,' muttered the cabbie. 'Looks like that poor bastard has had his chips.'

Mulryan hadn't said anything. He knew that witnesses would describe the fight around the car and he hoped he hadn't left anything inside it to link him with the incident.

Now he had just returned from the hospital and his

right hand was encased in plaster from forearm to fingertips. It felt like a useless club of lead dangling at the end of his arm and it was going to be some time before he stopped trying to do things with it. His nose was going to be a bigger problem. The doctor at accidents and emergencies had informed him it was broken in two places and would have to be reset at a later date. Meanwhile, it resembled something like a squashed potato, clinging tenaciously to his face. The black and purple bruises extended up around his eyes in clownish rings that not even a pair of dark glasses could mask and it hurt him to even breath. Consequently, he had to walk around with his mouth hanging open, making noises like a scuba diver.

He had told the doctor that he'd been in a fight with a relative and didn't want the police involved. He'd handle the matter himself. He felt ridiculous, totally humiliated by his situation. The only thing that kept him going was the cold, sweet certainty, that sooner or later, he would have his revenge.

He closed the door quietly behind him and stood for a moment in the opulent hallway, beneath the huge cut-glass chandelier that Mr Winters had imported from France. The door to the living room opened and Mrs Winters looked out at him. Her eyes opened wide in shock and her hands flew up to her cheeks, while her crimson lips formed a tiny circle of concern.

'Ooh, Eddie! Whatever's happened?' She hurried towards him, full of maternal concern, a thin, whey-faced woman, with bouffant hair coloured an improbable shade of blue. She fussed around him, shocked by the severity of his injuries. 'Lou said you'd been in a car accident, but he told me it wasn't serious.'

'Oh, it's not so bad, Mrs W!' He raised his right hand and she seized on it like a trophy, cradling it in her own hands and tutting enthusiastically at the sight of it.

'Really, Eddie, you've got to take better care of yourself! We can't have you getting into all these scrapes, can we? What would your mother say if she knew?' She wagged a painted fingernail in admonition. 'They're all maniacs out on the road these days! Lou says Vince was driving.'

'That's right, Mrs W. He's had the worst of it, I think. Fractured skull, I shouldn't be surprised.'

'Oh, that's terrible!' Mrs Winters shook her head despairingly. 'Well, it's just a blessing he wasn't *killed*.' She narrowed her eyes and looked at Mulryan sharply. 'He wasn't killed, was he? Only, I heard Lou on the phone talking to the police, telling them that Vince didn't work for us anymore, that he sacked him months ago. I don't like that kind of double dealing. Vince *is* all right, isn't he?'

Mulryan shifted on his feet uncomfortably.

'I don't really know, Mrs W. I expect so.'

'Mmmm, well . . .' She patted Mulryan's good hand. 'You're going to have to take it easy for a while. I keep telling Lou, he's giving you far too much to do. You want to get your feet up and have a nice rest.'

'I will, soon,' Mulryan assured her. 'Is Mr Winters about?'

Mrs Winters adopted a disapproving look, pursing her lips into a crimson dot. 'In his room,' she said quietly. 'He's watching those films again.' She crossed her arms over her skinny chest and raised her eyes towards the chandelier. She didn't approve of the films.

'I think I'll go on up,' said Mulryan.

'He doesn't like being disturbed when he's watching his films,' she said doubtfully.

'I know. All the same, I reckon I'll go up.'

Mulryan turned towards the big, curved flight of stairs. Mrs Winters stared up at him for a moment, then shook her head and went back into the sitting room. Mulryan reached the landing and walked along it, his feet sinking into the deep pile of the carpet. As he approached the door of Winters' office, he could hear sounds from within; a sinewy jazz-funk backing interspersed with grunts and groans.

Mulryan paused at the door, raised his right hand to knock and found himself looking at a chunk of plaster of Paris. He sighed, lifted his other hand and knocked gently. There was no answer. He waited a few moments and then opened the door.

Winters was sitting on an expansive leather sofa in front of a huge television screen. Caught unaware he was frantically rearranging his silk dressing gown. 'For Christ's sake, Eddie!' Winters' face was purple with indignation. 'Can't you see I'm busy?'

Mulryan gazed at his employer blankly. 'Sorry, Mr Winters. But I just got back from the horsepiddle . . .'

'The what?' Winters grabbed the remote and jabbed at a button, abruptly changing the pornographic television image to three bobbing glove puppets. A grinning female presenter was teaching them a song.

Winters hit the off-switch and the screen went black, sending the dancing puppets into oblivion. He turned in his seat and studied Mulryan's face. He grinned unpleasantly. 'Christ, what did the bastard hit you with? An articulated lorry?'

Mulryan reddened beneath his bruises, glanced at his feet. 'He tricked me, Mr Winters. It wasn't fair. He used my own trick on me and I fell for it.'

'What about the hand?' asked Winters.

'Broke every finger. I'll 'ave to wear this thing for weeks.'

Winters chuckled. 'Who'd have thought it, eh?' He shook his head. 'Ah, well, it only goes to show, even the smallest worm can turn.' He finished arranging his clothing. 'Well, he's slipped the net now, hasn't he?'

Mulryan stepped forward.

'But I know where he was headed, Mr Winters. Malaga. I saw the flight details and everything.'

Winters shrugged. 'Forget it,' he said.

'Forget it?' Mulryan looked astonished. 'But . . . I can track him down. Might take a bit of time, but—'

Winters shook his head.

'I said forget it, Eddie. Let's face it, the bastard hasn't got my nine grand or any way of getting it. That's why he skipped the country. It would cost me too much to track him down, and besides, I've plenty of work for you here. I'm not paying for you to get a sodding sun-tan in Spain. Right?'

Mulryan considered this for a moment.

'No,' he said. 'No, I'm goin' after him. It's a professional thing. A matter of honour. I can't just let it go.'

'Oh yes you can,' said Winters firmly. 'Consider it finished, Eddie. If the little twat ever shows his face around here again, then you can be my guest. But Malaga? Do me a favour! Besides, he owes a couple of grand to The Armenian.' He raised his eyebrows meaningfully. 'And you know *his* reputation. *He's* got this big thing about *honour*. Stupid git!'

'It's not stupid,' said Mulryan, tonelessly. 'In this business there has to be some kind of *code*.'

Winters grinned. 'Is that a fact? Well, don't worry on that score, I'll phone and let The Armenian know where Doyle is headed. You can be sure that he won't let it go. He'll probably bring the poor sod back in a duty-free bag.'

Mulryan took another step forward.

'You don't understand, Mr Winters. I'm not askin' you. I'm just explainin' what's going to happen. I have to go after Doyle, it's as simple as that.'

Winters sighed. 'Perhaps I'm not making myself clear, Eddie. Read my lips. YOU AIN'T GOING! I understand you're angry about what's happened but those are the breaks. I can't spare you right now, there's plenty here to keep you occupied. You've got a score to settle – do it in your own time, not mine.'

Mulryan frowned, then brightened. 'All right then. I'd like a holiday please.'

Winters' eyebrows lifted. 'You what?' he cried.

'A holiday. Time to recuperate from my injuries. I ain't

never asked for time off before. Not in two years. These 'ere bones will mend quicker in a hot climate. They say Spain's very nice this time o' year.'

Winters' face darkened. 'Do they? Do they in fuckin' deed? Forget it, Eddie. There's no vacations in this line of work. Don't forget, you've just cost me a lot of money. Vince is in hospital, there's a car written off, I'll have all the hassle of finding a new driver. And you're not exactly a lot of use with your hand like that, are you? Now, it was your balls-up and I don't intend to be left in the lurch over this . . .'

'A holiday with full pay,' said Mulryan, as though he hadn't heard a word. 'A month should be enough, I reckon. Shouldn't take longer than that to track him down. And then I'll be ready to start work again.'

Winters was beginning to get nervous. Something in Mulryan's detached manner was rattling him.

'No way!' he growled. 'If you think I'm going to pay you to go swanning off to bleedin' Spain, you've got another—'

He broke off as Mulryan leaned forward and picked up the remote control from the coffee table. The screen flickered into life and now there were four glove puppets capering about to some jaunty music. Mulryan smiled, warming to his theme.

'All work and no play,' he said. 'You know the saying, Mr Winters. My old mum always used to say—'

'Fuck your old mum!' snapped Winters. He got up off the sofa, intending to storm out of the room. But Mulryan's expression stopped him in his tracks. He had never seen such a look on his face before. The genial grin had vanished, to be replaced by a look of total horror. The bruises around his nose looked shockingly black against his pale skin. His eyes were bulging. On the screen, the puppets were leaping up and down.

'What did you say?' whispered Mulryan, hoarsely.

'Uh . . . listen, Eddie, I didn't mean—'

'Are you suggesting that I should . . . that with my own mother, I could . . .'

'God, no. Eddie, for Christ's sake, it's just an expression!'

'You want me to . . .' Eddie seemed lost for words. '*My* mother?' he roared. 'My blessed mother?'

Winters cowered. He opened his mouth to say something. Mulryan struck him across the face with the back of his right hand, the plaster-cast making a dull thwacking sound against his jaw. Winters fell sideways and struck the soft pile carpet. Mulryan walked over to Winters and grabbed him left-handed, by the back of his neck. As he lifted him up, Winters' toupee slid forward over his eyes. His jaw hinged to one side and bubbles of blood foamed from his open mouth. A couple of stray teeth plopped to the carpet with barely a sound.

Mulryan pulled Winters forward and held his smashed face within inches of the television screen. Winters made a protesting noise, somewhere between a snigger and a belch. A big bubble of blood welled from his nostrils, then popped.

'Egggiiie,' he groaned. 'Pwweeease. Pwweeeease . . .'

Mulryan slammed Winters' face into the screen. There was a dull, crumpling noise, and lines scarred the glass surface but it didn't shatter. Not the first time, not the fourth. It was only on the sixth attempt that Winters' head went through into the electrical darkness beyond. There was a dull thud of implosion, a cloud of smoke and then flames were dancing in Winters' toupee. After a few moments, his hands stopped gesticulating. Mulryan looked down at Winters' hunched figure, vaguely surprised by how it had turned out. He hadn't meant it to go like this at all but supposed he'd just have to make the best of it.

Turning aside, he walked across to the far wall, where there was a painting of wild horses running through the surf. Wrenching it off the wall, he revealed a recessed safe. He knew the combination, Winters had never made any secret of it. He unlocked it, revealing thick wads of money. He had no idea how much was there, he didn't particularly care, he only wanted enough for his mission. He wasn't a thief.

He was just beginning to fill his pockets when the door opened and Mrs Winters came in. She froze, her eyes wide, her mouth hanging open in incomprehension as flames flickered on the shoulders of her husband's silk dressing gown. As she watched, a blue dart of fire clambered up the curtains beside the ruined television.

'Lou?' she whispered. 'Eddie, what's happened?'

He crossed the room to her quickly, a reassuring smile on his face. He didn't want her to scream, that was important.

'Mrs W, come and sit down a minute while I explain,' he said.

'But ... the fire ...'

'Just for a moment, dear.' He put an arm around her and tried to lead her to the sofa. She didn't want to go. She dragged her feet, her body resisting, so he picked her up like a little girl and took her to the sofa and laid her down. He really liked Mrs W. He liked her but he couldn't afford to have her go telling stories to the police. She had suddenly acquired the dubious status of a loose end. She stared at him with frightened eyes. 'What ... what are you going to do?' she whispered, hoarsely.

'I'm sorry, Mrs W,' he said. 'I really am. If he'd only listened to me ... All I wanted was a holiday.'

'E ... Eddie?' She opened her mouth to scream.

There was no time. He lifted his right arm and brought it down hard on her forehead. The impact sent needles of pain through his hand. He grunted, looked at her. He wasn't sure if she was dead, so he gritted his teeth and did it again. This time the front of her skull cracked open and grey stuff squirted out. Her eyes were open in surprise, staring at him.

'You naughty boy!' she said and he jumped to his feet, frightened. He watched her anxiously for a moment but all that came from her lips now was a slow exhalation and a dry, rattling sound. Then nothing. He felt bad. He had never killed a woman before. Doyle's fault, he told himself. Doyle was to blame for everything that happened now. He would be called to atone for his sins sooner or later.

He hurried back to the safe, finished filling his pockets. Then he closed it, hung the picture back on the wall.

Glancing around the room, he saw that the fire was taking hold. There was a horrible acrid smell, like burning fat. He went out of the room, across the landing and down the stairs, telling himself that he daren't linger here.

His passport was in order, Winters had made him apply for one when he'd first started working for him, explaining that it might at some point be necessary to travel abroad. The need had never arisen till now. He was beginning to feel quite excited. He couldn't remember when he had last had a holiday. The thing was to get away from here before the fire really took hold. It would take the authorities some time to sort out exactly what was left in the blackened ruins of the house. By then, hopefully, he'd be in Spain.

He opened the front door and somebody was standing on the step, somebody he'd met a couple of times before. It was the big Scottish enforcer who worked for The Armenian. He was standing there with his hands in his pockets, a puzzled expression on his thin face. He gazed at Mulryan for a moment then raised his eyebrows as his nostrils caught the smell of smoke.

'Hello, Eddie,' said McGiver. 'I've been trying to get hold of you all day.' He took in Mulryan's damaged face and then his gaze lifted over his shoulder to where clouds of smoke were billowing out on to the top of the landing. 'Oh dear,' he said. 'Did I call at an inconvenient moment?'

Mulryan frowned. This was a complication he hadn't expected. He considered punching McGiver out and dragging him back inside but it wouldn't be easy. The Scotsman was built like a brick shithouse. McGiver was in the same line of work though and on reflection, Mulryan decided to observe the unspoken code of honour that existed between such men.

'We'd better not hang about here,' he said at last.

McGiver nodded. He had seen enough to get the general idea. 'Where's Lou?' he inquired.

Mulryan flicked his head back in the direction of the staircase.

'He's in there,' he said. 'We had er . . . a bit of a disagreement.'

'Christ!' McGiver looked impressed. He thought for a moment. 'You got anywhere to go?' he asked.

'I'm planning to go to Spain,' said Mulryan.

'After Doyle?'

Mulryan stared at McGiver for a moment, then nodded.

'After Doyle,' he admitted.

'That'll take a bit of time to organize. Tell you what, you'd better come along to my place. You're going to need somewhere to lie low for a while.' He took hold of Mulryan's arm and drew him out on to the step. Mulryan reached back and pulled the door shut behind him.

'I reckon I'll take my chances, 'he said.

'Don't be daft. When this place goes up there'll be a lot of people wanting to ask you questions. Relax, I'm not going to grass you up.'

'I know that. But this is a personal matter, no reason for you to get involved.'

'The Armenian wants Doyle taken care of. And since it looks like we're both after the same feller, it makes sense to team up. Don't you think?'

Mulryan considered it for a moment. He would have liked more time to make his mind up. But smoke was already coming from under the gap in the door.

'OK,' he grunted. The two men walked away from the house, along the drive to the gates. Glancing back, Mulryan saw that smoke was now spilling out of the upstairs windows. But the nearest neighbours were four hundred yards away. By the time they noticed anything, it would be too late to do much about it.

McGiver was shaking his head.

'What exactly happened?' he asked.

'Lou made a remark about my mother. A filthy remark. I don't like anybody saying things about my mother.'

'I'll bear that in mind,' said McGiver.

They turned left out of the gate and walked quickly away. Behind them there was a dull crash as the first of the windows blew out. Black smoke began to rise into the clear sky.

'Jesus,' muttered McGiver. 'A big place like that, you'd think he'd have installed smoke alarms, wouldn't you?'

'Penny pincher,' muttered Mulryan. 'He always was.' He glanced back thoughtfully at the house. 'His wife was nice though. Like a mother to me, she was.'

McGiver noted the use of the past tense. He shrugged.

'Some days are like that,' he observed.

They didn't speak much after that.

PART TWO

JACK FLUSH

Chapter Ten

After half an hour or so in the air, stewardesses started ferrying out the in-flight meal. A greasy, unappetizing aroma permeated the cabin. Jack abandoned the idea of eating and settled instead for a double Scotch. Bored, he took out a pack of playing cards and tried a game of patience, but it wouldn't come out right as he kept getting stuck with a handful of useless cards.

The guy next to him didn't seem interested in food either. Ten minutes after take-off, he'd got one of the attaché cases down from the luggage locker and had opened it up to reveal a lap-top computer. He'd immediately set about using it, his hands flying frantically across the keyboard, as though he was in some kind of race. The tiny LCD screen filled up with processed words, which went marching upwards in neatly ordered ranks. Eventually, he seemed satisfied with what he'd done. He stored the information, closed up the case and set it down at his feet. Then he summoned a stewardess and asked for a glass of mineral water. He eyed Jack's whisky, wistfully.

'Rather have one of those,' he said, with a grin.

Jack studied him for a moment. He was bored with cards and a little conversation might help to pass the time.

'So why not?' he inquired.

'Hmm?' The man looked startled as though he hadn't expected his remark to elicit any response.

'Why not have a drink?' Jack prompted him. 'Listen, I hate drinking alone. If you're on a budget, I'll stand you a round.'

The man smiled. 'Oh, it's nothing like that. It's just that the doctors warned me off booze months ago. Said it was bad for me.'

Jack shrugged. 'I suppose it's bad for *everyone* but surely it can't hurt in moderation?'

The man looked doubtful. 'I'm not the kind that can drink just one,' he explained.

Jack nodded.

'I know what you mean,' he said. 'I suffer from the same condition.' There was a brief pause as he cast about for something else to say. 'Going on holiday?' he asked.

'No. Working trip. I'm a journalist.'

'Yeah? Which paper you with?'

'I'm a freelancer. Frank Nolan's the name. Maybe you heard of me?'

'Rings a bell.' It didn't. Jack was just being pleasant. 'Explains the business with the lap-top.'

'Life-support system,' said Frank and he really sounded as though he meant it. 'It's all in there, diary, accounts, notes . . . don't know how I ever managed with pen and paper. I was just getting down a few thoughts . . .' He raised his eyebrows slightly. 'Sorry, I didn't catch your name.'

'That's right, you didn't.'

Frank smiled slyly. 'Sorry. Some kind of secret is it?'

Jack shook his head, decided he was being too careful. 'No, of course not. It's Jack. Jack Doyle.'

Frank seemed to consider this for a moment. 'Good name,' he said. 'Sounds like the hero of an American cop show. You're *not* a cop, are you?'

'No, I'm a . . .' Jack paused, a little unsure of what to say about himself. He reviewed the options in his head. *I'm a bankrupt ex-businessman who just made the dumbest move of my life.* Not too impressive that one. How about, *I'm the guy who barely made it on to the plane with my bollocks intact?* Interesting, but not the kind of thing you wanted to mention to a total stranger. Or maybe just, *I'm running for my life and I haven't got the faintest idea of my next move.* A conversation stopper if there ever was one. He decided to play safe. 'I'm a complete layabout,' he concluded.

'Oh, I doubt that. A genuine complete bum would never admit to it. I ought to know, I've been acquainted with a few of them in my time.'

The stewardess brought the mineral water and Frank took it with an air of resignation. Ice tinkled in the glass. Frank sipped at it and sighed.

'If you really stretch your imagination,' he said, 'you can pretend this stuff is gin and tonic.'

'Gin your tipple, then?'

'Used to be. Then the old ticker started performing tricks on me. It's never been much use, even when I was a kid. Lately its been about as dependable as a five quid watch.' Frank tapped himself on the chest and looked suddenly thoughtful. Jack surmised that despite his jovial manner, his health was every bit as bad as it could be.

Impulsively, Jack pulled back his sleeve to reveal his wrist-watch. 'Look at this,' he said.

'A Rolex,' observed Frank. 'Very nice.'

Jack shook his head. 'A *bootleg* Rolex. Cost me a fiver in a pub three years ago. Never had a problem with it. Before that, I had a *genuine* Rolex and the bloody thing was always in and out of the repairers.'

Frank looked vaguely bemused.

'So what's your point?' he asked.

'Well . . . I'm not sure. Just that you shouldn't be so quick to write off a five quid watch, I suppose.' Jack spread his hands in a helpless gesture and Frank chuckled.

'I'll bear it in mind,' he said. 'Actually, it's a relief. I thought for a minute there you were going to try and sell it to me!'

Jack laughed. 'Don't think I haven't considered it,' he said. He made an effort to steer the conversation in a less depressing direction. 'So, what's your work in Spain?' he asked. 'Doing a travel piece?'

'Not exactly. Something bigger. Biggest break of my life, tell you the truth.'

'Yeah?' Jack was intrigued. With his own career well and truly down the toilet, it was strangely comforting to hear about somebody who was on the up. 'Want to tell me about it? Or is it some kind of secret?'

Frank grinned, acknowledging the dig. 'No, it's not exactly a secret. Fact is, I've been bursting to tell somebody about it.' He looked doubtful for a moment. 'You're not connected with the publishing industry in any way, are you?'

'Me? I can barely write my own name!'

'OK, I suppose it can't do any harm.' Frank glanced around as though nervous of being overheard. He lowered his voice. 'I'm ghost-writing an autobiography,' he said. 'Should be worth a packet when it's finished. Ever heard of a guy called Tony Gorman?'

Jack was suitably impressed. Yes, he had heard of him.

'*The* Tony Gorman? The bank robber?'

'That's the guy. A living legend. People like me have been chasing the bastard for years, trying to get him to spill the beans. I mean, it's a great story, right? There he is, living it up on the "Costa del Crime", the man who pulled off the biggest bank raid in history.'

'Right. He's supposed to have got away with millions, isn't he?'

'Nobody really knows how much. They undersold it at the time, the official line was five million, but nobody ever really believed that. I think they were too embarrassed to admit the truth.'

'And they could never pin it on him?'

'Nope. He's sitting pretty. Police can't extradite him, they've tried and failed, time after time. Everybody wants to know the details, how he pulled it off, how he got out of the country with all that loot.'

'I seem to remember there was something on the telly a few years back. They sent a camera crew out to follow him around, one of those watchdog programmes.'

'Yeah, I saw it. But they got zilch out of him, apart from him nearly throwing a punch at one of the cameramen. Thing is, he's intriguing. He's Jack-the-Lad, right, cockney barrow boy made good. Publishers have been creaming their collective jeans over the prospect of a book for years. And now, out of the blue, it's right there on a plate ... and I'm the man he's going to talk to.' Frank grinned, sipped at his water. He looked very pleased with himself.

'Nice one,' admitted Jack. 'So what's he really like?'

Frank shrugged. 'Won't know that till I meet him.'

'What, you mean you haven't—'

'Not so much as a phone call. I've never met him. I've only spoken with his so-called "business manager", a guy called Bill Farnell. He's fixed it all up on Gorman's behalf.'

'So how ... no offence, Frank, but how did he come to offer this to you?'

'No offence taken. I mean, obviously he could have had anybody he wanted. From what Bill Farnell told me, Gorman saw some pieces I did in *Esquire*. A series about famous criminals. Ronnie Biggs, the Krays, Ruth Ellis ... people like that. Well, he must've liked what he saw, 'cos he instructed Farnell to get me over there, money no object! The plan is, I go over, all expenses paid and put my arse down in five-star luxury – the Hotel Excelsior in Puerto Banus, for Christ's sake! I meet up with Gorman and his pals, get to know them, hang out with them, experience how the other half lives ... oh, and somewhere along the way, I write the book. When it's done, Farnell negotiates for a publishing deal which guarantees me a big, fat twenty-five per cent of what it makes. And believe me, it'll make buckets.'

Jack let out a whistle.

'Sounds great,' he said. 'How long will it take to write it?'

Frank shrugged.

'Oh ... eight months, a year. Maybe longer if I put my mind to it.' He laughed at his own good fortune. 'Meanwhile, I'm living it up in that hotel, taking the odd dip in the pool, investigating the local colour ... research, you understand, purely research ... while ol' Tony takes care of the tab.' He sighed contentedly. 'Beats the shit out of knocking up stories in a dingy bedsit in Finsbury Park!'

'Jesus, I should think it does!' Jack sighed. 'Why can't I chance into something like that?'

'It's easy,' Frank told him. 'All you have to do is pray hard enough. I know I have, every night for the last five years.'

They both laughed. Jack decided that he liked Frank and was amazed to discover that he didn't begrudge him his success, not one little bit.

'Where does this Gorman character live?' he asked.

'Where do you think, man? Marbella! Yachts, swimming pools and wall-to-wall ex-pat criminals. No self-respecting bank robber would live anywhere else!'

Jack sensed an opportunity. He remembered that Leo King had mentioned Marbella. He had business connections there. Maybe if he mentioned Leo's name enough times around the area, he might do himself some good. And if Frank Nolan was going to be staying there, he could be a useful contact.

'Hey, now there's a coincidence!' he said.

'What is?'

'That's where I'm headed.'

'To Marbella? You got business there too?'

'No, I'm just getting away for a few weeks. Heard it was a good place for a holiday.'

'Well, we'll have to look each other up some time.'

'Yeah, maybe have a couple of drinks . . .' Jack glanced at Frank's Perrier water. 'Sorry,' he said. 'I forgot.'

'Don't worry. Listen, how are you getting there?'

'Hadn't thought about it. A taxi, I suppose. Why, do you want to share one?'

'Relax, *compadre*! It just so happens I'm picking up a hire car at the airport. I'll give you a lift, no problem.'

'Oh no, I couldn't . . .'

'Sure you could! Anyway, you can earn your ride by being the navigator, I'm hopeless with maps.'

'Well, that's very decent of you Frank. Thanks, I appreciate it.'

Frank raised his glass of mineral water. 'To Mr Gorman,' he said. 'Our passport to pleasure.'

Chapter Eleven

'Right,' said Frank. 'Let's see what she can do!' He'd hired a tough-looking vehicle, a chunky, four-wheel drive Mitsubishi Shogun in a fetching shade of green. But Jack could see that the ride through Malaga had been pretty stressful for him, unfamiliar as he was with the town's chaotic one-way systems. Jack had offered to drive a couple of times, but Frank would hear none of it. He was intent on playing the genial host to the hilt.

Still, it was a relief for both men when they finally escaped on to deserted country roads, unwinding like a ribbon across the arid landscape. Dusty boulder-strewn hills stretched to the horizon, dotted here and there with occasional clumps of cacti and scrub. Frank had spurned the straightforward drive down the busy coast highway and had asked Jack to plot a route inland along little used minor roads. He was in no great hurry to get to the hotel, he said, and he wanted to take a look at the country and put the Mitsubishi through its paces. Like a kid with a new toy he was throwing the jeep recklessly around the curves.

They wound their way uphill through scruffy little villages, kicking up clouds of red dust in their wake. Jack had intended heading for a village called Mijas but they must have taken a wrong turn somewhere. Now the jeep was grinding upwards through the foothills of the Serrania de Ronda, flanked by wild slopes of verdant scrub. Everywhere seemed deserted and Jack reminded himself that they were smack dab in the middle of the afternoon siesta. He didn't much like the look of Frank, who was sweating profusely in the fierce heat. Though he was making a big show of enjoying himself, his thin face was pale and flecked with beads of perspiration.

'Hey, man, this is the life!' he told Jack. 'You think I could afford a motor like this at home? No way!'

'What do you normally drive?' Jack asked him.

'A clapped out old Chevette. Thing doesn't go above sixty miles an hour, even on a downhill stretch . . . but this baby can move!'

He got his foot well down and the speedometer edged up to around sixty, the jeep bucketing alarmingly on the pitted surface of the road. Jack braced himself in his seat and wondered if accepting the lift had been such a smart move. At the time, his only thought had been to get out of Malaga with all speed. But he hadn't bargained on speed like this.

They crested a steep rise and swooped down into a valley, the road running straight now for some distance. Frank grinned, pushed the accelerator down to the floorboards.

'I feel the need for speed,' he said, in a fake American

accent. Jack recognized the quote from *Top Gun* just as the jeep lost contact with the road's surface. For a few moments it felt as if they really were flying. The Mitsubishi came down with a thud and the tyres span for an instant before making proper contact. The jeep accelerated to around eighty miles an hour. Jack could feel his seat pushing at his spine.

It happened suddenly. One instant, the road ahead was clear as far as the eye could see. The next, the skinny brown dog was virtually under their front bumper.

'Fuck!' said Frank. He wrenched the wheel hard to the left and hit the brake, missing the fortunate dog by a hair's breadth. The jeep went into a long, sliding skid, wheels screeching in protest. It stalled to a halt some sixty yards further down the road and both men were thrown forward in their seats and then snapped back by their belts.

Frank slumped over the wheel and let out a long breath. 'Where in Jesus did that mutt come from?' he asked the world in general.

'Dunno. You all right?'

Frank lifted his head and looked at Jack. His face had the colour of old parchment.

'Bloody thing scared the shit out of me,' he mumbled.

'Why don't you let me take over for a while? You don't look so good.'

Frank nodded reluctantly.

'Maybe you're right,' he admitted. 'I feel like I could use a rest.' His breathing was very shallow now, his chest rising and falling, as he strove to control it. He slipped a hand into the pocket of his jeans and then stiffened in surprise. His eyes widened in panic.

'What's the matter?' Jack asked him.

'My pills! My fuckin' nitroglycerine! They're not here . . . Jesus, I must have dropped them on the plane!'

Jack stared at him, unsure of how serious a problem this was.

'All right, calm down a moment. Check again . . .'

Frank's breathing was getting more frantic now, hoarse gasps escaping from his open mouth. He began to grope in his other pockets and a fat droplet of sweat fell from his forehead.

'Jesus Christ,' he gasped. 'Oh Jesus, what'll I do . . .?' He stared imploringly at Jack for a moment, then seemed to remember something. He laughed with relief. 'What am I talking about, I've got more of them.' He pointed into the back of the jeep. 'In my case. Always carry some for an emergency . . . hey man, think you could—?'

'Sure!' Jack unclipped his belt, threw open the door and went around to the back. He tried the rear door handle, then realized it was locked. He walked back to the driver's side and opened Frank's door. 'I need the—'

He broke off in alarm. Frank was leaning back in his seat now, his face staring up towards the roof of the jeep. His breathing sounded like it was coming through an aqualung. Jack grabbed the keys from the ignition and ran around to the back. Fumbling the unfamiliar keys into the lock, he got the door open and grabbed an attaché case. He unlatched it and found himself looking at the portable computer. It wasn't going to be much use to Frank now. Jack pushed it aside and opened the second case, trying not to listen to the hideous whooping noises coming from the front of the jeep. He popped it open and the contents spilled out in a jumble. Sheets of paper, a mini-cassette recorder, a Filofax, a traveller's washbag... but no tin, no fucking tin! Surely Frank wouldn't have put them in the big suitcase he collected at the airport? The washbag, maybe the washbag... He unzipped it and strewed toothbrush, razor and soap around the interior of the jeep in his clumsy haste. And then he found the tin, tucked into a small compartment. He yanked it out and ran back to the passenger door, climbed into his seat.

'OK, mate, I got them!' He stared in horror at Frank. He was arching up out of his seat and his hands had become agonized talons that clawed ineffectually at his own chest. His mouth was wide open and the sound that emerged from it was a hideous gargling, the unmistakable rattle of approaching death.

'Frank, for God's sake, hold on!' Jack fumbled with the tin's dispenser and shook a pill out on to the palm of his hand. He put one arm around Frank's shoulders and tried to force the pill into his mouth, but it just got pushed out by the tongue, which was now protruding over his bottom lip. A violent spasm shook his body and the heels of his boots hammered up and down on the jeep's brake and accelerator, making a rythmic clunking. Then, abruptly, he stilled. His teeth clicked together and a last, surprised breath whistled between them. He sank slowly down into his seat.

Jack took his arm away and sat there watching Frank. He looked calm now. His eyes were still open, though his skin had darkened to an ugly grey. Illogically, Jack kept expecting him to turn his head and smile, say 'Jesus, that was a close thing!' But he just sat there, gazing through the fly-splashed windscreen at the deserted road ahead.

And then a panic claimed Jack. He was suddenly horribly aware that he was shut up in an enclosed space with a dead body at his side. He kicked open the door and scrambled out of the jeep, his own heart jolting, and took to his heels. He knew he should be trying to do something, thumping Frank's chest or clamping his mouth over those blue lips in a desperate attempt to breathe life back into his corpse. But he couldn't even think about that. All of a sudden, his proximity to death had made him aware of his own mortality and the thought had terrified him. He ran for some distance over the scorched grass, his shoes thudding on the dry earth. Then he stopped and looked back at the jeep.

A deep silence fell; then gradually, he became aware of sound. The rhythmic chirruping of cicadas, the buzz of horseflies, the rattle of branches in a nearby olive tree as a light breeze stirred the foliage.

And Frank was dead. As abruptly as he'd stepped into Jack's life, he had bowed out of it and all when he was on the verge of pulling off something big. Part of Jack had genuinely liked him and another part had clung to Frank, seeing him as a potential meal ticket.

Perhaps he still could be.

The thought had risen unbidden from Jack's subconscious mind. He tried to shake it away, but it nagged at him, as persistent as the horseflies which now buzzed inquisitively around his head. *Yes, perhaps he still could be . . .*

He began to walk back to the jeep, marvelling at how one half of him was already weighing up the possibilities, while the other half stood back appalled.

He replayed snatches of an earlier conversation in his head. Frank's voice, exuberant, elated, unaware that he was within hours of his own death. *'I've never met him. I've only spoken with his so-called "business manager", a guy called Bill Farnell . . . the plan is, I go over, all expenses paid . . . the Hotel Excelsior . . . for Christ's sake! . . . a big, fat twenty-five per cent . . . eight months, a year. Maybe longer if I put my mind to it.'*

Another voice now, deep inside him. *No, no! You've got to be kidding! You're not a fucking writer, for God's sake, how could you ever hope to pull it off?*

And then, as if answering. *Don't actually have to write anything! But I could stall for a while. Live in the style to which I'm accustomed, at least till something else comes up. Who would ever know I wasn't Frank Nolan?*

He had reached the jeep now. He stared in through the open door. He was illogically surprised to see that Frank hadn't moved a muscle. Gingerly, his skin crawling with apprehension, he climbed back into the passenger seat and closed the door. There was Frank's passport, sticking out of the breast pocket of his shirt. Jack took it carefully between thumb and forefinger and pulled at it. There was resistance where the shirt fabric was stretched taut. He pulled harder and got it free, opened it to the photograph. Taken some years back it showed a plumper, more healthy Frank Nolan. Anonymous face, dark hair, keen eyes ... it could easily have been a younger Jack Doyle. Well, couldn't it?

He transferred the passport to his own pocket. Encouraged now, he began to search Frank's clothing, taking out anything that might serve to identify the body. Keys. A handful of change. A small penknife. What about a wallet, there ought to be a wallet ... ah, there it was, stuffed into his back pocket. He tilted the body forward and cringed as Frank's head smacked against the steering wheel with a dull clunk.

'Sorry,' said Jack and felt foolish. He tugged the wallet out. Everything was here. A lot of Spanish money. Credit cards. Membership of the NUJ.

He felt guilty now and tried to rationalize. Frank would approve of this, he really would! He was so fired up over this great opportunity, he'd want somebody to benefit from it, surely to God?

The growl of a car engine set his nerves jittering. He glanced over his shoulder and saw it coming up behind him, a rusty old pickup truck stirring the surface of the road into thick red clouds.

Don't panic he told himself. *Act natural, they've no reason to stop.*

He sat back, then realized that Frank's head was still slumped on the wheel. He grabbed Frank by the collar and jerked him savagely upright. Frank's head thumped against the back of his seat. There was a jagged cut on his forehead, which wasn't bleeding. Jack turned to face the body as though chatting to it and the pickup swept on past without slowing.

Jack remembered to breathe. He gave the pockets a final check, found nothing more. He considered exchanging his passport for Frank's but thought better of it. He'd need that when he dumped his new identity. All right then, one last thing. He got out of the jeep and walked around to the driver's side, glanced quickly up and down the road, ensuring that the coast was clear. Then he opened the driver's door and took Frank firmly under his arms. The pools of sweat there felt like ice and Jack nearly lost his nerve.

He shrugged off his fear and wrenched up, lifting the body out of the seat and across to the passenger side. He got in behind the wheel, started the engine and began to drive slowly along, looking for somewhere to hide the body. Even if he'd had a spade it would have been pointless to try digging a grave in this parched soil.

He drove for perhaps half a mile. A couple of cars passed him on the road, coming in the opposite direction, but other than that, he didn't see a soul. Then, off to his left, he spotted a large outcrop of rocks, some thirty yards in from the road. A few stunted olive trees grew around it and he saw that there was a deep crevice between the boulders, a few feet from the ground. It wasn't ideal but he was in no position to be choosy. He stopped the jeep, got out and walked around to the passenger side. He glanced quickly up and down again, took a firm grip around Frank's waist and heaved him out of the vehicle. Frank's heels came down on the surface of the road with a clump. Thin as he was, his body was disconcertingly heavy.

Jack began to drag him off the road and across the field, throwing nervous glances to left and right, but nobody came. He looked back over his shoulder and dragged Frank to the edge of the boulders. Laying the body down, he flexed his shoulders and examined the crevice, a long v-shaped slot in the rocks, dropping away behind a flat ledge. It was narrow but he judged he could get Frank into it if he laid him on his side. He stooped and gathered Frank in his arms, lifted him up on to the ledge. He manoeuvred the body over the hole and pushed it down into the cleft.

The head and torso went in with no difficulty but the legs were too long by about six inches and the feet remained sticking up above the level of the crevice. In different circumstances the effect would have been comical. Jack reached down and attempted to bend Frank's legs at the knees, but still couldn't make up the length. Sweating now, he unlaced Frank's shoes and removed them, dropped them in beside the body. He still needed to gain a couple of inches. He decided to look for a better hiding place but when he reached down to try and lift Frank's body clear again, he found that it was wedged firmly in place and he couldn't get sufficient purchase on it. He was going to have to make the best of a bad job.

Desperately, he climbed up on to the ledge and stood

on Frank's ankles, steadying himself by holding on to the rocks that rose in front of him. He shifted his weight, bouncing up and down with increasing ferocity, until he was rewarded with a dull, dry snap that sent a jolt of revulsion through his stomach. The feet hinged abruptly over on themselves and he was able to tread them into the shaded darkness below.

Jack climbed down, stood back a moment and peered into the crevice. As an afterthought, he reached in and closed Frank's eyes. The lids made a dry, clicking sound as they came down, but it was good not to have to look at them as he piled rocks on to the face. He moved around the boulders, collecting more and more of them and after about an hour's hard work, he had the whole body more or less covered. He stepped back a short distance and studied the effect critically, decided that it would pass muster provided nobody came too close.

He felt totally exhausted now and there was a dull pulse of nausea at the back of his throat. He wondered if he ought to say a prayer or something, but he wasn't religious and he doubted if Frank had been. So he simply said, 'Thanks for the chance, mate. I'll try not to waste it.'

The afternoon was fading fast, the sun creeping wearily towards the horizon, trailing long shadows in its wake. Jack walked back to the jeep and packed Frank's scattered belongings into his attaché case. Then he climbed into the driver's seat, started up the engine and drove away from the grave of Frank Nolan, without looking back.

Chapter Twelve

Tony Gorman walked out on to the high diving board and stood there for a moment, composing himself, sucking in the thick roll of his belly where it jutted over the top of his Union Jack bathing trunks. He looked down to his left, across the broad sweep of the patio, to where Lisa sat at the round table, thumbing listlessly through a copy of *Elle*. She had her shades on and a cigarette drooped from her lips. Beside her stood her fourth Martini of the afternoon, already half consumed.

Gorman made a small sound of irritation. She wasn't watching him and that was annoying.

'Oy!' he called down to her. 'Watch this!'

Raising himself on his toes, he extended his brawny arms in front of him, snatched a breath and launched himself from the board. He hurtled towards the pool, but lost his balance half way down. He flailed his legs in a desperate attempt to keep himself vertical but it was to no avail. Striking the water almost horizontally, he swamped the sides of the pool. The impact drove the breath out of him, making him open his mouth and he got a generous helping of chlorinated water for his trouble.

He sank, struck out blindly for a moment and then surfaced in an ungainly doggy paddle, coughing and spluttering. Flicking the water back out of his eyes he glanced towards Lisa, but she was still looking at her magazine, totally unaware of his existence. Her fault, he decided. If she'd bothered to watch him, the dive would have been better.

'Fuck it!' he said. He struck out for the shallow end of the pool, his arms machine gunning the water. By the time he reached the rail he was exhausted, the breath exploding from his chest in a series of shallow gasps. He hung there for a few moments, collecting himself, remembering a time when he'd do twenty lengths without breaking sweat. Too much drink and too many fags, he told himself. He couldn't blame it on the other. That was supposed to be good exercise.

Moving to the ladder, he hauled himself on to the side of the pool and padded over to Lisa. He slipped on the towelling robe that hung over the vacant chair and sat down heavily. Lisa still wasn't looking at him, pretending to be absorbed in a magazine she'd read a dozen times before. Gorman studied her profile, noticing the tight set of her lips around the cigarette, the ghost of a bruise on her left cheek, just below the edge of her shades.

Jesus, so she was still stewing over that, days after the event, as though it was his fault, as though she hadn't asked for it . . .

He grabbed a packet of Marlboro off the table,

jammed one in his mouth and lit it with his solid gold Ronson. He thought wistfully of his yacht and the night he'd spent there with Josie, just a couple of days back. Now there was a woman who knew how to behave, a woman who knew how to make a bloke happy. He'd need to organize another of those therapy sessions soon.

He glanced guiltily at Lisa but she was still reading. He tried to remember what it had been like when they were first married. Christ, it shouldn't be that difficult, it was only, what, eight or nine years ago? He was surprised to discover that he was unsure of the date.

'Eh, babe,' he said. ''Ow long we been married?'

'Too long.' Her American accent deadpan, not missing a beat, not even glancing up from her magazine as she replied. She was feeling pretty confident today, perhaps because he hadn't had a drink yet, wanting to keep himself clear headed to meet the writer. Except the bloke still hadn't shown up at the Excelsior. Typical. You couldn't depend on anybody any more. Maybe, he should sink a couple of stiff ones and see how Lisa's confidence held up then. She'd been meeker a few nights back, oh yes, humble as you like. He'd stood over her with his fists raised, that close, that fucking close to giving her a real thumping and she'd cowered there in the corner, her hands up to protect that fashion model face of hers and then, she hadn't even had the guts to look him in the eye.

He blew out a cloud of smoke and stared at Lisa for a moment.

'All right,' he said quietly, 'what's the problem? Which

particular bug have you got up your arse this time?'

She glanced up from the magazine and he saw his own face reflected in duplicate in her mirrored shades.

'You know what's wrong with me,' she snapped.

'Christ, 'ow many times I got to tell you? I was drunk, wasn't I? I'd 'ad a skinful. I've said I'm sorry.'

'Not as sorry as I am,' she said quietly. She went back to *Elle*, flicked over the page with a flourish.

He knew what she was thinking. *It used to be me in this magazine, yes, my face advertising these cosmetics, my body looking terrific in those designer swimsuits. But I gave it all up to marry you. And now I wish to God I hadn't.*

He bit his lip, not wanting to lose his temper.

'Tell you what, why don't you get Angelito to take you into Marbelly? Buy yourself a new outfit or some-fink, 'stead of sittin' round 'ere drinking yourself stupid.'

'I don't want to go into Mar*belly*, thank you.' Putting his London accent on, the way he always pronounced it, trying to make him feel like an oik. He persevered.

'Gordon Bennett, Lisa, you 'aven't been out for months. There must be somethin' you want!'

She raised her head again and this time she slipped off the shades, giving him a good eyeful of that bruise on her cheek. 'There is something I want,' she growled. 'But it's the one thing you won't give me.'

He sneered. 'You can fuckin' forget that, gel,' he said. 'You're my wife. When we was wed, you took *vows*. Don't forget that.'

'Vows?' She tilted back her head and laughed, displaying perfect teeth that lately Gorman had felt like kicking down her perfect throat. 'Excuse me, but I haven't noticed you observing any vows lately. I don't recall anything in the ceremony about that slag you take aboard *The Duchess* for the occasional bout of extramarital humping.'

He leant forward across the table and pointed a finger at her.

'Don't call her a slag,' he said quietly. 'I've told you before, Josie is just a mate. P'raps if you paid me a bit more attention, I wouldn't need to go lookin' for a little companionship.'

Josie could be pretty persuasive when she put her mind to it. Sixteen years old and she knew more tricks than a happy hour hooker. Not that she put out for anybody else. He'd got her solemn promise on that. It was more important than ever now that she was pregnant . . .

'Oh, so it's companionship, is it? What a delightful euphemism. Do rabbits have companions, I wonder?' asked Lisa.

He stared at her, bewildered.

'Rabbits?' he echoed. 'What you on about? Who mentioned rabbits, for Christ's sake?'

'Never mind,' she said dismissively. 'You wouldn't understand.' She picked up her Martini and raised it to her lips, drank it down in one. Then she took a small brass bell from the table and rang it.

'Jesus,' said Gorman in disgust. 'When I first met you, you didn't 'ave more than the occasional glass of wine. Now you put it away like a bleedin' docker!'

'I've had a good tutor,' she told him.

'You know your trouble, don't you? You think you're too good for the rest of the world.'

She leaned back in her chair, closed her eyes.

'Funny,' she said. 'I never used to.'

Jorge, the young houseboy, came out through the French windows, carrying another Martini on a silver tray. *Typical*, thought Gorman, *no need to ask if she* wants *another one, goes without saying.* Jorge set the drink down, collected the empty glass and looked inquiringly at Gorman.

'Something for you, Señor Gorman?'

He shook his head, though he would have killed for a double whisky right now. He had recently set himself a new regime, no alcohol before sundown and he had largely stuck to it, though in reality, he tended to drink twice as much to make up for lost time. And with the writer arriving today, he was anxious to make a good impression.

The curtains at the French windows parted again and Bill Farnell came out, immaculate as ever in his pinstripe business suit, despite the heat. He wasn't even breaking sweat. He looked a lot younger than his forty-five years, his black hair and moustache immaculately trimmed, his tall frame not carrying an ounce of excess weight. Another American addicted to physical exercise and clean living. He strolled over to the table, looking slightly perplexed. Gorman raised his eyebrows inquiringly and Farnell shook his head.

'Still hasn't arrived,' he said. 'I left a message for him to call me.'

'Bleedin' 'ell. What can be keeping him?'

'Must have got lost,' suggested Farnell. 'I checked with the airport, the flight arrived on schedule. And he definitely picked up his hire car as planned. It's not a long drive, he really should have been at the Excelsior an hour ago at the latest.'

'Maybe he stopped to do some sightseeing,' said Lisa.

'What sightseeing? There's nothin' between the airport and Marbelly but a road and a few fuckin' tourist villages. Who'd want to look at that?'

'Perhaps he isn't even heading this way. Perhaps he's taken your free flight and hire car and he's treating himself to a nice little holiday in sunny Spain. Maybe he's got better things to do than scribble down the life story of Tony Gorman.'

Gorman frowned and glanced at Farnell who smiled, shook his head.

'He'll be along soon,' he assured Gorman. 'Believe me, he was thrilled to be chosen. He told me it was a dream assignment, something he would kill for.'

'There, you see!' said Gorman triumphantly. He stubbed out his cigarette like a visual exclamation mark.

'I don't get it,' said Lisa. 'A book? You've never expressed any interest before.'

'Never thought of it before,' said Gorman, matter-of-factly. 'Then I read these articles by this Nolan geezer . . . He's got this way of writin', see. Hard to explain but it's like . . . uh . . .' He gestured helplessly and looked to Farnell for assistance.

'Mythic,' he suggested. 'He talks of outlaws rather than villains, Lisa. Makes comparisons between people like Tony here and the great heroes of folklore. Robin Hood, Billy the Kid, Cu Chulainn . . .'

'Koo who?' asked Gorman, mystified.

Lisa sniggered. 'Oh, that's a pretty picture,' she said, '*Tony the Kid*? Hardly. But *Tony the Hood*, now, I can see that comparison.' She glanced at Farnell. 'You honestly think anybody would be interested in reading it?'

'I *know* they will be, Lisa. I've already had some very productive talks with most of the major British and American publishers. They all seem to think that Frank Nolan is the ideal writer for the project. And of course, it will be excellent publicity for the club. It's doing OK at the moment, but it's like I've been telling Tony, we should be aiming for a more exclusive clientele.'

'Instead of the sleazy jerks who are currently hanging out there,' observed Lisa. 'Well, I wish you both every success!'

'You can't stand it, can you!' sneered Gorman, leaning forwards across the table. 'You just hate to see me getting the limelight. It's always got right up your nose, ennit? Me, Tony Gorman, the kid from the East End, rubbin' shoulders with the rich and famous!' He waved a hand at her dismissively, then turned to face Farnell and opened his bathrobe to display his sucked-in stomach. 'What d'yer reckon, Bill? I fink I've lost a few pounds off the ol' tum, don't you?'

'Looking good, Tony, looking good!'

Gorman stood up. 'Go on,' he said. 'Punch me in the stomach!'

Farnell looked doubtful.

'Go on! Give me your best shot. I can take it.'

Farnell smiled foolishly, and gave Gorman a playful tap with his knuckles.

'No,' Gorman urged him. 'I mean a proper belt, go on! I've got belly muscles like iron. Go on, my son, hit me!'

Farnell stared at Gorman. He glanced at Lisa. She was watching closely, an expectant smile on her face. Farnell shrugged. He turned back and popped a sharp jab into Gorman's stomach. He folded like a paper bag, doubling up over Farnell's arm as a whoosh of air exploded from his mouth. His face went very red.

'Jesus, Tony, you all right?' Farnell bent over him in concern. Gorman straightened up again, with an unconvincing laugh, displaying clenched teeth.

'Ha! Had yer ... fooled! Just pullin ... yer leg!' He sat down heavily in his seat and stared off at the pool for a moment, while he struggled to regain his breathing.

Lisa laughed mockingly and he snapped around to glare at her, his eyes suddenly clear and very dangerous.

'Somethin' funny?' he growled.

Lisa stopped laughing, like somebody had pulled a plug. She stared down at her hands for a moment, not wanting to challenge his gaze. She reached for her Martini.

'Make that your last drink before dinner,' he warned her. 'I don't want this guy thinking that I'm married to a sponge! Got that?'

She nodded, dumbly. She put her shades back on and

161

went back to flicking aimlessly through the magazine. It was suddenly very quiet on the patio. Gorman sat there, absent-mindedly stroking his stomach.

'Where the fuck *is* that guy?' he muttered. 'What's he playin' at?'

Chapter Thirteen

Tam McGiver pulled the tab on a can of Special Brew and took a generous swallow from the contents. He set the can down on the table, belched appreciatively then smiled at Eddie Mulryan who was sitting across from him. Mulryan was winding black insulation tape around the cracked plaster-cast on his hand, the tip of his tongue extending from between his teeth as he worked. He looked a fright, McGiver thought, his squashed nose a livid mass of purple and yellow bruises. Who would have thought that somebody like Jack Doyle was capable of inflicting that kind of damage on a man as big and powerful as Mulryan? It only went to show that a cornered animal should never be underestimated.

McGiver had stripped down to his vest and he scratched absent-mindedly at the matting of thick, wiry hair that sprouted from his chest. Mulryan hadn't even taken his coat off, had refused anything stronger than tea and was studiously affecting the attitude that he had only entered McGiver's flat on sufferance. But for all his size, the man wasn't stupid, he must have realized that

163

this was a relatively safe haven in a city that had suddenly become a very hot place for him to be.

The smell of frying bacon wafted in from the kitchen where Sandra was preparing dinner. She hadn't commented on McGiver's unexpected house guest, but then she knew better than that. McGiver had always subscribed to the view that a man's house was his castle and that those who shared it on a regular basis were merely servants. Sandra had lived here for close on two years now and any uppity qualities she had initially possessed had long ago been beaten out of her. If McGiver chose to bring somebody home – and that included other women – it was his business and nobody else's.

He took another swig of lager and then nodded at Mulryan's smashed hand.

'You ought to get a doctor to take another look at that,' he said. 'I could arrange it, you know, there's a few that owe me a favour.'

Mulryan shook his head stubbornly.

'I reckon it'll be all right,' he muttered.

McGiver shrugged. 'Suit y'self,' he said. 'But if we're going to be travelling around Spain, it won't help if you get ill. And they say the doctors out there are butchers.'

Mulryan stopped winding tape and regarded McGiver thoughtfully.

' "We?" ' he echoed. 'Who said anything about "we?" '

McGiver sighed. 'Look, Eddie, don't give me a hard time over this, OK? The Armenian has instructed me to find out Doyle's whereabouts and to go and pay him off. Now, you tell me he's gone to Spain. Fine, The Armenian wouldn't care if it was the moon, he'd still expect me to follow it up. As far as I'm concerned, it's just a free holiday on the "Costa del Sunshine".'

'It's more than that to me!' Mulryan assured him. 'I owe Doyle. It's a personal matter and I'll be damned if I let somebody else have the pleasure of rubbing him out.'

McGiver shook his head. 'Listen, I don't particularly care who handles that part of it; only that I see it's done. I have no axe to grind. But I'm buggered if I'm going to pass off an opportunity like this one. I haven't been out of the country in years. So, what I suggest is that we work together to track him down. And when we find him, he's all yours.'

Mulryan frowned. He looked doubtful.

'That's easily said,' he murmured. 'How do I know you'll keep your word?'

'Well, now, you're going to have to trust me, aren't you? Tell you the truth, the situation you're in right now, I don't think you've got a lot of choice in the matter. Jesus, haven't I just brought you to my own flat because you were in trouble?'

Mulryan shrugged. 'I suppose.'

'What exactly happened back there, anyway? You said something about your mother . . .'

'It wasn't just that. Winters told me that I couldn't go after Doyle. He said that we should just leave things to you. Then I told him I'd take a holiday and sort things out and he wasn't going to let me do that either . . . I suppose I . . . just saw red.'

'And you killed him?'

'Him and his wife. She came in after I'd done him and I . . . sort of panicked, I suppose.'

'Jesus.' McGiver shook his head. 'And was it you started the fire?'

'No, that just sort of happened. When Winters' head went through the television screen . . .'

'What?' McGiver glanced at him sharply, then gave a short barking laugh. 'That's one way of getting on the telly!' he quipped. 'Christ, Eddie, you really went for broke didn't you?'

Mulryan nodded glumly.

'I regret it,' he said. 'It's the one time in my life I've ever acted unprofessional. It's just that when I think of the way Doyle tricked me, it makes me . . . it makes me so angry.' He tore a strip of tape off with the fingernails on his good hand.

'Yeah, well . . . don't worry, Eddie, you'll have your revenge. It tastes all the sweeter for having to wait for it.' McGiver looked at the can in his hand for a moment, reflecting that since his brother Alex's death, he'd never really stopped taking *his* revenge. He took a little more of it just about every day of his life and the weird thing was that it was never really enough to satisfy him. However much he glutted himself on it, he still craved more. He made a mental effort to cast his thoughts aside. 'So,' he said, 'where in Spain was he headed?'

'Malaga. I know the flight number and everything.'

'Hmm. Well, it's a big town, as far as I can remember. And since he must have realized that you know his destination, it's unlikely that he'll hang around there.

We may have quite a search on our hands.'

'We'll find him,' said Mulryan. 'I'll sniff him out.'

McGiver smirked. 'Not with that nose, you won't! It's a pity he isn't the one with the bruises. Might make him easier to find.'

'He has a bandaged hand. I cut him with a knife a couple of days ago.'

'That might help. First things first, we'll have to book a flight. I take it your passport is in order?'

'Yes. Trouble is, it's back at my place. I don't know if it'll be safe to go and get it.'

Sandra came through from the kitchen, carrying two heaped plates of bacon, egg and sausage. She was a big-boned, fleshy woman with long coppery curls, held back from her face by an elastic grip. Despite the lateness of the hour she was wearing a white towelling gown over a black nylon slip. The stub of a cigarette drooped from her full, red-painted lips.

She set the plates down in front of the men and Mulryan noticed that there was something distinctly odd about her right hand; but he only got a glimpse of it before she snatched it away, turned on her heel and went back into the kitchen; she re-emerged moments later carrying a tin tray, containing cups, cutlery, bread and butter and a teapot covered with a cat-shaped cosy. She set it down between the men then stood there, as if awaiting further instructions. Mulryan noticed that now she had put the right hand into the pocket of her gown as though she had noticed him trying to get a look at it.

'Ketchup,' grunted McGiver, irritably. Again, she

turned on her heel and trudged obediently back into the kitchen. McGiver gave Mulryan a sly wink. 'The food's not much cop but the service is great!' he said. He laughed unpleasantly.

Mulryan stared down at his plate. He didn't have much of an appetite. He kept getting an image of Mrs Winters' pale face staring up at him, her white forehead leaking blood and brains, her eyes full of reproach, her painted lips working around her final words. *You naughty boy!* As though chiding him for some foolish little misdemeanour. Somehow, that was the worst thing of all.

'Get it down you, pal,' McGiver advised him. 'Life always looks better with a full belly.' He took a slice of bread, folded it and prodded one corner into an egg yolk. It burst, squirting its thick yellow glop across his plate. Sandra reappeared and handed him a bottle of sauce. Presumably not hungry herself, she moved across to a leather sofa and slumped down in front of a large television set. She reached for the remote control and gestured the set into life. An Australian soap opera was in full swing, a couple of gawky looking kids lying on a beach and discussing the problems of somebody called Jessica.

McGiver strafed his food with generous explosions of tomato sauce.

'Switch it over, will you,' he grunted. 'News.'

Sandra made a small sound of irritation at the back of her throat but she hit the appropriate button and the picture changed; another Australian soap, grinning teenagers in garish shirts, who had just organized a surprise leaving party for somebody called Keith.

McGiver rolled his eyes up to the ceiling.

'Load of bleeding shite,' he observed. 'Beats me why the fuck anybody bothers to pay the licence any more.' He gazed at Mulryan who was picking half heartedly at his food. 'Don't worry, I'll arrange to collect your passport. You'll probably want some other stuff too. You can write a list and I'll get Sandra to collect it later.'

Mulryan glanced at her uncertainly.

'Well . . . if it wouldn't be too much trouble . . .'

'Don't worry about it! You don't mind, do you, hen?'

Sandra gave some kind of reply, half sigh, half grunt. She stubbed the butt of her cigarette into an ashtray and immediately lit another. Then she picked up a file from the arm of the sofa and began to work on the nails of her left hand, not really looking at what she was doing.

'After you've been up to Eddie's place, you can run another errand for me,' McGiver told her. 'I want you to go to a travel agent and book a couple of tickets to Malaga. Get the earliest available flight.'

Sandra seemed to perk up a little at this. Her thickly pencilled eyebrows arched quizzically.

'We going to Spain?' she asked.

'No, stupid.' McGiver dropped a rasher of bacon on to a slice of bread and folded it over. 'The tickets are for me and him. The two of us are going on a wee business trip.' He bit into his sandwich and chewed noisily for a moment. He swallowed. 'You'd better arrange for some traveller's cheques too. I'll write down the details for you.'

'OK.' She was uninterested again, her voice flat, toneless. She returned her gaze to the television screen. The soap's credits were playing out over an irritating theme song about love and understanding.

'Load of fucking bollocks,' observed McGiver bitterly. 'See, the trouble with most people in this world is that they'll put up with any amount of shite, rather than stand up and say what they *want*. People have to shape the life they want. It's no use whining about how crap things are, you've got to grab life by the balls and—' He broke off as the familiar music for the local news programme interrupted his tirade. 'Hey, look, Eddie, you might be seeing yourself in a minute! Sandra, turn the fucking volume up!'

The item was featured well down in the pecking order and was allotted little more than lip service. The male newscaster simply reported that a man and his wife had perished in a house fire at their luxury home in Wimbledon. The fire brigade had yet to establish the cause of the blaze but fire officers were treating it as 'suspicious'.

'Christ,' muttered McGiver. 'You can't get much past those bastards. Next thing you know, they'll be wanting to talk to you. The sooner you get out of the country, the better.' He gestured at Sandra, miming his thumb on an imaginary button.

'Oh, Tam,' she protested. 'I wanted to watch—'

'Off!' he snapped and that dangerous look was back in his eyes. The screen flickered and went dead.

McGiver pushed his empty plate away and leaned back in his chair with a sigh of contentment. 'Tab!' he commanded.

Sandra got up from the sofa and came across to him. She put a cigarette between his lips and torched it with a plastic lighter. McGiver puffed out a cloud of smoke, then swivelled sideways and patted his knees, indicating that she should sit down. She did as he suggested. She sat there, looking blankly at Mulryan who was still trying to eat his dinner.

'She's a good girl, this one,' observed McGiver, giving Sandra a slap on the rump. 'Well behaved, wouldn't you say, Eddie?'

Mulryan glanced up from his meal, bemused. He couldn't think of a suitable reply. McGiver went on anyway. He reached around Sandra's waist and untied the cord of her robe, allowing it to fall open. Mulryan reddened and looked down at his food again, as though he had just noticed something of great interest on his plate.

'The thing about Sandra is, she does whatever she's told. But she wasn't always like that . . . were you, hen?'

Sandra shook her head, her face expressionless.

'I had to work on her,' explained McGiver. '*Customise* her. Like you do with a car, you know? I remember one occasion when she made a very rude two-finger gesture to me. She wouldn't do it now. Now she's a good girl. She does what I tell her, don't you, hen?'

Sandra nodded.

'What's up?' demanded McGiver. 'Cat got your tongue? You do what I tell you, don't you?'

'Yes, Tam.' The voice flat, lacking any spark of life.

'You know, Eddie, there's some fellers who'd be a wee bit nervous about going off to Spain and leaving their woman here alone. While the cat's away ... isn't that how the saying goes? While the cat's away ...?'

He prodded Sandra with his elbow.

'The mice will play,' she finished dutifully.

'That's right! But see, now, I don't worry about that, not for one minute. Oh, I dare say there've been times in the past when Sandra might have been tempted by forbidden fruit but ... not any more, eh, hen? Here, Sandra, why don't you show Eddie your tits?'

Mulryan spluttered, nearly choked on his food. His face, already red, shaded to a deep, hot crimson.

''Ere, now look ... I don't think I ...'

McGiver gestured him to silence.

'Oh, but she's got lovely tits, they're well worth a look! It's no problem, is it, Sandra?'

She shook her head. Still staring impassively at Mulryan, she reached up her hands, pulled the straps of her slip over her shoulders and let it fall to her waist.

Mulryan stared. He didn't want to but he couldn't help it. It wasn't so much Sandra's naked breasts. No, it was the crudely tattooed words etched into the breasts themselves, rising and falling across the curves in ugly, blue letters. PROPERTY OF TAM MCGIVER, they read. Mulryan pushed his half eaten meal away. What little appetite he'd had was suddenly gone. He sat there, gazing across the table at McGiver who was grinning wolfishly back at him, the cold grey eyes gauging Mulryan's shock, relishing it, enjoying the flavour of it. There was a silence that seemed to last an eternity.

'Cover yourself up,' said McGiver at last. Sandra

raised her right hand to pull at her slip and Mulryan found himself focusing on it. He was suddenly shocked all over again. He had finally realized what was odd about that hand. It was missing two fingers.

Chapter Fourteen

Jack brought the Mitsubishi to a halt outside the illuminated entrance to the Hotel Excelsior. He sat there looking apprehensively at its glass doorway, flanked between massive marble columns, and began to wish that he'd stopped for a wash and a change of clothes somewhere along the way. Glancing at his hands by the light of the dashboard he saw they were filthy, the nails ingrained with grime, the bandage on his left hand hanging in bloody tatters.

Away to his right was the marina of Puerto Banus, where a huge selection of ostentatious yachts and cruisers rode at anchor, overtly advertising the kind of wealth that congregated here. He thought about driving on and abandoning his planned deception but he knew that he would have trouble booking into any hotel in his present state and besides, this one was already paid for. So he climbed grimly out of the vehicle and went around to unload his newly acquired luggage.

Instantly, a uniformed doorman appeared on the steps, looking faintly ludicrous in a crimson, military styled overcoat. He gave an imperious wave of his white gloved hand and a couple of porters came running out of the entrance to commandeer Jack's luggage. They cast doubtful glances at his dishevelled appearance but it was hardly their place to comment on it. Jack handed the keys to one of them and turned to stroll, as casually as possible, up the steps to the entrance.

A couple of people emerged from the swing doors, a young Spanish couple, the man clothed in elegant casuals that somehow contrived to give an impression of wealth, the woman wearing a skimpy, designer mini-dress, diamonds glittering at her ears and throat. They stared openly at Jack in passing, as though he had just stepped out of a spacecraft.

He passed on through the entrance and into the reception area. A broad expanse of marble floor lay between him and the desk and he crossed it slowly, cringing inwardly at the hollow clunk of his own footsteps. There were strategically placed potted palms ranged about the room and overhead, a massive chandelier provided more light than was strictly comfortable. An old couple sitting on a rattan sofa nearby peered down their noses at him, as if he'd arrived smeared in excrement. There was nothing for it but to walk on to the desk, where an impeccably attired clerk stood waiting for him, his expression suggesting that some horrible mistake had occurred. There was a clatter behind Jack and he turned to see that the porters were bringing in his baggage. He hoped to God he'd got the right hotel.

'Señor?' The desk clerk was a plump man with a

clipped moustache and a head that was symmetrically bald on top, as though he scissored a neat, straight wedge out of it every morning.

Jack leaned an arm on the mahogany counter and adopted what he hoped was a casual pose.

'I believe you have a room for me?' he said.

'I'm sorry, Señor, we are fully booked.'

'No, no, a *reservation*. In the name of Jack—' He broke off, silently cursing his own stupidity. 'In the name of Frank Nolan.'

'Meester Jack-Frank Nolan?'

'No, just *Frank* Nolan.'

The man frowned, gave Jack a suspicious look. 'I will have to check,' he announced.

'So check,' said Jack irritably. 'The name should be there.'

The man scanned the book in front of him, his lips drawn into a disapproving pout. Then his expression changed dramatically. His eyes seemed to light up and the pout was replaced by an oily smile of welcome. 'Ah *si*, Señor Nolan! You are the guest of Señor Gorman, yes?'

Jack relaxed a little, returned the man's smile.

'That's right. Had a little trouble getting here.' He indicated his filthy clothes and spread his hands in a gesture of helplessness. 'Got lost on some back road and drove my car into a ditch. Had to dig my way out!'

'Oh no!' Now the man was looking at Jack's bandaged hand. 'You have injured yourself!'

'Er . . . yeah. Did it when I was digging the car out.'

The clerk reached for a telephone. 'I will call out a doctor immediately!'

'No!' Jack had reached across the counter to put his hand on the man's wrist. 'No, really, there's no need. It's just a scratch. I can take care of it myself.'

The man stared at him. 'You are sure?'

'Positive. Once I've cleaned myself up I'll be as good as new.'

'As you wish, Señor. Please, accept my humble apologies for our terrible roads.' He looked like he might be about to break down and cry. 'It is not like this in your country, I think?'

Jack didn't know what to say to this, so he just shrugged and gave the man a vacant smile.

'Please to sign in, Señor Nolan.' The man pushed the book towards Jack and turned aside to get a key from the rack. Jack just made a meaningless squiggle for his signature and wrote down the address in Finsbury Park that he had memorized from Frank's passport. The clerk turned back with that gracious smile still plastered all over his face. It was a wonder his lips didn't crack.

'We have put you in apartment 216,' he said. 'I think, Señor, you will find it most agreeable, but if there is any problem please call down and we will find you something else.'

'I thought you said you were fully booked?'

The man spread his hands in a meaningless gesture. 'Señor Gorman is a well respected *patron* of the hotel,' he said, by way of explanation. He bowed from the waist as if in the presence of royalty, then beckoned to one of the porters and handed him the keys.

'Oh, one more thing. Señor Farnell has called for you, several times. He asks if you would ring him as soon as you arrive.' He handed Jack a compliment slip with a phone number written on it.

'Thanks.' Jack pushed the note into his pocket and followed the porter towards the elevator.

'I hope you enjoy your stay with us, Señor Nolan,' said the desk clerk.

Jesus, thought Jack. *So do I, mate. So do I.*

The apartment was up on the second floor and it was palatial enough to convince Jack that he had hit on a good thing. After he had got rid of the porter, he stood there on the deep pile carpet, gazing thoughtfully around the place. He wondered how much it was costing to keep him here and told himself that for a few days at least, it was going to be a very comfortable hideaway.

The main room featured a television and stereo system, an oak dining table with six elegant chairs and a comfortable looking leather sofa and armchair. Sliding glass doors gave out on to a balcony which afforded a pleasing view of the floodlit marina and the scores of bars and restaurants that surrounded it. Up on a higher level, there was a king-size bed that looked very inviting just at the moment; and through an adjoining door, he found a large bathroom, tiled from floor to ceiling in black marble. Without further ado, he ran the shower nice and hot. He stripped his clothes off and flung them unceremoniously into a corner. Then he stood beneath the rush of water and washed away the sweat and dust of travel with the hotel's complimentary soap and shampoo.

When he emerged ten minutes later, he felt almost human, his skin tingling from the vigorous scrubbing he had given it. He unpicked the sodden bandage from his hand and gingerly cleaned out the wound, the pain driving away any thought of sleep. He found a clean dressing in a first-aid kit in the bathroom cabinet and carefully wound it around the hand. He regarded his reflection in the mirror and rubbed his fingers thoughtfully across several day's growth of beard, wondering if he should use Frank's razor. On reflection, he decided to leave it be. A decent beard was the best disguise going and might help to explain why he didn't look much like his passport photograph.

Jack's own clothes were filthy so he walked into the main room and threw Frank's cases on to the bed, so he could unpack their contents. It was evident that clothes were going to be a problem. Frank had been about his height but a good deal leaner, which meant that the various jackets and trousers in the big case were far too tight for him. Eventually, he found a loose-fitting tracksuit which he could get into without too much discomfort.

He turned his attention to one of Frank's attaché cases, the one he had rifled when he was looking for pills. He found a couple of glossy magazines tucked away at the back of it. Flicking through them, he found the articles that Frank had mentioned, the biographies of famous criminals that had so impressed Tony Gorman. He threw these on to the bed, telling himself that he would do well to memorize their contents. After all, *he* was supposed to have written them.

He found a couple of bank statements folded into one compartment and discovered that despite Frank's protests to the contrary, he was a relatively wealthy man. There were several credit cards in Frank's wallet and Jack supposed that this was the solution to his wardrobe problem. He would buy new clothes at the first opportunity. After all, he reasoned, the money wasn't going to be any use to Frank now, was it?

Jack sighed. No sense in sweating it, he decided. He told himself that if the worst came to the worst, he could just get in that hire car and drive in the opposite direction. He could destroy Frank's passport and belongings and be himself again. Some prospect.

Now he opened Frank's portable computer. He hit the 'on' switch and the screen lit up with columns of names. Scanning them, Jack could see that they were all documents, most of them with self explanatory names. He chose one labelled GORMAN and punched the EDIT command. He was cheered to see that the screen filled up with a formidable array of information. Frank had evidently done considerable homework and for that, Jack was very grateful. There was a detailed summary of Tony Gorman's history, from his innocuous birth in Bethnal Green in 1951, to his most recent exploits. Jack noted that he'd taken up residence in Marbella in 1978, a few months before he'd been implicated in the infamous bank robbery. He'd been lucky to get out of the country.

His three accomplices on the job had all been picked up before they could follow his example and were still serving time back in Britain.

Gorman had married in Marbella in 1980 and had engaged the services of Bill Farnell one year later. Just two years ago, the duo had opened a nightclub in Marbella called, appropriately enough, TONY'S. After this entry there followed a series of Latin-American sounding names, with question marks after them and several mentions of somebody, or something, called *The Duchess*, together with a list of dates ranging back over the past eight years. This meant nothing to Jack, so he exited the document and tried looking at a few more.

Frank Nolan had been busy. Here was a chapter-by-chapter outline of the proposed autobiography. Very useful to have, under the circumstances ...

The phone rang, making Jack start. He looked at it warily but after some hesitation, he decided he'd better answer it. He picked up the receiver.

'Yes?' he said.

'Señor Nolan? I have a call for you. Please hold on, I will put it through.'

A pause. Then; 'Mr Nolan?'

'Speaking.'

'You made it then! This is Bill Farnell. Tony and I were beginning to worry. What happened?'

'Oh, I had a little trouble with the car. Not used to driving on the right-hand side, I guess. Drove it into a ditch.'

'Christ! You OK? I mean, you weren't injured or anything?'

'No. I'm fine thanks. Just scratched my hand, that's all. But I had to dig the rear wheel out of the dirt, which took quite some time. I would have called you straightaway, but I needed to get cleaned up.'

'Don't worry, just so long as you're safe. You . . . you sound different.'

Jack tensed.

'Do I? How do you mean?'

'Don't know exactly. Your voice sounds . . . well, just different.'

'I'm closer now, remember. Some of those long-distance lines do strange things to the voice.'

'That right? Maybe we just had a bad connection. Anyway, Tony's very anxious to meet you. Wants you to come right over for food and drinks. Don't worry about bringing any work with you, this is just to see how the two of you get along. Tell you what, I'll send a driver to pick you up. Sounds like you've had enough of our roads for one night.'

'Oh, there's no need, really!'

'I insist. He'll be there in about half an hour. See you later.'

The receiver was replaced. Jack put down his own handset. He tried to remember if Frank Nolan had any distinctive characteristics in his voice, but already the man was fading from his memory. He'd just have to try and wing it. He lay back on the bed and picked up another of the magazines. Thumbing through it, he came to an article about Ronald Biggs. He resolved to use the next half hour usefully. If Tony Gorman started talking about his writing it would be useful if Jack could display at least a working knowledge of it.

Jack was pleased to discover that 'he' was very readable. It was good to be so talented. That helped.

Chapter Fifteen

Angelito parked the grey Mercedes in the forecourt of the Excelsior and sat there for a moment, finishing his cigarette and studying his reflection critically in the driving mirror. He let the cigarette droop from his lips, narrowed his eyes and reached up a hand to smooth his long black hair into place. Then he removed the cigarette and smiled, what he called his 'movie-star smile', his white, even teeth dazzling against his tanned skin.

Hey, but he was looking good tonight! Maybe when Señor Gorman's book was finished, they'd make it into a movie in Hollywood and maybe, just maybe, they'd find a part in it for him. Others had told Angelito that he sometimes got ideas above his station, but he refused to listen to that kind of talk. The way he figured it, a guy could go as far and as high as he pushed himself. Señor Gorman was always saying how he'd started with nothing and look at him now; a fine house, a beautiful wife and money enough to buy whatever he desired. And *he* hadn't been blessed with movie-star looks.

Angelito flicked the stub of his Marlboro through the

open window and got out of the car. He secured the door and walked across to the hotel entrance, his hand-tooled cowboy boots clicking on the asphalt. He was wearing a red western-styled shirt under a loose fitting Levi jacket, which hid the bulge of the .38 pistol where it fitted snugly into the soft leather holster tucked under his left arm. He hooked his thumbs into the leather belt with the Harley Davidson buckle and walked the way he had seen John Travolta walk in a movie once, a slow, swaggering strut, swinging his hips from side to side as though walking to a funky musical accompaniment.

He went in through the swing doors and traversed the marble floor of the reception area. The metal tips of his heels clacked loudly in the silence and heads turned to look at him, but he kind of enjoyed that.

'*Si*, Señor?' The guy at the desk had a superior look on his face. Angelito gave him the snake-eyes and the man's gaze flicked nervously aside, reluctant to return the stare.

Angelito grinned. 'Señor Gorman sent me. I'm to collect a Señor Nolan, an *Ingles.*' He noted how the clerk's expression changed when Gorman's name was mentioned, how the man became immediately attentive, servile. One day, Angelito thought, *his* name would have the same effect. He had aspirations and he believed it was all just a matter of time. You kept your eyes open, watching for opportunities and when one came along, you grabbed it with both hands and didn't let go, no matter what. Señor Gorman had told him that so many times, probably believing that Angelito would never dare to act on his advice. But the time was coming when he would do something about it . . .

'Señor Nolan is in room 216,' announced the desk clerk. 'We gave him one of our best apartments, I'm sure he'll find it most comfortable.'

Angelito shrugged, as if to say that it was of no consequence to him whether the *Ingles* was comfortable or not. But he knew that Tony Gorman owned a very large chunk of the Excelsior Hotel and its management was keen to keep him sweet.

'I'll go on up.'

'Perhaps I should phone to say you're coming?' suggested the clerk.

'Do that,' said Angelito, without turning back to face the man.

Entering the elevator, Angelito decided he didn't much like the look of the lift attendant. He was a skinny, ape-like boy, around eighteen years old. His uniform was several sizes too big for him and his cheeks were pitted with pussy explosions of chronic acne. As Angelito stepped in, he noticed the boy glance down at the cowboy boots with a barely disguised smile.

'Somethin' funny?' he growled.

The boy glanced up, his blue eyes wide with surprise.

'Eh, no señor!'

'You sure? You fuckin' sure?' Angelito leaned closer to the kid and gave him the snake-eyed look.

The kid swallowed noisily and his flesh turned several shades paler beneath its fiery blemishes.

'S . . . s . . . second floor,' he announced. The doors

pinged as they slid open. Grinning, Angelito walked out of the lift and strutted along the corridor beyond. He found room 216 and rapped his knuckles on the hardwood door.

'Just a minute.' Some scuffling sounds from within. Then the door opened and the *Ingles* peeped out at him. 'Yes?'

'Señor Gorman sent me. You are Señor Nolan, yes?'

Jack nodded. 'Come in, I won't be a minute.' He turned away and Angelito was able to appraise him as he followed him into the room. Odd looking guy, dressed in a scruffy jogsuit that seemed to be several sizes too small for him. A bandage around the palm of his left hand. He seemed nervous, a little unsure of himself as he searched out his wallet from a case on the bed. Angelito settled into an armchair.

'Good trip over?' he asked; not that he was interested, it was just the kind of thing you were expected to say.

'A nightmare, if you want to know the truth. Anyway, I guess I'm ready to go.'

Angelito's expression of disbelief must have spoken louder than words because the *Ingles* looked doubtfully down at his jogging trousers and scuffed shoes. 'You're right,' he said. 'I can't go to dinner like this.'

'Hey man, I didn't say anything!'

'You didn't have to. I mean, Christ, you don't think I normally dress like this, do you?'

Angelito shrugged. 'I wouldn't know,' he said.

'The bloody airline lost my luggage . . . don't ask me how, but it got put on the wrong plane! Can't get it back for a few days.'

Angelito stared at him. 'Jesus,' he muttered. 'You ain't having much luck on this trip, are you?'

Jack shook his head. He looked at Angelito for a moment.

'Would you know of any good clothes shops around here?' he asked.

Angelito grinned. 'Sure. Good shops, right here in Puerto Banus. Little pricey maybe . . .'

Jack frowned. 'Well, that doesn't matter. OK if we make a stop on the way to Mr Gorman's? I'll try to be as quick as I can.'

'Whatever you say. I can phone from the car, tell 'em we're gonna be late.'

'Hmm. Well listen, er . . . I'm sorry, what's your name?'

'Angelito. Friends call me Angel.'

'Yes, well, I'd appreciate it if you didn't say anything about this. They probably already feel bad about me having that little accident back on the road. I don't want them thinking I'm a total waste of time, do I?'

Angelito frowned. 'OK. Listen though, this place I take you. Tell them you're a guest of Señor Gorman. Should be good for a big discount.'

'Think so?'

'I know so. That goes for any place around here. His name means a lot.'

'OK. Let's go shall we?'

In the elevator going down, Angelito was pleased to note that the kid in the ill-fitting uniform kept his gaze fixed resolutely to the floor the whole time.

Angelito smoked a Marlboro while he waited outside

the boutique. It was an up-market place called LORCA'S, all high-tech metal and neon strip lighting. Through the window, he could see the *Ingles* pointing to various out-fits, while the two men who ran the shop rushed around in a frenzy, trying to please him, their pony-tails bobbing.

Angelito glanced at his Rolex and noted that fifteen minutes had already slipped by. He picked up the car phone and dialled home. He had considered backing up Jack's story and promptly dismissed the idea. For one thing, he'd have to make up some story and he frankly couldn't be bothered with it. For another, he wasn't about to risk lying to his employers. If they found out, he'd be in the shit with them. He wasn't above practising deception, of course, he'd done it often enough when there was something in it for him. Right now, all he stood to gain was the gratitude of the *Ingles*. Gratitude was an overrated commodity. You couldn't spend it and you couldn't eat it. In Angelito's book, it wasn't worth a flying fuck.

Bill Farnell answered the phone.

'Hello, Mr Gorman's residence.'

'Señor Farnell? It's Angel. We're gonna be a little bit late.'

'Jesus, what's the problem now?' Farnell sounded peeved.

'Señor Nolan wanted to buy some clothes. I'm outside LORCA'S waiting for him.'

'Clothes? The fuck he want clothes for?'

'Dumb airline lost his bags. He won't get them back for a few days.'

'The hell, you say! Boy, he must be regretting coming already.'

Angelito chuckled. 'That's what I said. Oh, listen, he asked me not to mention this. Figured you might feel bad.'

'Hmm. OK, I'll make sure not to admire his dress sense. I hope you told him to mention Tony's name.'

'Sure, I did. Maybe he will too. I don't know, he's a strange one . . .'

'How do you mean, strange?'

'Kind of weird, you know? Maybe all writers are like that. I never met one before.'

'Me neither. Anyway, thanks for calling. I'll tell Maximillian to hold back on the dinner for a while. See you later.'

Angelito put down the phone and flicked the stub of his cigarette out of the window.

The passenger door opened and there was the *Ingles*, looking like an entirely different person. He had on an Armani suit in blue silk, a crisp white shirt and a silk tie, hand-printed with Aztec designs. He was carrying several more bags with the LORCA logo emblazoned on them.

'What do you think?' he asked. He seemed more confident now, as though he had put on new skin.

'Hey, man, you look good,' said Angelito. 'You look better than good. You look *sharp*!'

The *Ingles* grinned. 'OK if I stow this other stuff in the back?'

'Sure, throw it in there. Hey, what's that, a leather

jacket? Fuck man, looks like you bought the entire shop!'

Jack shrugged, climbed into the passenger seat. 'Well, you can't take it with you,' he observed.

'Ain't that a fact.' Angelito hit the starter, let out the clutch and accelerated away from the curb.

Jack felt better now that he'd sorted out his clothing. He had never been more aware of how important it was to present the right image. Losing his suits had been like losing his identity. Now he was back in control and beginning to believe that he could handle this deception.

Angelito had been right about mentioning Gorman's name. The proprietors of LORCA'S had been servile enough when he walked in there. At the mention of Tony Gorman, they'd all but had their tongues up his arse. Jack had paid by American Express, scribbling down the Frank Nolan signature he had practised back at the hotel, as though he'd been writing it all his life.

Now Jack was on his way to his first meeting with Tony Gorman and in a strange kind of way, he was looking forward to it. Angelito had the speedo cranked up way over the limit, driving in a blatantly macho style that was doubtless designed to impress the new arrival. Recent memories of the consequences of speeding prevented Jack from responding with anything but the stomping of an imaginary brake pedal every time the Mercedes approached a bend in the road.

Jack couldn't quite believe Angelito. He wondered if his narcissism was just a front, though it certainly appeared to be genuine enough. The man kept throwing admiring glances into his driving mirror, occasionally reaching up a hand to pat his hair into place. Then he would grin at Jack, displaying those even, white teeth. What happened to a guy like that when he got old and fat? It really didn't bear thinking about. Now Angelito was looking at him intently and Jack sensed a conversation welling up in his mouth.

'Tell me, Señor. Does it pay well, writing?'

'It seems to.' Jack hoped he had managed to keep the tone of genuine surprise out of his voice. 'What about driving? That pay well?'

Angelito's lip curled in a sneer. 'Oh, I do more than just drive. Tell you the truth, I been asking Señor Gorman to get somebody else, you know, a proper chauffeur. See, he don't drive himself, never learned and neither does Señor Farnell. I think that's pathetic, don't you? Two grown men and they can't drive a car. Do you drive? Oh sure, you managed to put that hire car into a ditch, right?'

Jack decided to ignore the mocking tone in Angelito's voice.

'Dog ran right out in front of me,' he explained. 'You know how it is. So, what else do you do for Tony?'

'I am . . . what does he call it? His "right-hand man". I take care of business, you know?'

'I thought that was Bill Farnell's job,' said Jack, with exaggerated innocence.

Angelito laughed. 'Eh, man, not that kind of business! Señor Gorman's an important guy. He has many enemies.

So, when he goes somewhere, I watch out for him. He has a name for it, he says I'm his—'

'—Minder,' finished Jack; and thought of Eddie Mulryan.

'Hey, that's right! You got a minder, back in the UK?'

'No, I look after myself.'

'Maybe you should think about getting one. Big-shot writer and all.'

'Oh, I'm not that important. How long you been working for Tony?'

'Aroun' two years now . . . hey, is this for the book?'

Jack shrugged. 'Could be. Why, you want to be in it?'

'Sure!' Angelito seemed genuinely pleased at the prospect. 'Even better, how about when they make a movie? You think there'd be a part for me?'

Jack tried not to smile. This guy would probably benefit from the occasional visit with reality. 'Well, now, that's not really for me to say, is it? A film's a long way in the future. I think maybe we'd better concentrate on getting the book finished first.'

Angelito drove on for some distance in silence. In the light of the dashboard, his face was scowling.

'Something wrong?' Jack asked him.

'It's just that I wouldn't want no chicken-shit actor to play me. Far as I'm concerned, if I couldn't do it myself, there's only one guy in the world right for the part.'

'Yeah, who's that?'

'Can't you guess, man? A lot of people say he looks like me.'

'Well now, I'm not sure . . .'

'Come on, man, it's obvious! He's a real famous movie star. He's got this walk, right, and he's just about the best dancer ever. Oh, you know who I'm talking about, don't you?'

Jack gazed at him blankly. 'Fred Astaire?' he ventured.

Angelito looked like he might be about to throw up.

'Fred Astaire?' he exploded. 'What are you talking about, man, that guy's about ninety! Hell, I heard he was dead! You think I look like him?'

'Well no, but you said, a famous dancer . . .'

'Hey fuck man, why don't you try Sammy Davis Junior, he was a dancer also! No, I'm talking about John Travolta. See, watch.' He made a slow grin and narrowed his eyes. 'You see the likeness?'

'Now you mention it . . .'

'Yeah, well that's the guy who should play me, see? You think he'd be interested?'

'I think you should ask *him*,' said Jack quietly.

'Yeah, maybe I'll do that. You know where I could get in touch with him?'

Jack didn't have an answer to that. He was relieved when the car turned off the main road, sped along a narrow uphill driveway and approached a set of tall iron gates. Angelito took out a small remote control device and keyed in a four figure code. The gates swung silently back to admit them. They drove slowly up an approach that was flanked by date palms. They passed a full-size tennis court on their left and then a huge, meticulously tended garden.

The house was a sprawling, hacienda-style property,

painted brilliant white. It was lit by strategically placed spotlights and seemed to have been created solely to advertise the fact that the people who lived here were disgustingly rich and didn't lose a single night's sleep over it. As they drove around the side of the house, to a large flagged parking area, Jack got a look at the swimming pool, shimmering invitingly in the beam of overhead lights.

'It ain't much,' said Angelito. 'But we call it home.'

He got out of the car and Jack followed. A figure emerged from the French windows at the rear of the house, a tanned, solid-looking man with jet black hair and an immaculately trimmed moustache. He smiled good naturedly and hurried forward to shake Jack's hand.

'Frank!' he said. 'Great to meet you at last! I'm Bill Farnell.'

Jack shook the proffered hand, deciding that Farnell was exerting just a little more grip than was strictly necessary. 'I'm sorry about all the delay. I can hardly believe I'm here at last.'

Farnell gestured at Jack's bandaged hand.

'That looks a bit more than a scratch.'

For a moment, Jack's mind filled with the image of Eddie Mulryan's placid expression as he'd pushed the stiletto blade into his palm. He made a mental effort to banish the image and he forced a weak smile.

'It's nothing. Anyway, I'm right-handed.'

Farnell slipped an arm around Jack's shoulders and steered him towards the house.

'We'd better take good care of you, while you're here. Wouldn't want any more accidents to happen while you're staying with us. Come on, let's go inside. Tony's there and he's just dying to meet you!'

Chapter Sixteen

Jack's first impression of Tony Gorman was a flash of recognition. Of course, he'd never met the man before, but he'd met plenty like him, the East End boy made good and gone to seed.

Gorman had posed himself at the stone fireplace in the hacienda-style lounge, one elbow up on the mantel, legs nonchalantly crossed. He had a cigarette in one hand and a glass of whisky in the other. He was dressed in expensive casuals; white silk slacks, hand-tooled sandals, a garish designer T-shirt worn out of the trousers in a vain attempt to disguise his beer belly. He had a plump, tanned face that was fast acquiring an extra chin, a prominent nose that was veined with purple blood vessels. His deep-set blue eyes still glittered with all the suss of the cockney street trader he used to be. His hair, prematurely grey and wiry was slicked back to his skull and visibly thinning at the front. Jack noticed that he wore a lot of gold; a chunky chain bracelet around his left wrist, a collection of signet rings on each hand and the inevitable ingot-shaped medallion around his thick neck.

'Frankie boy!' he bellowed. 'We'd about given you up, son! We was goin' to send out a bleedin' search party!'

The cockney accent was overdone, Jack thought. Like so many ex-pats, Gorman had worked his East End origins up into a parody of the real thing. He came across like a cockney stand-up comedian, all mouth and no integrity. Now he was striding across the terracotta tiles, one meaty hand extended to shake. He gripped Jack's hand and pumped it up and down with exaggerated ferocity, talking the whole time.

'I 'ear you 'ad a bit of bovver gettin' down to Marbelly! Honest, the bleedin' roads round 'ere, you can't trust 'em, knowarramean? See, what it is, Frank, right, if a bleedin' donkey falls into a pot 'ole, they leave it to rot and call that maintenance!' He threw back his head and laughed raucously. Jack noticed that Bill Farnell and Angelito were chuckling too, so he did his best to force a feeble smile. He opened his mouth to say something but Gorman was off again.

'You know what? I oughta 'ave sent Angel to pick you up from the airport.' He glanced at Angelito who had dropped into a vacant armchair. 'Angel, why didn't you offer? Let's face it, you do bugger all else to earn your keep!' Angelito scowled and Gorman laughed again. 'Oh, look out, I've 'urt his feelin's now. Bugger'll sulk about it for a week!' He turned back to face Jack. ''Ere, what am I thinking' of? I bet you could use a drink, couldn't yer? What'll you 'ave? Jorge? JORGE!? Where is that lad? He's never around when you want 'im! Now, let's see, Frankie boy, you look like a whisky man to me. You know, I once 'ad this bet with a publican, ran a place in the Mile End Road. Told 'im I could tell a bloke's drink just by lookin' at 'im. "Bollocks!" he said, "'ere's a tenner says you can't guess ten people in a row!" "Right," I says.'

Gorman had evidently told the story many times, but he worked his meagre audience like a professional comic, using his hands, keeping up plenty of eye contact.

'So I sits there and these punters are comin' in one after the other and I'm goin', "This one's a pint of bitter!" or "This one's a gin and tonic," and all that . . . and of course, jammy bleeder, I get's nine in a row. Come's time for the last one and this old geezer walks in and I says, "This one will 'ave a rum and blackcurrant and he'll ask you to put three cocktail cherries in it." "Bollocks!" says the publican. "'Ere's another twenty says he won't!" "Done!" I says. Old geezer staggers up to the counter, asks for a rum and blackcurrant wiv three cherries in it. The publican is flabbergasted. "'Ow the fuck did you know that?" he asks me. "Intuition," I says. Then I turns to the old geezer and I says, "'Ello, Dad, 'aven't seen you for ages!" ' Again the laugh, a near hysterical bellow of mirth.

'That's one for the book!' exclaimed Bill Farnell. 'We gotta put that one in Tony!'

'Yeah.' Gorman glanced irritably around. 'Where's Jorge for Christ's sake?' He turned, glanced over his shoulder. 'Lisa, get Mr Nolan a drink, would you?'

Jack turned in surprise, noting the woman for the first time. She sat apart from the others, slumped back in a leather sofa, a tall, lean woman with straight, honey-blonde hair that hung to her shoulders. She was wearing dark glasses and cradling a drink in her beautifully mani-cured hands. Jack thought she looked slightly sozzled; but she got obediently to her feet and moved unsteadily towards the well-stocked bar behind her.

'What'll it be, Mr Nolan?' There was a twang of an American accent in her voice, which was otherwise dead, toneless, as though she didn't give a damn what Jack was drinking.

'Whisky is fine, thanks. A little dry ginger, if you have it.'

She stepped in behind the bar to fix the drink.

'See, didn't I say you looked like a whisky man!' Gorman slapped Jack heartily on the shoulder. 'I can pick 'em, me! Well . . .' He made an expansive gesture at his surroundings. 'What d'yer think of my little hideaway?'

Jack took the opportunity to gaze around the room. It was surprisingly tasteful, charcoal leather furniture and terracotta tiles, against rough-plastered white-painted walls, which were hung with abstract paintings and hand-woven rugs. Jack would have been willing to bet that it wasn't Gorman who had designed it. There were little touches of him here and there, however. A few copies of the *Daily Mirror* lying on a coffee table, some darts trophies ranged on the mantelpiece and a brightly illuminated Wurlitzer juke box set against one wall, shockingly out of place with its sophisticated sur-roundings.

'It's perfect,' said Jack. 'I wouldn't mind something like this myself.'

'Oh, it's easy, Frankie boy, all you've got to do is rob a bank!' Again, with the laugh, already becoming a major irritation. 'You 'ear that, Bill, this one's ambitious, I like that! Tell you what, Frankie, once we've sewed up this book-and-movie deal, you'll be able to *buy* something similar! You know, I picked this place up for twenty grand, a few years back. 'Course, I made a few improvements and that but now it's worth...' He paused, glanced at Bill Farnell uncertainly.

'Three-quarters of a million,' responded Farnell, without batting an eyelid.

'Yeah, three-quarters of a million! Not bad for an old barrow-boy, eh?'

'Did you really start out as a barrow-boy?' asked Jack. 'I mean, I know that's what it says in all the bio's, but—'

'Oh, it's straight-up, God's honest!' insisted Gorman. 'I left school at fifteen with not a sustificate to me name and I got a stall in Berwick Street market. Don't know if you're familiar with it?'

'Er... yes, I've been there,' said Jack.

'Sold all sorts, mostly knock-off. Started doin' the odd bit of petty thievin', just to make ends meet. But see, the four of us, we always 'ad this ambition to pull off one big job. The biggest, you know? What I said was, we might as well 'ang for a sheep as for a lamb. So we did it. We just up and did it. 'Course, the others didn't make it away clear, but I tell you what, I made sure their families was well looked after. When those fellers get out, they're going to be rich men. None of 'em will ever have to work again.'

'You think any of them bears a grudge?' asked Jack.

There was an uncomfortable silence. Lisa came over and pressed a glass into Jack's hand. She gave him a look as she did this, a tired smile and it seemed to light her whole face. Jack was pleasantly surprised to note that close up, she was quite beautiful, the effect only marred by a faint purple discolouration on one cheek. He thought also that there was something disturbingly familiar about her but he couldn't place it. Perhaps she simply reminded him of someone else.

'So, you're the writer,' she said quietly. Her eyes were hidden behind the mirrored shades but he had the impression that they were burning into him. 'Funny, you don't *look* like one.'

Jack smiled, nervously. 'What does a writer look like?' he asked her.

'Oh . . . threadbare. Rumpled. Balding little men in tweed suits. I've known a few writers in my time. I once had lunch with Graham Greene.'

'Really?' Jack did his best to look suitably impressed. 'What was he like?'

She shrugged. 'Like a writer,' she said. She tilted her own drink to her lips, what looked like a vodka Martini. She took a slug at it, half emptying the glass.

'You'll 'ave to excuse my wife,' said Gorman, slipping an arm around her waist. 'She's feelin' a little out of sorts today, aren't you dear?'

Jack noticed how Lisa's body flinched under Gorman's

204

hand, the way her mouth turned down in a scowl of contempt. 'Angel hasn't got a drink, darlin',' added Gorman, quietly.

'So?' she snapped. 'Who am I, the fucking home help?'

There was an awkward silence. Then Angelito got up from his chair with an exaggerated sigh and walked over to the bar to help himself. Gorman was attempting to mask his anger with a thin smile, but his eyes were blazing.

'My husband gets confused sometimes,' Lisa told Jack. 'He gets me mixed up with the servants. But they get paid to be treated like shit.'

The temperature in the room seemed to drop several degrees.

'Talkin' of servants,' muttered Gorman, 'where the fuck is Jorge? Dinner should be ready by now, Bill, could you . . .?'

'Sure, Tony.' Bill Farnell nodded to Jack and strolled out of the room. Lisa pulled herself out of her husband's embrace and headed back to the bar for a refill, draining her glass as she went. Gorman glared after her.

'Take it easy,' he hissed. 'It's not a bloody race.'

She threw a glance at him, over her shoulder. She didn't actually say 'fuck you' but it was there in her eyes and the tight set of her mouth. Gorman turned back to Jack and gave him another kind of look, the eyes raised upwards.

'You married?' he asked quietly.

Jack shook his head.

'Lucky bleeder,' he said and he winked, slyly.

Bill Farnell reappeared and announced that dinner was about to be served.

'Thank God for that!' exclaimed Gorman, draining his drink. 'Me belly thinks me throat's been cut!' He threw a meaty arm around Jack's shoulders and steered him across the room. 'Let's eat,' he said. 'And you can tell us all about this book you're going to write . . .'

Jack took a deep breath and went into his prepared routine.

'What I need, Tony, is time to just sit down and talk with you. If it's OK, I'd like to make tapes. All I need is for you to just rap about whichever subject we've chosen for the day. I've already got an outline down on computer, but what I need now is information, as much as you can give me. I'll sift through the tapes and put in what I feel are the essential parts.'

Jack glanced around the table. Gorman and Farnell were giving him their full attention. Lisa was playing with the remains of her onion soup, stirring it into complex patterns with her spoon. She seemed bored and was gulping down glasses of white wine at an almost indecent speed. Angelito had not been invited to join them and had remained in the lounge with his drink. Jack imagined that he was probably listening at the door.

Jorge came in and cleared away the remains of the first course. He was in a snotty mood because Gorman had bawled him out about his non-appearance earlier in the proceedings. He turned and flounced out of the room without a word.

'Touchy little faggot,' muttered Gorman. 'Honestly, these kids, I don't know where we get them from.' He studied his hands for a moment, playing with a chunky gold ring on his right index finger. 'Anyway, Frank, I don't see any real problems,' he said. 'I mean, I won't be available every day, I've got a lot of other business to attend to . . . it's best you phone me each morning and we'll work out times and places.'

'How long do you envisage it taking?' asked Farnell.

'Very hard to say,' replied Jack. 'Almost impossible. In my experience, a book takes as long as it takes. It's not a thing you can hurry.'

'No, no, 'course not!' agreed Gorman. 'After all, we want it to be good, don't we, Bill? It's got to be *right*.'

Farnell nodded. 'If I could make a suggestion, Frank . . .?'

'By all means.'

'Maybe we could see it chapter by chapter, as it's written.'

'Er . . . well, I don't usually work that way.'

'Just so we can make sure you're on the right track.'

'Or not too close to the truth!' said Lisa, unexpectedly. Everyone looked at her. She raised a mock toast to her husband and drank it down.

'But that's exactly what we *do* want,' retorted Gorman. 'I don't want a bleedin' whitewash, do I? *The Tony Gorman Story*, exactly as it happened, warts and all. Bill's been into the . . . the . . .' He waved a hand, unsure of his words.

'Legal implications?' suggested Farnell.

'Yeah, right, imprecations, all of that stuff. And we're happy that they can't touch me for anything I say in the book. I mean, I could confess to bein' Jack the Ripper and there's nothin' they could do about it.'

'Have you ever killed anybody?' asked Jack, sure that this would have been one of Frank Nolan's first questions.

'Who, me?' Gorman's eyes widened clownishly. 'Do me a favour! Not my style, Frankie, never was.'

'But a guard was killed during the bank raid wasn't he?'

'Well, yeah, but that wasn't me! That was Jimmy McIntosh. 'Course, he never admitted it in court, that's why the three of them went down for as long as they did, 'cos old Jimmy stuck the boot into that guard. I'll tell you somethin' nobody's ever heard before. I went into that bank with a shotgun, right, but it wasn't even loaded, it was just for show! See, I've never been involved in premedicated violence, not in my whole career. I'm not a violent person, Frank.'

Lisa sniggered loudly and Jack found himself wondering about that bruise on her cheek. Gorman glanced at her irritably.

''Course, *everybody* loses their rag once in a while,' he added. 'See, what it is, Frank, a bloke like me gets a lot of pressure. People think it's easy bein' a millionaire but it ain't. I mean, for one thing, everybody you meet is out to shaft you up the arse. Everybody. Bill here and Angel, next door, they're the only two people I can really trust in the world.'

208

Jack wondered if Gorman had excluded Lisa accidentally or on purpose. She didn't seem in the least surprised that she hadn't been mentioned. She had lit a cigarette now and was staring up at the ceiling, as though she had just noticed it for the first time. Jack was intrigued by her. Even stewed as she was, she gave out an impression of intelligence and sophistication. What was a woman like that doing with Tony Gorman, for Christ's sake? How did she ever get involved with him? And how did she keep from going crazy?

Gorman was still talking. He never seemed to stop talking.

'What I'd like, Frankie boy, what I'd *really* like, is for you to be one of the people I can trust, you know? I mean, put it like this, you've got yourself a cushy little number 'ere, 'aven't you? A free vacation in Spain, a five-star hotel, a car, all provided by yours truly. Now, there are some people, Frankie, who'd take advantage of all that, drag their feet a bit and enjoy *la Dolly Vito*, as the dagos call it. But I know you're a professional, Frankie, I've seen your work and it's good . . .'

'It's better than good,' interjected Farnell, hastily.

'Yeah, it's fuckin' magic. That stuff you wrote on Biggsie, for instance. I mean, I know Ron and 'ees a waste of space, but you made 'im seem . . .' He struggled for words. 'Mistalogical,' he said. 'And I also know, you're not going to let me down. When I read that first chapter you bring in, I'm going to be blown away by it. Then I'm not going to resent all the money I've spent bringing you over here . . . am I?'

Jack had kept a broad smile plastered to his face all the way through the speech. By the end of it, the smile was beginning to ache around the edges.

Jorge arrived with the main course arranged on a hot trolley. He began to set the food out.

'Roast beef and Yorkshire pud!' roared Gorman enthusiastically. He rubbed his plump hands together. 'Me favourite!' He leaned across the table and grinned at Jack. 'None of that dago muck in this house,' he said. 'I like good, plain, English cookin'.'

'Me too,' agreed Jack; and noticed the look of doubt that came into Gorman's eyes. An instant later, Jorge slid a plate in front of Jack. It contained a muddy brown heap of rice and vegetables. 'At least . . . that's what I *used* to like before I got ill,' he added hastily. He hoped the dismay he felt didn't show on his face.

'I trust that's all right for you, Frank,' said Farnell. 'Our chef, Maximillian, doesn't have much experience of macrobiotic cuisine. I sent Angelito out for a cookbook, just to be on the safe side.'

'It looks. . . delicious!' enthused Jack, as sincerely as he could. 'You shouldn't have gone to so much trouble.'

'You can't take too much trouble where health is concerned,' observed Farnell. 'It's low cholesterol and salt free, just as you requested. After all, we don't want you dropping down with a heart attack in the middle of the book, do we?'

Jack laughed hollowly.

'That wouldn't do at all,' he admitted. He scooped up a forkful of brown gunge and put it into his mouth. It was like chewing sawdust. He forced a smile and made an appreciative 'mmm' noise. He had difficulty swallowing and took a gulp of wine to help it on its way. At least, he reflected, he seemed to be allowed to take a drink. Damn Frank Nolan and his weak heart ... but then, he reflected, without it, he wouldn't even be here. He reminded himself glumly not to smoke a cigarette in their presence. Glancing up, he noticed that Lisa was watching him, a faint smile on her lips. He'd have felt a lot happier if he could have seen her eyes.

'Dunno 'ow you stick it,' said Gorman, from around a mouthful of Yorkshire pudding. A rivulet of gravy trickled sluggishly down his chin. 'The old ticker, eh? It's funny, you *look* healthy enough.'

'I'm feeling a lot better,' said Jack. 'I think the Spanish climate agrees with me.'

''Course it does, son, 'course it does! It's the best fuckin' climate in the world! You should think seriously about movin' out here. Don't get me wrong, I miss London, 'course I do. I miss the pubs and clubs, fish n' chips from a newspaper, Tubby Isaacs' pie n' mash, jellied eels, though they tell me you can 'ardly get 'em anywhere these days ... but the weather! Jesus, that's one thing I can do without. Bleedin' miserable rain all the time. It beats me 'ow anybody stays over there. I love Spain, me!'

Jack felt like laughing at that one. Gorman loved Spain so much he ate only English food, referred to the locals as 'dagos' and had the *Daily Mirror* delivered to his door. He would probably have given his right arm to go back to Britain, but knew only too well that the police would be waiting for him. Meanwhile, if this was supposed to be exile, it did seem a pretty agreeable existence.

'Now, about the film . . .' said Gorman, waving his knife.

Jack sensed he was about to edge out into deep water. He scooped up a forkful of food, thought better of it and took a gulp of wine instead.

'It, er . . . may be a bit premature to talk about the film,' he said.

Gorman looked dismayed. 'But I thought your publishers said it was a natural for a film deal?'

'Oh, it *is*,' Jack assured him. 'Of course it is. But film deals aren't made overnight, Tony.'

'I know that! But we got to think about it, ain't we? It don't 'arm to discuss the possibilities.'

'I suppose not,' admitted Jack, glumly. 'Angelito already mentioned it on the way over here.'

'Did he now?' Gorman seemed amused. 'That kid's a scream, I swear! What exactly did he say?'

Jack outlined Angelito's concern about which particular actor should portray him. The story caused considerable amusement. Even Lisa smiled and Jack felt like telling her that she should smile more often. It did something magical to her face.

'Good old Angel!' observed Gorman. 'That kid thinks he's James fuckin' Dean!'

'John Travolta,' Jack corrected him.

'Yeah, right. But see, although it's a bit funny comin'

from him, the kid's got a good point. I've been thinkin' along similar lines lately, I really 'ave. I asked myself, "Tony, if they made a film of your life, which actor could they get to play you?" '

'Robert Redford,' suggested Lisa brightly; and then went into that drunken snigger she had used earlier. Gorman fixed her with a look but refused to acknowledge that she was taking the piss.

'No good,' he said, as though he'd already considered the possibility. 'For one thing, he's a Yank. And for another, he's too bleedin' old. The story starts wiv me as a young geezer, right? So it's got to be a young actor, who can also look older wiv make-up and that. Just as important, he's got to be a *Brit*. I am not goin' to be played by some Yank wiv a Dick Van Dyke cockney accent. "Gor glimey guv'nor! Strike a bleedin' light!" ' Jack surmised that the latter lines were an attempt to demonstrate Dick Van Dyke's approach to the problem, but it was hard to tell, since it didn't sound much different to Gorman's usual accent.

'We could perhaps use a young pop star,' suggested Farnell.

'You must be jokin'! I saw that thing they did on Buster Edwards. Jesus, I kept waitin' for the bugger to burst into song! No, that's a non-starter, Bill! I'm not bein' played by some poofta wiv a record in the hit parade!' He spread his hands in a gesture of helplessness. 'But who is there, eh? Bob Hoskins? Bald and fat! Michael Caine? It's all he can do to get about wivout a zimmer frame! I was wonderin' about that young lad who played the Irish cripple, you know, the one that got the Oscar. He might make a decent job of it . . .'

This was too much for Lisa. She tilted back her chair and began to laugh uproariously.

'What's so fuckin' funny?' bellowed Gorman, glaring venom at her.

She shook her head, attempted to take a gulp of wine, then splurted it all over the table, as she started laughing again.

'Bill, she's pissed!' yelled Gorman. 'Get 'er the fuck out of 'ere!'

Farnell got obediently to his feet and went over to help Lisa up from her chair. Jack could see that she wasn't so very drunk, just helpless with mirth.

'Come on, honey,' coaxed Farnell. 'I think it's your bedtime.' He steered her towards the exit.

'Daniel Day Lewis *is* Tony Gorman,' she shouted gleefully. 'Christ, they'd have to break out a second Oscar for that performance!'

'Get 'er out!' snapped Gorman, spraying bits of his dinner across the table. His face was purple with fury now. Farnell attempted to jostle her out of the room, but she paused by the door and glanced back at Jack. She reached up a hand and removed her shades. It was only then, looking into her beautiful turquoise eyes that he finally realized who she reminded him of. It hit him like a jolt of white hot electricity, making him snatch in his breath and hold it.

Catherine! Oh God, she was the image of Catherine! The likeness was so striking that he almost cried out, but somehow he managed to get control of himself. He had the uncanny impression that everything else in the room had momentarily evaporated, leaving just the two of them. He made an effort to be more logical and told himself that no, she wasn't exactly Catherine's double ... the hair was different of course and she was older than Catherine had been when she died. Mostly the likeness was around the eyes ... they had the same distinctive colouring, the same piercing intensity. And something else, something that happily he had never seen in Catherine's eyes. Pain. Pain and a kind of baffled rage. And as he watched, they were filling with tears, tears that welled up and ran in two trickles down her cheeks. Jack felt a strong desire to get up from his seat, to go and comfort her, tell her that everything would be all right. But he couldn't do that. He could only stare at her, dumbstruck.

'You'll have to excuse me, Mr Nolan,' she said. 'I have a few drinks and then I say what I think. It never seems to go down very well.' She forced a smile. 'I hope you enjoy your stay here. I'll ... I'll say goodnight.'

'Goodnight, Mrs Gorman,' he said.

She let Farnell guide her out of the room.

Gorman was staring down at the remains of his dinner.

'That bitch,' he said. 'I don't know what it is wiv that woman. Everythin' I do, she tries to fuck it up for me. It's jealousy, there's no other word for it!' He gestured helplessly, then looked up at Jack. 'Take my advice, son. Stay single. I wish to God I was, I really do.' He shook his head. 'She's ruined it now, she's completely blown the mood! Tell you what, why don't we meet tomorrow at my golf club? I'll send Angel over to pick you up, you can bring your tape recorder and we'll make a start.' He glanced down at Jack's plate. 'You've 'ardly touched your food,' he observed.

'No . . . I guess I'm just not very hungry. To be honest, I'm a little tired from the flight.'

'Yeah, of course, you must be. I'll get Angel to run you back to your hotel, eh? An early night and you'll be as right as rain. Wait'll you 'ear the stories I've got for you. This is gonna be some book!'

Back at the hotel, Jack flopped on his bed with a sigh of relief. He dialled room service and ordered a rare steak. This vegetarian business was going to be the hardest bit to pull off, he decided. He switched on the portable computer and set about doing some homework for the following day. He tried to concentrate but couldn't rid himself of the image of Lisa Gorman's beautiful eyes filling with tears; couldn't shake off the notion that it was somehow Catherine he was seeing.

Stupid, of course, Catherine was long dead and nobody could ever take her place. He didn't know Lisa Gorman at all, she was just some unfortunate woman who had got her life inextricably mixed up with an obnoxious crook of a husband. If she was unhappy with the arrangement, that was her look-out. It wasn't up to him to go sailing in there like a latter-day Sir bloody Lancelot.

And yet . . . he wanted to know more about her. He wanted to spend a little time with her, talking to her, listening to the sound of her voice. He could always pass it off as research for the book, couldn't he? After all, where was the harm in that? It wasn't as if he fancied her or anything stupid like that . . .

A waiter arrived with the steak and he realized that he wasn't so enthralled with Lisa Gorman that his appetite was affected. In fact, he thought that he had never tasted anything so wonderful in his entire life.

Chapter Seventeen

Mulryan was nervous. He had never been in a plane before and his naïve concept of what it would be like was shattered the moment the aircraft left the runway. He was horribly aware of the thousands of feet of empty air, just below the soles of his shoes and a sensation of cold, churning nausea began to rise in his gut.

Now, a mere fifteen minutes into the two-and-a-half hour flight, he sat rigid in his seat, belted in tight, his body sweating profusely beneath the heavy overcoat that he had steadfastly refused to take off. He kept his gaze fixed resolutely on the seat in front of him, because to glance out of the window at the grey wash of ocean far below was to invite an all pervading giddiness to take hold of him.

He risked a glance across the aisle to where McGiver was sitting. At such short notice they hadn't been able to book seats together. Mulryan saw to his amazement that the Scotsman was fast asleep, his arms crossed, his bony head drooping forward on to his chest. Lord, how could *anybody* fall asleep in such circumstances?

In the elasticated magazine holder in front of Mulryan, a brightly laminated card showed smiling people inflating lifejackets and gleefully jumping out of emergency exits, as though it was the most natural thing in the world. Beside this, was a carefully folded brown paper bag. He could guess what that was for and he grimly anticipated having to use it before very much longer.

He and McGiver had had to wait three days before a suitable flight became available and Mulryan had spent the time sitting around the apartment while McGiver was at work, mostly just playing cards with Sandra or watching old black-and-white movies on the television. It had been the longest three days of his life. Sandra wasn't much of a conversationalist, she seemed to be constantly afraid that her remarks might be reported back to McGiver. She spent her life treading on eggshells, afraid of setting off his hairtrigger temper and suffering the inevitable consequences. Mulryan concluded that McGiver's impending absence was probably the answer to all her prayers. He'd already started to regret having hooked up with McGiver and he told himself repeatedly, that once they got to Spain, things would be different.

The captain's voice crackled from the speaker, announcing that the plane was passing into some turbulence and that the passengers might expect a bit of a bumpy ride. Mulryan closed his eyes and groaned dismally.

'Are you all right dear?' The elderly woman sitting to his left looked concerned.

What little colour was left in Mulryan's face drained away, as though somebody had pulled out a plug in his belly button. He took the paper bag and placed it in his lap.

'Oh dear, air travel doesn't agree with you, does it?' observed the woman. 'Nerves, is it?'

Mulryan nodded. 'I never thought . . . it would be like this.'

The woman glanced around in a furtive manner, reached into her handbag and took out a small bottle of pills. 'Try a couple of these,' she said. 'They'll help.'

Mulryan eyed the bottle suspiciously. 'What are they?' he asked.

'Tranquilizers. I get them on prescription. I used to take Valium but these are much better. I take one in the morning and just float through the rest of the day.' She smiled dreamily, totally unruffled by the bucketing and lurching of the plane. 'I'm nervous of flying too,' she explained. 'Honestly!'

Mulryan took the bottle, uncapped it, shook several pills on to the palm of his hand and gulped them down. He handed the bottle back to the woman who was looking at him uncertainly.

'How many did you take?' she asked.

Mulryan shrugged. He hadn't noticed.

'How long do they take to work?' he asked.

'Not long . . .' The woman was looking at the warning on the label which advised against taking more than two pills at any one time. She frowned, shook off her doubts. He was a big fellow, it would probably be all right.

221

'Are you heading off on holiday?' she asked. 'You're dressed more like a businessman.'

Mulryan nodded.

'Yes, business,' he agreed. 'There's somebody out in Spain . . . I got to meet up with him.'

'That's nice. I'm just going up to Torremolinos for a couple of weeks. I go every year. It was always our favourite place, me and Fred. Fred was my husband, but he's been gone two years now, God rest him. I always go to the same hotel and I always make sure and book early, so I can have the same room. On the first night, I order a glass of Amontillado sherry and I stand there in that room and do you know what I say? It's silly really . . . but I say, "Here's to you, Fred!" And I sort of drink a little toast to him.'

Mulryan concentrated on her voice. It was soft and soothing and though the accent was quite different, he decided that it sounded like his mother's voice. She seemed happy enough to talk and as she rattled on, her voice acquired a strange, spatial quality. Remarkably, the tension in Mulryan's guts began to recede.

'. . . there's a lovely waiter at the hotel, José, he's called. He has the darkest brown eyes and a lovely black moustache. I always say he looks like Ronald Colman in *Lost Horizon*. Do you know that one? It's all set in the snow, Tibet, I think it was, and they find this place called Shangri La, which is funny, because there's a Chinese restaurant called that just down the road from where I live and nobody ever grows old there . . . not the restaurant, in the film, I mean, only this one fellow . . . and I can never remember the name of the actor, but it's not Ronald Colman, it's the one *with* him, he falls in love with this beautiful young girl and they set off through the snow to try and leave Shangri La and the strangest thing happens . . .'

The strangest thing was happening to Mulryan. His insides were melting into a warm, agreeable blob, the tense muscles relaxing into the glow. He smiled, nodded, no longer making much sense of what she was saying. Even the dull throb in his broken fingers seemed to be fading. Her words were fragmenting, dissolving, so that he could only pick out the odd phrase.

'. . . jug of *sangría*! And . . .

. . . José always seats me first, he says . . .

. . . bring tea-bags and a little water heater because you can't get a decent . . .'

Mulryan sighed. He didn't realize it, but his head was tilting sideways by degrees, until it rested on the woman's shoulder. She didn't seem to mind, she just kept right on talking.

Something strange was happening . . . Eddie was growing smaller and smaller, his clothes loosening on his frame as his body shrank, he was climbing into her lap, where she sat in the kitchen rocker, he was snuggling into the soft clean smell of her pinafore and taking solace from the smell of apples and pastry he found there. He was whimpering and crying and his backside was one mass of pain, the skin raw with welts. But what hurt most was the injustice of it all. Her big, capable hands moved over him, soothing his grief.

'Hush now, Eddie, don't take on so! Your daddy didn't

mean to go at you so hard, he just lost his temper, that's all. I didn't tell him about the bed, but he must've found out somehow.'

'It wa . . . wasn't the bed, Ma. T'was the riddle. I got it wrong again.'

'Just the riddle? What's got into that man?' She thought for a moment. 'Eddie, did you tell him anything? About last night? About the dream?'

Eddie sniffed, hung his head. He was eight years old and he had betrayed his mother. He felt about as miserable as any eight year old could be expected to feel.

'Yes, 'm.' he said forlornly. 'I didn't mean to. I thought maybe he wouldn't keep on hittin' me. But he jus' got angrier. Called me a liar.'

His mother's body relaxed and she let out a sigh.

'Well, that just goes to show you,' she said firmly. 'You told me you wouldn't say anything. Now I kept my part of the bargain but you didn't keep yours, did you? Supposin' I just went to your father and told him about you wettin' the bed? What do you suppose he'd have to say about that, eh?'

Eddie was terrified. Fresh teardrops welled in his eyes.

'Please, 'm! Don't tell 'im! Don't! I'll be good from now on, I promise. I won't wet the bed no more, please don't tell Dad!'

'All right, all right!' She patted his head gently. 'I won't tell him, not this time. But you think on, my lad. Try and be a good boy from now on.'

'I will, Ma, I promise.'

It had all happened last night. Eddie was big for his

*age and perhaps that was why people expected him to act
more grown up than he did. Besides, he had tried to go
to the bathroom, he'd had every intention of using the
toilet! He'd woken in the early hours, wrenched from sleep
by the urgent message he was getting from his bladder. He
lay there for a while, peering around the room in the red
glow from his night light. The big old house creaked and
ticked and a sea breeze stirred the curtains at the open
window, allowing flashes of moonlight to draw patterns
on the bare floorboards. Out beyond the promenade, the
sea moved restlessly against the shore, insistent watery
sounds, making his own predicament more acute. Sometimes Eddie saw strange faces in the patterned curtains,
monster faces that winked and leered at him, but tonight
the pattern was just a pattern, shifting restlessly in the
breeze.*

*At last, he could wait no longer. He threw aside his
blankets and climbed out of bed. He moved across to the
door and peeped out on to the landing. The bathroom was
at the far end of it, past the door to his parents' room. Dad
was away fishing tonight. He had set out early from St Ives
that morning, dressed in his souwester and big boots. They
were going out into the deep water, he told Eddie, trawling
for mackerel. Eddie had seen his dad to the door and
before leaving, his father had set him a riddle to solve.
This made Eddie uneasy. His dad always expected him to
work out the answer by himself and sometimes got very
angry if he failed. He had knelt beside Eddie and spoken
slowly, so that the boy wouldn't forget any of it, looking at
him all the time with those mean grey eyes.*

'As I was going to St Ives, I met a man with seven wives . . .'

Eddie nodded confidently. Yes, he'd remember that bit. After all it was where they lived.

'Every wife had seven sacks. Every sack had seven cats. Every cat had seven kits . . .'

Eddie repeated the phrases haltingly, sensing that it was going to be tricky.

'Kits, cats, sacks and wives . . . how many were going to St Ives?'

Dad got back to his feet and tousled Eddie's hair.

'See if you can work it out by the time I get back tomorrow,' his dad said, meaningfully. And with a wave, he set off for the quayside.

Now, wandering along the dark landing, Eddie went over the riddle in his head for the umpteenth time. He thought that he had worked it out, but he wanted to be sure. At first he had thought the answer was twenty-eight. Seven kits, seven cats, seven sacks, seven wives. Then he remembered to add the man who was married to the wives, plus the man who was telling the story. That made thirty. He was sure he hadn't forgotten anything else.

As he came level with his mother's door, he hesitated. There were noises from within. Sounds of pain perhaps? Long groans and grunts and a strange rhythmic creaking. He thought that some of the sounds might have come from his mother, but they were not the kind of sounds he had ever heard her make before. There was something disturbing about them, as though she was no longer his mother, as if she had changed into something else, some-

thing wild and frightening. Then he heard her speak. 'Yes, yes, yes!' she gasped, her voice clipped, urgent. There was a long deep groan, which put Eddie more in mind of his father. Now the creaking had stopped, there was the sound of muffled laughter and a shushing noise.

A twinge in his bladder reminded Eddie of why he was out of bed in the first place, but still he hesitated, undecided whether to carry on going to the bathroom or to open his mother's door and find out what was happening in there. As he stood pondering, the decision was made for him. The bedroom door opened and a man stepped on to the landing.

Eddie shrank back in fear. The man was huge, naked in the uncertain light, his body shimmering with sweat and covered with a thick layer of dark hair. Eddie had never seen him before. He stopped in his tracks when he saw Eddie and his face split into a grin, his dazzling teeth gleaming like an inverted crescent moon.

The hairy man winked at Eddie and called over his shoulder into the dark room.

'Meg, I think we got ourselves an audience here!'

A pause, then his mother's voice, cold and angry.

'Go back to bed, Eddie!'

'But Mum, I—'

'Bed, Eddie! Now! You're . . . you're dreaming again.'

The hairy man threw back his head and laughed, his deep voice booming. 'Dreaming! Boy, that's a good one!' He strolled towards the bathroom, went in and closed the door.

Eddie threw a last despairing look at the bathroom

door, then turned and ran back to his room. He clambered into bed, pulled the covers up over his head. The pain in his bladder was awful now, he couldn't hold it back any longer. He relaxed involuntarily and the warm wetness pulsed across his thighs, soaking into his pyjamas and the sheet beneath him. The stink of ammonia filled his nostrils. He lay in the spreading pool of wetness, unable to sleep now, afraid to sleep, afraid of what his mother would say when she discovered this mess. He hadn't wet the bed in months. And when his dad found out . . . Dad got very angry when he did baby things like that. There was a big leather belt in his wardrobe and when Eddie did baby things, his father would take him up to the bedroom and beat him hard with the belt until Eddie screamed for him to stop. Perhaps, Eddie thought, if he could solve the riddle, if he could get it right this time, maybe his dad wouldn't be angry, perhaps he'd leave the belt hanging in the wardrobe.

He began to whimper, his eyes filling with tears.

'As I was goin' to St Ives . . .' he whispered.

The door creaked slowly open. Eddie tensed, expecting to see the hairy man come into his room, but it was his mother, looking slightly bedraggled in her dressing gown. She came and stood beside the bed.

'You've been dreaming, Eddie,' she said tonelessly. 'You woke me up with your crying . . .' Her nose wrinkled as she caught the smell emanating from the bed. 'Eddie?' she asked. She took hold of the sheets and pulled them back. 'Oh, Eddie!' she cried. 'Honestly!'

He stared up at her, his face pale in the moonlight.

'I was gonna use the bathroom, Ma!' he pleaded. *'But that man was in there, he—'*

'What man?' asked his mother, coldly. *'There's nobody in the bathroom. I told you, you've been dreaming again.'*

'But I saw him!'

'No! I told you. Come on, get out of those wet things, we'll 'ave to strip the bed. I don't know what your father will say . . .'

'Please don't tell him, Ma!' Eddie was pleading now, his eyes big and frightened. *'Please don't tell him I wet. He'll get out the strap.'*

His mother's eyes narrowed.

'I won't tell him,' she said quietly. *'We'll get everything cleaned up and he won't know a thing . . . if you don't tell him about the dream you had. About what you thought you saw.'*

'I won't, Ma. I won't, I promise.' He would have agreed to anything right then. Anything at all. His mother smiled thinly, began to strip the soiled sheets off the bed. *'All right then, Eddie, off to the bathroom now and get yourself cleaned up.'*

Sniffing, he went across the landing and into the bathroom. The light was already on in there. He stripped off his pyjamas and went to the sink to wash himself down. The bathroom seemed the same as usual but there was a strange smell in there, a thick animal odour of sweat. Eddie rubbed soap into the flannel and washed it across his body carefully, then dried himself on a towel.

When he came out on to the landing, his mother was padding down the staircase with her arms full of bed linen. Eddie noticed that she had decided to change the sheets on her bed too.

'Kits, cats, sacks and wives,' he said to himself. He was sure now. The answer was thirty.

The following afternoon, Eddie was playing in the yard with his fire engine; or at least, he was glumly going through the motions. Really, he was waiting with mounting apprehension. When his dad called him from the bedroom window, he nearly jumped out of his skin. He went obediently up the stairs, his stomach a tight knot. There was a raw smell in the bedroom. His dad was sitting on the edge of the bed, dressed in his vest and longjohns. The stub of a cigarette coiled smoke from between his nicotine-stained fingers. He was studying Eddie intently and that mean look was in his eyes again. Perhaps the fishing had been bad, it always seemed to be lately. A half empty whisky bottle stood on the bedside cabinet and when Eddie stepped closer, there was a powerful smell on his dad's breath.

'Now then,' he said quietly. 'You got an answer for me?'

Eddie swallowed nervously, nodded. 'Yes Dad,' he said.

'How many were going to St Ives?'

'Thirty,' said Eddie, hopefully.

His father looked at him, a sad, hopeless look.

'Wrong,' he said. 'Think again, lad. As I was going to St Ives.'

Eddie nodded, tried not to panic.

'T . . . twenty-eight,' he gasped. 'Or twenty-nine!'

Again his father shook his head.

'I'll give you one last chance, boy,' he growled. 'Listen to me. As I was going to St Ives. Now, how many is that?'

Eddie shook his head, frightened.

'I . . . I dunno, Dad. I thought thirty. Seven wives, seven cats and . . .'

His father got up from the bed. He went over to the wardrobe and opened it.

'. . . s . . . seven kits . . . that makes twenty-eight . . .'

The leather belt hung there like a great snake, sleeping for the moment but easily awakened. His father reached out and took hold of it, stretched it between his powerful hands.

'. . . and then there was the man married to the wives . . . and the man telling the story . . . so . . . so it must be thirty.'

His father turned back to face him.

'The answer is one,' he said. 'As I was going. It doesn't say that any of the others were going, does it? They might just as easily have been coming back.'

Eddie stared at his father in dismay.

'But . . . but that's a trick question!' he cried. 'That's not fair!'

'Fair?' His father laughed unpleasantly. 'What's ever fair, lad? Who said life had to be fair?' He approached his son slowly, his eyes seeming to blaze now with some deep-rooted pain all of his own. He was going to share that pain with Eddie. He was going to pass it on like a disease. He raised his arm and desperate now, Eddie used the only knowledge he had that he thought might save him.

'Dad, there was someone here last night!'

His father froze, his arm upraised.

'What?' he whispered.

'There was a man. A hairy man. I saw him! He came out of Mum's room. He had no clothes on. He—'

Eddie gave a yelp of surprise and pain, as the belt lashed him across the ribs.

'You little liar!' yelled his father. 'You dirty little liar!'

'Dad, no, listen to me, please!'

But then the blows were raining down on him, the thick belt stinging where it hit, sending explosions of pain through his body. He threw his arms up across his face and tried to run, but he was knocked back against the wall, the hard leather lashing at his arms, his bare legs, his backside. And he was screaming and the belt, ah, the belt, fire blossoming and pulsing, alive on his skin . . .

A woman's voice gasping in his ear, 'No, you're hurting me! Please, please!' Mulryan woke to the unfamiliar rumble of aircraft noise and the sight of the folded paper bag in his lap. 'Make 'im stop, Ma,' he groaned. 'Make 'im stop! He's gonna kill me!' He was groggy and stupid with tranquilizers. A stewardess was leaning over the two passengers to see what all the commotion was about.

'My arm! Please, you're hurting my arm!'

Mulryan came suddenly to his senses and stared at the woman beside him. She was badly shaken and her face held an expression of pain. He saw that his left hand was clutching her arm, the thick fingers digging into her, leaving livid white spots against the tanned flesh. He glanced around, saw the concerned face of the stewardess gazing down at him. Behind her, across the aisle, Tam McGiver had woken up and was glaring daggers at him.

'Oh, dear!' Mulryan was horrified. He released his grip, made an apologetic gesture. 'Oh ... I'm sorry. I'm so sorry. I think I must have been dreaming. I think I ...'

A sudden wrench of nausea twisted like a coil in his stomach and he felt acid burning at the back of his throat. He made a desperate grab for the paper bag, fumbling with his broken hand. He got it open just in time to vomit the contents of his stomach into it. He sat there, hunched miserably in his seat, while the stewardess hurried off to get a flannel.

'One,' he groaned, spitting out bile. 'Only one going to St Ives. A trick question d'you see? It's not fair, is it?'

'No,' agreed the old woman, whole-heartedly, as she glanced hopefully down the aisle for a vacant seat. 'No, I don't suppose it is ...'

PART THREE

JACK OF HEARTS

Chapter Eighteen

Jack breakfasted on the balcony in the early morning sunshine. He chose a full English breakfast with mounds of thickly buttered toast and cup after cup of hot, sweet tea. Afterwards, he smoked a cigarette and felt distinctly like a naughty school-kid, enjoying an illicit fag. He wondered how poor Frank Nolan had endured his daily regime of tasteless meals and careful habits.

Jack had never really given much thought to his health. Until recently, it was something he had simply taken for granted. Eddie Mulryan had changed all that, making him shockingly aware of his own mortality. He wondered what Mulryan was doing now. He might already be in Malaga, Jack thought glumly. He would arrive there sooner or later, that much was certain; and when he did arrive, it would be in Jack's best interests to have put as many miles as possible behind him.

He was uncomfortably aware that three days had already slipped by, days spent waiting on Tony Gorman for the promised first interview. Gorman, it seemed, always had some kind of excuse. Three times it had been set up, three times it had been cancelled at short notice. Not that Jack was particularly bothered about that. Talking to Gorman was a prospect he could happily live without. Besides, it had given him an excuse to spend his days hanging around Gorman's villa, making small-talk with Lisa, a much more appealing proposition, even though she didn't give much away. She was an enigma, that one. The more Jack saw of her, the more he recognized the powerful fascination she was exerting on him, though he doubted that she was even aware of it.

He glanced over the balcony at the Mitsubishi, parked in the forecourt below. Why not, he thought, just get straight in the jeep and head north, while the going was good? But then he thought about Lisa's turquoise eyes, the desperate pleading message he had perceived in them that first night he had met her and he knew, God help him, that he was not ready to go yet. She had made no mention of the incident, had given him no intimation that she thought of him as anything other than one of her husband's hired hands and yet, there was something about her . . .

In that instant, Jack hated himself, mooning about like some lovesick kid when he ought to be intent on preserving his own skin. Why had it been her of all people? Perhaps if she hadn't taken off those bloody shades he wouldn't have noticed the resemblance to Catherine. He'd have been driving north right now, living off Frank's credit cards and looking for a new life . . .

The phone rang, interrupting his thoughts. He stubbed out his cigarette and went inside. Probably Bill Farnell, phoning to explain why Gorman wasn't available for interview this afternoon. He sat on the bed and picked up the receiver.

'Yes?' he enquired.

'Señor Nolan? I have a call for you from London, England. One moment please!'

In the few seconds interval, Jack's brain went into overdrive. Somebody calling from England, somebody who knew Frank, knew his voice! Shit, what to do? Then;

'Hello, Frank, it's Peter! Frank, you there?'

Desperate, Jack launched into what he hoped was a fair impersonation of a Spanish accent.

''Ello? No, Señor Nolan 'ees not here. He just step outside for one moment. You want, I call him?'

'Er . . . yes, please. Tell him Peter Sinclair is calling, would you?'

'Peetair Seenclair. Yes, I tell him. Pleese, what is your business with Señor Nolan? He tell me he take no personal calls.'

'It's not personal. I'm his literary agent.'

'Hees agent? Right, OK, one moment pleese!'

Jack got up and paced about the room, weighing up the possible pitfalls. An agent might talk technical. Jack might let something slip. But if he didn't speak to the guy now, he would only call again, maybe at a more inconvenient moment, maybe when Jack had somebody with him. Perhaps this guy had been expecting Frank to call him. Jack didn't want anybody getting suspicious, asking embarrassing questions . . . best to try and brazen it out. But his voice, what about his voice?

He had a flash of inspiration. Clutching his nose between thumb and forefinger, he lifted the telephone to his mouth.

'Hello Peder,' he said. 'Thangs for callig!'

'Jesus. Have you got a cold or something?'

'An absolute stinker. Just hid me this morning. Wod cad I do for you?'

'Just phoning to see if you're OK . . . hey, who was that on the phone just now?'

'A wader. I asked him to ged the phobe while I was id the bathroom.'

'Sounded like Manuel from *Fawlty Towers*! So, did you make contact with Gorman yet?'

'Yes. I been ub at his villa the las' three days. Preddy fancy place. We talked about the book mostly. And the filb.'

'Yes, that's the idea. Tell him any shit he wants to hear. Play him along.'

Odd, thought Jack. *Almost as if this was some kind of scam.*

'Did you see *The Duchess* yet?'

'I did. She's still beaudiful. Biggest green eyes you ever saw . . .'

There was a puzzled silence at the other end of the line.

'What are you blathering about? What eyes?'

'His wife, Lisa. She—'

'You idiot, I mean *The Duchess*! His yacht! Have you managed to get aboard yet?'

'Uh . . . no, nod yet.' Alarm bells were going off in

Jack's head. Now he remembered seeing those words on Frank's computer screen, together with a series of dates. 'Bud er . . . I'm working on it,' he added, cagily.

'Good. If a chance doesn't come up in the next few days, try and force the issue. Say you want to check out his lifestyle, some crap like that. Listen, Frank, this is important. I hear our friend Mr Martinez is due to be paying Gorman a visit in a few days time.'

'Martinez? Right . . .' More bells. Hadn't Jack seen that name too?

'*The Duchess* is booked to sail three weeks from now. Martinez is almost certainly bringing in another delivery of cocaine. You can bet that Gorman will have it put aboard for delivery to his network in England. But don't blow the whistle unless you're one hundred per cent certain that it's there.'

Blow the whistle? What the fuck . . . ?

'Once they're out of the harbour, it'll be difficult to pin it on Gorman, he's a slippery bastard at the best of times. It'd be best if you could actually call in the Spanish authorities just as the gear's being loaded. If we can't get him extradited, then we'll let the Spaniards put him away. Then you can sit back and write the story of how you nailed Tony Gorman. I reckon we'll both be able to retire on that one.'

Jack listened glumly. The telephone handset seemed suddenly heavy. As if life wasn't complicated enough. He had thought he was just pretending to be somebody he wasn't. But no, he was pretending to be somebody who was pretending to be somebody he wasn't. He thought again about the Mitsubishi and pictured himself driving. Fast.

'How's your health, apart from the cold?' asked Peter.

'Never bedder,' replied Jack. But he didn't feel particularly great at that moment.

'That's good. We don't want you dropping dead in the middle of all this, do we?' Peter laughed and Jack did his level best to join in, but that joke was becoming less funny every time he heard it.

'The er . . . police?' ventured Jack.

'Don't worry, they've promised not to do anything to compromise you. Strictly low profile. But when you're one hundred per cent certain that you've got him, just call the number and give the password. Ten minutes later, Gorman's villa is going to be crawling with *Los Puercos*.'

'Los—?'

'Spanish piggies, dear boy. Hey, are you all right? You don't seem quite with it today.'

'Oh, jus' wagged out frob dis code,' Jack assured him. 'I'll be all ride in a day or so. I jus need to—' He broke off at the sound of a knock on the door. He lowered his voice. 'Peder, godda go now. Somebody ad the door. Bye.' He put down the phone, released his nose with a sense of relief and moving across to the door, he opened it. Angelito was standing in the corridor, a wide grin on his suntanned face.

'Hey, man, you ready to roll? Señor Gorman is waiting to talk to you.'

Jack frowned. 'You mean he's not too busy today?'

He tried to keep the note of hope out of his voice, but Angelito just looked at him blankly. 'I'll get my stuff together,' said Jack.

Angelito followed him into the room, glancing quizzically around.

'I thought I heard you talkin' to somebody.'

Jack nodded towards the phone.

'My agent,' he said.

'Eh, you got an agent, man? Far out! Like in Hollywood, huh? Say, you think I should get an agent?' Jack shrugged. Angelito moved closer, lowered his voice. 'We didn' get the chance to talk much when you first arrived, but if there's anything you want that's not on the menu ... maybe a woman, maybe a little nose candy, that kind of thing, I can *fix* it for you – if you know what I mean.'

Jack slipped on his jacket. 'That's good to know,' he said. 'How about a bullet proof vest?'

Angelito stared at him dully for a moment. Then the grin returned.

'Hey, man, you make a joke, huh? You're a really funny guy, you know that?' Angelito turned his head to look through the window on to the balcony and his eyes narrowed suspiciously. Jack followed his gaze, saw the breakfast things still sitting on the table, the leftover bacon scraps on the side of the plate.

'Hey, I thought you didn't eat regular food,' muttered Angelito.

'I don't,' Jack assured him.

'Then how come ...?'

'Had company last night.' Jack waggled his eyebrows meaningfully. 'You should have offered your services a little earlier, Angel. I got bored and I met a good looking chick in the bar. Local girl, very pretty. I sent her on her way with a good breakfast inside her.' He leered suggestively, slapped Angelito on the shoulder, knowing it was exactly the kind of macho bullshit he'd respond to. Sure enough, Angelito seemed instantly reassured.

'Hey, you're full of surprises, you know that?'

'That's what *she* said! Come on, we'd better not keep Mr Gorman waiting.'

They headed for the door. Outside, Jack turned back to lock up and allowed himself a sly exhalation of air. One of these days, he wasn't going to be able to come up with a convincing excuse. It was getting too bloody complicated being Frank Nolan.

They drove over to Gorman's golf club. Angelito kept up his usual stream of self-obsessed patter but Jack wasn't really listening. He just kept nodding occasionally and saying 'uh huh' at regular intervals. Meanwhile, he was trying to think.

So he had unwittingly wandered into the midst of a set-up. Great. Just perfect. Gorman was still up to his old tricks and Nolan and Sinclair had cooked up some scheme to implicate him with the Spanish authorities. When Jack had met Frank Nolan on the plane, Frank had simply repeated his cover story. He was a genuine writer sure enough but he had omitted to mention that this particular assignment fell into the realms of investigative journalism.

Sinclair had said something about a phone number and a password. Real James Bond stuff. And presumably out there somewhere, the Spanish equivalent of a SWAT team was on hold, just waiting for Jack's call. Well, let them wait. Jack wasn't inclined to be a hero, particularly when he'd be left with the problem of explaining exactly how he had come by his new identity. A few miles down the road, the body of Frank Nolan must have been stinking up the landscape by now. As if that wasn't enough to sweat over, there was the unseen spectre of Eddie Mulryan, lurking somewhere over the horizon like Jack's worst nightmare. And here he was, *en route* to a nice restful game of golf. Jesus! Why was he still here? Because of some hare-brained notion about a woman who resembled his dead girlfriend? Pathetic!

All right, he thought. I'll do this thing with Gorman. Then back to the hotel in the Mitsubishi and gone. History. Lisa would just have to make the best of her life under her own steam. But those eyes, man! Those beautiful, sad, pleading eyes . . .

Angelito turned off the road, in through a set of wrought iron gates. They motored along a broad driveway, flanked by date palms and then pulled up in front of a low, white clubhouse. There were a lot of ostentatious vehicles parked out front, Rolls, Porsches, BMWs. They may as well have put up a sign saying MILLIONAIRES ONLY! Angelito got out of the car and Jack followed. Angelito led the way around the side of the clubhouse to a patio area, where they found Tony Gorman sitting at a table, smoking a Marlboro and sipping Perrier water. He looked faintly ludicrous in a flat cap, a red Fred Perry sports shirt and a pair of loud yellow check trousers.

'Frankie boy! Good to see ya! Sorry about the 'old-ups, the last couple of days. Bit of unexpected business came up. You want a glass of over-priced tap water before we start?'

'No thanks, I just had breakfast.'

'OK, let's step out on the green, shall we? I never thought to ask, do you play?'

Jack shook his head.

'I'll just watch,' he said.

Gorman shrugged. He motioned to Angelito to collect the leather golf caddie that stood off to one side of the patio. He began to stroll towards the green and Jack fell into step. Angelito followed, towing the caddie. Gorman glanced at Jack expectantly and Jack reminded himself that he'd better start making like a writer. He took the mini-recorder out of his jacket pocket and checked that there was a fresh tape in it. Then he turned uncertainly to look at Gorman.

'Where shall we start?' he asked.

Gorman chuckled. 'You tell me, you're the bleedin' writer!'

'Yes, of course.' Jack thought for a moment. 'Well, let's go right back to the very beginning, shall we?' He switched on the machine. 'Where were you born?' he asked.

'I don't remember, I was very young at the time!' Gorman threw back his head and brayed laughter and Jack felt like stuffing the tape-recorder into his mouth. 'No, no, seriously . . . in Bethnal Green. Not in an 'orsepiddle or nothin', me old lady 'ad me and me two brothers at 'ome in bed. Everyone did in those days. Number 11, Jubilee Street, that was our address.'

'Tell me about your mother.'

'She was a doll . . . an absolute doll. Me old man barely 'ad much to do with bringin' us up. He was there, but only in body. More interested in the boozer and the bettin' shops. The ol' Duchess kept us going, fed us, clothed us, put us through school and that . . .'

'The Duchess?'

'Yeah, that's what we called 'er.'

'Isn't that also the name of your boat?'

'My *yacht*, son, not a bleedin' boat. But yeah, I named it in honour of me old mum. She's been dead these twenty years and more, Gawd rest 'er soul. There was never another one like Polly. They broke the mould, d'yer know what I mean? I wished she could 'ave lived to see me pull off that big robbery. She'd 'ave been so proud.'

'Umm . . . yes, I suppose so. What was your childhood like?'

''Ard. Very 'ard. We didn't 'ave nothin'. We lived on welfare and me mum took in washin'. In the winter, we couldn't afford a fire. Mum would suck peppermints and we'd all sit around 'er mouth!' Again the braying laugh.

They had reached the first green now. Gorman stooped to plant a tee and a ball, then took a lot of time selecting a club. Angelito watched impassively, his hands in his pockets, his mouth working around a wad of chewing gum. Jack decided he'd better ask another question.

'So, do you remember much about those early years?'

'I remember the gangs,' said Gorman, wistfully. 'Every street 'ad one. Ours was called the Jubilee Street Mashers. No, honest, it was! We reckoned we was the 'ardest lot going. Our rivals was called . . . The Wolves or The Foxes, something like that. We spent all our spare time kicking the shit out of each other. Then a bunch of coons moved into the neighbourhood and we joined forces and spent all our spare time kicking the shit out of *them*!' He grinned. ''Appy days!' he said.

He selected a club and stepped up to the tee, sizing up the shot carefully, making restless little swings just above the ball.

'Did you—'

'Jus' a sec, son!' Gorman was preparing for the real shot. He lifted the club up to above his shoulder and swung hard. The club kicked up a chunk of turf, two inches in front of the ball, which was merely dislodged from the tee. 'Shit!' said Gorman emphatically. He turned to glance irritably at Jack. 'You spoiled me concentration,' he said.

'Sorry . . . so, you could say the gangs were training for your later life of crime.'

'Eh?'

'The gangs were . . .'

'Oh yeah, true enough. In fact, you could go so far as to say that there was no real difference. See, I met Jimmy McIntosh in that gang. And Vince Ryan and Harry Lyneham. Well, the four of us was a team from the word go. As we got older, the gang still ran together, but it

248

got more serious, more organized. We started knocking over grocery stores, chemists, newsagents. By day, we worked the barrows, right, but by night, well, we did what we'd always done. An' we was always careful, the filth never came anywhere near us. I'm proud to say that to this day, I've got no proven criminal record. And like I told you before, we always dreamed of pulling off the big one. So the bank was always on the agenda. It just took a bit of time to pull the threads together.'

He bent and replaced the ball on the tee; then gave Jack a sober look, as if warning him not to make a sound. Jack nodded. Gorman turned back, got into his stance and began to size up the shot. He took his time over this one, painstakingly practising it before committing himself. Jack watched with mounting impatience. At last, Gorman brought the club up and swung hard at the ball. He sliced it and it shot sideways, narrowly missing Angelito's head. It hit the trunk of a tree, rebounded and finally rolled to a halt a few inches from Gorman's shoes.

'Shit!' he said again, but whether it was merely an exclamation of disgust or a comment on his own ability, Jack couldn't be sure. Gorman retrieved the ball, his face set in a studied scowl. Clearly, he was going to make this shot if it killed him.

Jack attempted to fill the silence with a question.

'Do you feel responsible for your friends being in prison?'

'Fuck, no! Why should I? We planned it together, I can't even remember whose idea it was originally. Probably Harry Lyneham's, he was the real brains of the outfit. I was just the one that got away. See, I'd planned for it all in advance. I 'ad me trading company all set up over 'ere before we ever did the job, I'd taken up residence and all that. Soon as we 'ad that money I was out of the country quicker than a greased turd. The other lads was stubborn though. They didn't wanna leave Blighty. I told 'em not to be stupid. I said, sooner or later, the filth will close the net and you'll all be knack-ered. The three of 'em came over 'ere for a while to try it out, but they couldn't stick it. Started whining about all the things they couldn't do 'ere. Eventually ended up complaining about the bleedin' weather! Can you credit it? "It's too 'ot," they kept sayin'. Too bleedin' 'ot! I ask you! So the silly buggers went back to England, where it soon got a good deal 'otter for 'em. The Old Bill picked 'em off one by one.'

'You must have been sweating it then?'

'No, not really. Like I said, by that time I'd taken up citizenship, adn' I? And I knew the lads would never grass me up, not for all the promises the filth made 'em. We was a gang, see, we 'ad that sort of honour between us. The scuffers knew I was involved, but they 'ad no real proof. I tell you what, when them lads finally get out, will I 'ave a welcome for them! I've got money invested in all their names. They'll be set up for life.'

'What's left of it,' Jack corrected him. 'How much did you actually get away with?'

Gorman grinned. 'That's a good question, Frank. That's never really come out, 'as it? The bank said five million, but that's bullshit. They didn' 'ave the bottle to admit 'ow much we really got.'

'So, want to set the record straight?'

'All right. It was fourteen million.' He smiled. 'And don't forget, that was over ten years ago, when fourteen million could still buy a few things.'

'It can now,' said Jack. 'So, your split was a fourth share of that?'

'Oh, officially it was. But it all came over 'ere, every last penny. All invested in various deals. Like I said, the lads' shares are still workin' for 'em. And I'm still doin' the business with my cut.'

'Business?'

'*Legitimate* business, of course! These days I'm as straight as a rod. There's the club, the casino, couple of 'otels. Lot of tourist properties. A boating firm, shares in this golf club . . . you name it. 'Ow much d'you think I'm worth, these days? Go on, 'ave a guess!'

Jack shrugged. 'I wouldn't have the first idea,' he said.

'No, me neither!' he chuckled. 'Bill could tell you, I expect. The last time I asked him he said it was in the region of forty-five million. Not a bad little region if you ask me.'

'So why don't you retire?' asked Jack. 'Surely forty-five million is enough for anyone.'

'Do me a favour, son. You can never 'ave enough.'

He stooped and set the ball on the tee with great precision, the tip of his tongue protruding from his mouth. 'Right, you bastard,' he whispered. 'You're goin' down that bleedin' fairway.'

Poor bugger, thought Jack. Worth forty-five million

and he can't even hit a golf ball in a straight line. There was a certain irony there. He watched as Gorman sized up the ball with infinite care, wiggling his backside, making little stabbing motions with the club. He took a deep breath, raised the club and—

'Hey, Tony!'

Gorman let out a yelp of baffled rage as the club slipped from his hands and went spinning, end over end, down the fairway. He turned angrily to glare at the approaching figure of Bill Farnell.

'For fuck's sake, Bill, I'm tryin' to 'ave a game of golf 'ere!' He did a little dance of exasperation, grinding his spiked shoes into the turf. In his red shirt and checked trousers, Jack thought he looked like a manic version of Rupert Bear and he had to work hard at not laughing. 'Don't you know better than to sneak up on somebody like that? Christ!'

'I'm sorry, Tony.' Farnell looked strangely out of place, dressed in an immaculate suit. 'Something came up.'

'Something will come up in a minute!' fumed Gorman. ''Ave you ever tried walkin' around with a golf club shoved up yer arse? 'Cos believe me, I'm that far from doin' it. *Sideways!*'

Farnell smiled sheepishly. 'Aww, now Tony, you know I wouldn't interrupt your game unless it was important.'

'Yeah, yeah, tell me about it!' Gorman stared sulkily down the fairway and put his hands on his hips. Farnell glanced quickly at Jack, clearly uncomfortable that he was present. 'It's er . . . our South American friend. I've just had a call that he's arriving this afternoon.'

'This afternoon? He's three bleedin' days early!'

'Yeah, some last minute change of plan. At any rate, I think we should be in Malaga to greet him.'

Gorman nodded. 'I suppose you're right, Bill. You'll 'ave to excuse my little show of temperature. I was tryin' to concentrate on me game.' He sighed, glanced apologetically at Jack. 'I'm afraid we'll 'ave to finish there for now, Frankie boy. One of my business associates has turned up unexpected.'

'That's OK. I've got plenty to work with for the time being.'

'Good. We'll drop you off at your hotel on the way back.' Gorman hesitated, as though he had just remembered something. 'Shit,' he said.

'What's the matter?' asked Farnell.

'I promised Lisa she could 'ave Angelito to drive her this afternoon. She wanted to do a bit of shoppin'.'

'She could get a taxi,' suggested Farnell.

Gorman looked doubtful. 'I don't like lettin' 'er out unsupervised,' he said. Jack noted that he could have been talking about a child or a dog. 'I mean, look what 'appened last time. Pissed out of 'er 'ead in some back-street dive. You can't trust a dago taxi driver to keep 'er out of trouble.'

'Why not let me drive her?' said Jack; and was astonished at his own stupidity. Hadn't he planned to do a runner that afternoon?

'Oh, I dunno.' Gorman looked at him thoughtfully. 'Nice of you to offer and all that, but she can be a right pain in the arse sometimes.'

'I haven't got anything planned,' Jack assured him. 'And besides, I'll need to talk to her sooner or later. For the book.'

Now Gorman looked positively affronted. 'I dunno if I want 'er sticking her four-penneth in,' he protested. 'It's *my* book. It's not meant to be about her.'

'Oh, I mean, just for trivial stuff really. Background. The house, the furnishings, you know, *women's* stuff. Of course, if she tells me anything you don't agree with, it doesn't have to go in. After all, you and Bill will be editing it.'

'Well . . .' Gorman was softening.

'I think it's a great idea,' said Farnell. 'You don't want her in one of her depressions when Mr Martinez is around, do you?'

'No, I suppose not.' Gorman sighed. 'OK, Frankie, thanks a million. I owe you one. You can take one of the spare cars up at the house.' He took Jack's arm and drew him aside a little, as if confiding a secret. 'I know it's not really your job, mate, but try and keep her off the booze, will you? I mean, one or two drinks is all right but if she goes past that in the daytime, she can be a right bloody handful. And keep an eye out. She might try and give you the slip. She's done that with Angel before now. Oh, and don't forget . . .' He gave Jack a sly wink. 'She's a married woman. Knowarramean?'

Jack looked suitably horrified.

'Christ, Mr Gorman, I hope you don't think that I—'

''Course not, Frankie, 'course not! I mean, you don't look *that* stupid!' He grinned meaningfully, then turned away. He motioned to Angelito to follow them with the caddie. Angelito looked thoughtfully towards the discarded club, lying some distance away.

'Shall I fetch that, Señor Gorman?'

'Nah, leave it! Bleedin' thing's bent.'

Angelito nodded.

'Yeah, I thought it looked kinda funny when you got it out of the caddie.'

Jack studied Angelito with interest. He was beginning to understand how the man held down his job with the Gorman outfit. He could tell a lie without batting an eyelid. Maybe the two of them had something in common after all.

Chapter Nineteen

Tam McGiver led the way through the airport building, sweating slightly in his heavy jacket. Eddie Mulryan stumbled after him, still groggy from the pills but a lot happier for being safely back on terra firma, which here seemed to consist of acres of shiny oatmeal tiles, polished like a skating rink.

Mulryan's little display on the plane had displeased McGiver, who thought they should be keeping a lower profile than that. Mulryan felt too washed out to care. He slumped down on a wooden bench while McGiver went into the baggage area to get their luggage. Massive octagonal columns supported the roof and a series of serpentine conveyer belts wound in and out of them. McGiver retrieved the bags and brought them across to the bench. He sat down beside Mulryan and stared blankly around, unsure for the moment of his next move.

Mulryan noticed the old woman from the plane and thought about apologizing to her again, but she so obviously wanted to avoid him, he promptly abandoned the idea. The two men watched as she hurried past and into a waiting taxi.

257

'Silly old cow,' muttered McGiver ungraciously. 'I think you scared the shit out of her. It's a wonder you didn't break her fucking arm the way you were squeezing it.'

Mulryan grunted. He sat slumped on the bench, cradling his plaster-cast in his lap. The strained expression on his face suggested that his broken hand had started aching again.

'You OK?' McGiver asked him. 'You still look like shit.'

'I'll be fine,' Mulryan assured him. He shook his head as if making an effort to shrug off his daze. 'What now?' he wondered aloud.

McGiver unfolded a free tourist map of the area on his lap and sat there staring at it thoughtfully.

'What indeed? As you can see, Malaga's a big place. But I'm certain that Doyle won't be here anyway.'

'You reckon?'

'Aye. Put yourself in his place. Would *you* hang around?'

'I suppose not.' Mulryan reached up his good hand to scratch at his head. 'All right, let's think it through, logical like. He's a man on his own, so far as we know he doesn't know anybody over here. He arrives in a strange airport in the middle of the day. What's the first thing he needs?'

'A drink?' suggested McGiver.

Mulryan glared at him. 'Transport! He's going to need some kind of transport.'

McGiver nodded. 'Makes sense, I suppose.' He traced a nicotine stained finger across the face of the map. 'Well, there's a bus and a train station nearby,' he observed.

Mulryan looked doubtful. 'I can't see Doyle travelling by public transport,' he muttered. 'As I understand it, he was a big wheel once. Old habits die hard. And by my reckoning, he's probably still got a few bob in his pocket.'

McGiver frowned. He nodded towards the busy taxi rank.

'I suppose we could start by questioning that lot. One of those taxi drivers might remember picking up a man with a bandaged hand ... that's if we can find a dago that speaks the Queen's English.'

'Maybe.' But Mulryan still looked unconvinced. He was staring through a glass doorway off to his right. Following his gaze, McGiver saw that it led to an adjoining room. The illuminated signs of car hire firms were clearly visible.

'Good thinking,' he muttered. 'Why go by taxi when you can be your own driver?'

Mulryan got to his feet, more confident now. He led McGiver through the swing door into the area beyond. There were a dozen open counters clustered in a square. Avis and Hertz had the lion's share of the space, but there were smaller, local firms too, and it was to one of these that Mulryan headed.

'Leave the talking to me,' he said to McGiver as he approached the counter. The receptionist, a pretty, dark-haired young woman, regarded the two men with a professional smile of welcome; a smile that wavered slightly when she registered the battered purple face of one of them.

'*Buenos días*, Señors. Welcome to Spain!'

Mulryan rewarded her with a smile every bit as professional as her own. 'Good-day, Miss. I wonder if you 8can help me?'

'Eh, yes Señor, you have a reservation?'

'Oh, now don't you speak marvellous English!' He turned to glance at McGiver. 'Doesn't she speak good English?'

McGiver nodded, slightly bemused.

'Excellent,' he said.

Mulryan turned back to the young woman with a conspiratorial air. 'I'd be willing to bet you've spent some time over in my country,' he said.

The girl nodded, delighted by his observation. 'Oh yes, I live for two years in Hammersmith, London.'

'Is that right, now! Well, I could tell, instantly.' Mulryan took out a white handkerchief and mopped at his perspiring face. 'Goodness, it's very hot today,' he said. 'Is it always as hot as this, here?'

The girl smiled vaguely at him. 'The weather just now is hotter than usual for the time of year. But very good for a holiday, yes? You would like a car, Señor?'

'Oh, no, no, I just wanted to ask you a few questions, my dear. This is a police matter. The *British* police, you understand?'

'Yes, of course, Señor.'

Mulryan fumbled in his breast pocket with his left hand. He took out his wallet and flipped it open briefly, giving her just a glimpse of the police badge that he carried in there. He'd liberated it from a copper some years back and had since doctored it up with his own passport photograph and details. It had got him past a lot of locked doors back in Britain and the receptionist seemed suitably impressed by it. She sat a little straighter in her seat and paid attention.

'I'm Detective Inspector Mulryan,' he said. 'This is Detective Sergeant McGiver.' The girl was intent on the badge, so she didn't notice the look of stunned bewilderment that flitted briefly across McGiver's face. 'We're looking for a suspect, an Englishman name of Jack Doyle. He would have arrived here around midday on Friday and it's just possible he might have hired a car from you.'

'I will check, Señor.' The girl reached under the counter and pulled out a stack of files. She started going through the columns of figures with quiet deliberation. 'I was on duty, Friday,' she told Mulryan. 'But I don't think . . . Doyle, you say? How do you spell this?'

Mulryan spelled it for her. She shook her head. 'No. Nobody by that name, I'm sorry.'

'Well, of course, he could have used another name.'

'You have no photograph of this man? I'm good at remembering faces.'

Mulryan smiled, apologetically.

'I'm afraid not. He's around five-foot-ten . . . er . . . that's just under two metres to you . . . dark hair, quite good looking I suppose. I know you young girls always remember the good looking ones!'

The girl simpered, fluttered her eyelashes.

'We get a lot of good looking men calling here,' she said. 'I can't be expected to remember them all!'

'Hmm. Oh, one other thing, he would have had a bandage around his left hand.'

'No, Señor, I'm sorry. I don't think I saw him.'

'OK. Thanks anyway.'

Mulryan nodded graciously and moved across to the next counter. McGiver followed and watched in mute disbelief as the big man went through the entire routine again, line for line. 'Oh what wonderful English! Doesn't she speak great English? I'm Detective Inspector Mulryan . . .' By the time McGiver had heard it through a second time, he was almost beginning to believe it himself. But it wasn't until the fourth attempt that Mulryan finally struck paydirt.

The woman at this counter seemed to be a clone of her three predecessors, she had the same straight black hair, the same dark brown eyes; but those eyes projected an unmistakable flash of recognition when Mulryan got to the bit about the bandaged hand. He leaned forward expectantly.

'That rings a bell, doesn't it?'

'Señor?'

'That means something to you!'

She nodded. 'I think . . . yes, there *was* a man that day . . . I remember the bandage. Now I come to think of it, he seemed very nervous. He stood off to one side while the other man signed the papers.'

'The *other* man?'

'Yes, another Englishman, I think.'

'You have his name?'

She frowned, opened a thick file on the counter top

and started leafing through it. She found the relevant page and moved an elegantly manicured fingernail down a computer printout. 'It was very busy on Friday. I think the car was a Mitsubishi Shogun ... ah, yes, I'm sure now, he took a jeep. The problem is, there were two jeeps went out around that time and I can't quite remember which one your man was with. Let me see now. One was a Mr Michael Reynolds, staying at the ... yes, the Hotel Estragon in Torremolinos ... and there was also a Mr Frank Nolan, staying at the Excelsior in Puerto Banus.'

'You can't be sure which one?'

She shook her head. 'No, I'm sorry. It was very busy around that time. If you would like to come back in a couple of hours, my friend Pilar will be on duty. She was working with me, that day, maybe she would remember.'

'Oh, I don't think that will be necessary, my dear, you've done very well. Saved me a lot of time. I wonder, would you be so kind as to write that information down for me?' He gestured vaguely at his shattered hand.

She made a sympathetic face. 'Of course, Señor.' She wrote the names and addresses out neatly on a compliment slip and pushed it across the counter to him. 'This man, you are looking for. He ... he did this to you?' She gestured self consciously at Mulryan's battered face.

Mulryan nodded. 'Oh, he's a dangerous man, Miss. A villain.' He pushed the scrap of paper carefully into his pocket. 'Thanks very much for your help. I appreciate it, I really do.'

'A pleasure. I hope you find him, soon.'

'Oh, I will,' Mulryan assured her. 'Come along, Sergeant.' He turned and led McGiver back into the main building.

'That was bloody brilliant!' McGiver said. 'Jesus, if I hadn't seen it with my own eyes! Where the fuck did you get that badge from? It looked like the real thing!'

'It *is* the real thing,' Mulryan assured him. 'I . . . er . . . persuaded a bent copper to accidentally lose it – if you know what I mean. Comes in handy sometimes.'

'Christ, I'll bet it does!'

Mulryan took out the slip of paper and stared at it thoughtfully.

'Thing is, which of these names should we check out first?'

McGiver took the paper from him and tore it into two strips. He handed one strip back to Mulryan.

'You go after the one in Torremolinos . . . I'll take the other guy.'

Mulryan frowned. He clearly didn't like the idea.

'We ought to stick together,' he said.

'Nonsense! We might miss Doyle if we go after the wrong one. It makes more sense to split up.'

'Yes, but supposing you get to Doyle before I do?'

McGiver gave Mulryan a twisted grin. 'Relax! I've already told you, I don't have an axe to grind. If I latch on to him first, I'll just keep an eye on him until you get there. There's no problem on that score.'

'Well, I don't know . . .'

'Come on, Eddie, we're wasting time here. What do you want me to do, swear on the Bible?'

Mulryan thought for a moment. Then he shook his head.

'I want you to swear on your mother's grave,' he said.

McGiver stared at him. 'Are you joking?' he asked.

'No, I'm serious. On your mother's grave.'

McGiver shrugged. 'OK, if that's what it takes . . .'

'Say it then.'

'Say what?'

'Say, "I swear on my Mother's grave, I won't kill Jack Doyle." '

'For Christ's sake, man!'

'Say it, or we go together!'

McGiver sighed. He spread his hands in a gesture of helplessness. But then he repeated the line, quietly, self-consciously. 'Want me to add "cross my heart and hope to die?" ' he asked cuttingly.

Mulryan ignored the taunt.

'No, that'll do for now.' He picked up his suitcase. 'Where will we meet up?' he asked.

'Whatever happens, I'll check in to this . . .' McGiver glanced at his scrap of paper, '. . . Hotel Excelsior. You can get a message to me there. If for any reason I have to move on, I'll leave directions for you.'

Mulryan nodded. 'Right then. Hopefully, I'll see you soon. Don't forget that promise now.' He moved towards the exit. McGiver watched as Mulryan approached the next taxi in the rank, showed the slip of paper to the driver and climbed into the back seat, pushing his case in ahead of him. McGiver grinned. Poor dope didn't realize he'd just been conned. Probably didn't even know that there was a world of difference between Torremolinos and Puerto Banus.

Like the difference between brown ale and champagne, thought McGiver, as he watched Mulryan's taxi drive away, the big man waving briefly from the rear of the car. McGiver waved back, grinning all over his face now. The major flaw in Mulryan's personality was that he operated by a kind of moral code and clearly expected everybody else to do the same. He obviously believed that McGiver would stand by an oath made on his mother's grave. But for one thing, McGiver's mother was a boozy old whore who didn't deserve anybody's respect. And for another, so far as McGiver was aware, the old cow wasn't even dead yet.

Laughing, he collected his own suitcase and made his way out to the taxi rank.

'Puerto Banus,' he told the taxi driver. 'The Hotel Excelsior. And don't spare the fuckin' horsepower!'

Chapter Twenty

Jack found Lisa lounging beside the swimming pool. She was wearing a black bikini, the inevitable shades and a broad-brimmed straw hat. She was reading a thick paperback book, one of those historical romances judging by the cover, all ripped bodices and steamy passions. She glanced up in surprise as Jack approached.

'Hello,' she said. 'What are you doing here?'

'I'm your driver for the day,' he told her.

She studied him for a moment. 'You're kidding.'

He shook his head. 'Something came up and Tony needed Angelito to drive.'

She glanced down at her book for a moment, her mouth twisted into a frown of disapproval. Then she snapped her gaze back up to his.

'So now he's got you working as an unpaid chauffeur!'

'Not at all. I volunteered.'

'Did you? Now, why would you do a thing like that, I wonder?' She drummed her fingers on the arm of the lounger, as though considering a possible motive. 'What came up that was so important?'

'Some guy called Mr Martinez? He arrived earlier than expected. Angel's driving Tony and Bill to the airport to meet him. They're all inside now, getting changed.'

'Hmmph!' She wrinkled her nose, as though she had just encountered a disagreeable odour. 'Martinez. That sleaze bucket. I suppose that means he'll be running around here like a randy dog for the next couple of days.'

Jack smiled. 'Something tells me he's not your favourite person in the world.'

'Very astute.' She sighed deeply. 'Listen, don't worry about driving me. It doesn't really matter.'

'Oh, but I want to!' he insisted. 'We can talk. It er . . . would be useful for the book.'

'Oh, right. The book. Let's not forget about the book.' She seemed to find this mildly amusing. 'OK, give me a minute to get dressed.' She set down her novel, got gracefully to her feet and walked back towards the house, her hips swinging, as though she was prowling the catwalk at a fashion show. Jack watched the sway of her buttocks and wondered if she practised that walk in her spare time. He suspected that she did.

She approached the French windows and almost collided with Angelito as he came out. He had changed his western-style clothes for the traditional black suit and peaked cap of a chauffeur. He leaned close to Lisa and said something to her, but she pushed past him and went inside. He turned his head and stared after her for a moment, an expression of irritation on his face. Then he seemed to remember Jack. He reached for his Marlboros, lit one up and strolled over to the pool, the familiar grin back on his face.

'Too hot for this freakin' suit,' he observed. He proffered his cigarettes. 'Smoke?' he asked.

'Why not?' Jack took a cigarette instinctively and had it in his mouth, before he remembered that up till now, he'd made a point of not smoking in front of Gorman and his crew. 'I shouldn't really,' he said. 'But I guess one won't hurt.'

Angelito didn't say anything. He lit Jack's cigarette with a gold Ronson, then displayed the lighter proudly. It was inscribed, 'To Angel, from Tony'.

'Present,' he said. 'Señor Gorman thinks real highly of me. He's bought me a lot of stuff.'

'That's nice for you,' said Jack.

They stood for a moment, looking at each other.

'How's it goin' with the book?' asked Angelito.

'Too early to say yet.'

'Must take a lot of thinking out, huh? You know, I always thought about writing, myself. Trouble is, I can't spell. Never could. What about you?'

'I get by.'

'You gonna ask Señora Gorman to help you with the book?'

Jack shrugged. 'Maybe.'

There was a small puddle of water beside the pool. Angelito put the toe of his shoe into it and began to trace out a design, pulling off long streaks that made it look like a big spider.

'She's a fine looking woman, huh?'

'I guess she's OK,' admitted Jack.

'Oh, you're tellin' me you didn't notice?' Angelito grinned slyly. 'Come on, you're a man, sure you noticed.

I notice things too. Like, I noticed you were pretty quick offering to take my place today.'

Jack looked at him sharply. 'So, what of it?'

'Hey, man, no offence! I'm just saying, is all. You know, Señor Gorman, he doesn't care about her so much these days. He doesn't see these little things. But I see everything, you know? I got the snake eyes and I'm always watching.'

'Well, that's fascinating, Angelito. Is there some point to this or are you just airing your tonsils?'

'Hey, man, I tol' you, stay cool. I'm just gonna give you a little friendly advice, is all. You don' want to make an enemy out of Señor Gorman. I mean, listen, man, you got everything on a plate here. Be a shame to fuck it all up on account of some woman, huh?'

Jack slipped his right hand into his pocket, knowing that if he left it out, he was liable to take a swing at Angelito.

'I can assure you, I have no intention—'

'Sure, sure, is OK. But listen, man, there was this other guy, see, he got friendly with Señora Gorman. Maybe a little too friendly, I don' know, but I tell you, the craziest thing, he went swimming one night. Must've swum out too far, 'cos we never seen him round here again. Maybe he's down at the bottom of the sea, fucking fishes!' He laughed at this, tilting back his handsome face and cackling gleefully.

Jack was about to say something caustic but Gorman and Farnell stepped out through the French windows, deep in conversation. Jack casually flicked the stub of his cigarette into the pool before they noticed him smoking. Gorman had changed into a blue silk suit and his plump face already looked red and sweaty. He glanced at Jack and grimaced.

'Like a gorilla's armpit today!' he observed. 'Beats me why the 'ell we've 'ad to get dressed up like a trio of tarts. You'd think royalty was payin' a visit. 'Ere, Frankie boy!' He threw a set of car keys and Jack snatched his hand from his pocket, just in time to catch them.

'Good reflexes,' said Farnell, smiling.

'Them's for the Volvo down the drive,' explained Gorman. 'I expect 'er ladyship will be out in due course. I'm sorry for the interruption. Listen, I thought you might like to visit the club tomorrow night. See 'ow the other 'alf lives!'

'Yeah, that sounds OK.'

'All right, see you later. Be good!' The three men strolled off towards the limousine, Angelito flinging back a last, spiteful grin at Jack. Jack found himself wondering if Angelito had something going with Lisa himself and was simply warning off the competition.

More complications. Just what he needed. He watched as the grey limo purred away along the drive.

He wondered vaguely why he was still hanging around here. Then Lisa appeared and the question was answered. She had put on a shapely, button-through mini-dress in red silk and had used lipstick of the same shade. She strolled towards him through the languid heat of afternoon and he felt desire, crawling like a lizard in the pit of his stomach. He turned aside, so she wouldn't read it on his face. They walked towards the car. Crickets chattered in the silence, a dry, restless rhythm throbbing from the trees that lined the driveway. Jack spoke and his tongue felt dry and leaden.

'Where shall we go then?' he asked her.

'Where the hell else is there to go?' she said. 'Puerto Banus.'

He unlocked the passenger door of the black Volvo and held it open for her. She slid into the seat, the red dress riding up to reveal her perfectly tanned thighs. Jack glanced away, not wanting to be caught staring at her legs. He closed the door, walked around the rear of the car and got into the driver's seat. He started the engine and they coasted slowly towards the open gates.

'So, how come you don't drive yourself?' he asked her.

'Big girl like me?' she added, mockingly. 'Oh well, let's just say that Tony prefers me helpless. If he gave *me* the car keys, I might just keep right on going.'

Jack nodded. He glanced at her but couldn't be sure she was looking at him. Those damned mirrored shades.

'Would you do me a favour?' he asked her.

'Depends,' she said.

'Would you take the glasses off?'

'Why?'

'Because I like to see people's eyes when I talk to them.'

She grimaced, but she reached up and removed them. Those startling turquoise eyes were regarding him now, appraising him, sizing him up. *She might be a tigress*, Jack thought, *surveying a potential meal*. Or maybe that was just wishful thinking.

'You know, you have beautiful eyes,' he told her. 'I er . . . understand that you were a fashion model at one time.'

'Do you indeed?' she asked sharply.

'Yes. I think Bill mentioned it.'

'Oh, right.' She turned to glance out of the window. 'What made you give it up?'

She gave a hollow laugh. 'That's a long story,' she told him.

'It's OK. I've got plenty of time.'

Lisa smiled wistfully. 'You know, not so long ago, somebody told me I could go back to it if I wanted to. I told him I was too old now, they only want the kids, but he said, no, I still looked great, I could make the grade if I really wanted to.'

Jack turned left out of the main gates and on to the road.

'Was this the same guy who went swimming late at night?' he asked.

'No, this was . . .' She turned in her seat, gave him a sharp look. 'Who told you about that?' she demanded.

'Angelito. He just kind of mentioned it in passing.'

'Did he now? Asshole!'

'Is it true?'

'That he went swimming? Sure.'

'And was never seen again?'

She nodded. 'It doesn't mean anything. The current was bad where Gary went in. I must have told him a dozen times not to swim there. It was an accident, I'm sure of that.' But then she looked thoughtful, like maybe she didn't really believe what she was saying.

'Excuse me, but there seems to be an element of doubt in your mind. And Angelito implied that you were having some kind of an affair with this guy.'

'Gary and I were close, that's all. He was an employee of Tony's, an accountant. We had a few laughs together. Angelito was jealous of him.'

'Jealous? Why would he be jealous?'

Lisa glanced at him sharply. 'You don't beat about the bush, do you?'

Jack shrugged. 'I'm a writer, it's my job to ask questions. What's the matter, you worried that I might put it in the book?'

She laughed bitterly. 'I don't give a damn what you put in the book,' she assured him. 'But something tells me that you'll only give them what they want to hear. And I don't think you'd go shooting off your mouth to Tony, either. I don't know why, but there's something about you that I feel I can trust.'

'So tell me why Angelito would be jealous of you and this Gary.'

She sighed. 'OK, what it is, I made a mistake with Angel once. I'd had a few drinks, we were in the house alone and we started fooling around. It was just the one time, you understand and I must have been crazy to have gone along with it. Anyhow, it was a unique experience.'

'Unique?'

'Well, it's not every day you get to watch a man make love to himself.'

They shared a laugh then and he thought he felt an invisible barrier crashing down between them.

'That boy *is* kind of self-obsessed, isn't he?'

'Just a little! Anyway, ever since then, he's been trying for a repeat prescription, but the plain truth is, I'm not interested. For reasons I can't begin to fathom, he gets very possessive about me. So I guess he was just trying to throw a scare into you.'

'Yeah, I figured that's what it was. Does Tony know about you and Angelito?'

'You kidding? That boy may be a first class asshole, but I wouldn't like to see him dead.'

'Like Gary, you mean?'

'Hey, I was talking figuratively. Tony is capable of a lot of bad shit, but I don't think he'd ever go that far, not really.'

Lisa took out her cigarettes and offered Jack one. He shook his head but pushed in the lighter on the dash.

'So, tell me,' Jack said. 'About you and Tony.'

'What's to tell?' she asked.

'Well, for instance, why are the two of you together? There doesn't seem to be all that much between you.'

'I wish there *was*,' she said. 'Like, for instance, the Mediterranean.'

The lighter popped out of the dash with a click. Lisa took it and lit her cigarette. She inhaled, blew out smoke.

'Well, it's obvious to anyone that you don't have a lot of time for each other. I suppose you must have once, but it doesn't add up somehow. You're so different to him. Makes me wonder how the two of you ever got together in the first place.'

'This for the book?' she asked him.

'No. It's for my own edification.'

'Well, it's pretty straightforward. I made a mistake, that's all. I was eighteen years old, at the top of my profession and about as naïve as they come. I was in Marbella doing a fashion shoot and somebody introduced me to Tony. He'd only just come out here and he was everybody's blue-eyed boy. All the publicity about the robbery was going around, reporters were falling over themselves to get to him. He had the kind of buzz about him that you associate with a pop star. And ... well, he was different then, you know? He was ...'

She inhaled on her cigarette, as though seeking inspiration.

'You've seen that movie, *Alfie*? You know the character of that guy in the film, kind of charming, sneaky, sexy, all at the same time? Tony had that quality about him then. I know it's hard to believe but he was a real charmer. And me, I was as green as a dollar bill. I drank it all in and I thought I'd found somebody extraordinary, somebody *exciting*.' She laughed bitterly. 'By the time I woke up to what was really happening, I was a married woman ... and already a prisoner.'

Jack glanced at her. 'A little strong maybe?'

'No, not at all. It's exactly what I am. This little trip we're having, it's just time out for good behaviour. But somebody always has to go with me. A chaperon. A minder. You think I've ever been allowed to go further than the local bar? Never. Tony keeps me on a string, like a pet dog.'

'Did you ever talk to him about it?'

She seemed amused by that. 'I can't expect you to understand,' she said. 'You've probably never been held back in your entire life. Neither was I, until I was married. You see, in my naïvety, I just assumed that I'd be able to continue with my career after the debris of the wedding had settled in. But no, Tony didn't care for that idea.' She slipped effortlessly into a cruelly accurate impersonation of her husband.

'I don't want you paradin' round like a tart for other blokes! We don't need the money and you oughta be 'appy stayin' 'ome and keepin' 'ouse! 'Olidays! 'Oo needs 'olidays, we're livin' on the bleedin' Costa del Sol ain't we?'

She smiled sadly. 'I tried to make it work for the first couple of years, I really did. I was stupid enough to believe that I owed it to the marriage. Then we discovered that I couldn't have children. You can imagine Tony's reaction to that. It was as though I'd duped him, married him under false pretences. I suggested adoption, but no, he wouldn't hear of it. Said he wasn't prepared to take in some dago kid and pretend it was his own.'

'He might come round to it,' said Jack.

'Oh, no, not Tony. He's found his own solution to that particular problem.'

'What do you mean?'

'Forget it, it doesn't matter . . . you probably wouldn't believe me anyway.'

'Try me.'

'Well . . .' She sighed. 'He's got this mistress. Some local tramp name of Josie. She's barely more than a kid herself. Tony takes her to parties, shows her off to all his friends, has her set up in a swish apartment in Marbella. Last time I saw her, she seemed to have filled out a bit. I believe the happy event is pencilled in for August.'

'Jesus,' said Jack quietly.

'Quite. Now, I don't suppose for one moment that any of this stuff will find its way into the book . . .'

Jack ignored the remark. 'Divorce him,' he said.

'What?'

'Just divorce him. Christ, you've got more than enough grounds for it.'

She laughed. 'Please, Mr Nolan, be serious! Do you honestly think he'd give me a divorce? I'm one of his possessions now. Like the paintings he buys and stores away in a bank vault. He doesn't know anything about art, you understand, but sometimes he likes to bring them out to impress his friends. I serve a similar function. His tame ex-fashion model. He let's them look all they want but they can't touch, oh no! I'm his property. And remember, he knows that if he granted a divorce, I could legally get half of what he's worth. Losing that would hurt him far more than losing me.'

Jack thought for a moment.

'Then you should just run out on him.'

'I've tried that, twice. The first time they picked me up in Malaga. The second time I did better, I got as far as Seville.'

'Well, maybe third time lucky,' said Jack. 'You could come with me.'

She stared at him for a moment. 'What do you mean?'

'I mean I'm leaving soon and I'd be quite happy to take you along for the ride. No strings, you can do whatever you want once we're clear.'

She stared at him.

'What are you talking about?' she demanded. 'The book . . .'

'Screw the book! It doesn't mean that much to me. Anyway, the thing is, I've already made up my mind to run out on the deal. Let's just say I don't much care for the set-up. If you want to come along, you're welcome.'

She chewed her lip nervously for a moment.

'This doesn't make sense,' she said quietly. 'Why would you do that for me? What are you, some kind of modern-day Sir Galahad? Or is it that you're not exactly what you seem? You know, I had a feeling about you the first time I saw you. You didn't strike me as a writer, you didn't then and you still don't. And then there was that business with the vegetarian food. I was watching your face, you looked like you were trying to swallow dog shit. I thought then that you weren't used to eating that kind of stuff.'

Jack ignored her insinuations. 'You coming with me or what?' he asked her.

'He'd come after us, you know . . . or more likely, he'd *send* somebody after us.'

'Maybe. But you didn't answer the question.'

'I'll have to think about it,' she told him.

'Don't take too long,' he advised her. They were coming into the outskirts of Puerto Banus now, white-painted villas flanking the road. 'Where to?' he asked.

'Your hotel,' she replied.

He glanced at her in surprise. 'Why?' he demanded.

'You want to fuck me, don't you?'

For a moment, he nearly lost control of the car. 'Jesus,' he said.

'Well, yes or no?'

'I've heard it put more romantically,' he protested.

'Maybe, but I don't have much time for romance these days. Most guys who start mouthing off to me about how horrified they are by my predicament are usually after one thing. They're looking to get laid. Once they've had that, they generally change the subject and get very nervous about who my husband is. So, I'll give you what you so obviously want. Then I'll see what you have to say.'

'Supposing I said I wasn't interested in fucking you?'

'You'd be lying,' she said bluntly.

He thought about it for a moment. 'Yes,' he said. 'I suppose I would at that.'

They went up separately. It seemed safer, for both of them.

Jack paced around his hotel room, as keyed up and jumpy as a teenager on a first date. He had fallen into this assignation with surprising ease, but now that it was imminent, he couldn't help but consider the implications. He was about to have sex with the wife of one of the richest crooks on the 'Costa del Crime'; a man who could doubtless have Jack rubbed out simply by snapping his fingers. By all accounts, the last person who had tried this had by now been recycled into the local fish population. And meanwhile, time was passing and a certain Eddie Mulryan was surely getting closer . . .

'Crazy,' muttered Jack. 'You've finally flipped, boy!'

But then he heard Lisa's gentle knock on the door and all his doubts were instantly forgotten in the excitement of being close to her. He opened the door and she strolled into the room, removing the mirrored shades which she had worn down in the foyer.

'I don't think anybody recognized me,' she told him disconcertingly. She stood for a moment, gazing curiously around the room. 'Nice,' she said approvingly. 'My husband has obviously given you the best. Now let's see what I can do.'

She took his hand and led him across to the bed. Then turning, she stepped up close to him and kissed him hard on the lips, pushing her tongue into his mouth, her hands moving up and down his body, unbuttoning his shirt, unbuckling his belt. He reached for the fastenings on her dress and fumbled them open. He was startled by the delicious shock of her bare breasts against his hands. She was naked beneath the red silk. She had come prepared for this, not wanting to waste any time.

Now she was easing him back on to the bed, her mouth was against his, she was unzipping his fly . . .

'No!' he said, pushing her away from him. He sat up, shaking his head. She lay there on the bed, looking at him in surprise.

'Something wrong?' she asked him.

'Everything's wrong. It's not that I don't want to, it's just . . . too fast for me. Can't we . . . take our time about this? Have a drink, maybe just talk?'

Now she was staring at him. 'Talk?' she echoed. 'Jesus, what's the matter, you're not in *love* with me or anything?'

He didn't answer that. He got up from the bed, buckled his belt and went over to the drinks cabinet.

'What will you have?' he asked her. 'There's just about everything here.'

'Vodka Martini. Ice if you have it.' He busied himself making a couple of drinks. Lisa lit a cigarette and lay there watching him thoughtfully. She inhaled smoke and blew it out of her mouth in a slow stream.

'So, what about you?' she murmured. 'Since you're so keen to talk. We've heard all about little old me. But what does Frank Nolan do when he's at home?'

'Not much.'

'Come on, don't be evasive! I spilled my guts to you, didn't I? Let's hear the low-down on a writer's life. Where do you get your inspiration, do you work to a regular routine, who are your influences? Those are the kind of questions they usually ask, I believe.'

Jack poured whisky into his own glass. 'It's boring,' he concluded. 'I really don't want to go into it.'

'A writer that doesn't like to talk about writing?' Her eyes mocked him. 'A rare creature indeed! All right, let's get down to the nitty gritty, shall we?'

He shrugged. 'By all means,' he said.

'Is there a Mrs Nolan, tucked away back in England?'

Jack shook his head. He brought the drinks back to the bed, sat beside her and handed her a glass.

'Well then, is there someone special? A girlfriend?'

Again Jack shook his head. Lisa looked doubtful.

'How come?' she wanted to know. 'I mean, you're a good looking guy, you have an interesting job . . . you're not gay, are you?'

Jack laughed. 'No,' he said.

'So how come there isn't somebody? Don't tell me you've been saving yourself, waiting for the right lady to come along!'

'No, of course not. There *was* somebody special. She . . . she died.'

Lisa grimaced. 'Oh, that's too bad. What happened?'

'Catherine . . . was killed in a road accident. It was round Christmas, the year before last. She . . .' He shook his head, sipped at his drink. 'I still find it difficult to talk about her,' he apologized.

'Jeez, I know how *that* feels! When Gary drowned, I couldn't speak to anyone for months. So this Catherine, you were deeply in love with her, I suppose? Going to be married, the whole shebang?'

Jack nodded. 'Kind of thing,' he said. He reached into his breast pocket, took out his wallet and extracted a small photograph. He handed it to Lisa. 'That was taken a couple of weeks before she died,' he said.

She took the picture from him and studied it for a moment. She opened her mouth to say something complimentary; but then her eyes widened in surprise and she glanced sharply at Jack.

'My *God*!' she whispered. 'She . . . she looks kind of like me, doesn't she?'

Jack didn't say anything. He sat there, watching her. He saw an expression of bafflement pass over her face. Then she seemed to become angry.

'Say, what *is* this? There's something pretty weird going on here! Is that why you're so keen to help me? Because . . . because I look like this girl that you used to go out with? I mean, just what the *fuck* is this all about?'

'I don't know,' he told her. 'I honestly don't.' He took the photograph back from her and put it carefully into his wallet. 'The first time I saw you without your shades it struck me that you *were* the image of Catherine. You were crying and I . . . well, you *touched* me somehow. I guess I just felt sorry for you. I wanted to help.'

'Yeah?' She stubbed out her cigarette in the bedside ashtray. 'What makes you think I need any help?'

He took another pull at his drink.

'Lisa, from what I've seen, I *know* you need help. You're stuck in a relationship with a guy who doesn't give a shit about you. You've got an obvious drink problem and you think so little of yourself that you would have slept with me just for the opportunity to get away from here.'

She sneered. 'And what are you, some kind of fucking saint? That why you pushed me away just now? Because I didn't compare favourably to your Catherine? Had some idea in the back of your mind that I'd be just like her, I suppose! But I blew it by coming on too strong!'

Jack shook his head sadly.

'Catherine is dead,' he told her. 'I would never expect anyone to fill her shoes. I'll admit that the resemblance *was* the first thing that caught my attention, but that was all. My offer of help was perfectly genuine. So is the way I feel about you.'

She gazed at him in genuine surprise.

'And how *do* you feel about me?'

'Excited whenever you're near. Breathless, jumpy, sick to my stomach. All the classic symptoms.'

She looked doubtful.

'But you barely even know me,' she protested. 'Isn't it just that I remind you of her?'

'I don't think so.'

'You sure?'

He thought about it. 'Fairly,' he admitted.

'So if you feel so strongly about me, why push me away?'

'Because I wanted you to know how I felt. So you knew this wasn't just some sleazy business transaction. And I . . . I wanted to feel ready for you.'

She frowned, gazed at him from beneath half lowered eyelids.

'And do you feel ready now?' she murmured.

He set down his drink on the floor and took her in his arms. He kissed her gently on the mouth, holding the kiss for a long time, waiting for the tension to melt out of her body. After a few moments it did. She relaxed, began to return his kisses hungrily. He lifted a hand to stroke her hair and eased her down onto the bed, detaching his mouth long enough to draw breath and to kiss her neck, enjoying the clean smell of her, the warmth of her body as he undid the buttons on her silk dress, revealing the firm tanned flesh beneath.

She reached for his belt a second time but now, she was in no great hurry, knowing as he did, that they could take their own sweet time over this, that they had the whole afternoon ahead of them.

They lay naked under the covers. Jack smoked a cigarette with her, all his pretences down now, the two of them laughing at the terrible movie cliché of it but reluctantly admitting that a cigarette never tasted better than just after making love. They were both feeling pleased with themselves and for a while they talked about trivial things, not wanting to break the spell. It was Lisa who finally steered the conversation back to more serious matters.

'So,' she said quietly. 'What says the great lover now? This the part of the story where you decide to go back to your book and forget this ever happened?'

'No,' he said firmly. 'The offer still stands.'

'Oh but aren't you the reckless one!' She smiled, reached up a hand to stroke his face. Then she sighed. 'It's no use, I can't just up and go. I wouldn't have a penny.'

'So? Neither would I. But we'd manage.' He was feeling reckless all right.

'You don't understand.' Her voice harder now, all emotion gone from it. 'That bastard owes me. I won't let him get away clean, it wouldn't be right. How soon are you planning to leave?'

'How about like *now*?'

She frowned, shook her head. 'If you could wait a couple more days . . .'

'Why? What difference would that make?'

'Because maybe . . . just maybe, we could leave with a million dollars to help us on our way. It would be a lot less than he owes me, but I could make do with that. How about you?'

He considered for a moment. 'Yeah, I dare say I could manage on a million. What's on your mind?'

She outlined her plan to him, talking slowly, calmly, making it all sound so easy. He listened to her, interrupting only occasionally to clarify some point and as she talked, he began to believe that they could do it.

'Yes,' he said, when she had finished. 'Yes, I think it could work. You're sure about this money?'

'Oh, I should know the routine by now. I've seen it happen often enough.'

'All right,' he said. 'Let's go for it.'

They sealed the bargain by making love again, while the clock on the wall crept all too quickly around the hour, the second hand stealing a precious minute with every circle it made. This time it was even better. This time she came too. Afterwards, they dressed, went out and did some shopping. Actually, there was only one item that Lisa wanted to buy. An attaché case.

Chapter Twenty-One

Gorman waited in the car with Angelito while Farnell walked into the arrivals lounge to meet Raul Martinez. It was unbearably hot in the car and Gorman sat there sweating, aware of two prickly pools of moisture beneath his armpits. He lit up a cigarette and puffed clouds of smoke out through the open window, wondering why Martinez had shown up earlier than expected, but he didn't feel unduly worried. The man was untouchable.

Martinez was a cultural attaché with the Colombian government and made regular trips to embassies and arts centres the world over. Malaga was a regular destination for him. He tended to show up four or five times a year and he always had something to sell. Like all diplomats, he enjoyed the enviable luxury of being able to breeze through customs without having to submit his luggage for inspection. This was just as well. On his last visit, he'd brought two suitcases that were stuffed with carefully sealed packages of high grade cocaine.

Gorman hated drugs, almost as much as he hated the people who used them, but he had no aversion to a good business deal. For a mere million dollars outlay, he'd eventually recouped seven million, once contacts in Miami had adulterated the coke with baby powder and sold it on to customers in the film and music world. There was little personal risk involved. Over the years, Gorman had made a series of contacts and acquaintances and had ensured that all the right palms got regularly greased.

To all intents and purposes, he was now a model citizen, going about his legitimate business. He sometimes wondered if a time would come when he would stop wanting to make deals, but somehow, he doubted it. It was all he had left to give his life an illusion of excitement. Of course, it wasn't the same as being personally involved. He still looked back at the London bank raid as the most exciting time of his life. He remembered vividly, sitting in the car outside the bank, waiting for the signal to go in. His entire body had been tingling with a buzz of electricity and between his legs he felt the beginnings of an erection. It had made him want to laugh out loud, the thought of going into that bank with a boner in his trousers.

Then it was all happening, they were charging inside, brandishing shotguns, screaming through their balaclavas at the punters to get down on the floor. Some brainless security guard had made a lunge for the alarm bell and Jimmy McIntosh had taken the guy out, calm as you please, smacking him hard across the back of the head with a baseball bat. The guard went down like a bundle of discarded laundry, blood trickling from his ears and nobody else had tried anything funny after that.

Then they were hustling the tubby, bespectacled manager into the vault, the man so frightened he could hardly breathe and the massive steel doors opened and they all stood there looking at wall-to-wall money . . .

Gorman still dreamed about that moment. The doors opening and the delicious smell of printed paper wafting out at him, the sweet smell of excess. At that moment, he was floating on an air of unreality and his hands had been shaking as he threw wad after wad into sacks, knowing that he'd finally cracked it, that from this moment his life would never be the same again. He had felt a brief, intoxicating spasm in his loins and glancing down, he realized that he'd come in his pants. He had started laughing hysterically, his hands still scooping wealth and his mates must have thought he had gone crazy. Perhaps he had, it didn't matter, nothing mattered any more.

Then they were racing out to the van they'd faked up with a Securicor logo, masks off now, dressed in their uniforms, straining under the weight of the sacks. The crowd in the street hadn't so much as batted an eyelid as they loaded up the loot, the people inside the bank too scared to even lift their eyes from the floor. A doddle. An absolute fucking doddle.

They'd driven to the lock-up in Fulham, most of them lying on the sacks in the back and they'd exchanged looks in the light of their torches and suddenly, they'd all started whooping and screaming like madmen, astonished and delighted that it had all gone without a hitch, that they'd pulled it off, they'd actually been and gone and done it.

These days it was all clinical, distant, no more than a row of figures on paper that Farnell occasionally passed over for his perusal. Yes, he was still making a killing but it couldn't compare to the adrenalin rush of taking it yourself, standing face-to-face with the people you were robbing and relishing the smell of their fear. The bank job had made Gorman feel like the most powerful man on Earth. Everything that had happened since had somehow contrived to make him feel impotent.

Raul Martinez stepped out through the main entrance with Farnell. Behind them, a couple of porters struggled with the diplomat's cases. Gorman studied Martinez as he walked across the car-park. He had never liked this dapper little man, with his bushy moustache and closely clipped hair. He was wearing a nicely cut white suit and a waistcoat from which a silver watch chain dangled. He wore stack-heeled shoes, deeply unfashionable but essential for a man who was so self-conscious about his height. He was chatting with Farnell, waving his free hand around as he talked. In the other hand, he carried an attaché case.

'Look at that greasy little fucker,' said Gorman, to Angelito. 'Actually carrying his own case today. Must be a first.'

'I guess he's got somethin' important in it, boss.'

'Yeah, well you'd better get out and do your chauffeur routine. You know 'ow he likes the red carpet treatment.'

Angelito scowled, but got obediently out of the car

and walked around to open the back door.

Martinez sauntered up to the car and grinned in at Gorman.

'Hey, amigo!'

''Ello, Raul, 'old mate! 'Ow yer doin'?'

'Fine, Tony, just fine. Hey, you are lookin' good!'

'Nah, put on a bit of weight, en' I?'

'No, I don't think so.' Angelito opened the rear door and Martinez slipped in beside Gorman. The two men appraised each other for a moment and then Martinez opened his arms for the hug. Gorman hated this ritual, but knew it was expected. He took Martinez's thin frame in his arms and pulled him close, turning his head sideways so he wouldn't have to see the man's dumb expression as they embraced. He noticed Angelito and Farnell exchanging sly grins and he fumed inwardly. Martinez smelled of a mixture of cigar smoke and expensive cologne. Gorman patted him self-consciously on the back and then pulled away, relieved to have got the ordeal over. Farnell climbed into the front passenger seat and closed the door.

'Well,' said Gorman. 'You gave us a bit of a surprise, Raul. Why the early arrival?'

Martinez gestured an apology.

'I'm sorry, Tony. My employers got into something of a panic. They wanted me to leave immediately. This business with Chico Estevez . . .'

'Who?'

'You haven't heard? He's a folk singer, a huge star in Colombia. He's touring Spain and he got busted for drug

293

possession in a hotel in Malaga. They wanted me to fly straight over and smooth things out.'

Gorman laughed gleefully.

'Bloody 'ell, they sure sent the right man for the job! What you gonna do, take over supplying 'im?'

Martinez showed his teeth, but there was no amusement in his eyes. Angelito had stowed the cases in the boot and he got back into the driver's seat. 'Where to?' he asked.

Gorman raised his eyebrows at Martinez.

'Police headquarters,' he said. 'I've got to go and arrange bail for Chico. Make a few contributions to some unofficial police charities.' He patted his attaché case. 'But I didn't want to go in there carrying what's in here, you understand?'

Angelito put the car into gear and drove off.

'So what have you got for us?' asked Gorman.

'Something very special,' said Martinez, with a wink. He glanced quickly out of the window, as if to assure himself that there were no police around. Then he set the combination of the lock and opened the case. There was a small velvet bag amongst the other contents. He untied the loop and shook out the contents into the case.

'Fuck me,' said Gorman, quietly.

It was a collection of diamonds, some twenty or so of them, ranging in size from tiny glittering specks, to one or two that were only a little smaller than quails' eggs. They reflected the sun, filling the interior of the car with a myriad flecks of light. Martinez picked up the largest of them and handed it to Gorman. He weighed it in his hand appreciatively. As he did so, he caught a glimpse of Angelito's eyes in the driving mirror. They were big and round, like the diamond.

'That one's over thirty carats,' said Martinez, matter-of-factly.

'That so? Real, are they?'

Martinez looked offended. 'Of course they're real! Do you honestly think I'd bring them to you if they were not?'

Gorman laughed, shook his head, held up a hand in a gesture of peace.

'Only kiddin', Raul, honest! 'Ow did you 'appen to come by these?'

'A quick fingered friend of mine liberated them from a private collection in Cartagena, just over a week ago. They were too hot to sell in Colombia, so he looked for a friend who could get them out of the country, pronto. I told him I would help him out for a small commission.'

'Big 'arted Raul!' observed Gorman. 'What makes me think this "small commission" is going to be at least fifty per cent of the asking price?'

'*Twenty* per cent,' Martinez corrected him. 'I'm not a greedy man.'

'Not much, you aren't. What *is* the asking price, by the way?'

'Three million dollars, American.'

Gorman stared at him. 'Strewth, 'ow much?'

'That's a fair price,' Martinez assured him. 'They've been valued at eight million.'

'Maybe so, son, maybe so. But they're not goin' to be

easy to get shut of, are they? It's gonna take time and trouble to get 'em fenced and after all that, we'll probably 'ave to let 'em go for a lot less than they're worth. See, it's not like the old nose-powder, is it, Raul? You know you've got a guaranteed market for that. Plus, it's disposable evidence, ten minutes after you've flogged it, it's disappeared up some twat's 'ooter. Diamonds, I'm not so sure about. I gotta think about profit margins.'

'You could do it easy, Tony. A man with your contacts, it's just a matter of—'

'Stop tryin' to butter me up, Raul. Three million is totally out of the question.'

They drove in silence for a few moments.

'Maybe I could go two and a half,' ventured Martinez, cautiously.

'Maybe you could go *one* and a half. Sounds more reasonable to me.'

Martinez shook his head. 'I'd rather take them back to Colombia,' he snarled. 'Two and a half, Tony, that's a good price. Come on, you'll make a lot of money on this deal, believe me.'

'I dunno. I just don't know.' Gorman mopped at his brow with a white handkerchief. 'Tell you what, Raul, 'ere's what I'll do. I'll 'ave a geezer I know check these out, all right? I mean, I don't know diamonds from dog shit, do I? If my man agrees with your valuation and can't see any major problems in fencin' 'em, I'll take 'em off yer 'ands for two million dollars, tops. And I do mean tops.'

Martinez seemed to ponder this for a few moments, though Gorman suspected that this was the price he had always expected to settle on. The haggling was a kind of ritual between them, it would have been unthinkable to simply agree on a price straight away. Now Martinez gave a slow sigh.

'Very well, Tony. Two million. You got yourself a bargain there.' He began to scoop the diamonds back into the bag.

'Thing is,' muttered Gorman, 'what d'yer want me to do wiv 'em in the meantime?'

'Take them back to your place, put them in the safe. It's OK, I know you are a man of honour . . . and anyway, I have a complete inventory of what's in here, just in case any should be mislaid, while your "geezer" is "checking them out" . . . I'll want payment in the usual way.'

'That's a fair bit of cash to get me 'ands on, old son. Used notes, I suppose?'

'Of course.'

'Hmm. 'Ow long you gonna be around, then?'

'Four days . . . that's how long I've got to clear the Chico Estevez mess up. But I'll have time for a little recreation, too.' He leaned closer, lowered his voice. 'The English girl you fixed me up with last time. Fiona, was it? You know, the skinny one . . . she around?'

'I dare say we can dig her up for you. We're all takin' a trip up to the club tomorrow night, so I'll make sure Angelito gives her a bell. She's a bit of a wild one, her. I dunno what Mrs Martinez would make of her, do you?'

Martinez grinned sheepishly. 'Talking of wives, where is the lovely Lisa today?'

'She's out shoppin'. Don't worry, she'll be here later

on.' Gorman thought for a moment. 'Listen, Raul, there's a geezer 'angin' about with me at the moment. A writer, name of Frank Nolan. 'Ees doin' a book about me.'

Martinez raised his eyebrows. 'A book? Eh, Tony, you're famous enough already, why you want to be more famous?'

Gorman shrugged. 'Just an idea me and Bill cooked up. But it goes without sayin' that as far as this guy's concerned, I run a straight ship here. I'm a legitimate businessman. If he asks you any questions, just tell him you're an old friend what's stayin' with me for a couple of days. OK?'

Martinez showed his perfect teeth. 'Sure, Tony, anything you say.'

'The police station,' announced Angelito. He pulled the car to a halt in front of the main entrance. Martinez handed Gorman the bag of diamonds.

'Take good care of them,' he said. 'Now I go and put on a show for the uniforms. Is my tie straight?'

'It's the only thing about you that is,' observed Gorman, caustically.

Martinez chuckled. He snapped shut the attaché case and got out of the car. He closed the door and leaned in at the window. 'See you later on,' he said. 'And you won't forget . . . Fiona?'

'Don't worry, Raul. We'll fix you up.'

Martinez turned and walked jauntily up the steps of the police station.

'He doesn't change much,' observed Farnell quietly.

'Nah. Greasy little turd.' Gorman rattled the bag of

diamonds thoughtfully. 'What's so special about this Fiona, anyway? Skinny streak of pelican shit, far as I can remember.'

'Yeah, but she takes it up the ass,' said Angelito. '*Prefers* it that way.'

'That a fact?' Gorman grinned. 'Pervy little twat, so that's his poison is it? Tell you what, Bill, might be an idea to get some photos of that. 'Ave the two of 'em put in the guest room tonight and get Diego to film 'em through the two-way mirror. No, better still, tell 'im to shoot a video.'

Farnell looked doubtful.

'What's your thinking on this, Tony? After all, Raul is a good customer, you don't want to do anything to spoil that.'

'Relax, it's just a bit of insurance. In case he ever *stops* being a good customer. Besides, we'll 'ave some laughs watching that ugly little dip-shit goin' at it, won't we Angel?' He slapped Angelito on the shoulder. 'Come on, let's get back to the old 'omestead, I wanna get out of this bleedin' suit. Besides, I don't like hangin' about in front of this place, it makes me nervous.'

Angelito pulled the car out into heavy traffic.

'No need to worry on that score,' Farnell assured him. 'All the cops that matter are sitting right in your pocket.'

'Old 'abits die 'ard,' Gorman said. He leaned forward and dropped the bag of diamonds into Farnell's lap. ''Ere's a few marbles to play with. Get 'em checked out, will you? I don't think for one moment that Raul would try and pull a fast one, but it's as well to be sure, ennit?

If they check out OK, make arrangements to pick up two million in cash and put it in the safe at 'ome.'

'They'll be difficult to get rid of,' observed Farnell.

'Might not bother just yet. Might just pop 'em in a vault and forget about 'em for a few years. Somethin' to 'and on to me kids, knowarramean?'

'But you haven't—' Farnell checked himself. 'Tony, what are you going to do about that? Lisa could cause some real problems when she finds out . . . that's if she hasn't worked it out already.'

Tony smiled confidently. 'I'll 'andle Lisa,' he said. 'You just leave all that to me. That one knows which side 'er bread's buttered. In the end, she'll do what she's told. If she knows what's good for her. Come on, Angel, get yer bleedin' foot down, the day will be gone by the time we get back!'

Angelito did as he was told. The limousine picked up speed, heading now in the general direction of home.

Chapter Twenty-Two

Eddie Mulryan trudged through the winding streets of the unfamiliar town. The sunlight seemed to ricochet off every white-painted surface and his body was slowly cooking inside his heavy clothes. It reminded him of when he was a child, the hours he'd spent with an old magnifying glass, directing a little spot of searing heat on to the backs of luckless insects, watching in fascination as their shiny bodies crumpled and smoked, before bursting briefly into flames. He thought he knew how they must have felt.

He had decided against going straight to the hotel. The taxi had dropped him on a busy main street, where bars, discos and gift shops throbbed with the noise of amplified rock music. He had moved instinctively away from that, wandering along quieter back streets, looking for somewhere to rest. He had to be ready to square up to Doyle and right now, he felt near to exhaustion. He needed some sleep, he needed to freshen up and he needed a knife, since he hadn't wanted to risk smuggling one through customs. Once those things were taken care of, he'd be ready. Before any of that though, he wanted a cold drink. He felt dehydrated and his throat was raw from his sickness on the plane. He didn't understand how anybody could live in this climate.

He glanced around, squinting in the afternoon haze and he spotted a sign halfway down a nearby sidestreet. PEPE'S PUB it read. Responding to the familiar English word, he made his way towards it and paused to look at a large framed display by the open door. It consisted of photographs of plates of food, fake waxy-looking portions of fish and greasy white chips, hamburgers that looked like they would break the teeth of anybody unwary enough to take a bite of them. Printed at the bottom of the board in big letters were the words WE SPEAK ENGLISH! He also noticed a small sign on the wall, advertising the fact that there were rooms to rent here.

There were half a dozen plastic chairs and tables set outside but they were empty. He threaded his way through them and went inside, stepping into the cool gloom with a sigh of relief. He was greeted by a burst of raucous laughter and he hesitated a moment, unsure of himself. There was a long wooden bar stretching away from him and down at the far end of it, a half dozen young men were standing about in what was clearly an advanced state of inebriation. They all had close-cropped hair and some of them were wearing Union Jack T-shirts and shorts. There was an ultra-violet light above their shaved heads which gave their faces an unnerving skull-like quality. Mulryan thought he had never seen such an ugly bunch, but he decided that their evident patriotism was quite reassuring. What confused him was that they seemed to be laughing at him.

'Fackin' hell,' said the nearest of them, a tall, skinny lad, with tattoos on his neck. ''E finks 'ees in bleedin' Siberia!' This signalled another bout of laughter, the youths throwing back their heads and barking like a pack of dogs.

'Now, you lads just shut up or get out!' said a voice from behind the counter. Mulryan forgot about the youths instantly, as he detected a pleasingly familiar accent. A woman came slowly towards him on the other side of the bar, a big boned woman with red hair that had been teased up into a beehive. She was wearing a frilly silk blouse in a vivid shade of orange and a short black skirt that showed her ample legs well above the knee. She had black-painted eyebrows and a cupid's bow mouth, coloured a deep crimson. She was smiling at Mulryan and he was shocked, because she reminded him of photographs he'd seen of his mother when she was younger. Most women reminded him of his mother in some way, but here the resemblance was uncanny. He set down his case and moved closer to the bar.

'Now then, lover, what's your pleasure?'

The young men sniggered loudly but Mulryan took no notice.

'A glass of lemonade please. Plenty of ice, if it's no trouble.'

The woman raised her arched eyebrows and smiled delightedly.

'Well now, if I'm not mistaken, that's a Cornishman's lilt!'

Mulryan nodded.

'And yours would be . . . Devon?' he ventured.

'Spot on,' she said. 'Teignmouth, born and bred. It's a small world and no mistake.'

'Fack me, I fink these two 'ave fallen in love!' said one of the youths.

The woman snapped him a look over her shoulder. 'I warned you!' she growled.

The youths made oohing noises and laughed again. She turned back to face Mulryan. 'Take no notice of 'em,' she advised. 'They're louts. This town is famous for 'em.' She took a tall glass, half filled it with crushed ice and topped it up with lemonade. Mulryan's throat clicked in anticipation.

'You look all 'ot and bothered,' said the woman. 'Why don't you take off that coat if you're staying?'

Mulryan considered this. He had stubbornly resisted it so far, but now this woman had suggested it to him, it didn't seem such a terrible idea. He slipped off his overcoat, folded it carefully and laid it across a chair. The woman nodded her approval. Mulryan took the glass and tilted it to his lips, draining its contents in one easy swallow.

'Another one?' she asked him.

Mulryan nodded and watched as she refilled his glass.

'Looks like you been in the wars,' she observed.

'That's a fact.'

'My name's Rosie,' she said. 'Rosie Quigly.'

'I'm Eddie Mulryan.' He thought for a moment. 'Bless me,' he said. 'We sound like a pair, don't we? Eddie and Rosie.'

She tilted back her head and chuckled. *A nice, musical sound,* Mulryan thought.

'You're new round 'ere,' she observed.

'Just got in.'

'Where you stayin' then?'

'Dunno yet.' He glanced around the bar. 'Sign says you take guests here.'

Rosie frowned, leaned forward across the bar.

'Do yourself a favour, lover. Go somewhere else. They don't keep this place as clean as you might like.'

'You don't live 'ere, then?'

'Bless you, no! I just *work* 'ere.' She threw a glance down to the end of the bar. 'Not for much longer if I can 'elp it. No, I've got a nice little *pension* at the other end of town. It ain't much but it's clean and nobody bothers me there.'

Mulryan drank his lemonade, slowly this time, relishing the sharp taste.

''Ow long you worked 'ere, then?' he asked.

'Not long. Coupla days. I was in Malaga 'afore that. Got a bit fed up with it, but I didn't know when I was well off. Since then it's been nothing but skivvying for these bloody oiks. "Lager louts", they call 'em. I could think of a better name. Honest, I can stand anything but plain rudeness, that makes my blood boil.'

'Oy!' shouted a voice. 'Darlin'! 'Ows about a bit a service down 'ere?'

'You see?' said Rosie quietly. She turned and her voice rose by several decibels. ''Old yer bloody 'orses, can't you see I'm busy?'

The yobs made the oohing sound again.

'You don't look so busy to me,' observed one of them. 'You're just chatting up Nanook of the North, there! Get yer tits out and bring 'em over 'ere where they'll be appreciated!'

'You watch your language!' snapped Rosie. 'Anyway, you 'aven't paid for your last round, yet!'

'I'll pay yer, darlin',' said the youth with the tattoos. He reached a hand down and pulled at his crotch. 'Come and sit on this for a minute. You'll be buying us a round after that!'

Another of the youths, a tubby lad with a smattering of acne around his nose, mimed the act of throwing up. 'No fanks!' he said. 'Be like chucking a sausage up the Channel Tunnel!'

They dissolved into laughter again. Mulryan looked at Rosie for a moment, saw tears of humiliation in her eyes. He finished his drink and set the empty glass carefully down on the bar.

Rosie must have guessed at his intentions.

'Leave it,' she said quietly. 'They're not worth it.'

Mulryan gave her a reassuring smile. Then he began to walk slowly along the bar towards the yobs. He kept the smile on his face, an open, good-natured smile.

'Look out, it's alive!' sniggered one of them.

Mulryan kept walking.

'What you lookin' at?' asked Tattoos. He stepped back from the bar, squaring up to Mulryan.

'I'm looking at a very rude young man. Somebody who's surely old enough to know better than behave like a snotty-nosed little brat.'

'Wot?' The youth's jaw dropped. *He's probably never been spoken to like that in his entire life*, thought Mulryan. He came to a halt in front of them.

'You see, there's really no excuse for rudeness. I was always raised to be polite to my elders and betters and I've no doubt you were. But for some reason, you've forgotten it. So somebody like me has to remind you. I'm good at reminding people. My old mum always used to say that politeness costs nothing. Now, there's a lady behind that bar, doin' her level best to serve you lads and you've said some very hurtful things to her. I want you all to apologize to her and after that, if you want another drink, you're to say "please" and "thank you" and generally deport yourselves in a pleasant manner.'

'Yeah?' sneered Tattoos. ''Oos gonna make us?'

Mulryan looked slowly around the bar, then back at the youth.

'There doesn't seem to be anybody else 'ere,' he observed. 'So I suppose it'll 'ave to be me.'

Tattoos sneered derisively.

'Fack off, Grandad,' he said; and his friends laughed.

'Oh dear,' said Mulryan quietly. 'You obviously weren't listening.'

Tattoos stepped forward. He was performing for his mates now.

'Why don't you piss off back to the other end of the bar and drink your lemonade?' he said.

Mulryan's smile broadened. 'Because I'm still waiting for you to apologize to the lady.'

'Lady? I can't see no lady. Just a fat slag with big tits.' More laughter. They were really enjoying themselves now.

Mulryan sighed. 'Nobody here by that description, sonny. Now I've asked twice, I won't ask a third time.'

Tattoos seemed to lose patience. He took another step forward and extended a hand to push Mulryan in the chest. Mulryan moved quickly for a big man. He brought a foot up suddenly, driving the toe of his boot into the youth's testicles. Tattoos howled and jumped so high, his cropped head hit the low ceiling, leaving a round indentation in the plaster. He came down on his feet, his face screwed into a mask of agony, his hands clawing at his genitals. Mulryan struck him back-handed across the mouth with his plaster-cast. Teeth pinged off the glasses hanging over the bar and Tattoos fell sideways. His head struck the brass footrail with a loud, gonging sound.

Then it was very quiet. The other youths stood frozen, mouths open, staring down at their fallen comrade. He was gazing up at the ceiling, stunned. Blood was fountaining upwards from his mashed lips, then running down either side of his head to collect in a pool on the tiled floor.

Mulryan shook his head, tutted loudly.

'Now, you see what happens when you're rude?' he said. 'It's regrettable. Violence is always regrettable, but sometimes it's the only thing that gets through to people. Now . . . I wonder if any of you have anything to say to the lady behind the bar?' He reached out his left hand and placed it gently on the shoulder of the nearest youth, the tubby one. 'Perhaps you'd like to start the ball rolling?' he suggested.

The youth looked up at him and Mulryan noted a brief flash of defiance in his eyes. Mulryan, still smiling, shifted his weight slightly and stood on Tattoos' nose. It made a brief crunching sound and blood squirted out from under Mulryan's heel.

'Oops,' he said. 'Clumsy me.'

The tubby youth twitched like he had been jolted with a cattle prod. The anger dissolved from his eyes to be replaced by naked fear. 'I'm sorry,' he gasped, his voice toneless.

'Not to *me*, you daft 'apeth. To the lady.'

The youth raised his eyes to look at Rosie. 'I'm sorry,' he repeated. 'We didn't mean any harm, did we lads?'

There was a general murmur of agreement. Mulryan patted the youth on the shoulder.

'There now, that wasn't so difficult, was it? Who's next, I wonder?'

Now they were all jabbering their apologies, apart from Tattoos who was making a kind of bubbling, groaning sound.

'Good lads,' Mulryan congratulated them. 'It takes a real man to say he was wrong! Now, 'ere's what I think you should do. Gather up your friend here and get him back to wherever you're staying. Put some ice in a flannel and hold it to his face. Oh and his . . . other bits. You'll find the swelling will go down in no time. He might want to see a dentist about his teeth though. And I hope you'll all think on and treat ladies with a bit of respect from now on.'

'We will,' the tubby youth assured him.

Mulryan watched as they picked up their friend and half carried, half dragged him out of the door. He took a towel off the counter and dropped it into the blood on the floor with an expression of distaste. Then he strolled back to his place at the bar. Rosie was watching him, her cheeks flushed with excitement, her eyes wide.

'There now,' said Mulryan. 'A bit quieter in here. I believe I'll have another lemonade.'

She fixed it for him, her hands trembling slightly as she got the ice into the glass. 'You know how to handle yourself,' she observed.

He shrugged, didn't say anything.

'They might go to the police,' she added.

He grinned. 'I doubt it. Can you picture a young rip like that, admitting that he's been dusted by an old codger like me?'

She laughed then, that deep, fruity chuckle that he was already acquiring a liking for.

'I been thinkin',' she said, 'you *could* stay at my place, if'n you like. It's not a palace, but it's clean and cosy and there's room enough for two little ones like us.' She handed him the lemonade. He savoured it for a moment, relishing the tinkling ice just below his top lip, the way it made his breath cloud. Then he took a long swallow of its contents and smacked his lips.

'Why not?' he said. There was something about Rosie that made him feel reckless. 'What time do you get off?'

She considered the question for all of three seconds.

'Now,' she said. 'I was thinking of giving it up, anyway.'

He glanced around the empty bar.

310

'You can't just up and leave, surely?'

''Course I can! I'll just take what I'm owed and leave a note for my boss. I'll say something better came up. I can get a job like this one, any time.'

He nodded. 'True enough, I suppose.' He finished the lemonade and set down the empty glass. 'How much do I owe you?' he asked.

'It's on the house,' she assured him.

'Very kind.' He thought for a moment. 'Tell you what, Rosie. Can you drive a car?'

'Sure. Why?'

''Cause I just might have a job for you, myself. Yes, I reckon I might, at that.'

She was intrigued. 'Doin' what?'

'Drivin',' he said. 'You know, like a chauffeur.' He held up his broken hand. 'Can't do it myself, as you can see.'

She looked doubtful. 'Would I 'ave to wear a uniform?'

'No, I reckon you'll do just as you are. Tell you what, you get your stuff together and we'll talk about it on the way to your place.'

'All right.' She opened the cash register and extracted a pile of cash. She smiled at Mulryan. 'A little bonus,' she explained. 'For my trouble.'

'Won't they miss it?'

'No. They don't keep a proper check on their takings. If anyone asks, I'll say we had a quiet day.'

Mulryan watched her thoughtfully. The more he saw of Rosie, the more he liked her. He wondered if fate had directed his steps into the little bar. Perhaps this meeting was always meant to happen. She came out from behind the bar. Collecting his suitcase and over-coat, Mulryan followed her out into the street. He was surprised to see that the shadows of afternoon were already lengthening as the sun began to sink below the horizon. Night was fast approaching and he felt inexplic-ably excited at the prospect.

Rosie had turned back to padlock the steel shutters across the doorway. She posted her bunch of keys in through the letterbox.

'Good bloody riddance,' she muttered. 'Come on, lover, it's just along the road a bit!' She took his hand and led him down the street and for a moment, he felt like a child, accompanying his mother home after a hectic day out. It was a nice warm feeling and for the moment at least, Jack Doyle was the last thing on his mind.

Chapter Twenty-Three

It had been a strange evening. After taking Lisa back to the Villa Gorman, he'd spent the larger part of the evening sitting with Bill Farnell on the patio, chatting about 'background' material for the book. Jack was getting so much into the role he was beginning to believe that he really could write the damned thing.

Gorman was nowhere to be seen, he'd sloped off somewhere with the mysterious Mr Martinez. Lisa, meanwhile, with no more than a monosyllabic farewell to Jack, had taken her solitary 'package' into the house and hadn't come out again. Jack was obliged to sit there, hoping that his guilt didn't show in his face, while Bill Farnell chattered on and on about the valuable work he did on Gorman's behalf. It was clearly a favourite subject and Jack was only required to nod and smile at regular intervals.

Around nine o'clock, Gorman, Angelito and Raul Martinez finally put in an appearance. Jack took an instant dislike to Martinez. The man was sickeningly obsequious and his sole mission in life seemed to be to crawl up Gorman's backside and die happily. Gorman responded with his usual oafish good humour but it was painfully apparent that he didn't much care for Martinez either. They all sat and drank for a few minutes before Gorman apologetically told Jack that he, Martinez and Farnell had some private business to discuss and that Angelito would be happy to drive him back to his hotel.

Now, slumped in the passenger seat of the grey limo and staring into the twin beams of the headlights, Jack was finally free to think back to his afternoon with Lisa. It had been so much more than just sex and he knew now that he was in deep; maybe too deep. What had initially been a powerful attraction was quickly blossoming into something more than that. He was finally beginning to accept the idea that he was falling for her. He hated to admit it, even to himself. His life was currently complicated enough.

Angelito seemed to be in a bad mood, staring sullenly at the road ahead and making no attempt at conversation. All in all it was a relief when they finally pulled into the floodlit forecourt of the Excelsior. Jack let himself out of the car and it was only then that Angelito chose to speak.

'Have a good shopping trip today?' he sneered.

Jack glanced at him sharply, then shrugged, decided the kid was just fishing, he didn't really know anything.

'Fine thanks,' Jack told him. 'Mrs Gorman and I had a long talk. Your name came up, once or twice.'

'Yeah?' Angelito looked thoughtful. 'What'd she say about me?'

Jack grinned. 'Wouldn't you like to know!' he concluded.

He slammed the door and strolled across the forecourt to the hotel entrance. The limo's tyres squealed as Angelito took off in a hurry. Jack paused to watch as it turned out on to the main highway and accelerated away into the night, Angelito working off his frustration with his usual macho display. Jack smiled ruefully. There were no worries on that score, he decided. Angelito was hardly likely to say anything to Gorman if he was guilty himself of having dallied with Lisa. Besides, the kid had a cushy number going for him there, he wasn't going to jeopardize it over something like this.

Jack climbed the steps of the entrance and the glass doors slid open with a hiss of cool air. The foyer was crowded, smartly dressed couples moving around the entrance of what appeared to be the hotel's ballroom. Jack could hear the strains of some crappy cabaret music coming from inside. He winced, decided he'd go straight up to his room, take a shower and have an early night. He began to walk towards the reception desk to collect his keys but he'd only taken a few steps when he froze in his tracks, every nerve in his body shrilling a warning.

A familiar figure was sitting on one of the leather sofas in the lobby, a thin, ugly man with closely cropped hair. He was holding a magazine but was making no pretence at reading it. Instead he was staring intently at Jack over the top of it, his pale lips twisting into a crooked smile. As Jack stood there, momentarily stunned, Tam McGiver got to his feet and began to cross the marble floor towards him.

Panic took over, galvanizing Jack into some semblance of action. He turned on his heel and made for the exit, fumbling in his jacket pocket for his car keys as he did so. OK, no problem, he told himself, he'd go straight out to the Mitsubishi and get the fuck out of here . . .

That was when he remembered he'd left the car keys in his hotel room. Fear jolted through him like an electric prod; an instant later, the glass doors parted again and he stumbled out into the night. He stood for a moment at the top of the steps, hesitant, unsure of what to do for the best. He glanced back through the open doors and saw McGiver moving towards him, that confident smile on his pockmarked face.

'Christ!' Jack willed his feet to move, descended the stone steps at a brisk trot and acting impulsively, ran around the side of the hotel towards the lights of the harbour. Here, the cafés, bars and shops were in full swing, pop music blasting out from a dozen hidden speakers. The waterside teemed with crowds of people, a mixture of young locals and well-to-do holidaymakers, dressed in expensive casuals and out looking to scare up some excitement.

Jack meanwhile was getting more than enough of that commodity. He dodged and weaved through the crowd, occasionally throwing frantic glances over his shoulder to ensure that McGiver was still in pursuit. Jack had no plan worth speaking of, just the vague idea that he might be able to double back somewhere and lose the Scotsman in the crush. It was strange but he'd been so keyed up about Eddie Mulryan, he hadn't even considered

McGiver. The man seemed to be matching him easily, striding along on those long legs and looking vaguely amused by it all.

Keep running, his expression seemed to say. *I'll catch you sooner or later.*

Jack thought of the last time he'd seen McGiver, the man lifting the big coal hammer to pound somebody's knee. He thought of the way the knee had split open like a piece of rotten fruit and his stomach turned over.

Jack reached a tight knot of people clustered around the entrance of a café bar and was obliged to push and shove his way through them, horribly aware that the gap between him and McGiver was narrowing by the second. In trying to pass by, Jack inadvertently jostled a young woman, spilling the glass of wine she was holding and the man with her shouted at Jack in heated Spanish; but there was no time to stop and argue the toss. Jack cleared the obstruction, noticed the mouth of an alleyway on his left and took the opportunity to duck into it. He began to run uphill between rows of shuttered white-painted houses. He climbed a short flight of steps and took another turning, this time to his right. He paused to listen and heard the thudding of footsteps racing in pursuit.

He swore viciously and moved on along a cobbled street, realizing that he was moving parallel to the water-front. A thick sweat of fear was soaking into the fabric of his shirt as he saw to his consternation that the way ahead ended in a narrow cul-de-sac. He glanced wildly about, spotted another narrow passage to his right leading back down to the harbour. He threw himself into it, his footsteps echoing in the enclosed space. He emerged back on the waterfront several hundred yards lower down than he had left it.

Ahead of him now, he could see a small bunch of teenagers heading down a flight of steps into the illuminated entrance of a club. The wall was garishly painted with a mural depicting punky-looking devils capering against a background of flames and above this, trails of smoke formed letters announcing that this was NICK'S CELLAR. Jack could feel the sonic rumble of music running through the ground beneath his feet and without stopping to think it through, he ran to the steps and went down them, tagging on to the kids that were now disappearing through the doorway. McGiver wouldn't expect him to come down here, he told himself, he'd carry on along the waterfront. Then Jack could double back and grab his car keys . . .

He followed the last kid through a set of swing doors and the music jumped several notches in volume. He found himself in a dimly lit hallway, the walls papered in imitation red velvet. There was a cubicle on the right, lit by a single ultraviolet spotlight. A big, muscular man in an ill fitting tuxedo, sat in the cubicle, taking the money from the kids. He had short hair and wore dark glasses. The ultraviolet picked out flecks of dandruff on his shoulders. He thrust the stub of a ticket into Jack's hand and demanded the sum of three thousand pesetas. Jack fumbled out his wallet and shoved the money at the man, all the while throwing anxious glances over his shoulder. He put the ticket stub into his pocket and moved along the hall. He pushed open another set of swing doors and descended a flight of stone steps into the cellar itself.

The music struck him like a clenched fist, a brutish, bellowing cacophony of fuzz, feedback and synthesized noise. There was some kind of vocal in there too, he decided, but the way it was mixed it was just more racket. As he came down the stairs, a wave of heat rose up to swamp him, coaxing even more sweat from his already open pores. He saw that the cellar was packed to bursting with a sea of dancing kids. A sophisticated lighting rack above their heads blitzed, strafed and strobed them with explosions of coloured light. Up at the top end of the club, the band were crammed on to a tiny stage area. Jack could see several musicians crouched over their respective instruments, long hair thrashing and flailing in the strobes. At stage front a young woman, dressed in a grubby white nightie and sporting a painted face was screaming incomprehensible lyrics into a microphone. The result sounded not unlike a jet aircraft taking off and Jack's ears were literally vibrating to the din.

He hesitated at the bottom step and turned to look back up at the doorway above him. Senseless to get caught up in that crush if he could avoid it. He'd just wait here a few minutes and hopefully . . .

The swing doors opened and Tam McGiver stood there, looking down into the chaos. He spotted Jack and smiled, raised one hand in a beckoning gesture. Jack shook his head, started to back away. McGiver began to descend the stairs. When Jack reached the edges of the crowd, he turned and began to shoulder his way frantically through it. It was a near impossible task. The kids were lost in the music, heads down, limbs flailing, oblivious to Jack's clumsy attempts to get by them. The uncertain lighting was disorientating, making him trip and stumble over other people's feet. Nevertheless, he plunged on, pushing and shoving people bodily out of his path. He felt like he was wading through a sea of humanity and whenever he looked over his shoulder, McGiver was following, his pock-marked face blue, red, orange, green as the lights moved through their programmed sequence.

As Jack neared the stage, progress became even more difficult. Here, the band's more avid fans were gathered shoulder to shoulder in front of their heroes, leaping and thrashing to the manic, supercharged beat. The noise was hellish. Jack spotted a small gap between two spike-headed dancers and attempted to force his way into it.

He was held fast between them as the rhythm seemed to crank up a couple of notches. An arm came around his shoulders and he winced, believing for a moment that it was McGiver who had grabbed him but then he realized that one of the youths had latched on to him. Before he could do anything a second arm encircled him from the other side and he realized that this was some ritual dance that he was caught up in. He struggled to escape but then he was pulled hard to the left and he had to concentrate on moving his feet to avoid falling over. Glancing up, confused by the sudden turn of events, he saw he was now part of a large circle that had formed, as if by magic, in front of the stage. He was horrified to see McGiver's grinning face on the other side of the circle, moving away to his right, his big arms thrown around the shoulders of two girls.

The circle stopped turning to the left; now it turned in the other direction. Jack persuaded his feet to adjust to the new steps while he searched frantically for McGiver. There he was, moving back to the left, his eyes fixed on Jack with deadly intent. Now the circle stopped moving and there was a frozen moment while both sides regarded each other gleefully. The music hit a major chord and as if at some signal, the two youths on either side of Jack ran towards the opposite side of the circle, which in turn came lunging back at them. Jack tried to dig his heels in but the impetus carried him forward. In a flash of strobe light, he saw McGiver's grinning face only feet away from him . . .

In the last instant, the two sides snapped back again and other points of the circle spilled in to fill the breach. Jack struggled to free himself from the grip of the two youths who seemed to be too drunk or too stoned to notice. Again he was whipped forward towards the waiting line ahead of him. This time the charge wasn't halted soon enough and Jack felt himself cannon into somebody straight ahead of him. Whoever it was stumbled and fell and Jack and several other people went sprawling over them. He hit the ground with an oath, rolled away from the youths who were holding him and scrambled uneasily to his feet. He backed up until he was right beside the stage, standing at the feet of the gyrating female singer.

At that instant the music changed abruptly. The other instruments cut off, leaving just the drummer hammering out a merciless, speed-freak rhythm. All the lights snapped out save for one white strobe flickering to the beat. Jack saw laughing, carnival faces on all sides of him, snapshot impressions of people jerking past him in a frenzied parody of life, kids clambering up on to the stage to dance with the singer, fallen kids getting back to their feet, everyone laughing insanely, arms flailing, hair thrashing like gorgons. And then, from amidst the heap of crumpled figures at Jack's feet, one familiar face rising like a beast from the depths, mouth smiling in a shark's grin as he got himself carefully upright, his eyes reflecting the flashing of the strobe.

He was moving towards Jack now like a demented marionette, his hand going down, down to his pocket, gone for an instant then re-emerging in a series of stabbing motions, holding something that flashed silver in the half light and Jack waiting, frozen, his heart pounding in time to the drummer's adrenalin-fuelled beat.

McGiver stepped forward now, one arm raised to slash at Jack's throat with the razor and the strobe picked out his face in perfect detail, cadaverous shadows under the cheeks, teeth exposed, open mouth trailing harpstrings of saliva, eyes blazing in feral joy as his arm began to descend in a series of chops and Jack cringing, waiting for the edge of the razor to slice into him . . .

And then a body seemed to come out of nowhere, falling backwards through the air and cannoning into McGiver, knocking him off his feet. Just some luckless kid who'd lost his footing on the narrow stage and had taken a tumble. McGiver went down hard, the drummer hit a climax on the cymbals and the lights came up again, the whole band steaming back in for the final chorus. The audience reacted as though they'd been plugged into the mains, dancing with renewed vigour.

Jack just turned and pushed his way around the edge of the stage. He saw a curtained doorway ahead of him and went to it, stepped through into a long corridor and the stink of fried onions. There was some kind of kitchen off to his right, a store room to his left. Up ahead of him was what could only be a back exit. Gratefully, he headed for it, threw the door open and stepped out into the welcome cool of the evening.

The relief was short-lived. He stood there staring ahead of him, hardly believing what had happened. He was in a small concrete yard, wedged between the sheer walls of two other buildings. There was only one way out, a long flight of stone steps leading down into the water. The sea looked deep and distinctly choppy. A reasonable swimmer could doubtless dive in and make it to safety further along the beach, but Jack wasn't a reasonable swimmer by any stretch of the imagination. In fact, he was no kind of swimmer at all.

Fighting panic, he glanced back through the open doorway and saw McGiver at the end of the hall, moving rapidly towards him. Desperately, Jack moved to his left, pressing his back up against a row of metal dustbins that stood to one side of the open door. He edged in there, out of sight and instinctively, one hand groped behind him, closing around the handle of a bin lid. He stood waiting and the ocean roared in the silence.

Hit the fucker as he comes through the door. Don't give him a chance to . . .

The heavy wooden door was kicked suddenly wide open with a force that slammed it against Jack's body, catching his forehead a glancing blow. He reeled against the bins with an oath, the breath driven out of him, stars dancing in front of his eyes. The door swung shut again and McGiver stood there, grinning at Jack like the angel of death.

'You must think I came down with the last shower,' he observed. 'That was quite a chase you gave me. And what a surprise to find *you* in the Hotel Excelsior. Undergone a wee change of name since you left England, I see.'

Jack lifted his bandaged hand to rub at his forehead.

'Listen,' he said. 'The two thousand . . . I can pay you now. With interest if you like.'

McGiver raised his eyebrows.

'Is that a fact? Well, that's nice to know. I could do with some more spending money while I'm here.'

'No . . . but . . . The Armenian . . . you could take it back for him. Then we'd be quits, right?'

McGiver laughed derisively.

'I'm afraid it doesn't work like that, pal. The Armenian put the finger on you. That means he's washed his hands of the whole thing. He isn't expecting me to come back with the money. Just your balls on a plate.'

Jack felt his body temperature drop several degrees,

but he fought to keep control of himself. He moved the bandaged hand back and forth over his forehead, feigning dizziness.

'But . . . but that's stupid. You don't *want* to kill me, do you? The Armenian would be none the wiser.'

'Oh yeah? And what's to say you wouldn't turn up back in London in a few months time, drop me right in it? Besides, who says I don't want to kill you. Could be I'd enjoy it.'

Jack groaned. He swayed back against the bins, threw out one arm to steady himself. Once again his good hand closed on the handle of the bin lid. 'How . . . how did you find me?' he muttered. 'Eddie Mulryan tell you where I was headed. He's with you, is he?'

McGiver sneered. 'Eddie who?' he muttered. He slipped a hand into his pocket and it emerged holding the cut-throat razor he had used earlier. 'I work alone, pal. Always have, always will.' He lifted the razor so Jack could get a better look at it. 'Like it?' he asked. 'I took it off a Paki, back in London. Had to break his arm first. Just a wee lad he was, but I have to admit he had balls. He tried to cut *me* with it, but I told him that when you use a razor you have to have the element—'

He slashed at Jack's face mid sentence, almost catching him off guard; but Jack reacted instinctively, snatching the bin lid up and whirling it around in front of him like a shield. The razor's edge struck sparks off the rusty metal and glanced aside, throwing McGiver slightly off balance. Jack knew he'd get only one opportunity and he didn't hesitate. He launched a savage kick into McGiver's testicles. His toe cap connected with a meaty thud and McGiver's face contorted into a mask of white agony. He dropped the razor and both hands went down to clutch at his groin. He stood there at the top of the flight of steps, opened his mouth and made a thin, agonized sound from between clenched teeth. It sounded oddly like a kettle coming to the boil.

Jack made the teeth his target. He thrust forward with the bin lid, putting all his strength into the blow. The galvanized metal clanged against McGiver's mouth and he fell backwards, poleaxed. His shoulders slammed against the concrete steps and he began to slide down them like a toboggan, his shaved head jerking like a puppet as it glanced off every step along the way. By the time he hit the water, his skull resembled a split water melon. He sank head first to his waist then slowed. His legs began to kick feebly and Jack could see his fingers clawing helplessly at the slippery green steps like a pair of fleshy crabs. Bubbles rose in the water above his head but he seemed to be too disorientated to know what was happening to him. He slipped down another couple of steps.

Jack stood there, still holding the bin lid, staring down in disbelief at what he had done. He felt an irrational urge to go down and help McGiver, pull him back up out of the water. He even started to descend the steps but then, with a last bubble of exhaled air, McGiver sank as far as his knees. His hands were gesticulating helplessly beneath the surface.

The restless waves sucked back for a moment and Jack

could see the pock-marked face staring up from the shallow water in shocked surprise. Then the next wave folded over him and his heels slipped anchor off the steps. His body drifted down and away and when the next wave pulled back, there was no sign that he had ever been there.

Jack turned away, feeling sick to his stomach. He stumbled back to the bins and lifted the lid to replace it. Something white embedded in the underside of the lid caught his attention. He looked closer and saw to his disgust that it was a tooth. His stomach churning, he wrenched the thing free and flung it into the water. He replaced the bin lid and glanced quickly around the yard. He found the razor and that too he flung far out into the depths of the sea. His horrified gaze kept returning to the place where McGiver had gone in, some irrational expectation of seeing him wading out, battered but far from defeated. But though Jack lingered for several more minutes, nothing emerged from the dark water.

He opened the door and slipped back along the empty hall. He went through the curtained doorway into the cellar, where the band were blasting out another anthem of anarchy and destruction. Jack pushed his way back through the crowd, feeling exhausted now, wanting nothing more than to go back to his hotel and sleep.

At least, he told himself, there was one consolation in all this, Eddie Mulryan seemed to be out of the picture, McGiver hadn't seemed to even recognize the name. Provided the Scotsman's body drifted far away from here, there was surely nothing to tie it to Jack. At any rate, he could risk the few more days he and Lisa needed to put their plan into operation.

Maybe everything was going to be all right, after all.

Chapter Twenty-Four

Eddie Mulryan surveyed his reflection doubtfully in the mirror of the cramped changing cubicle. He had never worn clothes like this before and he thought he looked clownish. The short-sleeved Bermuda shirt had a garish red pattern that looked as though somebody had bled all over it. The white cotton beach pants were cut high on the leg, revealing the tan leather sandals, from which his misshapen toes protruded. Admittedly, he felt a lot cooler but he wasn't sure that he'd have the confidence to walk down the street looking like this.

Rosie's voice called through the curtain.

'Are you ready, lover? Come out and let me see!'

'I don't know about this, Rosie. I really don't.'

'Silly. *Everybody* dresses like that here! Now come on out and let me have a look!'

Rosie could make him do anything. He had realized that after spending just one night with her. He'd never thought about women in that way before, had never had the slightest interest in doing the kind of things he saw people doing on the television. Kissing and that. Indeed, it would never have occurred to him to do those things with Rosie if she hadn't taken the initiative, almost the moment he'd stepped into her little apartment. She'd pounced on him – there was no other word for it – *pounced* on him and started kissing him and pulling at his clothes and putting her hands on to the most intimate parts of his body, even *downstairs*. He hadn't resisted, hadn't tried to push her off, even when she'd removed both their clothes and had straddled him naked on the bed. She started working her hips up and down in a frenzied rhythm, while he lay there staring at her in bemused silence.

At first, it hadn't been at all successful. His cock had remained stubbornly flaccid, despite all her efforts. Eddie had told himself she'd get fed up in a minute and would leave him be. But then, something extraordinary had happened. She looked down at him with a strange gleam in her eye.

'I know what you need,' she said. She got up and walked over to a small wardrobe and as Eddie watched in astonishment, she picked out a broad leather belt and stretched it between her fists, making it snap. It was just like being a child again, waiting for his dad to come and leather him and instantly, he felt a stirring in his loins, his cock beginning to harden. Rosie noticed it. She came back to the bed, a triumphant smile on her face.

'Oh, you bad boy,' she whispered. 'I knew you were like me. I knew it!'

The first crack of the belt across his thighs had brought him to full erection. She bestrode him again, lashing down with the belt whenever the mood took her and the thrill, the sheer, all-pervading ecstasy that filled him was a unique experience in his life. He had quickly come to orgasm, grunting and gasping like a big animal and it was all he could do to keep from screaming with the unexpected joy of it. Gasping for breath, her skin shining beneath a film of sweat, she had detached herself from him and lain down on the bed beside him. Then she handed him the belt.

'My turn,' she said.

Now, in the cubicle, Eddie closed his eyes for shame and felt the colour rising into his face as he remembered that long night and how they had gone turn and turn about, until their bodies were mottled with weals and bruises and at last, satiated, they slept side by side like babies. It made him feel like some kind of Christopher Columbus, enthralled and astonished by the discovery of a world he hadn't realized existed.

'Eddie, what's taking you so long?'

The curtain was pulled aside and Rosie stepped into the booth. He turned awkwardly to face her.

'Rosie, I really don't know about this,' he mumbled.

'Oh, lover, don't you just look the bee's knees!' Now she was pulling him out into the boutique, oblivious to the amused stares of the other shoppers, she was turning him around to face an even bigger mirror. 'Just look!' she enthused. 'Just look at yourself! Who's a pretty boy then? Or at least you *will* be when all them bruises heal up. And here, I've found the perfect finishing touch!' She plopped a straw fedora on his head and tilted it to a rakish angle. 'There now, isn't that just the business? Don't you just look the proper gentleman?'

He regarded his reflection dubiously and was astonished to find that he was softening to the idea.

'It's certainly more *comfortable*,' he admitted.

'Of course it is, lover! Now, if you'd just try on the shorts . . .'

'Oh no, Rosie, no! I couldn't, I just couldn't!' He had to put his foot down somewhere. 'I think I could just about get up the courage to go out like this, but shorts! I haven't worn those since I was a little boy.'

She smiled, winked at him lasciviously.

'Afraid the bruises will show, eh?'

He glanced nervously around.

'Rosie! For goodness sakes!'

She laughed heartily, amused by his shyness. 'Come on now, let's have them put your old things in a bag and we'll take the new you for a stroll around town.'

'But people will stare at me!'

'You'll get the odd admiring glance, I shouldn't wonder. A real man always does. But those girls will just have to keep their hands to themselves, you're *mine*!'

For the first ten minutes, Eddie could barely raise his eyes from the pavement; but then the feeling passed and he began to walk along with growing confidence. People did look at him, it was true, but he soon discovered that all he had to do was return the glance and the eyes simply fell away. Anyway, they were bound to stare. The bruises around his flattened nose still looked a fright.

A shop window caught his eye, the brilliant flash of

332

sunlight on metal, drawing him like a magnet. He took Rosie's hand and moved closer. The window display consisted of knives, knives and more knives. He had never seen so many blades in his life. He stood there, mesmerized by the sight.

'Toledo steel,' Rosie said. 'Best steel in Spain. Do you like knives, lover?'

He nodded dumbly.

'Do you want one?'

'I do,' he replied.

She nodded, smiled. She didn't seem to find this in the least bit unusual. 'Let's go in and choose you one,' she said. 'Only this will be my treat. I'd like to buy you something.'

He protested but she would not be swayed on the matter. They went inside and Eddie spent the best part of an hour examining the extensive range of weapons, while Rosie looked on proudly, beaming like a mother presiding over a son's first present.

In the end, Eddie chose a beautifully crafted hunting knife. It was bigger than he was used to but he thought it would make up for the comparative clumsiness of his left hand. The knife had a moulded bone handle and a broad, eight-inch blade with a jagged ridge running along the top of it. Eddie tested the edge with his thumb. It was as sharp as a razor. The knife came with a soft leather sheath that could easily be belted around his waist, beneath the hem of his Bermuda shirt. The shop had an engraving service and Rosie insisted on getting the knife inscribed. She sent Eddie off to look at a display at the far end of the shop. When the knife was ready, she brought it over to show him. Etched into the blade in elegant letters were nine words:

Eddie, love Rosie – the first cut is the deepest.

'It's beautiful,' said Eddie; and he almost felt like crying.

They went straight from the knife shop to a car hire bureau. Eddie told Rosie to pick out any vehicle that took her fancy. She chose a red Polo convertible. She signed all the documents and Eddie handed over the cash. Ten minutes later they were driving out on to the street of Torremolinos with the top rolled down. Rosie had put on a pair of sunglasses with pink frames. Her beehive was coming loose in the wind, but she didn't seem to mind.

'Where to?' she asked Eddie.

'Do you know the Hotel Estragon?'

'Piece of cake,' she said. She turned left on to the main road. Eddie was strapping the knife to his belt with great difficulty.

'Am I allowed to ask why we're going there?' she asked.

'I'm lookin' for a bloke.'

'What bloke?'

Eddie held up his shattered hand. 'Feller who did this,' he said.

She gazed at him for a moment, then scowled.

'You in some kind of trouble, then?'

'No. He is, when I find him. But listen, Rosie, I might need a little help with this. If I go in there askin' about room numbers and such, with all these bruises on my face, I'm goin' to stick out like a sore thumb . . .'

'I'll sort it, lover. What name is it?'

Eddie glanced at a slip of paper. 'Michael Reynolds. If it isn't him, there's another feller called Frank Nolan, in a place called Puerto Banus.'

Rosie's face lit up. 'Oh, I hope it's there! I *love* Puerto Banus, it's dead posh . . . a bit too pricey for me, though.'

'We'll go there anyway,' he promised her. 'Sooner or later.'

'Oh, Eddie, could we?'

''Course we could. Nothing's too good for you, Princess. But as they say in the movies, "business before pleasure".'

The Hotel Estragon was a tourist hotel on the sea front, brand spanking new, twenty-five stories of shimmering white concrete, dwarfing the surrounding date palms. There was a crazy golf course and a kidney-shaped swimming pool. Rosie pulled into the forecourt, gave Eddie a kiss on the cheek and strolled in through the entrance. Five minutes later, she was back, smiling and pleased with herself.

'Room 2108' she told him. 'That's up on the twenty-first floor.' She gazed upwards at the dazzling edifice of concrete and glass, the countless square balconies climbing dizzily towards heaven. 'Long way up,' she observed.

'Thanks, sweetie. I shan't be long.' Mulryan got out of the car and started towards the hotel. Then he hesitated, glanced back over his shoulder. 'Might be an idea to keep that ol' engine a runnin',' he added.

She looked at him, concern in her eyes.

'Will it be dangerous?' she asked.

He smiled, winked. 'Not for me,' he said.

He walked up to the entrance and went in through the revolving glass doors. The foyer was crowded, a host of new arrivals clustered around the reception desk. There was an argument in progress, something about a double booking. A tubby American was complaining loudly about how the hotel had ruined his holiday and everybody's attention was focused on him. Mulryan went straight to the self-service elevator and rode up to the twenty-first floor, without stopping. That was good, he told himself, nobody to identify him later. He wandered along the deserted corridor, found room 2108 and tapped politely on the door. He waited.

After a few moments, it opened. A thin, middle-aged man peered out at him through horn-rimmed glasses. He wore a blue towelling robe and his hair was wet as though he'd just taken a shower.

Mulryan favoured him with his sweetest smile. 'Mr Reynolds? Mr Michael Reynolds?'

Reynolds' eyes widened and then he returned the smile.

'You're early,' he observed. He took Mulryan by the arm and pulled him into the room. He moved to the door and glanced up and down the hallway, before stepping back and closing it behind him. 'You're a new face,' he said. 'But I think you'll do.' He walked slowly around Mulryan, eyeing him appreciatively. 'Yes, I'm sure you will.' He fingered Mulryan's plaster-cast curiously. 'We've been in a fight, haven't we? Do you like to fight?'

Mulryan stared at the man, bemused.

'Mr Reynolds, I—'

'Yes, yes, don't speak, you'll spoil it for me!' Reynolds was still circling him. 'My, but you're a big fellow, aren't you? And English, too. I like that. I don't speak much Spanish and I like to talk. I need to be understood. Nobody back home seems to understand . . . now look, I wasn't quite ready for you. Give me a couple of seconds, will you? Just wait right here . . . no, no, don't take the hat off, it's perfect!'

Reynolds turned and hurried through an adjoining doorway into the bathroom. 'So, where have you come from?' he shouted through.

'Cornwall,' said Mulryan. He stood awkwardly in the unfamiliar room, staring uncertainly at his surroundings. *The man seemed to have been expecting him,* he thought; *but how was that possible?*

'No, silly! Where in Spain?'

'Oh . . . right here in Torremolinos. Now listen, Mr Reynolds . . .'

'Georgina!'

'I beg your pardon?'

'Call me Georgina!'

Eddie frowned. 'Georgina?' he echoed.

'It's my holiday name. Why, don't you like it?'

Mulryan shrugged. 'It's all right, I suppose. Funny sort of name for a bloke.'

Reynolds laughed. 'Oh, I *like* you!' he said. 'I can see we're going to have fun together. Right, I'm ready for you now.' He came back and stood in the bathroom doorway, then untied the robe and let it fall to the floor. He struck an exaggerated fashion pose, one hand on his hip, the other lifted to the back of his neck. 'Ta-daa!' he exclaimed.

Mulryan stared. 'Bloody hell!' he said.

Reynolds was wearing a black lace bra, matching panties and a long black wig. He had painted his lips a deep shade of crimson. Now he was advancing towards Mulryan, moving very slowly, his hands on his hips. 'What do you think?' he asked. He was using a different voice now, a soft, husky tone.

Mulryan spluttered. 'I . . . I . . .'

Reynolds put a hand on Mulryan's arm and looked at him intently.

'Let me tell you what I require from you,' he whispered. 'I want you to be rough with me. Do you understand? I want to be chastised. Don't hold back. You can make me do anything you want. I'm your slave.' He dropped to his knees and began to pull at Mulryan's trousers. 'Now let's see what you've got for me,' he said.

Mulryan stared down at Reynolds for a moment in total disbelief. Then, instinctively, he brought down his plaster-cast hard on the top of the man's head. Reynolds grunted and went down flat on his face. Mulryan stopped, grabbed him by the back of the neck and jerked him back to his feet. He brought a knee up hard between the man's legs, driving the breath out of him. Then he flung Reynolds backwards across the room. His legs connected with a low coffee table and he fell in an ungainly sprawl of arms, legs and splintered wood. He lay on his back, gasping for breath. Mulryan came forward and stood over him.

Reynolds drew back his lips in what amounted to a cross between a grin and a grimace.

'Perhaps . . . not quite . . . *so* rough,' he groaned.

Mulryan shook his head. He crouched down and put one knee against Reynolds' chest.

'Mr Reynolds, I don't know who you think I am. But I'm afraid you've made an unfortunate mistake.'

Reynolds' eyes narrowed. 'You're . . . you're not from the agency?'

'No, sir, I'm afraid not.'

'But you came up here . . . you knew my name . . . and I asked them to send a big man . . .' His eyes widened in horror. 'My God, you're not a policeman are you?'

Mulryan didn't answer that one.

'I came to ask you a few questions,' he said.

'Listen . . . this was . . . a joke! . . . yes, a practical joke, that's all. I mean, you don't think I really . . . Christ, I've a wife and kids back in England! I wouldn't want them to find out about this, they . . . they . . . they might get the wrong idea.'

Mulryan silenced him by putting a finger to the man's lips.

'I believe you arrived here Friday on a plane from Gatwick. Is that correct?'

Reynolds nodded, his eyes bulging.

'And you hired a car at the airport? A . . . Mitsubishi?'

'Yes. Surely the papers were in order? It was a reputable company, I always use them!'

'And you gave a lift to somebody, didn't you? A young English lad you met on the plane.'

Now Reynolds looked puzzled.

'No. I didn't meet anybody on the plane.'

Mulryan leaned closer. 'You sure, Mr Reynolds?'

'Absolutely! Oh, I'd never give lifts! You can't be too careful, can you? There are some weird people about.'

Mulryan smiled. He reached left handed behind his back and pulled out the knife. He lifted it up to Reynolds' face, gave him a good look at the jagged blade.

'Oh, you're right there, Mr Reynolds. Yes you are! But you see now, I have to be sure you're not lying to me. It could be that this man told you not to tell anyone about him. It could be you made some kind of deal with him.'

'No, no, I swear!' Reynolds couldn't take his eyes off the knife. His body was trembling under Mulryan's knee. 'I drove straight here, I didn't give a lift to anyone. All right, I have done in the past, I'll admit that, you know, young boys thumbing at the side of the road, that kind of thing. But this time there wasn't anybody, not a soul! I'd tell you if there was.'

'Yes,' said Mulryan quietly. 'I believe you would.' He got to his feet and slipped the knife back into its sheath. 'You've been very co-operative, thanks very much.'

Reynolds let out a long sigh of relief. He lay there, fighting to get his breathing back to normal.

'You're . . . you're not a policeman,' he observed.

'No,' said Mulryan.

For the first time, a flash of indignation appeared in Reynolds' eyes.

'Well, then, who the hell are you? What's the idea of coming up here and threatening me?'

Mulryan smiled. 'I wasn't threatening you.'

'Yes you were! My God, you just half killed me!' He rubbed the top of his wig ruefully. 'You could have broken my skull. I've a good mind to report this incident!'

Mulryan shrugged. He was thinking. He was wondering if Reynolds would tell anyone about this visit. A man with a battered face and a plaster-cast on his hand was just too easily recognized. Maybe Reynolds was a loose end he couldn't afford to leave untied. He reached out and helped Reynolds to his feet.

'It's just that they told me at the agency, you liked a bit of rough treatment. A bit of danger. I thought I'd come early, give you a surprise.'

Reynolds stared at him. 'Then you ... you *are* from the agency?'

Mulryan nodded. 'Yes. But I'm new there. You're my first client and I ... I'm afraid I've messed things up. You see, I thought I'd just do the kind of thing that *I* like myself.'

Reynolds was confused now. 'That's the kind of thing you like? Being terrorized?'

Mulryan nodded. 'I suppose I just assumed that you would too.' He spread his hands in a gesture of apology. 'I'm sorry, Mr Reynolds. I misjudged the situation. I'll understand if you don't want to see me again.'

'Well, let's not be in such a hurry ...' Reynolds took a step towards Mulryan, then winced as he registered the pain in his battered body. Now the adrenalin of fear had left him, he was becoming aware of his injuries.

'You all right?' Mulryan asked him.

'A bit sore, I'm afraid. You're . . . you're very strong, aren't you?'

'You told me to be rough.'

'Yes, I know . . .' He gave Mulryan a nervous look. 'But there's a limit, my friend. That business with the knife . . .'

'You don't like that?'

'I was terrified! I thought . . .'

Mulryan looked mortified. 'I think I'd better just go,' he said.

'No, wait! Hang on a minute . . . we . . . we could have a drink and we could talk about this . . . I mean, looking back at it, it *was* kind of exciting. But I think you've got to let people know what you're planning to do. It's all about make-believe, of course, but there's a very fine line between excitement and fear. Let's not be hasty. Perhaps if we talked, we could find a way to make it work.'

Mulryan smiled. 'That's very kind of you,' he said.

'Not at all!' Reynolds returned the smile, reassured by Mulryan's explanation. 'Well, look, I've got some wine in the fridge.'

Mulryan glanced quickly across the room. The fridge was a short distance away, about six feet from the open doors leading to the balcony.

'Wine is always welcome,' said Mulryan. 'Look, I'm sorry about this misunderstanding. Perhaps we could try again . . . and this time, you could tell me exactly what you want.'

Reynolds' smile broadened.

'Why not? You know, I *do* like you. The moment you stepped through the door, I liked what I saw. And I think your basic idea was a good one, I like to be physical, you know?'

'Some of my friends are like that,' said Mulryan. 'I've one friend who likes to be beaten with a leather belt.'

'Really? My goodness . . .' Reynolds reached up and settled his wig straighter on his head. 'I must look a sight for sore eyes,' he said. 'You know, these holidays, they're just a bit of fun. A way of letting my hair down. Back home, I work in an office and everything is so . . . so rigid. I don't know what my colleagues would say if they saw me dressed in this ridiculous outfit. They'd probably say I was some kind of . . . of deviant.'

'Not at all,' Mulryan assured him. 'I think you look very nice.'

Reynolds simpered. 'Yes . . . well . . . I'll get those drinks, shall I?' He turned and limped towards the fridge, still talking. 'I think what you shouldn't lose is that element of surprise. If we could just think of some way of making that work . . .'

Mulryan walked quickly up behind him and grabbed him around the waist.

'Ooh!' gasped Reynolds, excitedly.

Mulryan lifted him clear of the ground and walked towards the balcony. As he stepped through the doorway into the open sunlight, Reynolds got his first inkling of what was about to happen. He went rigid in the big man's arms.

'Oh no,' he whispered. 'You wouldn't . . .'

'Nothing personal,' Mulryan assured him, and threw him head first over the rail.

The skinny white body in bra and pants went hurtling downwards without a sound. Mulryan peered over the rail and noted with a sense of surprise, the blue outline of the swimming pool far below. He could see tiny figures splashing in the clear water. Reynolds was falling towards the pool and Mulryan quickly calculated his probability of survival. Even into the deep end, from a height of twenty-one stories, there seemed to be little hope. Reynolds must have spotted the water too. Now his dwindling figure appeared to be running in mid air, arms flailing as if in an attempt to propel him closer to it. The black wig detached itself from his head and went whirling off at a tangent, like something alive. Mulryan smiled, reminded of the antics of Wil E. Coyote in his favourite cartoon series. In the cartoon, the coyote always struck the ground in a puff of clean white dust . . .

Reynolds nearly made it. He struck the tiled edge of the pool horizontally, with an impact that was audible up on the balcony. His body snapped across the middle and bounced upwards, folding like a jack-knife, heels against the back of his head. He smashed down into the water and sank like a stone, trailing clouds of crimson into the turquoise. There were tiny screams from below as the bathers began to hurriedly vacate the pool.

Mulryan ducked back out of sight and went into the room. He took a handkerchief from his pocket and used it to open the door. He glanced each way along the corridor before letting himself out. He took the elevator down to the ground floor, noting that he made comparatively slow progress compared with Reynolds.

Rosie was waiting for him in the forecourt. She had the engine running as instructed, but Eddie seemed relaxed, unhurried. Away to the left, there was a commotion going on around the pool, people scrambling in all directions, children crying. Rosie could hear the wail of an ambulance siren off in the distance. Eddie climbed into the passenger seat and gave Rosie a peck on the cheek.

'What's goin' on?' she asked him suspiciously.

'Probably been an accident in the pool,' he told her. 'Anyway, we've been on a wild goose chase here. How d'yer fancy that trip to this Porto Wotsit?'

'When?' she asked delightedly.

He smiled. 'Why not now?'

'What, this minute?' She frowned. 'Eddie, I can't just up and leave. I'll have to pack a few things for the trip, do a bit of shopping and such.'

Eddie looked doubtful.

'I don't want to hang around too long,' he told her. 'I'm supposed to be meeting up with someone. A business associate.'

Rosie put a plump hand on his knee and regarded him from beneath lowered eyelashes.

'It's only early,' she reminded him. 'It's a short drive to Puerto Banus. I could pack up a few things and still get us there in good time. What difference can a few hours make, eh?'

Eddie swallowed with some difficulty. There was a

strange swirly feeling in the pit of his stomach.

'Oh, well . . . I suppose it can't hurt,' he admitted. 'Just a few hours, mind.'

'That's a good boy,' said Rosie. 'Too much rushing about is no use to anyone. Remember the hare and the tortoise! The hare went racing in and got into trouble, didn't he? But the old tortoise went plodding along and won the race in the end.'

Smiling, she removed her hand from his knee, put the car into gear and drove away. Down by the pool, women were screaming.

Chapter Twenty-Five

It's only a dream, Jack reminded himself, but that didn't help much. It was too vivid, too firmly entrenched in recent experience. *He was standing there at the top of the long flight of stone steps, gazing down into the dark fathoms of water, knowing that against all odds, McGiver wasn't finished, he was simply waiting beneath the surface, biding his time.*

And, sure enough, an instant later, the thin pock-marked face gliding eerily up out of the sea, a grin like a cold crescent moon on his waxy lips, his bony head split wide open like a water-melon, grey wrinkled matter oozing out of the crack as he lifted a finger and beckoned to Jack.

'Come on in,' he said. 'The water's lovely.'

And then, inevitably, as they always did in dreams, the steps crumbling, turning to powder beneath Jack's feet, precipitating him downwards towards the water's edge where McGiver waited to enfold him in his icy arms . . .

The trilling of the telephone rescued him not a moment

too soon. Jack flung out an arm and clumsily retrieved the hand-set from beside the bed, made a kind of grunting sound into the receiver.

'Señor Nolan?' The voice of the ever obsequious desk clerk cutting into his hazy thoughts. 'Señora Gorman is on the line for you.'

'Uh?' Jack shook his head, made an attempt to focus. He gazed around the still unfamiliar room, piecing it all together like a jigsaw puzzle. 'Uh, yeah. Put her through, will you?'

A pause: then the sound of Lisa's voice, soft, husky, effectively dispelling all thoughts of sleep.

'Hey there! Did I wake you?'

'Yes, but that's OK. I wasn't enjoying it.'

'Shame on you! It's after midday.'

'I had a restless night.'

'Poor baby. Sounds like I should have been there.'

'It might have helped . . .' Jack frowned. 'Should we be talking like this?'

'Relax. There's nobody else around. Tony's taking a swim, Angelito and Bill are out somewhere, wheeling and dealing. Actually, it was Bill asked me to give you a call, remind you about tonight.'

'Tonight?'

'Yes, we're all going up to the club, remember? Hey, you *did* have a rough night, didn't you?'

'You'll never know how rough,' he told her. He sat up now and threw back the sheets. Reaching for a bathrobe, he slipped it on and carried the phone across the room to the open doors of the patio. He stepped out into the glare of the sun, propped his elbows on the balustrade and squinted down to the hotel forecourt. Rows of shiny cars were lined up like toys on the hot black tarmac.

'About our little arrangement,' he heard her say. 'It looks like everything will come together the day after tomorrow. Think you can wait that long?'

'I guess so. My circumstances have changed considerably since last night. Some of the pressure's off.'

'Oh? You're being very mysterious.'

'I don't mean to be.'

'By the way, I overheard something this morning. It's two million dollars, not one.'

'That's nice. One each.' The conversation was starting to seem surreal so he changed the subject. 'What are you wearing?' he asked her.

'Huh?'

'You heard me. What are you wearing?'

'Oh, well let me see now. I have on a bathrobe . . .'

'Snap! What kind of bathrobe?'

'Silk.'

'Yeah? Mine's just plain old towelling. What's *under* the robe?'

'Nothing much – just me.'

Jesus. Thinking back to the other afternoon, the warmth of her naked body against his, the way she had moaned beneath him, her eyes squeezed shut, her hips arching . . . knowing now that he'd risk just about anything to experience that again. Two million dollars? Christ, he'd risk it for a buck and a half.

'What are your plans for the day?' she asked him.

'Number one, take a cold shower.'

She laughed at that. Down in the forecourt, a red Polo convertible turned in off the main road and pulled into a vacant slot. 'We'd better curtail this conversation,' she warned him. 'I don't know if I can stand too much of this.'

He grinned, turned away from the rail, sat down on a wooden recliner. He was aware that he was becoming hard under his bathrobe.

'Maybe you could come over, help me with that shower.'

'God, I wish I could. But I've some things to organize. *Fiscal* arrangements.' A pause. 'Look, I'd better go. We'll pick you up around seven.'

'There's no need. I have the jeep, I've barely had the chance to use it yet.'

'Oh, you'll get your chance, hotshot, the day after tomorrow. Besides, you're Tony's tame writer. Think he's going to miss the opportunity to show you off? Listen, I have to ask this. You aren't going to go soft on me are you?'

He slipped a hand beneath the folds of his bathrobe and smiled. 'No chance of that,' he said.

She caught the inference and seemed to become irritated.

'No, damn it, I'm serious! You won't back out at the last minute? If we go for this thing, it's all or nothing. It'll be too late to change your mind.'

He considered this for a moment. Ah, what the hell, he decided. He didn't have any other pressing engagements.

'Count me in.'

'That's what I hoped you'd say. See you tonight.'

She put down the phone and he followed suit. Jack reached for his cigarettes and lighter on the table top, lit one up, exhaled smoke.

So that's it, he decided. He was going through with it. Up until a moment ago, he'd had the chance to call the whole thing off. Now he was past the point of no return, he was in on the scam. God help him if it went wrong. What worried him more than anything was that the money didn't seem to matter so much. It was simply the icing on the cake. It was Lisa he wanted. He was sure of that now.

'Jesus,' he murmured. 'You poor bastard.'

He stubbed out the half-smoked cigarette and went in to take his shower.

Mulryan sat in the baking interior of the car, waiting for Rosie. He was aware of a dull throbbing ache in his injured hand and when he lifted the plaster-cast to his nose and sniffed, there was a bad, sickly sweet odour coming from it. He remembered McGiver's warning about having the hand reset before he left England, about how the doctors in Spain were all butchers. He shrugged away the thought. Get this business sorted out and have the hand looked at when he was back home. A few more days wouldn't hurt.

Rosie came out of the hotel entrance, a puzzled expression on her face. She walked across to the car, opened the door and slid into the driver's seat.

'Well?' Eddie prompted her.

'Said they'd never heard of no Tam McGiver. No hrecord of him ever having checked in there. No messages left for you either.'

Eddie frowned.

'Doesn't make sense,' he protested. 'He told me he was going to be here. Unless there's another Hotel Excelsior somewhere around?'

She shook her head.

'This is the only one. Swankiest bloomin' place on the Costa.'

'What about the other feller? This Nolan character?'

'Oh, *he's* there. Been stayin' near on a week.'

Eddie removed his straw fedora and scratched thoughtfully at his head.

'I don't get it,' he confessed. 'McGiver was going to stay with Nolan until I got here. He said whatever happened, I'd find him here . . .'

'Maybe that was before he found out how much it costs,' suggested Rosie. 'Be an arm and a leg for a room in that joint.'

'Wouldn't make any difference. He was on expenses. No, there must have been some other reason why he didn't check in . . . maybe he figured it wasn't *safe*.'

'Safe?' Rosie was intrigued. 'Look, what's going on? You don't give much away, do you? All I know is you're lookin' for some bloke that broke your hand. But there must be more to it than that.'

'The less you know, the better,' he told her.

'It's not like . . . well, I know it sounds daft, but you're not like a secret agent or something?'

He smiled good naturedly.

'That kind of thing,' he said. 'So you'll appreciate I can't tell you very much, can I?'

She seemed satisfied with this explanation.

'So what do we do now, Eddie? Check into this place?'

Eddie shook his head.

'No, I don't think so. We'd best find somewhere close by. Somewhere smaller. Get ourselves settled in and hope that McGiver contacts us. I suppose another day or so can't make too much difference.'

'You're the boss,' said Rosie cheerfully. She started up the engine and drove out towards the exit. 'We passed a nice little place just up the coast road,' she told him.

He nodded, sat there cradling his aching hand in his lap. Despite his air of indifference he was worried. What had happened to McGiver? Had he got information from Nolan and headed off in pursuit of Doyle without leaving a message? Had he gone back on his oath? He'd better not have or it wouldn't just be Doyle that Eddie had to settle up with.

Still, for the moment he'd have to give the Scotsman the benefit of the doubt. Spend a day or so scouring the area for him, give him the opportunity to get in touch, if he needed to. And if nothing happened on that score, then Eddie would return to the hotel and have a quiet word with Nolan.

Maybe *he'd* be able to clear the whole thing up.

The boy stalked slowly along the beach with his bucket

and net, hunting for crabs. He was nine years old and bored. His parents were lying further up the beach, their plump bodies glistening beneath a covering of suntan oil. His younger sister was concentrating her energies on making the mother of all sandcastles, down by the shoreline. She had told him in no uncertain terms that crabs were gross and she had no intention of helping him. What was he going to do with them anyway, eat them? Yuck!

He'd patiently tried to explain to her that wasn't the point. You caught them, kept them in a bucket for a while, then let them go all at once, watching them skitter madly back towards the sea. Besides, he'd added, that wonderful sandcastle she was building would soon be washed away . . . but you couldn't tell her anything, so he'd set off on his hunt alone.

He arrived at a place where a flat ridge of smooth white rock angled down into the water, pitted here and there with a series of large, water-filled holes.

He moved to the nearest hollow and gazed down into the crystal clear water. He was encouraged by what he saw. There were no crabs in this one, but there were all manner of other things in there; shrimps, gloopy slug-like creatures, barnacles, even some tiny fish. He lowered his net carefully into the water and swept the largest of the fish into it. It flapped and struggled furiously as he eased it out into the fresh air, upended the net and dropped his catch into his bucket.

He stood up and turned to approach the next pool, much bigger than the first. He froze in amazed delight, hardly daring to believe what he saw. There were several good sized crabs crouched on a rock sticking up out of the water. The biggest of them was the size of a man's hand. Its claws were moving up and down in a brisk, rhythmic motion, making a dry clicking sound. The boy pictured himself carrying the crab back to show his father. Even *he* would be impressed. But first, of course, he had to catch it . . .

Snickety snack, snickety snack.

The crab's claws seemed to be tapping out an urgent morse code. The boy wondered if it was signalling to its smaller brethren. Perhaps this one was their leader and was issuing the day's orders. Crouching down, the boy began to approach the pool, setting down his flip-flops with great care, the net held out in front of him. He had already learned that crabs could be startled by quick movements. As if to emphasize the point, one of the smaller crabs slid off the white rock and into the water with an abrupt plop. But the big one seemed to take no notice, claws rising and falling, rising and falling.

Snickety snack, snickety snack.

The boy realized now that the crab wasn't communicating with the others. It was simply eating. They all were, but you couldn't hear the claws of the smaller crabs over the noise the big one was making.

Now the boy was at the very edge of the pool. He sank slowly to his bare knees, intent only on his target. A second smaller crab skittered off the smooth white rock into the pool but the boy didn't panic. He steadied his grip on the bamboo shaft of his net and began to inch it out across the intervening gap to his target. The big crab altered its position slightly but its pincers kept right on picking away at what it was eating.

Snickety snack, snickety snack.

The boy steadied himself, drew a breath. To achieve success, he needed to make a quick sideways sweep of the net, get the lip of it under the crab's body and flip it over backwards into the mesh. He'd get only one chance.

Snickety snack, snick—

The crab seemed to sense the boy's intentions. Its claws stopped suddenly, holding a lump of something red and rubbery inches away from its mouthparts.

NOW! The boy made his swing, arcing the net sideways across the still surface of the water, scraping the lip across the top of the rock which oddly didn't make a rock like sound, but there was no time to think about that now, because the crab was flipping over into the net, its pink legs pedalling frantically at the air as the green mesh enveloped it. The other crabs were dropping into the water as the boy lifted the net triumphantly into the air and for the first time he got a clear glimpse of the rock itself, only (*Mummy!*) it wasn't a rock at all, it was a thin white face staring up out of the water, (*No!*) not staring exactly because the eyes were pretty much gone, just ragged, tattered blobs of chewed matter where the crabs had been eating, (*Sick, feel sick!*) and the man's mouth wide open, teeth missing and a last crab, a tiny spider-like fellow skittering out from between the blue lips. (*No, no, no, no, no!*)

The boy was only dimly aware of warm urine pulsing

down his legs as he turned, dropped the net and ran frantically back in the direction of his parents, screaming at the top of his lungs.

On the rock, the big crab patiently disentangled itself from the net and began to march determinedly back towards the pool to resume its interrupted meal.

Chapter Twenty-Six

At seven P.M. sharp the limousine pulled up outside the Excelsior and Jack, who had been waiting in the reception area, walked out to it. Glancing in at the window, he saw that everybody was dressed in their best clothes and he was glad he opted to wear a suit. Angelito was at the wheel, sporting a white seventies-style three piece and a red satin shirt worn open necked to display a glitzy gold medallion. Bill Farnell sat beside him wearing a more sober outfit in blue silk. In the back seat, Tony Gorman wore a black Armani that must have set him back around a thousand quid and Lisa had on a chic clinging mini in bottle green crushed velvet. The daringly cut neck-line made Jack want to stare in undisguised admiration.

'Come on, son, shake a leg!' Gorman urged him. 'We're missing good drinking time 'ere!' He indicated an empty space beside Lisa and Jack climbed obligingly in. He was uncomfortably aware of Lisa's bare thigh hot against his and was terrified that his lust would be visible on his face; but Lisa was evidently astute at hiding her emotions. She had reverted to the familiar shades and bored expression and she kept her gaze fixed on the road ahead as the car moved out of the forecourt and on to the highway.

'Bit cramped in here,' observed Gorman. He indicated the bruise on Jack's forehead. 'You look like you've been in the wars again.'

'Bashed it on a cupboard door,' Jack told him.

'Christ, you're a bit accident prone aren't you? We'll 'ave to book you in to a padded cell.' He turned to face Lisa. 'By the way, I forgot to ask, 'ow was yer shoppin' trip?'

She scowled. 'Dreadful. I couldn't find anything I wanted!'

Gorman glanced at Jack and raised his hands in a gesture of helplessness. 'What d'yer do wiv 'em, eh Frankie? This one's got more plastic in her wallet than ICI an' she still can't find anything she wants to buy. I tell you what, I reckon the more dosh you've got, the 'arder it is to spend it.'

Lisa sneered. 'It would be nice to go shopping on my own, once in a while.'

'No, we tried that, remember? Found you pissed out of yer 'ead in some dive on the waterfront.'

'It wasn't a dive,' muttered Lisa. 'And I was only "pissed" in the American sense of the word.'

Gorman ignored her. He glanced apologetically at Jack.

'Must 'ave been a right bore for you, Frankie.'

'No, not at all. Gave me a chance to get the feel of

the place. Soak up a little atmosphere.' Jack noticed that Angelito was appraising him suspiciously in the rear-view mirror and he made an effort to change the subject. 'So, Tony . . . tell me all about the club.'

'Not much to tell,' Gorman leaned back in his seat and lit up a Marlboro. 'Been open now about two years. I thought it'd be nice to 'ave a place I could go any time, a little home from home. But since it was gonna 'ave my name on it, I figured it 'ad to be the best. We spent a fortune on it . . . Bill, 'ow much did we spend?'

Farnell half turned in his seat.

'Around two million dollars, I guess.'

'Yeah!' Gorman seemed pleased with the figure. He said it again, slowly, as though relishing the sound of it. 'Two . . . million . . . dollars. Bill would come to me and suggest cuttin' corners here and there and I'd say, "No, TONY'S 'as gotta be special!" So we didn't stint on nothin'.'

'And the place makes a profit?' asked Jack.

Gorman seemed unsure on this point. He glanced at Farnell.

'We're about approaching the break-even point. After all, it was a sizable investment. And you can't expect . . .'

'Mind you,' interrupted Gorman. 'We only cater for the jet-set. They've all been there, you know, all the *celebs*. And of course, people like that don't pay, do they? It's free publicity ennit? Lemme see now, we've 'ad the Rolling Stones in . . .'

Lisa looked at her husband scornfully.

'Bill Wyman called in once,' she corrected him. 'He

stayed ten minutes and that was only to ask directions to somewhere else . . .'

'So, it still counts! And er . . . lemme see . . . Rod Stewart, Elton John . . . Shakin' Stevens . . .'

'Jeanette McDonald and Nelson Eddy,' prompted Lisa.

Gorman gave her a look of disgust. 'All the big stars,' he persisted. 'And all wanting to be photographed with yours truly. Shakin' 'ands with the man who broke the biggest bank in England! Anyway, you'll see for yourself soon enough. It ain't far now.'

Darkness had fallen. The limo's headlights played on the oily black surface of the road. Streams of insects came whirling out of the night, to splatter their fragile bodies against the windscreen.

'Mr Martinez coming tonight?' asked Jack. He wasn't particularly interested, just felt obliged to keep the conversation going.

'Oh, he's meeting us there. Old Raul wouldn't miss the chance of a party, would he, Bill? By the way, Angel, did you fix up that little thing he asked about?'

Angelito nodded. All taken care of, boss.'

Lisa laughed. 'How touching. Raul's escort for the evening! Don't tell me, let me guess. It wouldn't be Fiona by any chance. She of the cocaine complexion and the unsanitary sexual habits? Wouldn't you think he'd be ready for a change by now?'

'Raul knows what he likes,' said Gorman. 'Who am I to argue?'

'Yes, but everybody needs a little variety now and

then . . . and there's so many willing ladies just there for the asking! I know, why don't you fix him up with that hot-assed little slut that's always hanging around the club?'

'Who's that?' asked Gorman suspiciously.

'Oh, what's her name? You know . . .' She waved her hands, feigning a poor memory. 'Oh yes, of course. Josie!'

Jack saw Gorman's face register a sudden rage, saw his right hand lift instinctively to strike Lisa. He tensed, knowing that if Gorman *did* hit her, he would be compelled to leap to her defence. But then the moment passed. Gorman's face relaxed and he let his hand fall to his side.

'Oh, you're a bundle of laughs tonight, ain't 'cha?' he said quietly.

'I try to lift the spirits,' she told him.

Gorman raised his eyebrows at Jack.

'What would you do with a woman like this, eh Frankie?'

For an instant, Jack experienced a vivid flashback. He lying naked on the bed, Lisa astride him, her head thrown back, her eyes squeezed shut as a violent orgasm shook her body. He made an effort to shrug off the recollection.

'I'd rather not get involved,' he said.

'But you *are* involved, aren't you?'

Jack sensed, rather than felt, Lisa flinch beside him. He turned to look steadily at Gorman.

'How do you mean?' he asked.

'Well, this book you're writing. It means you become

a part of it all, doesn't it? Almost like one of the family.'

Jack shrugged. 'I hadn't thought about it like that,' he said.

'Well, you *should* think about it. I must say we're all dying to see this first chapter you're putting together. When d'you reckon it'll be ready?'

'Soon,' said Jack.

A huge neon sign came into view on the right hand side of the road. Nestled amidst clumps of date palms, the word TONY'S was spelled out in loopy letters of electric blue light. Angelito turned in off the main road. The club, a long, low building of pink stucco was set a short distance back from the road, at the end of a short driveway. There was an illuminated door with a striped canvas awning over it. A couple of impassive bouncers, sweating in black tuxedos, stood at either side of the entrance. As Angelito drew the limousine to a halt, they moved down the short flight of steps to the car and opened the doors. Everyone got out and one of the goons took Angelito's place at the wheel, drove the car into a large parking lot that was already packed with expensive automobiles.

Gorman took Lisa's arm and drew her off to one side. He said something to her that Jack didn't catch, but judging by the stern expression on his face, he wasn't giving her a compliment. She shook his arm off and walked towards the entrance. Gorman nodded to the bouncer, a thick-set man with close-cropped hair and a nose that seemed to have been flattened to his face by years of fighting.

'Evenin', Bob. Good crowd in tonight?'

'Yes, Mr Gorman. Packed out.'

Gorman seemed pleased by this news. He followed Lisa towards the doors and the others fell into step. They went in at the entrance and Jack found himself in a plush foyer. There was burgundy carpet running from wall to wall and a long marble counter where a female cloak-room attendant in a skimpy outfit looked decidedly under-employed. A profusion of fake potted plants were arranged around the room and one wall was covered by a huge glass frame containing literally hundreds of photographs, all depicting Tony Gorman posing with various celebrities; pop stars, sporting personalities, Page Three girls. Jack noted that Gorman seemed to have the same expression in every picture, an inane grin; but his gradually expanding waistline and ballooning cheeks suggested that the pictures spanned some twenty years.

Here was a black and white shot of Gorman with Henry Cooper, taken in a London pub setting, the two of them looking slim and sartorial in their seventies-style suits. Gorman was miming a punch against Henry's chin and making a thumbs-up gesture with his free hand. Here was a threesome, a rare shot of Gorman and Lisa together, which must have dated from around the time of their marriage, Gorman still looking slim and hand-some in a rough sort of way, Lisa smiling adoringly up at him; but Jack noticed that Gorman had his arm around the third person in the shot, Lionel Blair and already he seemed barely aware of his wife's presence. And here was a recent picture, Gorman's latest incarnation, tubby, balding but still grinning for all he was worth as he clung on to the arm of Rod Stewart, the latter looking distinctly bored by the proceedings, as though wondering how best to extricate himself.

Jack became aware of a presence at his shoulder.

'What d'yer think?' asked Gorman, proudly.

'Pretty impressive. You know some famous people.'

Gorman shook his head. 'No, sunshine! Some famous people know *me*!'

He turned and led the way through a set of swing doors into the main lounge of the club. Music blared from a stage at the top end of it, a cheesy disco-cabaret band, currently churning out a lukewarm version of Abba's *Dancing Queen*. A couple of female singers sporting loose perms and glittery black jumpsuits were wriggling frantically as they sang, as though trying to rid themselves of some exotic species of insect that had crawled into their knickers. On a sizable dancefloor in front of the stage, several middle-aged couples were going through a startling series of contortions, waving their arms, shaking their buttocks, but in a controlled way, as though trying to avoid breaking sweat. Above them, a giant mirror ball peppered them with flecks of light.

Everyone seemed to be enjoying themselves but it struck Jack that he had just stepped back some twenty years in time. He watched amused as Angelito strode over to a couple of unaccompanied women on the floor and went into an uninhibited impersonation of John Travolta in *Saturday Night Fever*, right down the gesticulating hands and thrusting groin. In seconds, he had a gaggle of female admirers around him, all clapping their hands and urging him on.

'Look at Angel go!' Gorman shouted into Jack's ear. 'I wish I could move like that. They love him 'ere, they absolutely adore him!'

'He's ... quite a mover,' admitted Jack, fighting a powerful urge to laugh.

'That boy's like a son to me,' said Gorman, with uncharacteristic frankness. 'I'd trust him with my life.'

Jack stared at Gorman, wondering if he could be serious. Angelito had attributes, Jack supposed, but he wouldn't have listed loyalty as one of them.

Jack turned away to survey the rest of the club. The bar was a circular construction, all marble and mahogany, adorned with an incongruous collection of Brit paraphernalia – road signs, Union Jacks, Toby jugs, photographs of the Queen – Jack thought he had never seen anything quite so hideous. There was a crowd gathered around it and heads had turned to look at Gorman and his entourage, hands were going up in acknowledgement to the club's owner.

One face in particular jumped out at Jack, partly because it was the only black face in the club, but mostly because it was staring at him with an expression of sheer disbelief. For an instant, Jack was bewildered, unused to seeing this face anywhere other than the grey streets of Soho. Then he recognized Leo King and saw that he was lifting a hand to wave.

''Scuse me a moment, Tony,' he said. He crossed the room quickly before Leo had a chance to shout out to him. He grabbed Leo's hand and pumped it vigorously up and down.

'Leo, what the fuck are you doing here?'

'I could ask you the same question!' Leo's nasal Liverpudlian drawl was the same as ever. 'Bloody 'ell, Jack, I thought you—'

'Not Jack! My name's Frank, Frank Nolan, all right?'

Leo stared at him for a moment. 'What yer talkin' about?' he demanded.

'Listen to me! You call me by my real name and I'm dead! Frank Nolan. Say it. Say, "hello Frank!" '

Leo grinned, shook his head.

'Whatever you say . . . Frank.' Leo glanced over Jack's shoulder. ''Ere, isn't that Tony Gorman, you're with?'

'Yes. Listen, Leo, I'm a writer, OK? I'm here to ghost-write Gorman's autobiography. You know me as a writer . . .'

'Do I?' Leo reached up a hand and scratched his head. 'Sorry mate, this is all goin' a bit fast for me . . . I mean, I didn't know it was that easy to become a writer.'

'It's not. I've been one for years.'

'Christ, Jack, what the fuck have you got yourself mixed up in this time?'

'Never mind, you just have to—'

'Hey, Tony's comin' over!'

'Shit! Let me do the talking!'

'But, Jack . . .'

'Frank! For Christ's sake, get it right!'

Gorman appeared at Jack's shoulder, a curious smile on his face. Jack turned to meet him, grinning furiously.

'Tony! Let me introduce you to an old friend of mine from the smoke. Leo King. Tony Gorman.' The two men shook hands. 'Leo's from my neck of the woods, back home. I never thought I'd run into him here of all places!'

Leo smiled feebly. 'It's an honour, Mr Gorman,' he said. 'You've always been an 'ero of mine.'

Gorman brightened. 'Yeah? Are you a writer too?'

'Me? Oh no, I'm er ... I'm in the entertainment business.'

'Oh really? What brings you down 'ere then?'

Leo glanced uncertainly at Jack.

'Actually, I came down to see a bloke about some films.'

'Wot, you a director or something?'

'Er ... no, more of a distributor, really.'

Gorman looked impressed. 'Maybe I've seen one of your films?' he ventured. 'What's been one of your more successful ones?'

Leo thought for a moment. 'Well ... *Animal Farm's* been a big seller this season.'

'*Animal Farm*? That's a kiddie's film, isn't it?'

'Not my version,' Leo assured him. 'There's this woman right and she goes to a farm for 'er 'olidays—'

'Tony and I plan to make a film!' interrupted Jack. 'Isn't that right, Tony?'

'Not 'alf! Frank 'ere's got contacts at all the big film studios ... but I expect you know that already.'

'Yeah, he's er ... a man of many talents, our ... our *Frank*.'

Gorman smiled. 'Well, I'll leave you lads to chew over

old times. I'm dyin' for a drink. When yer ready, we'll be over in the VIP lounge ... see the glass doors over there?' He shook Leo's hand warmly. 'You take care now,' he said. He turned and moved away through the crowd, shaking hands with various people as he went.

'Christ,' said Leo. 'Tony friggin' Gorman.'

Jack slapped him on the shoulder. 'You laid it on a bit thick didn't you?' He mimicked Leo's nasal drawl. ' "You've always been an 'ero of mine, Mr Gorman!" '

Leo looked affronted.

'That was on the level actually! Listen, that bloke pulled off one of the biggest capers in history and got clean away with it, which makes him OK in my book. And you're in there pullin' his dick! I 'ope you know what you're doin' pal. What's all this crap about bein' a writer?'

'It's too complicated, Leo. Anyway, the less you know about it, the better. So, you're over here buying porno videos, is that it?'

Leo nodded. 'Bloke in Torremolinos offered me some locally-made vids. Very good rates and better quality than the Scandinavian stuff. So I've been over at his place checkin' 'em out. Afterwards, he offered to take me for a few drinks at the best club for miles. This is it.' He glanced glumly around for a few moments. 'Bit like an up-market Darby and Joan club, isn't it?'

Jack grinned. *Same old Leo*, he thought.

'Where's the bloke you came with?'

'God knows. He met some leggy tart in 'ere from one of his films. Dead friendly, the two of 'em. Five minutes later, he's givin' her an emergency tonsillectomy, if you know what I mean. Anyway, he said he was drivin' her home and he'd be back later. Probably dippin 'is wick, even as we speak. I expect it's the last I'll see of him tonight.'

'Well, let's get a couple of drinks, shall we?' Jack led the way to a gap at the bar and pulled out Frank's wallet. 'What'll you have?'

'Whisky and dry.' Leo raised his eyebrows at the evident wealth crammed in the wallet. 'You seem to be doin' very well for yerself all of a sudden,' he observed.

'Yeah, things are looking up.' Jack caught the attention of a barman and ordered the drinks, a coke for himself. Leo raised his eyebrows. 'Don't ask,' Jack warned him.

Leo cleared his throat. 'You know, I seem to remember a little matter of three hundred quid, lent to you for a certain card game.'

'I thought we wrote that off to experience.'

'Yeah, but you've obviously come up in the world, since then.'

'OK, no problem.'

'Plus interest?'

Jack glared at Leo. 'How much interest?'

Leo smiled, shrugged. 'Well, what say we call it five hundred?'

Jack scowled.

'Jesus, Leo, that's a bit steep isn't it?'

'Not really. Not when you consider I've just lied me guts out on your be'alf. And anyway, it's not as steep as Lou Winters' rates, is it? Actually, I've got a little bit of news concernin' our Lou. I think you'll be very interested to hear it.'

The drinks arrived and Jack paid with a five thousand peseta note. 'Keep the change,' he told the barman.

'Bloody hell, you *'ave* come up in the world, 'aven't ya?'

'So it would seem. What's this news about Lou Winters?'

'Cross me palm with silver an' I might tell ya!'

Jack sighed. He opened the compartment in the wallet where the big notes were stored and extracted the equivalent of five hundred pounds. He pressed the notes into Leo's hand.

'That should about cover it,' he observed. 'Now, Lou Winters . . .?'

'Doesn' exist,' finished Leo. 'He is, as the poets say, no more.'

'He's . . . he's dead?'

Leo nodded. 'There was a big fire up at his place. Him and his old lady, both burned to a crisp. Bad luck for them, but a great big slice of good luck for you. He isn't goin' to be collectin' on that debt after all. And then I 'eard, you stuffed yerself twice by borrowin' off The Armenian. So now you've got Tam McGiver to worry about.'

Jack shook his head.

'That's taken care of,' he assured him.

''Ow do you mean?'

'I er . . . paid him off.'

Leo looked impressed. 'When did this happen?' he asked.

'Just last night. He met up with me here and I gave him what I owed him and a bit more for his trouble. He said we could call it quits.'

'Well, it sounds like you can go 'ome whenever you want. I mean, Spain's all right for a visit, but you wouldn't wanna live 'ere, would ya?'

Jack sipped his coke contemplatively. 'What about Eddie Mulryan?' he asked.

'Now, there's a funny thing! Eddie's done a bunk. Nobody's seen 'ide nor 'air of 'im for over a week. The word is that there was somethin' suspicious about that fire and our Eddie might just 'ave some information about it.'

Jack nodded.

'You think he came after me?'

'Not necessarily. He could be anywhere.'

'I'm not so sure. I don't think he's the sort that gives up easily, whether Lou Winters is there to give him orders or not.'

'So if he turns up, you can pay him off as well.'

'I doubt it, Leo. Something tells me that Eddie Mulryan never took a bribe in his life. I figure I'll be moving on from here pretty soon. I've just got a couple of loose ends to tie up first.'

'Well, good luck to yer, mate. I don't know what's going on with you right now and frankly, I don't think I *want* to. But I tell you what I wouldn't mind. Tony Gorman's autograph. Now, where's that VIP lounge?' asked Leo, straightening his tie.

'Never mind that. You've got a pressing appointment, mate.'

''Ave I?'

'I'm afraid so. I can't afford to have you hanging around, Leo. You might say something without thinking. I mean, you wouldn't like to land me in the shit, would you?'

Leo seemed to be considering it.

Jack sighed. He took another of the big notes from his wallet and pushed it into Leo's top pocket. 'Why don't you go to a better club?' he suggested. 'I understand there are some very nice places just down the road.'

Leo smiled. 'You know, I could learn to love this new you. Look me up when you get back to the smoke. We'll 'ave a drink and show each other our holiday snaps. You er ... will be *coming* back, I suppose?'

'Maybe, maybe not. Tell you the truth, I've got this idea about going to a tropical island. Somewhere nice and quiet.'

Leo grinned, shook his head. He turned and disappeared into the crowd. Jack felt slightly wistful that he had to push Leo out. Once he'd got over the shock, it had been good having a familiar face around. He picked up his drink, moved away from the bar, skirted the dance-floor and made his way across to the VIP lounge.

The glass doors swished open, then slid shut behind him and the relentless din of the band was instantly reduced to a polite background noise. The lounge was furnished with soft leather sofas and low onyx tables. Venetian blinds on the glass windows ensured that people residing here wouldn't even have to look at the lesser mortals outside. A couple of white jacketed waiters prowled around on rubber soled shoes ready to take orders. Air conditioning purred.

Jack found Lisa sitting alone nursing a vodka Martini. He dropped down on the sofa beside her and gave her a quizzical look. 'Where is everybody?' he asked.

She nodded to the top end of the lounge, where Gorman, Farnell and Raul Martinez were sitting at another table with two women. Angelito was presumably still strutting his stuff on the dance-floor. One woman was tall and skinny as a beanpole. She had permed blonde hair and she was leaning against Martinez, laughing shrilly at some remark he was making. This, Jack decided, was Fiona. Next to her, across the table from Gorman, sat a pretty young Spanish girl with olive skin and straight black hair which hung to her shoulders. She must have been all of sixteen years old. Jack noticed how she kept glancing across at Lisa, a self-possessed smile on her lips, as though defying the older woman to say something.

'Josie, I presume,' murmured Jack.

Lisa nodded. 'Subtlety never was one of Tony's attributes,' she said. 'Don't worry, I'm used to it.'

Jack wished he could put his arm around her.

'Do you hate her?' he asked.

'Christ, no, I feel sorry for the poor bitch. She doesn't know what she's letting herself in for.' She sipped at her drink. 'Of course, it's just the final piece in Tony's self-protection scheme. He figured it worked for Ronald Biggs, so it'll work for him.' She shot a surreptitious glance at Jack. 'God, I'd like to go to bed with you, right now,' she whispered. 'I'm getting wet, just thinking.'

'Don't,' said Jack. 'For God's sake, Lisa, don't even talk about it.'

'Making you hard, am I?'

He closed his eyes for a moment, took a deep breath.

'Change the subject,' he pleaded.

'OK. Who was the guy you were talking to at the bar?'

'An old friend from London. He had to move on again. Listen, Lisa, I don't know how much longer I can hang around here . . . there's a guy from England and I've got a terrible feeling he's out here looking for me. It's possible he's still in Malaga, but then again, he's a smart cookie. He could be anywhere . . .'

She glanced at him sharply.

'I thought the pressure was off now?'

'I thought it was. Suddenly, I'm not so sure.'

'But you're a respectable writer, aren't you? Who would be looking for you?'

'It's complicated. Just take my word for it, I daren't waste any more time.'

She considered this for a moment.

'You won't have to,' she assured him. 'Bill's picking up Raul's money tomorrow. He'll put it in the safe at home. I figure I can make the switch tomorrow evening and be ready to leave late at night. All you'll have to do is drive over in the jeep and pick me up. With everyone asleep it'll give us a few hours start.'

'Sounds deceptively easy,' he said. 'How will you get into the safe?'

'Piece of cake. I know the combination. Tony doesn't realize I know it. Idiot has it written down on a slip of paper which he keeps taped to the bottom of a drawer in his desk. I memorized it months ago.'

'So you've been planning this for a long time? But you couldn't do it on your own.'

'Don't get sensitive on me. Let's just say I've been keeping my options open.' She closed her eyes for a moment, took another gulp at her drink. 'Trouble is, I can't think straight. I've got the cat scratch fever. You know what that is?'

He swallowed with difficulty. 'Uh huh,' he said. 'I've got it too. I wish there was some way we could . . .'

'Maybe there is. When Tony comes back to the table, tell him you'd like to take a look at *The Duchess*. Research and all that. He'll be entertaining Martinez at the house tomorrow, all the guys sitting around, drinking, telling dumb stories. He won't want to be bothered with it. But he hates having me around the place when they're all getting bombed, so maybe . . . just maybe, he'll assign me to show you around.'

Jack frowned. 'Jesus, I don't know, Lisa. It sounds risky. There'll be plenty of time for that once we're away from here.'

'I won't last that long! I swear, I'll explode first. Tell me you'll ask him or I promise you, I'll pull your pants down and fuck you right here, in front of all of them!'

'I'll ask,' said Jack, quickly.

The swing doors opened and Angelito came in, carrying a glass of something tall and non-alcoholic. He surveyed Jack and Lisa for a moment and then raised his eyebrows in an exaggerated manner. He came over and perched himself on the arm of the sofa, next to Lisa. Jack noticed that he looked immaculate, not a hair out of place, not a bead of sweat on his brow.

'Eh, I hope I'm not interrupting nothing,' he said. 'Only you two look like you're having a real deep conversation.'

'Yes,' agreed Lisa. 'We were just saying what a bozo you look on the dance-floor.'

Angelito showed his perfect teeth in a sneer.

'Maybe I should give *you* some dancing lessons,' he told her. 'You know, the lying down type.' He stared challengingly at Jack. 'Or maybe you found a new partner.'

Jack returned the stare. 'You know, I'm getting a little tired of your insinuations,' he said.

'That a fact?' Angelito leaned closer, keeping his voice quiet, confidential. 'Listen, I ain't stupid, you know? I can see what's going on even if Señor Gorman can't. Right now, you're his blue-eyed boy. But a word from me and he'd see things a whole lot different.'

Lisa smiled sweetly at him. 'Well now, Angelito, you're hardly in a position to say anything, are you? I could just tell him how you took advantage of me that time. How you forced me to have sex with you.'

Angelito chuckled. 'Think he'd believe you? He knows what you are, lady. He's got your number. Once a tramp, always a tramp, that's what he'd think. And if it comes to choosing between your word and mine, he—'

Angelito broke off in disbelief. Lisa had just upended the remains of her Martini into his lap. A dark stain was spreading across the crotch of his white trousers. He jumped to his feet spilling his own drink in the process. He grabbed a serviette from the table and started mopping ineffectually at the stain, his face white with anger.

'Clumsy me,' said Lisa.

'You did it on purpose, you bitch!' Angelito glared first at Lisa, then at Jack. 'You haven't heard the last of this,' he whispered.

'Oh, go and have another dance,' Lisa told him. 'I guarantee that every eye in the place will be on your crotch. That's what you like, isn't it?'

Angelito was about to say something else, but Gorman's voice called from across the room.

'Bloody hell, Angel, aren't you a bit old for that kind of thing?' Gorman's companions laughed at the poor joke. Angelito grinned desperately around the anger that was stuck in his throat.

'Little accident, boss,' he mumbled.

'Christ, must 'ave been the excitement!' More laughter, with which Angelito was obliged to join in. It didn't look very convincing, Jack thought. Angelito stumbled towards the exit, still mopping furiously. He paused at the door and looked back at Jack and Lisa. Jack could see the naked hatred in his eyes and he realized that Lisa had been too impetuous. Angelito would want revenge for this and he might not be too fussy about how he took it. He went out through the swing doors and the noise of the music blossomed briefly, before being abruptly cut off.

'Asshole,' murmured Lisa. She was smiling now, looking pleased with herself, but Jack was worried. Suddenly, tomorrow evening seemed a very long way off.

'Hey, Frankie boy, what you doin' there? Come on over, there's a couple of people want to meet you.'

Jack glanced apologetically at Lisa.

'Go,' she said beneath her breath. 'Butter them up. And remember, *The Duchess* . . .'

'Yeah,' muttered Jack. 'Right.'

He got to his feet and walked across the lounge as though he had all the time in the world.

Chapter Twenty-Seven

Jack lay on his back on the bed and watched calmly as Lisa lowered herself astride him. She never took her eyes from his face as she sank slowly on to the shaft of his cock, her wet warmth slowly closing around him.

He noticed that she had a tiny red birthmark on her left shoulder and he wondered how they had managed to conceal it from the cameras in her modelling days. He opened his mouth to speak but she touched the tips of her fingers to his lips, silencing him.

She began to move her hips in a slow, steady rhythm, concentrating hard. Beneath them the bed seemed to sway and dip as the yacht rode at anchor. A low moan escaped her and she quickened her rhythm slightly, her eyes closed now in rapt concentration. A light sweat already flecked her brow. Jack watched the motion of her breasts, bouncing enticingly as she got into her stride, lost to the rhythm and the search for the orgasm that she desired. He began to rise upwards to meet her thrusts, slamming his hardness into her, sensing that he too was close to coming.

The door behind her opened, framing a dark shape for an instant; a big, thick-set figure, the outline of a wide-brimmed hat. Then the door clicked shut again. Jack stared over Lisa's moving shoulders. Eddie Mulryan walked slowly towards the bed, smiling his sweet smile. He gave Jack a playful wink.

Jack opened his mouth to shout a warning, but again, Lisa put her fingers to his lips. He shook his head, tried to push her away from him but she was blind to everything but her own pleasure. Her buttocks slapped frenziedly against his stomach but fear was quickly killing his erection. He felt it dying inside her. Mulryan was standing directly behind her. He reached out his injured hand and took hold of Lisa's hair in his fingertips. She laughed, tilted back her head to offer a better grip. Jack tried to twist free but her weight kept him pinned to the bed. Now Mulryan's other hand moved into view. It held a knife, a big, broad-bladed knife that glittered dully in the gloom. Mulryan saw Jack staring and his grin widened, showing the dark gaps between his pink gums and his false teeth.

Jack tried to speak but now Lisa was cramming her whole hand over his mouth. She was laughing gleefully, like a child riding a merry-go-round.

Mulryan pulled the blade across her throat and the skin parted like processed cheese, a crescent-shaped opening in her neck widening to mirror Mulryan's grin. There was no blood. Mulryan wrenched harder at Lisa's hair and her head tore free from her neck. It hung from Mulryan's upraised arm and the expression on her face was still one of ecstatic pleasure. The tip of her tongue came out and licked along the red lips.

'Yum yum,' she said, her voice tiny now, metallic. Meanwhile, her headless body still bounced up and down on Jack's flaccid cock, her hand still holding his screams in check.

A spotlight burned out of the darkness and Mulryan stepped forward to take a bow.

'Abracadabra,' he said. He pointed to the open pit of Lisa's neck and made a flourish. White doves flapped out of the opening and went blundering up into the spotlight, two, six, eight, a dozen of them.

Jack heard the sounds of applause. Turning his head to the side, he saw a series of wooden benches, filled with spectators, rows of faces staring at him, some of them familiar. There was Tony Gorman raising a double whisky in a toast. Beside him, Angelito was eating a massive tub of popcorn. There was Bill Farnell, with one arm draped around Raul Martinez's shoulders. In the row behind them, Leo King sat politely beside Lou Winters and The Armenian. Lou's face was unnaturally white and he didn't seem to be enjoying the performance at all. The Armenian was reading *Country Life*. Leonard Riggs sat slightly to their left, wearing Jack's favourite suit. It was several sizes too big for him but he didn't seem to care. He was holding out a heart-shaped box of chocolates to Sammi and she was scooping up handfuls of them and cramming them into her mouth, smearing her red lipstick. There was one more familiar figure, up in the corner of the very back row, a thin, sickly looking fellow with mud in his hair. Frank Nolan lifted a hand to wave and he grinned feebly. Maggots squirmed between his teeth and dropped into his lap.

'And now, ladies and genn'elmen, for my next trick . . .'

Mulryan moved back to the bed. He took hold of Lisa's jerking body and flung it effortlessly aside. It struck a wall and smashed into clouds of white smoke. At last, Jack was able to scream. He opened his mouth and it filled with choking feathers. A white dove flapped out, beating its wings frantically in his face. He coughed, spat, tried to scream again. But another dove followed the first. Then another and another . . .

Jack woke making involuntary grabbing motions in front of him. It took several seconds to realize that he was in his hotel room, sitting up in bed. A thick sweat covered his body and the cotton sheets were glued to him like wet tissue paper. He remembered to breathe and flopped back on the bed with a gasp.

'Jesus,' he said quietly. He had thought the dream about Tam McGiver had been bad, but this one was in an entirely different league. It had seemed like he would never wake up from it. He reached for his cigarettes, fumbled one out and lit it with his Zippo lighter. Almost immediately, he wished he hadn't. His mouth was dry and stale.

He'd finally left the club around four A.M. At some point in the evening, he'd thrown Gorman the line about visiting *The Duchess* and it appeared to have worked like a charm. Lisa was to escort him there around midday.

Glancing at his watch, he saw that it was a little after ten A.M. With a sigh, he got out of bed and stumbled to the refrigerator. He uncapped a bottle of mineral water and took a long swig from its contents. He felt the water spread through his guts, as though they'd been stuffed with blotting paper and he grimaced as the chill liquid reached his stomach. Then he stumbled to the bathroom and showered himself awake.

He felt uneasy about this meeting with Lisa, but thinking of her also brought an undeniable thrill. His cock hardened as he soaped himself and he knew then that he would risk anything to keep the appointment. His nightmare had been the natural product of anxiety. He told himself that he didn't believe in omens. He was a gambler after all and lately, his luck seemed to be holding.

He walked back into the bathroom, towelling himself dry. The phone trilled and he went over to it. He lifted the receiver.

'Yes?' he said.

'Señor Nolan. I have Señor Sinclair on the line from London, England. One moment please.'

'Listen, tell him I already—'

Too late. The literary agent's voice came over the line, sounding pretty agitated.

'Frank, is that you? Where have you been for Christ's sake? I thought you were going to call me every day? What's happening down there? Frank? Well, for God's sake, say something will you?'

Jack scowled. He put the phone down again and stared

at it for a moment, chewing his thumbnail. Well, he reflected, he'd only have to bluff things out a few hours longer. Then he and Lisa were out of here.

He dressed quickly and went out of the room, locking the door behind him. He rode the elevator down to the lobby and strode past the reception desk, ignoring the calls of the clerk, who was holding a telephone receiver and waving frantically at him.

'Señor? Señor Nolan, your call from England? You were cut off, yes?'

Jack pushed out into the bright glare of late morning, slipping on a pair of shades as he went. He crossed the parking lot, aware of the heat already beginning to exude from the shiny black tarmac. He got into the Mitsubishi, opened all the windows to let a little air circulate and started up the engine. He put the car into gear and drove away in the direction of Gorman's villa.

'There's a spot,' said Eddie.

Rosie manoeuvred the Polo into the space recently vacated by Jack's Mitsubishi. She switched off the engine and gave Eddie a smile that was somewhat marred by the ugly black bruise at the side of her mouth. 'Want me to go in and ask, lover?'

He nodded, slightly perturbed. Now Rosie didn't look much more respectable than he did. He watched as she climbed out of the car and limped slowly across the forecourt. Things had got a little out of hand last night. After an afternoon spent wandering around Puerto Banus, in a fruitless search for Tam McGiver, the two of them had gone back to their hotel room and got straight into a lovemaking session. Now that all pretences were down, they'd really laid into each other.

Eddie had liberally scarred Rosie's back with the leather belt but the blow to her face had been an accident. She'd raised her head unexpectedly and got the full force of the buckle across her chin. She didn't seem to mind though. And she'd had plenty of opportunities to get her own back.

Eddie shifted uncomfortably in his seat. The raw welts on his buttocks had hurt like hell when he woke up that morning. Rosie had thought it best to go out and find a chemist, pick up some antiseptic. She had also purchased a local English language newspaper. Lying naked on the bed, Eddie had browsed through it while Rosie dabbed ointment on to his wounds. Then he'd suddenly cried out. He had just noticed a small news item about a dead body, washed up on the beach a few miles down the coast. The man's personal effects had identified him as a Mr Tam McGiver, a native of London, England.

'What's wrong?' Rosie had asked him.

'Er . . . nothin'.' He turned over the page before she got a chance to see what he was looking at. 'Must've nicked me with your fingernail,' he added.

'Sorry, lover.' She went on with her work.

Eddie scowled at the newspaper. Clearly it was time to have that little chat with Frank Nolan. As soon as Rosie had finished, Eddie announced his intention of going straight over to the Excelsior Hotel but Rosie wouldn't hear of it. She'd insisted that first the pair of them needed a good breakfast inside them. She'd led the way down to the hotel restaurant and munched her way steadfastly through several courses, while Eddie sat there watching the minutes tick away. Little wonder they were so late getting to the hotel.

Eddie was beginning to have mixed feelings about Rosie. Of course, he worshipped her, there was no doubt of that in his mind. But he was all too aware that she was slowing him down, complicating his life when he really ought to be concentrating all his attention on finding Jack Doyle. There could be no thought of abandoning the search. It was a matter of honour and Eddie would not be able to live with himself if he simply let it go. Once he had found Doyle and dealt with him accordingly, then he and Rosie could take all the time they needed for their little games.

But even that thought troubled him. Sooner or later, he realized, one of them was going to die. The games would get ever more violent and unpredictable. It only took one misplaced blow to end a life; and last night, they had both come close to losing all control . . .

Rosie came limping out of the exit, a disappointed frown on her face. She trudged across the car-park and climbed into the driving seat, grunting softly as she lowered her buttocks on to the upholstery.

'Mr Nolan's gone out,' she said. 'Bloke at the desk says we just missed him. Doesn't know when he'll be back.'

Eddie brought his fist down on the dashboard with a grunt of irritation. 'Damn it!' he said. 'If we hadn't stopped for breakfast . . .' He glared at her for a moment, then softened when he saw the look on her face. Her bottom lip was trembling.

'I'm sorry,' she said. 'I thought it was for the best.'

'Of course you did.' He felt terrible for having shouted at her. He reached out a hand to pat her knee reassuringly. 'It doesn't matter, sweetie, we can come back later.'

'Honestly?'

'Honestly. It's not a problem.' He sat for a moment, staring blankly at the hotel entrance.

'I suppose we could take another trip around town, have another look for your friend.'

'No point,' muttered Eddie. He glanced at her, warily. 'I mean, if he was around, he'd have got in touch by now, I reckon. P'raps you should go back to the hotel, sweetie. Rest up a little . . .'

'Oh no, I'm not tired! It's such a lovely day, Eddie, why don't we 'ave a bite of lunch down by the harbour?'

'Lunch?' Eddie stared at her. 'We only just had breakfast!'

'Well, just a snack, maybe. And a glass of wine. We could sit and look at the yachts.'

Eddie's resolution melted and he knew there was no hope for him.

'All right, whatever you say. We'll leave the car here, shall we?'

Rosie nodded, got out again. She looked wistful.

'It must be wonderful to be rich,' she said. 'Climb aboard a great big yacht and sail away forever.'

Eddie smiled fondly at her.

'I wish I 'ad the money to buy you one, love.'

'Don't be silly! I don't need nothin' like that. I got you.'

She took his hand and they walked slowly around the side of the hotel, to the long straight run of the harbour. A pavement café was open and they took seats out in the sunshine. Directly ahead of them, was what looked like the biggest, whitest yacht of them all. They could easily make out the name painted on her prow: *The Duchess*.

Jack drove in through the open metal gates and motored slowly along the drive. The patio area was deserted. He parked, got out of the car and went to look in through the open French windows. The lounge too, was empty, but he could hear the sounds of a television in the small adjoining room, Gorman's den.

'Hello?' called Jack.

'Through 'ere, Frankie boy!'

Jack found them sitting around in front of the huge colour television. Despite the relatively early hour, Gorman and Raul Martinez were evidently much the worse for drink. They had full glasses in their hands and glazed expressions on their faces. A well stocked drinks cabinet on the other side of the room appeared to have been well depleted. Only Angelito was sober. He was slumped in an armchair with his feet up on a stool and he looked decidedly bored. For some inexplicable reason, all three men were wearing brightly coloured shell-suits and trainers, as though they'd just returned from a jog.

'Party still going strong, I see,' said Jack.

'Jus' windin' down a bit,' Gorman assured him in a slurred voice. His face was mottled an unhealthy shade of red and he clearly hadn't shaved this morning. 'We like a little drink now and then, don't we lads?'

'We sure do,' agreed Martinez. 'Just once in a while.'

''Elp yourself if you want one, Frankie.'

Jack shook his head. 'No thanks. I'm driving Lisa up to *The Duchess*, remember?'

'Oh, yeah, right. She's a beauty, an absolute farkin' beauty.'

Jack stared at him. 'Lisa?' he asked.

'Not Lisa! *The Duchess*!' He laughed uproariously. 'Jesus, I tell you what, you could buy a hundred women for the price I paid for that yacht. Biggest boat in the bleedin' 'arbour! I oughta get out on it more, try and get me money's worth. Maybe we'll 'ave a little trip on it soon, eh Raul?'

'That'd be nice, Tony. Real nice.'

'Yeah, jus' the lads, eh? The ol' gang. All for one and one for all. Might cheer Angel up a bit.' He gave Angelito an accusing look. 'I dunno what's up wiv 'im, but we've barely 'ad a word out of 'im all day.' He leaned over the back of the chair and tousled Angelito's perfect hair. 'What's up, Angel? Whatsa matter, eh? Tell Uncle Tony!'

Angelito pouted, brushed Gorman's hand aside irritably.

'I'm trying to watch the film,' he complained.

Jack turned to look at the screen. It was an old Bette

Davis weepie, badly dubbed into Spanish. Davis and Paul Heinreid stood on a balcony. He was lighting two cigarettes. The music was slowly building to a climax. Gorman slipped a meaty arm around Angelito's shoulders and hugged him close. 'Less not arsk for the farkin' moon, Angel. We've already got the bleedin' stars!' He gave Angelito a noisy kiss on the cheek. Angelito scowled and pushed Gorman away, while Martinez laughed uproariously at his discomfort. Jack noticed that though Gorman had made a joke of it, the embrace had been considerably more intimate than was strictly necessary and that Angelito's discomfort was genuine. He was blushing furiously as though Gorman had made a real pass at him and Jack wondered if this could explain Gorman's evident adoration of his chauffeur. Last night, Gorman had claimed the boy was like a son to him, that he'd trust him with his life . . . maybe it was a less than fatherly relationship that he envisaged.

Gorman seemed to become aware of Angelito's discomfort and tried to mask it behind the usual bluster. As the end credits rolled, he jumped upright, applauding loudly. 'Christ, they don't write 'em like that, any more!' he bellowed. He continued to make oafish remarks during the commercial break, commenting on the size of a woman's breasts and what he wouldn't give for half an hour of her time. A man advertising a denture fixative was dismissed as, 'A cringing little arse-bandit,' while a woman in a swim-suit, advertising a low fat yoghurt, looked like she'd 'Shag like a rabbit.' Every remark seemed designed to point up his own masculinity, but whatever his motives, he soon had Martinez in stitches, while even Angelito gave a grudging smirk.

Jack glanced impatiently at his watch. 'Where exactly is Lisa?' he asked.

'Oh, she'll be along in a minute. Don't get yer knickers in a twist. 'Ave a drink, go on, one won't 'urt. 'Air of the dog and all that.'

Jack moved obligingly to the drinks cabinet, poured himself a coke and then surreptitiously added a small measure of Scotch. Perhaps, he reflected, it would help relax him a little.

A news bulletin came on, a sober looking moustachioed man in a grey suit. He spoke for a while, his expression grave and then the camera cut to an outside broadcast. The scene was a stretch of country road. Police cars and an ambulance were parked beside a cordoned off area. A press of uniformed men were gathered around a spot where a large outcrop of rock jutted up from the parched earth. It struck Jack instantly that there was something horribly familiar about this scene.

'Jesus,' said Gorman. 'That's just a few miles up the road, ennit?'

Angelito nodded. Now the men were man-handling something out of a crevice in the rock. You could see where machines had been used to chisel the opening wider. The view was obscured by the crowd but there were glimpses of a muddy, bloated corpse, the limbs stiff with rigor mortis. As it was hauled out into the open, a blanket was thrown over it but one hand jutted out, swollen like a white balloon. Jack had to make an effort not to cry out. He gulped down his drink and quickly helped himself to another.

'What they sayin' Angel?' asked Gorman. 'I can't follow it.'

Angelito translated as it went along. 'Body of a male Caucasian . . . late-twenties . . . found in the early hours of this morning. Body discovered by a local villager . . . dogs been trying to get at it. Jesus! Been lying there maybe five, six days. Police think the man died of natural causes.'

'Bollocks!' growled Gorman. 'Why would anybody stash a body in there if it was natural causes? Don't make sense.'

'Maybe he just crawled in there and died . . . no wait . . . ankles were broken, it says . . . and a mark on the forehead, but they think these happened *after* he died.' Angelito shrugged. 'Kind of weird, huh?'

Jack took another gulp of his drink and tried to ask the next question as calmly as possible. 'They er . . . know who he is, yet?'

Angelito shook his head. 'No ID. But they think he's an *Ingles*.'

'How would they know that?'

'Labels on his clothes, I guess.' Angelito turned his head and studied Jack for a moment. 'You gone a little pale,' he observed.

'Have I?' Jack shrugged. 'Well, things like that give me the creeps.'

'Yeah? Big crime writer like you?' Angelito seemed unconvinced. 'Funny thing, you been here around five or six days. Must have been out that way that you drove the car off the road. You remember, you injured your hand, digging it out of a ditch?'

Jack shrugged. 'So?'

'I don't know. Maybe you seen something funny, huh? Like a guy getting rid of a body.'

'No, of course I didn't! Christ, you think if I'd seen something like that, I wouldn't have mentioned it?'

''Course you would, Frankie!' said Gorman. 'Funny though, ennit? I mean, who'd go to the trouble to hide a bloke that's died of natural causes? What's the point? Unless . . . unless somebody didn't want anyone to know he's dead. Probably off somewhere spending his farkin' credit cards!' He shook his head, laughed. 'Anyway, I 'spect they'll find out who he is soon enough.'

Jack tried to look only mildly curious. 'Think so?'

'Of course! Modern forensics an' all that. Dental records, cloth samples . . . nah, it won't take 'em long.' He thought for a minute. ''Ere, that's funny. Wasn't some English bloke washed up on the beach only yesterday?'

'Scottish,' Angelito corrected him.

'Nah, the telly said he was from London . . .'

'Yeah, he lived in London.. But he was Scottish, the name was McKenzie or McDonald, somethin' like that.'

'Funny, though. I wonder if there's any connection . . .?'

The door opened and Lisa came in. Jack had never been so relieved to see anyone in his entire life.

'Ready to go, Mr Nolan?' she asked. She kept her voice flat, uninterested, as though the trip was a chore she was obliged to go through with.

He nodded.

'It's very good of you to take the time, Mrs Gorman,' he said.

'Now don't forget,' said Gorman, 'Make sure you show him *everything*.'

Lisa turned to face her husband and the ghost of a smile played upon her lips. 'I will,' she said.

Jack cringed inwardly, convinced that their intended deception was as transparent as glass. But Gorman didn't seem to have noticed anything amiss. He had transferred his attention to the television screen. Only Angelito watched Jack and Lisa as they went out of the door.

As they stepped out on to the patio, Bill Farnell was getting out of a taxi. He was carrying a black leather attaché case. He nodded to Jack and Lisa and went past them in through the French windows. Lisa flashed Jack a meaningful look.

He felt too nervous to register anything. They walked across to the Mitsubishi and climbed in. The leather upholstery was uncomfortably hot beneath them.

'Jesus,' muttered Jack.

'What's the matter?'

'They were asking me some sticky questions when you came in. I'm afraid they're going to put two and two together about me.'

She reached down a hand and squeezed his thigh reassuringly.

'They don't know anything,' she told him. 'They can't see past their next drink.'

'Maybe so. But Angelito hasn't been drinking. He's stone, cold sober.'

Jack started the engine, put the car into gear and drove slowly towards the gates. He wanted it all to be over. Soon it would be, one way or the other.

Chapter Twenty-Eight

Jack parked outside the Excelsior and he and Lisa got out. She led the way around the side of the building towards the harbour.

'We could just go up to your room, I guess,' she said. 'But we're supposed to be going aboard *The Duchess* and somebody might notice if we don't turn up.'

'Why don't we just go, right now?' suggested Jack. 'Get in the car and drive north.'

She glanced at him irritably. 'We already had this discussion, remember? I told you, I'm not going without the money. It's only a few more hours, what difference can it make?'

Jack frowned. 'I don't know. I've got a bad feeling, that's all. There was something on the television while I was waiting for you to come down. They found the body . . .'

'Body?' Lisa raised her eyebrows. 'What body?'

He shook his head. 'It's not what you're thinking,' he assured her. 'It's kind of complicated.'

She stared at him. 'Frank, would you mind telling me

exactly what you're talking about?'

'It's hard to explain,' he said. Then he shook his head. 'No, no it isn't. It's not hard to explain at all. It's very easy.'

'Frank?'

He had come to a decision. 'Listen,' he said, 'it's time I levelled with you.'

They had emerged into the marina now, ringed in by shops, bars and cafés. He indicated the nearest pavement café, grabbed Lisa's hand and led her towards it. He found an empty table and sat down with his back to the other diners. Lisa took a seat opposite him. Over Jack's shoulder, she watched with interest as an odd-looking couple got up to leave their table.

The man was huge and thick-set and looked like he'd been in the wars. His nose was a flattened grey lump on his face and one hand was encased in crumbling plaster which had been reinforced with lengths of insulating tape. He was wearing an outrageous Bermuda shirt and a broad-brimmed straw hat. The woman was big too, dressed in a garish red blouse and a skirt that revealed her long legs. She had her flaming red hair set in an outmoded beehive style and there was a nasty looking bruise at the side of her mouth.

Lisa covered a smile with her hand and prodded Jack playfully in the ribs. 'Don't look now, Frank, but there's the oddest looking couple you ever saw!' she told him.

He looked irritated. 'Never mind that now,' he said. 'Listen, I haven't been entirely honest with you. I haven't exactly lied to you either but . . . well, I feel I owe you an explanation.'

'I'm listening,' she said; but half of her attention remained with the odd-looking couple. They were walking slowly away now, hand in hand. They looked somehow like a pair of overgrown children.

'To begin with, my name isn't Frank Nolan. It's Jack. Jack Doyle.'

The big man paused and turned his head to glance back. He looked puzzled, as though he'd forgotten something or perhaps thought he'd heard somebody calling him. His eyes met Lisa's and she smiled sheepishly at him, embarrassed for having been caught staring. He returned the smile, his lips curving to reveal a set of perfect dentures. For some inexplicable reason, Lisa felt an abrupt chill tickle along the length of her spine. Then the beehive-woman said something and the big man nodded, turned away again. They set off along the marina at a leisurely stroll. Lisa made an effort to concentrate.

'Jack Doyle,' she repeated. 'That's a good name. I think I prefer it to Frank anyway . . .' She thought for a moment. 'But . . . if you're not Frank Nolan, then what—?'

'He's dead. The body I mentioned? It was on the news report while I was waiting for you. They found where I buried him.'

'Jesus!' Now Jack had her undivided attention. 'You . . . you *killed* somebody?'

'No, no, I promise you I didn't! The guy had a heart attack. He was giving me a lift to Marbella and he . . . well, he just died on me. It was really sudden, he just . . .' Jack shook his head. 'Anyway, I kind of borrowed his identity.'

'You kind of borrowed his—' Lisa sat back in her chair and stared at him for a moment. Then she threw back her head and laughed heartily. 'Oh, I'm going to like you,' she cried. 'You're just full of surprises, aren't you?'

'I try to lift the spirits,' he said, remembering something she'd once said to Gorman.

A waiter came. Jack ordered two coffees and two double brandies. The man scribbled on his pad and moved back inside the café.

Lisa studied Jack for a moment.

'I suppose the obvious question is "why?"' she said. 'Why would you want to take the identity of a stranger?'

Jack shrugged. 'Because I was going nowhere fast. I was broke and I owed serious money to some heavy people. Frank on the other hand seemed to have everything sewn up. Five star hotel, money, credit cards, a car ... everything that I didn't have. So I guess I just decided to try it for a day or so.'

'And he just happened to be a writer.' She thought for a moment. 'My God, Frank ... Jack ... I bet I made you nervous when I gave you that stuff about how you didn't look like a writer!'

He nodded. 'I've had better moments,' he admitted.

'But how did you ever hope to get away with it?'

'I didn't really. Not for long, anyway. I was just playing for time. I figured I'd buy a day or two, get my feet back on the ground and then take off for somewhere else. Only ... only then I met you and I decided maybe it was worth hanging on a little longer.'

She regarded him for a moment beneath half lowered eyelashes.

'Really?' she whispered.

'Really,' he said.

The waiter returned with the drinks and Jack and Lisa watched each other in uncomfortable silence while he arranged cups, glasses and napkins on the table. He seemed to take forever. When he had finally moved away, Lisa had another question.

'So, Mr Jack Doyle . . . if you're not a writer, what exactly are you?'

'I'm nothing much, Lisa. I'm a . . . well, if you really want to know the truth, I . . .'

A look of doubt came into her eyes. 'Oh no,' she said quietly. 'You're not a crook are you? Just tell me you're not a crook!'

'No, no, it's nothing like that! I'm a computer programmer. Or at least, I used to be. Had my own business and everything. Then, after my girlfriend died, I kind of went off the rails for a while. Tried my hand at gambling. But my luck turned bad, so now I'm . . . I'm just drifting, I guess.'

Lisa began to chuckle. The chuckle built gradually to a full laugh. 'Oh yes,' she said. 'Oh yes, it's perfect! Absolutely perfect! Tony thinks he's tied in with a famous author, but what he's really got . . . what he's really got . . . is a failed gambler! A drifter! God, I'd like to see his face when he finds out!'

Jack grimaced. 'Well, I wouldn't! That's why we've got to go tonight, money or no money. If the police come up with a name on that body and it goes out on the TV and radio . . .' He shook his head. 'It just doesn't bear thinking about.'

'Yes, I can see that it might make things the tiniest bit awkward,' she conceded.

'There's something else.'

'I'm all ears.'

'You remember I told you that there was somebody looking for me? Somebody from England? Well, *two* people, actually.'

She sipped at her brandy.

'Go on,' she urged him.

'One of them caught up with me the other night. We had a fight and . . . well, I killed him.'

She didn't say anything to that. She just looked at him.

'It was self-defence. He came at me with a razor and I hit him, hard. He fell into the water and drowned. It seems his body was washed up further down the coast.'

'Christ!'

'Don't worry. I don't think there's anything to connect me with him. The guy was a villain, he'd have killed me without a second thought. But I figure if we're going to go into this deal together, you should know everything.'

'So when you said that the pressure was off . . .?'

'That's what I was referring to. At the time, I figured the other guy wasn't a problem. Now I'm not so sure. I know that he left England some time ago and he's almost certainly looking for me.' He spread his hands in a gesture of helplessness. 'Anyway, that's everything, I think.'

She shook her head. 'It's enough to be going on with,'

she admitted. 'Let me get this straight. You're a failed computer programmer on the run. You stole a dead man's identity. You killed one guy and there's another enemy lurking in the woodwork. Did I miss anything?'

'Only one thing. I love you.'

'And because of that, I should trust you?'

'Well, I still think I'm your best chance of getting the hell away from here. But I'll understand if you want to pass on my offer.'

'The hell with that.' She tilted the glass of brandy and drained it in one swallow. 'We'll do it tonight,' she told him. 'You may not be Mr Perfect, but I'll take my chances. Here.' She reached into her bag and slipped Jack a small remote control handset.

A camera clicked.

'What's this for?' he asked.

'It's to open the gates, of course. I liberated it from Angelito's room when he wasn't around. You just key-in a four figure code and it's "open sesame"!' Now she took out a slip of paper and passed it to him. 'That's the code,' she said. 'Memorize and destroy!'

A camera clicked.

'So you *do* still want to come with me? Even now I've told you the truth and everything . . .'

She smiled. 'No offence, honey, but I'd make a run with Jack the Ripper if it meant getting out of that place.'

Jack looked offended. She placed a hand on his.

A camera clicked.

'Listen,' she said. 'We're adults. Let's be sensible about this. Right now, I like you very much. Maybe more than that. I know I fancy the pants right off you, but that doesn't mean things will work out between us. Hell, I've just spent a very long time in one kind of trap and I'm not particularly eager to get myself into another. So let's put this on a business level, what do you say?'

Jack shrugged. 'I guess it wouldn't hurt,' he admitted.

'OK, whatever happens, I swear to you that fifty per cent of whatever's in that attaché case is yours. When we land somewhere we both feel is safe, you can take your share and go, if you want to. Same applies to me. No strings, right?'

Jack frowned. 'I don't care about the money. You don't owe me anything.'

'Sure I do! You've offered to help me and its going to be dangerous. I wouldn't expect you to take a risk for nothing. Fifty per cent, Jack. That's the deal. Otherwise, all bets are off.'

He stared at her for a moment.

'I won't pretend it wouldn't come in useful,' he said.

'Sure. You'll be able to pay off that debt you mentioned.'

He shook his head. 'As I understand it, that one's been wiped clean. Only Eddie Mulryan seems to think I should still honour it.'

'Eddie who?'

'The guy that's still looking for me.'

'Spain's a big country,' she assured him. 'He isn't going to find you. Anyway, like I said. That's the deal. We split what's in the case, straight down the middle. Where we go from there, that's up to us.'

He smiled, nodded. 'OK,' he said. He raised his glass. 'I'll drink to that.'

She grinned, raised her drink. They touched glasses.

A camera clicked.

'Now,' said Jack. 'What about this boat?'

'It's right there,' said Lisa, nodding.

Jack turned his head. *The Duchess* towered above them, a huge gleaming hull of white steel.

'Ah,' said Jack. 'I should have known.' He slipped into a parody of Gorman's cockney accent. 'Biggest farkin' boat in the 'arbour!'

Lisa chuckled.

'You'll like *The Duchess*,' she whispered. 'In the master cabin there's the biggest, softest double bed you ever saw.'

'But I'm not feeling sleepy,' he told her.

'Good.' She leaned across the table and kissed him softly on the mouth. He reached up and slipped a hand behind her neck, pulling her to him.

A camera clicked, once, twice, three times, framing the image on high quality film.

Angelito lowered the camera and grinned. He was parked far away at the end of the marina, but the powerful telephoto lens had brought his subject up close enough to show every little detail. He got back into his car and put the camera down carefully on the passenger seat.

Now he had them. Now he'd show them the price they'd have to pay for laughing at him. His cousin,

Teresa, owned a photographic shop in Marbella. The place had its own darkroom. She'd assured Angelito that it would only take a couple of hours to process any film he brought in to her. He'd get her to do big blow ups, so there could be no mistaking the intimacy of that embrace.

And then he'd show them to Señor Gorman.

He put the car into gear and drove away, feeling happier than he'd felt in weeks.

PART FOUR

JACK OF DIAMONDS

Chapter Twenty-Nine

Jack walked in through the swing doors of the Excelsior, feeling refreshed and very much alive, as though every atom of his being had been taken apart, charged with adrenalin and pop-riveted back together again. The afternoon had gone all too quickly but it had served to reassure him that he was doing the right thing. He wanted Lisa. There was no way he would leave without her.

The moustachioed desk clerk waved to him as he crossed the lobby and reluctantly, Jack moved across to the counter.

'Señor Nolan, please. Señor Sinclair phone another two times for you. He asks you to call him urgently.'

Jack nodded. 'Yeah, I'll do that.' *Like hell I will*, he thought and turned to go.

'Oh, and a lady called for you also.'

Jack hesitated, turned back.

'A lady? What, she . . . she phoned?'

'No, Señor, she called here at the desk just after you went out. She ask for your room number, but of course,

I don't tell her. She said she will call again.'

Jack frowned. 'What did this lady look like?'

'Err . . . she was, you know . . .' He gestured ineffectually. 'She have the big hair.' He waved his hands a foot above his head. 'She is very . . . *grand* lady.'

Reading between the lines, Jack translated 'grand' to mean 'fat', though he couldn't be sure. He was totally nonplussed by this news. He didn't have the least idea who she could have been, but it made him feel distinctly nervous. She might be somebody who knew what Frank Nolan looked like, in which case, she wasn't a person he particularly wanted to meet. He leaned forward across the desk and adopted a conspiratorial air.

'Tell you what,' he said. 'I know this woman. She's a *fan*. You understand? A real nuisance. She follows me everywhere.'

The clerk nodded gravely.

'You are a movie actor, yes?'

Jack shook his head. 'No, a writer.' He made a few pen-like flourishes with one hand. 'This woman who called, she wants autographs, photos . . . things like that.'

'Ah, *si*!'

'So if she calls again, I'd really appreciate it if you could tell her I'm out, OK? Say you don't know where I've gone or when I'll be back. Would you do that for me?' Jack took out his wallet and extracted a ten thousand peseta note. He stuffed it gently into the man's breast pocket and smiled.

'No need to worry, Señor. I will make sure she does not disturb you.'

'Thanks. Appreciate it.'

Jack rode up in the elevator and let himself into his apartment. Once there, he couldn't settle. He knew that later this evening, Lisa would be making the switch. If all went well, she would be phoning him to arrange a pick up time. And then they would be taking off together, driving north to try and lose themselves in the vastness of Madrid, before flying on to the destination of their choice.

Just a few hours then. But how to pass it? Jack paced the floor for a while and then remembered the pack of playing cards in his bag. He found them and sat down on the bed to play a game of patience, a tried and tested way of passing the time. He shuffled the cards and turned the top one over.

It was the Jack of Diamonds.

Lisa stood on the landing and listened intently. Downstairs, she could hear the murmur of voices from the den. Gorman, Farnell and Martinez, very drunk now, talking in slurred tones. Angelito didn't seem to be around. A glance at her watch told her it was a little after six P.M. and she doubted that she'd ever get a better chance than this. She walked barefoot to her bedroom and got the attaché case from the back of the wardrobe. She'd already filled it with squares of cut newspaper, something she'd seen done in quite a few movies, but she had no idea if it was anything like the right weight. She told herself it didn't really matter. The deception only needed to work for a few hours.

She walked back out on to the landing and listened again. She could hear Gorman droning on, the tone of voice he always adopted when recounting a favourite anecdote. She knew from experience that such anecdotes had a habit of going on for hours.

She stopped at the door of the study and tried the handle. It was unlocked. She went inside and stood in the dark for a moment, steadying her breathing, before she reached out and switched on the light. She had expected to be nervous, but she actually felt scared, her breath jumping in her throat as she leaned back against the door.

'Come on,' she told herself. 'Get a grip for Christ's sake!' She crossed the room to the Monet oil painting hung on the far wall. She reached up, unlatched the hook at the side of the frame. The Monet hinged smoothly open to reveal the matt black safe, recessed in the chimney breast. Now the combination, a liquid crystal display that you altered by tapping keys. This was where it got hairy. Try to access the wrong code and alarm bells would start ringing all over the house. She couldn't be absolutely sure that Farnell hadn't altered the code at some point, though she seriously doubted it. Gorman would have grumbled if there'd been a new six digit code to memorize.

She keyed the numbers slowly, matching them to the sequence she had in her head, cringing every time she pressed, because the button emitted a high-pitched beep that seemed inordinately loud in the silence. Now, there it was. 7/6/1/4/2/8. She studied the reading a second time, wanting to be sure she had it right. She took a deep breath and pressed ENTER. There was a pause, then a sharp metallic click. The door unlocked.

She paused a moment, listened again. From downstairs a burst of raucous laughter. Biting her lip, she swung the door open. There was the attaché case. She reached up, hefted it down, noticing that it seemed far heavier than its replacement. She laid it flat on the ground and tested the latches. It wasn't even locked. She opened the case and nearly let out a scream of pure delight. The interior was crammed with neatly stacked wads of American dollars, each secured with a paper band. She was glad to see that they were hundred dollar bills that were grubby with use. Pretty untraceable, she decided. Two million dollars. Holy Jesus. She latched the case again, straightened up and lifted the substitute to put it in the safe. She hesitated.

There was something else in there, nestled among the legal documents and account books. A black velvet bag, the size of a grapefruit. Curious, she reached in and pulled it out. It made an attractive clicking sound. She put down her case and untied the bag's draw-string. She tipped some of the contents out on to her hand. Her eyes got big and round, reflecting the specks of light that glittered from the diamonds.

The sound of an approaching car made her snap her head up. She dropped the diamonds back into the bag and walked across to the window. She peeped out. The car was cruising up to the patio. As she watched, it came to a halt and Angelito got out. He had a large brown envelope tucked under his arm. Lisa had a sudden panic, thinking that he might notice the light on in the study; but he didn't even glance up as he hurried towards the house.

All right, no problem. She tucked the bag into the belt of her jeans and hurried back to the safe, lifted the substitute attaché case and stowed it inside. Shutting the door, she reset all the digits to zero, then swung back the painting and relatched the hook at the side. Now she picked up Farnell's case, walked back to the door and switched off the light. Easing the door open an inch or so, she peered out on to the landing. It was empty.

She stepped quickly out and pulled the door shut behind her. Again she listened. It seemed to have gone very quiet downstairs. Straining to hear, she could just discern Angelito's voice, talking in a low tone but she couldn't make out what he was saying. She started towards her room.

She was halfway across the landing when Gorman's bellow of rage stopped her in her tracks. There was the sudden, nerve-jangling sound of glass breaking. It set up a fluttering in her stomach, a sense of rising panic. Throwing caution to the winds, she ran to her room and threw open the door. Stumbling inside, she closed it behind her, aware now of the sound of a door slamming downstairs.

What the fuck was going on? She dropped to her knees beside the bed and fumbled out one of the suitcases she had packed earlier. She'd left room in this one for the attaché case. As she was attempting to cram it in amongst

416

the jumble of clothes, she became aware of footsteps crashing up the stairs.

'Dear God!' she whispered. She latched the suitcase, then remembered the velvet bag, sticking incriminatingly out of her belt. She pulled it free, threw open the case, jammed the bag into a corner.

Footsteps on the landing now, approaching the door.

She slammed the suitcase shut, thrust it back under the bed. Then she lunged across the room and threw herself into the seat at the dressing table mirror. She snatched up a hairbrush and began to brush at her long, honey-blonde hair, working methodically and staring at her reflection, hoping against hope that nothing in her expression would give her away.

The door opened and Gorman came in. He looked horrible, his face red and puffy with drink, his bloodshot eyes staring at Lisa's reflection. She noticed he was carrying a brown envelope. The same one Angelito had brought? She thought so. The conviction that something was terribly wrong began to creep over her but she was determined not to show any dismay. She kept moving the brush through her hair. Gorman was still staring at her and it was impossible to misconstrue the look of dumb hatred he was directing at her. She'd seen it before, usually when he had been drinking.

The silence seemed to go on for ever. At last, she was prompted to break it. 'This a social call?' she asked. 'Or is something wrong?'

'Wrong?' He laughed bitterly, began to pace up and down the room. 'Now what could possibly be wrong?'

His breathing was harsh, erratic. 'I was just wondering about something, that's all.'

'Oh?' She waited for him to continue.

'Yeah. What it is, see, I was finkin' about your little trip today. To *The Duchess*. Went all right, did it? I mean . . . you 'ad a good time, did'ya?'

Lisa shrugged. 'Not particularly. Bit of a bore, if you want to know the truth. I mean, it *was* your idea.'

'Yeah, right. My idea. All my idea.' He was still pacing restlessly. 'And what about Frankie-boy? Did he enjoy the trip?'

'Well, how would I know? He seemed interested. Made a lot of notes. You know, the things writers do.'

He stopped pacing. He came and stood directly behind her. He was smiling now. She didn't like that smile.

'Oh right. Notes. Yeah, he'd do that wouldn't he?' He reached out a hand to still the hairbrush. 'Tell me though, Lisa, I'm dead curious. How did he manage to take notes wiv both his 'ands up your skirt?'

She put down the hairbrush on the dresser.

'Don't be ridiculous,' she said quietly.

'Oh, I see. I've got the wrong idea 'ave I? Wrong end of the stick? That sorta thing?'

'Of course!' She turned in her seat and looked right at him. 'How could you think such a thing? Frank Nolan? Honestly, he's such a bore! I don't know what can have put that idea into your head.'

'Hmm.' He laughed, lightly now. 'I'm daft, aren't I? Fancy finkin' that you and him . . .' He shook his head. 'But you know me, Lisa, when I've 'ad a few. I keep finkin' stupid things.' He was tapping the brown envelope against his fingertips. She found that she couldn't take her eyes off it. 'Know what these are?' he asked her suddenly.

She shook her head.

'Go on. 'Ave a guess.'

'I really couldn't say.'

He handed her the envelope.

''Ave a look,' he suggested. 'Go on. Open it.'

There was another silence, so deep she thought she could hear the beating of her heart.

'Tony . . .' she began.

'Open it.' This time his tone was a command.

She opened the flap and pulled out the big, black and white enlargements. She examined them, her spirits sagging. She and Jack talking intently at the café table. Her hand resting on his. She handing him the remote control handset and a slip of paper. And then three shots of them kissing. Mouths opens, arms around each other. No way she could pass it off as a friendly peck. Nonetheless, she had to try. She had to try something.

'I can explain.' she said.

He hit her across the mouth with his fist, knocking her sideways off the seat. She struck the floor on her left side, trapping one arm beneath her body, her back slamming against one leg of the dressing table. She lay there stunned. Gorman came and stood over her, the grin manic now, showing his teeth, his eyes bulging grotesquely.

'You fucking whore!' he said. 'You dirty, lying bitch!'

419

'Tony!' she gasped. 'Listen to me, I—'

He kicked her, driving the toe of his boot hard into her stomach. She gasped as the air exploded from her lungs and she doubled over in pain. Now he was leaning forward, he had grabbed a handful of her hair, he was dragging her back to her feet.

'What did you do for him, eh? Did ya go down on 'im? Did ya fuck 'im? Was he good?' He snapped back an arm to throw another punch and desperately, Lisa brought her knee up into his groin. He bellowed with pain and doubled over, dropped to his knees. He made a horrible retching sound and was violently sick on the carpet.

'You filthy pig!' she gasped. 'Don't you . . . don't you ever touch me again! You hear?' She stood over him, fists clenched, her eyes blazing defiance. 'Jack's twice the man you ever were,' she screamed. 'And I'm going away with him!'

Gorman had finished being sick. He tilted his head to stare up at her, a dull gleam of intelligence in his red eyes. Vomit glistened on his chin.

'Jack?' he croaked.

She stared at him.

'I meant Frank,' she said.

He shook his head. 'Oh no. I don't think you did.'

Lisa heard a footstep behind her. Turning back, she saw Angelito leaning against the door frame, his arms crossed, an assured smile on his face.

'Need some help, Señor Gorman?'

Gorman was staggering to his feet now, he was trying

to grin. 'No, uh . . . she just caught me a lucky one, Angel, that's all. No problemo!' He limped over to Lisa and took her chin in his hand, made her look directly into his eyes. 'So, you're in love, are you? That's nice. Ain't that nice, Angel?'

'It's really sweet, boss!'

'Yeah, touchin'. You know what I fancy now, Angel? A swimmin' party. Ages since we had one of those, ennit?'

Lisa stared at him. 'A . . . swimming party?' she whispered.

'That's right. I seem to remember we last organized one for your mate, Gary. Very fond of a midnight swim, he was. Mind you, it's a good deal more difficult with your arms and legs tied.'

Lisa gasped, as though she'd been kicked in the stomach again. She had to fight to get out the next words. 'But . . . but you told me . . . you swore to me that it was an accident! That you didn't . . . know anything about it!'

Gorman leered. 'Come off it, Lisa. I saw the way things were between you two. Think I was just going to let it go? Think I was going to let him waltz in and fool around, right under my nose? No fuckin' chance!'

Lisa's eyes filled with tears. 'You bastard!' she shrieked. She lunged at Gorman, her hands outstretched to claw for his eyes but he slapped her back-handed across the face, stopping her in her tracks. She stood there, stunned. Then she was sobbing uncontrollably.

'I wonder if old Frankie boy's a good swimmer?' Gorman taunted her. 'Or should I say, Jackie boy? P'raps he'll explain that when we get 'im over 'ere.'

Lisa glared hatred at him.

'If you harm him in any way, I swear I'll . . .'

'What will you do, Lisa? Eh? Same as you did last time? Lock yourself away in your room for a couple of months and cry your little eyes out? Boo-hoo-hoo, poor little Lisa!' He thought for a moment, his grin widened. He was enjoying himself now. 'Tell you what. Since you love 'im so much . . . maybe this time, we'll let you *both* go swimmin'. Now wouldn't that be nice? Just the two of you, all alone in that big, dark ocean . . . unless of course, you can give me one good reason why you shouldn't join him.' He snapped his head to one side. 'Angel, tell Bill to give our Mr Nolan a ring. We want to see him right away. Bit of important business come up. Somethin' for the book. We'll see what he's got to say for himself.'

Angelito grinned. 'Yes boss,' he said. He hurried out of the room and down the stairs.

It was very quiet in the room now. Lisa could feel the tears burning her cheeks. She didn't want to cry in front of Gorman, but she couldn't help herself.

'Please,' she whispered. 'Please don't hurt him. You don't have to do that. He . . . he's harmless. I got him into this. Let him go and I'll . . . I'll be good. I'll do anything you want.'

'Anything?' asked Gorman quietly.

'Yes, anything.'

'Well . . . I'll tell you what I'd like you to do right now.' She nodded. 'What?' she asked him.

'Just shut the fuck up!' She saw the fist coming at her

and she tried to duck but it caught her on the left temple, a glancing blow. Darkness welled from the back of her head and she tried to outrun it but her legs were like silly putty and the darkness wrapped itself around her tenaciously, dragging her down on to the deep pile of the carpet and the black ocean that ebbed and flowed far beneath it.

Chapter Thirty

Something was wrong. Jack knew it with a dread certainty. Bill Farnell's tone had been too polite, too formal, a man desperately trying to assure the listener that everything was perfectly above board. It had been enough to convince Jack that it was time to go. He'd grabbed all his belongings and thrown them hastily into a suitcase, with every intention of leaping into his jeep and taking off for pastures new . . . and then he'd realized, quite suddenly, that he couldn't do it. He couldn't leave Lisa back there to carry the consequences of her attempted deception.

That had shocked him, driven the wind right out of his sails. He'd had to sit down on the bed, beside the scattered playing cards and consider all the implications. He, who'd never given a damn about anything or anyone since Catherine's death, now found that he cared enough about Lisa to risk everything for her. If he went in there, sure as anything, Gorman would be waiting for him. And what could he do to help Lisa then? He had no weapons, he was not particularly adept with his fists. Walking in to that house would simply place him in the same frying pan as Lisa. He thought about her previous lover, the man who'd been conveniently lost at sea and fear moved its cold fingers in his gut.

He studied his reflection in the wardrobe mirror and saw somebody he barely recognized. Somebody with a conscience. Somebody who cared more about a woman than he did about his own skin.

'Idiot,' he told his reflection. 'What are you trying to prove?'

The reflection gazed steadfastly back at him. He sighed. He picked up the suitcase from the bed. He wasn't sure why he was taking it. Maybe there'd be a chance for the two of them to make a run for it and he sure as hell wouldn't have time to call back here. He glanced quickly around the apartment. It had been a good place to hide out, if only for a few days. He went out of the door and walked to the elevator. He hummed a tune on his way down, surprised by his own calmness.

Jack dropped the keys off at the reception desk and told the clerk he was checking out. He told him to send the bill to Señor Gorman. What the hell? He had nothing to lose now anyway. The clerk seemed sorry to see him go.

'I hope you will come again, Señor,' he said.

'So do I,' Jack assured him.

'And if Señor Sinclair calls for you?'

'Tell him I died.'

'Señor?'

But Jack was already turning away.

He carried his case out to the jeep and loaded it into the back. It was dark now and Puerto Banus was just coming awake. Lights were clicking on in the shops and cafés around the marina. Jack thought about having one last drink for the road but decided against it. He'd need all his wits about him, he thought. But he was so preoccupied, he didn't notice the red Polo convertible that screeched to an abrupt halt a few yards behind him.

'What's wrong?' asked Rosie, surprised. She had been pulling into the car-park, when Eddie's good hand had reached out and squeezed her arm, obliging her to bring the car to an emergency stop.

'There,' he said quietly. Now he was leaning forward in his seat, staring through the windscreen at the man just ahead of him, illuminated in the glare of the head-lights. The man was climbing into the driving seat of a Mitsubishi jeep. Eddie let out a long, slow breath.

'Is that him, then?' asked Rosie. 'Frank Nolan?'

Eddie shook his head. He smiled coldly.

'No, sweetie. That's Doyle. Jack Doyle. That's the man I've been lookin' for.'

'But I thought you said . . .'

The Mitsubishi pulled smoothly out of its parking place and turned right on to the main road.

'Follow him,' said Eddie. 'Not too close now. Let's see where he's a goin' shall we? Sooner or later, he's goin' to be somewhere nice and quiet. And when he is . . .'

His grip on Rosie's arm was becoming painful, his huge fingers making white crescents on her tanned flesh.

She didn't mind. She slipped the car into first gear and began to follow the jeep.

'What you gonna do?' she asked him. 'When you catch up with him, like?'

'You just wait and see,' he told her. 'That'll be quite a party, I reckon.'

They drove for a mile or so, following the Mitsubishi's tail-lights. Then the jeep turned off the main road and moved along a deserted driveway. After a short distance, it approached a set of tall, iron gates, which swung magically open to admit it.

Rosie brought the Polo to a halt a short distance from the gates.

'What now?' she asked.

Eddie scratched his chin thoughtfully. 'We'll wait here,' he decided. 'Man's not going to stay in there all night, is he? And the drive up here is pretty quiet. Once he's finished his business in there, we'll be waiting for him. You may as well switch off the lights.'

She did as he suggested. Darkness settled around them. In the silence, she could hear the cicadas chirruping, a dry, raspy sound in the night. Eddie finally let go of her arm and she sat there, waiting for the feeling to come back to it. It was all right. She was exactly where she wanted to be.

Jack got out of the jeep and walked slowly towards the patio. Bill Farnell appeared at the French windows. He gave Jack an oily smile.

'Frank, glad you could make it! I know it's kind of

late, but there was something Tony wanted to talk over with you.' Again, the desperate show of *bonhomie*, the 'everything's just fine and dandy' bluster. He beckoned Jack towards him. 'Come on through, everyone's in the den.'

Appropriate, thought Jack, glumly. *That's where the wild beasts usually congregate.* Farnell was stepping back from the window to let him enter. He knew exactly what came next. Somebody, most probably Angelito, would be waiting for him behind the door frame. Pointless to try and evade it though. If he turned and ran, they'd get him just the same. He took a deep breath and stepped through the doorway. Right on queue there was the cold jab of a pistol barrel at the back of his neck.

'Hello Angel,' he said quietly.

'Shut up. Just keep walking.'

Jack did as he was told. He went through the lounge and dining room and in through the open doorway of the den. The others were there. Gorman was up on his feet, pacing nervously about, a glass of whisky in one hand. He looked well gone, Jack thought. His face was red and perspiring and the front of his gaudy red shell-suit was liberally splattered with what looked like dried vomit. Raul Martinez, similarly attired but considerably less dishevelled, sat in an armchair off to Gorman's left, watching the events with a detached curiosity. Then Jack saw Lisa. She was slumped in a chair and she looked like she'd gone three rounds with a heavyweight boxer. Her mouth was swollen up and one cheek was livid with bruises.

'Lisa!' He took a step towards her and a sudden explosion of pain flared in his right side. He caught his breath and dropped to his knees with a groan, dimly realizing that Angelito had just hit him in the kidneys with the gun barrel. He twisted around to face his tormentor and got a back-hander across the jaw for his trouble. He fell sideways and lay there looking up at Angelito. Beyond him, in the doorway, Bill Farnell was watching the proceedings with evident distaste. But Angelito was clearly enjoying himself, grinning his big movie-star grin.

'How you like that, big shot?' he asked.

'Very enjoyable,' Jack told him. 'I wonder if I could have another of those?'

He had the satisfaction of seeing Angelito's grin slip right off his face.

'Funny guy,' he snarled. He stepped forward to deliver a kick but Gorman's voice stilled him.

'All right, Angel, there's plenty of time for that! First, I wanna 'ave a little talk with *Jack* here.'

Jack twisted around to look at Gorman in surprise.

'Oh, didn' expect that, no? It's just that my dear wife let it slip, when she was tellin' me what a nice time the two of you 'ad aboard *The Duchess*.' He stepped closer to Jack. 'P'raps you'd like to begin by tellin' me who you are, exactly . . . and 'ow you come to be passin' yourself off as Frank Nolan.'

Jack sighed. He eased himself up into a sitting position, wincing at the pain in his side. He ran his tongue over his teeth to ensure that none of them were broken.

'It's quite simple, Tony . . .'

'*Mr Gorman* to you, arsehole! Only my friends call me *Tony*.'

'OK, it's quite simple, *Mr* Gorman. I'm a nobody. A gambler who lost his luck. I happened to get a lift to Marbella from Frank Nolan. He told me all about this great deal he'd made, living in luxury while he wrote your story. Then he died of a heart attack on route, so I buried him, took his identity and came to you instead. See. Easy!'

Gorman's eyes widened in disbelief. He seemed to be about to burst out laughing.

'You what? You buried 'im?'

'Boss,' said Angelito, 'that guy on the news the other day. You remember? I thought there was something goofy about it. And this one, asking all those questions . . .'

Gorman nodded.

'Yeah, that's right! Wanted to know if the cops would identify the body.' He crouched down and looked Jack straight in the eye. 'So, you thought you'd 'ave a go, did ya? Thought you'd just waltz in 'ere and pull my plonker? Jesus, you've got guts, I'll give you that! Eating my food, drinking my booze. Car and hotel paid for, oh, very nice. Very nice indeed! "Cut me off a slice of that, Guv, it'll go down a treat!" But then, not content with all that, you cap it all by 'aving my fuckin' wife!'

Jack shook his head.

'She's not your wife, Tony. Not any more. Can't you see that? You've lost her.'

'Not yet, I 'aven't! And it'll take more than a jumped up little prick like you to get 'er away from me, I can tell you! Pretty soon now, sunshine, you'll be dead and she'll still be my wife.'

'No I won't!' Lisa's voice, calm and authoritative. Gorman turned to look at her. 'If you kill him . . . then you may as well take a gun and finish me too. Because if you don't, I'll kill you. I swear it, I'll find a way, even if I have to wait years.' Her eyes filled with tears, but behind the wetness they blazed with anger. 'I love him,' she said. 'It's as simple as that.'

Gorman got to his feet and began to pace again.

'It is *not* simple!' he protested. 'Nothin' is that simple. Nothin'!' He went to swig down the remains of his whisky, but spilt some of it down his already filthy shell-suit. He seemed to abruptly lose his temper and he flung the glass at the nearest wall, showering the room with its fragments. 'Jesus, I can't believe this!' he roared. 'The ingratitude! The fuckin' ingratitude!' He rounded on Lisa, his slurred voice rising in volume. 'Everything I've done for you, you bitch! Bought you things. Given you everything you ever wanted . . .'

'So give me one more thing,' she told him. 'Give me my freedom.'

He raised a hand to strike her but she didn't flinch. She sat there, gazing defiantly at him. He hesitated, then slowly lowered his arm. Turning away, he walked back to face Jack, pointing at him.

'You're dead son,' he said matter-of-factly. 'You're history. You've cost me a lot, Jacko, now it's time to pay the bill. You got any final words to say to Lisa, you'd better say 'em now.'

Jack nodded. He looked at Lisa.

'Well,' he said. 'Here's another fine mess you've got me into.'

'Jack,' she whispered. 'I'm sorry.'

'It doesn't matter,' he assured her. 'Nothing matters aside from the fact that we had a little time together and that you made me realize that I wasn't quite beyond redemption. I've done some pretty cruddy things in my time, Lisa, things I'm not proud of. But I realized the other day that you mean more to me than just about anything and I'll always be proud of that . . .'

He was aware that he was rambling and also that he was playing for time, while he tried desperately to think of some possible avenue of escape. This time, he just didn't see one . . . unless . . .

A wild idea suggested itself to him and he snatched at it, knowing that at this stage in the game, he had nothing to lose.

'And I think you should go back to Angelito,' he added casually; but he flashed Lisa a meaningful look. 'Play along' it said. She was staring at him, her mouth slightly open. He wasn't sure if she'd registered it or not.

'What was that?' asked Gorman.

'Don't listen to him, boss!' snapped Angelito. 'Bastard would say anything to try and worm his way out of the shit!' Angelito lifted the gun and pressed it to Jack's head. 'What say I finish him right now, save us all a boat-trip?'

'Wait a minute!' snapped Gorman. He moved closer to Jack. 'What did you say?' he demanded.

Jack glanced up at him. He had to keep the expression right. Not surprise, no, no, that wouldn't be convincing. Mild disbelief. Yes, the eyes just so, the smile just the right side of arrogance. 'Oh, come on, Tony, don't pretend you don't know. I already figured it out, that's the set-up between you two, right? You've got Josie and he gets Lisa – sort of a reward for services rendered. I can understand that, it's only natural. How . . . how did you find out about us, by the way?'

Gorman looked confused, like he was trying to work out some complicated equation in his head.

'Er . . . Angel. He . . . he took some photographs.'

'Oh, right. It figures.' Jack turned to grin up at Angelito. 'Well, mate, I've got to hand it to you. You said you'd get her back and I guess you have.'

'Shut the fuck up!' Angelito told him. He looked at Gorman and laughed nervously. 'You can see what they're trying to do, huh?'

'Sure,' said Gorman; but he sounded doubtful.

'Oh, I get it,' said Jack. 'One of *those* arrangements! You both pretend it isn't happening. Well, whatever works for you, I guess. Angel, promise me you'll take good care of her from now on. You know, the only reason she came over to me is because you were too rough with her.'

'It was different with you,' said Lisa; and Jack could have reached out and kissed her. 'You were gentle, considerate. Angel just wanted to fuck for hours. The man's a non-stop sex machine . . .'

Gorman was looking at Angelito now.

'Hey, boss, come *on*!' Angelito looked around the room imploringly. 'I can't believe anybody's listening to this. I mean, it's obvious what they're trying to do, right? Jesus, as if I'd want to fuck *her*! My boss's wife. What do you think I am, crazy?'

'You don't have to pretend, Angel,' Lisa told him. 'Tony knows all about us. I told him, months ago.'

'You what?' Angelito looked totally bewildered now. 'You . . . you tol' him?'

'Yeah, that's right,' said Gorman quietly. 'I know all about it, Angel. And it's OK. When he's gone, you can go right back to it. I don't mind.'

'You . . . you don't?' Angelito grinned, a big, stupid grin. 'Hey, but you know, they make it sound like it was going on a long time. But it was only *once*.'

'Once?' echoed Gorman. 'Just the once was it? Funny, I got the impression . . .'

'Hey no, just the one time. And she wanted it, you know, she came on to me in the car and naturally I . . .' He shrugged, smiled, then looked unsure of himself. 'Just the one time, boss, I swear.' He turned his attention back to Jack. 'Shall I do it now, boss?' He cocked the trigger on the pistol. 'Just say the word and I'll finish him.'

Jack gritted his teeth, waited.

'No,' said Gorman. 'I want to do it. Give me the gun.'

Angelito looked disappointed. He stepped back and handed Gorman the heavy .38 automatic.

'I've never done this before,' said Gorman quietly. 'Where's the best place?'

'Side of the head, boss. Just pop it right in there.'

Gorman nodded sadly. He held the gun against Jack's temple. 'Here?' he asked.

'That's the place! Just squeeze the trigger, real gentle.'

Jack tensed, was suddenly aware of the frantic beating of his heart. An eternity seemed to pass while he knelt there, waiting. Then;

'Just the once?' asked Gorman.

Jack turned his head slightly and looked at him.

'What?' he murmured.

'Wasn't talking to you, sunshine.' Now Gorman lifted the pistol and held it up to Angelito's head. 'Just the fuckin' *once*?' he snarled.

Angelito's eyes widened in astonishment.

'Boss?' he whispered. 'Don't fool around with that—'

'Answer me you scumbag! You fucked my wife once?'

Too late, Angelito registered the impossibility of his situation. His mouth dropped open and a pathetic whining sound came out of it.

The bang of the gun was almost deafening in the enclosed space. The bullet punched a neat round hole in Angelito's temple and threw out a spray of blood and bone fragments behind him. He went staggering backwards on rubbery legs, his arms gesticulating wildly, his mouth opening and closing. To Jack it looked like a ghastly parody of his John Travolta routine at the disco. He flailed backwards for some ten feet before he struck the back wall. His knees buckled and he slid down in an untidy heap on the floor, leaving a thick crimson trail on the white plaster. He remained in a sitting position and the contents of his shattered skull continued to pulse out on to the tiles.

There was a terrible silence for several long minutes. Jack could hear the last reverberations of the shot ringing in his ears. He knelt there, trying not to look at Angelito's body. Then Farnell spoke, his face grey with shock.

'Jesus Christ, Tony . . .'

'Shut up!' yelled Gorman. 'Don't say a fucking word!' He was standing there, weaving unsteadily, the smoking gun hanging at his side. The room stank of cordite. He took a hesitant step forward and pointed at Angelito's body. 'I trusted that cunt!' he roared. 'He was like a son to me. I took 'im from nowhere and made him into somebody. Gave 'im good money . . . even gave 'im a solid gold lighter, specially inscribed . . . and how did he repay me? By shaggin' my wife, that's 'ow! I mean, can't I trust anybody? Can't I trust a single one of yer? Who else has had her, eh? You Bill? Raul?' He swung the gun between them like an incriminating finger and they cringed visibly, fearful of another killing shot.

Jack, still kneeling on the floor, watched Gorman carefully, waiting for a chance to tackle him.

'Well, I showed him, didn' I? I'm Tony Gorman! I'm the man what pulled off the crime of the century!' He extended his arm and sighted up on an imaginary target. 'Nobody messes with me!' He swung suddenly around until he had Lisa squarely in his sights. She stared back at him defiantly. 'Not you,' he whispered. 'Not ever again . . .'

Jack tensed himself, knowing it was now or never; but in that instant, Gorman swung around again, pointing the pistol straight at Jack's forehead. 'And not you, Jacko!' He grinned insanely, gave Jack a manic wink. Then a calm seemed to settle over him. He lowered the gun and walked across to the mantelpiece. He picked up a bottle of Scotch and took a leisurely swig from it. 'Now fuck off the pair of you,' he said.

Jack stared at him.

'What?' he gasped.

'You 'eard. Fuck off! If you want her so much, you can 'ave the moaning bitch. I'm well rid of 'er. But ... don't go thinking she's a catch. If she goes, she takes nothing with her, not a penny to her name. You want 'er, that's all you get, sunshine. I'll phone the bank in the mornin' and cancel every last one of 'er credit cards.'

Jack considered this for a moment.

'OK,' he said. He got uncertainly to his feet. 'That suits me.'

'Oh, does it now?' Gorman laughed. 'You don't know what you're lettin' yourself in for, son. A woman like Lisa, she's used to 'avin' things. The things that only money can buy. I bet you 'aven't got two brass farthings to rub together, 'ave you?'

'No,' admitted Jack. 'Frank Nolan has, but ...'

'But you can't go on being him for very much longer, can you? Specially when the cops will be getting an anonymous tip-off tomorrow, about that body they found down the road.'

'Think so?' asked Jack.

'You can depend on it.'

'OK, so we're skint. I can handle that.'

'Can you? Can you really? Well, let's see what the little lady has to say, shall we?' He turned to look at Lisa. 'What do you reckon? Think about it. No money, no cheque books, no credit cards. And don't even think about alimony, 'cos I'll see to it that you won't get a penny out of me, not even when I die. I'll leave everything to Josie and the kid. That's the deal, darlin'. 'Ow d'yer like them apples?'

Lisa stood up slowly.

'I'm not going empty handed,' she said.

Gorman laughed triumphantly. 'What did I tell you?' he asked Jack. 'See, she can't exist without what I can give 'er!'

Lisa ignored the taunt.

'I want to take one suitcase,' she said. 'There's things I need. Passport, make-up, some warm clothes . . .'

'Make-up? Warm clothes?' Gorman tilted back his head and roared laughter. 'Can you believe it, Jacko? Can you honestly believe it? I give 'er what she says she wants and she won't go without 'er fuckin' make-up! Oh, you kill me, Princess, you really do. Now if you're going, go, before I change my mind.'

Jack stepped across to her and took her by the arm.

'Come on, Lisa,' he said.

'No!' She was adamant. 'One godamned suitcase! After all the years you've taken from me, you owe me that much at least.'

They glared at each other in silence for a moment.

Gorman seemed to be debating whether or not to hit her again. Then he sagged, visibly. His eyes filled with tears.

'Get the suitcase,' he said quietly. 'I'll give you five minutes.'

Lisa nodded. She pushed past Farnell, walked quickly out of the room. Gorman moved across to the chair she had vacated and slumped down into it. He looked suddenly tired and rather frail. Jack moved across to the doorway and waited awkwardly. He kept one eye on the pistol in Gorman's hand.

'Thanks,' he said quietly.

Gorman glared at him. 'Don't thank me, you cunt! If I ever see you again, you'll be more than sorry. Understand?'

Jack nodded. 'I understand,' he said.

'You know what's really funny? I liked you, Jacko. I did. I thought we was going to be mates, you and me. I was glad it was you writin' my book. I thought we was kindred spirits.'

'Maybe we are,' said Jack; and was surprised to discover that he really meant it.

There was a long, long silence. Then Lisa appeared at the door. She had put on a suede jacket and was carrying a large suitcase. Jack stepped forward and took it from her. It was heavy. She looked into the room at Gorman but he was gazing at the tiled floor, as though searching for the answer to some unseen riddle.

'Let's go,' said Lisa.

Jack nodded. The two of them walked quickly through

the dining room and lounge and out into the night. Jack took big gulps of air. He opened the rear doors of the jeep and flung her case in beside his. He slammed the door, walked around to the front and climbed into the driver's seat. Lisa got in beside him.

'In case you were wondering why I was so intent on taking that case,' she said quietly. 'There's two million dollars in it. Oh, and some diamonds.'

Jack glanced at her, feigning surprise.

'No make-up?' he asked.

She smiled. 'I can always buy some,' she said.

He put the car into gear and drove towards the open gates. He accelerated along the driveway and headed down towards the road.

'I can hardly believe it,' he told Lisa. 'We've made it clear!'

Behind him in the darkness, two headlights flicked on and a red Polo convertible performed a ragged U-turn, before following in pursuit.

Raul Martinez waited until Gorman had put down the pistol and had walked across to the drinks cabinet to help himself to a Scotch. Then he cleared his throat politely.

'Uh . . . Tony?'

'What?'

'I think maybe is best I go,' he gestured vaguely at Angelito's body. 'You got some cleaning up to do and er . . . I think maybe is best, you know. I can phone for a taxi.'

'Sure, whatever.'

'But uh . . . I head back home in a couple of days, so I was thinking . . .'

Gorman sighed. He turned his head to look at Farnell. 'Get this arsehole his money, will you?' he snapped.

Farnell nodded. Martinez was clearly too nervous to bridle at being called an arsehole. He followed Farnell out of the room. Gorman filled a glass with whisky. He took a gulp of it and then moved across to look at Angelito's body. He noticed how the boy still had a perfect, movie-star grin on his face. Sitting there, it looked like he was beaming at an imaginary camera. It was a pity. He'd been a good driver and an even better dancer. Gorman was going to miss the dancing. He wondered about advertising for a female chauffeur, somebody who was also useful in a tight corner. A woman like that would be hard to find, he decided, but the interviews would be great fun.

Farnell came back into the room, his face furious.

'It's gone, Tony!' he gasped.

Gorman stared at him. 'What's gone?'

'The money. The fucking two million. Lisa must have taken it with her. The diamonds too . . . she must have known the combination of the safe!'

Gorman gazed at Farnell for a moment in complete bewilderment.

'You mean . . .'

'Gone. All of it. She's ripped us off!'

'*Make-up*,' said Gorman quietly.

'What?'

'One suitcase.' Gorman grinned. 'That was all she

wanted. One bloody suitcase.' He began to chuckle. 'Oh Jesus, Bill, you've got to 'and it to 'em, 'aven't yer? Cheeky fuckers!'

And now he was laughing fit to burst, fresh tears squeezing themselves down his red cheeks. 'Oh, Bill, it's brilliant! It's bloody brilliant! They conned me, Bill. They stood here face to face with me and they pulled it off!'

'Tony? Don't you think we should go after them?'

Gorman tilted back his head and roared.

'I do! Oh yes, I do, really, honestly! But Bill boy, you wanna know the truth? I can't be arsed. Two million quid? I reckon they've earned it. She stood there, face to face and she turned me over. Reckon she 'ad a good teacher, don't you? Besides . . .' He paused, glanced down at the body on the floor. 'I've gone and shot the bleedin' driver, 'aven't I?'

Bill just stood there staring and Gorman laughed and laughed, until the tears flooded down his cheeks.

Chapter Thirty-One

Jack drove slowly on the deserted roads, his gaze fixed to the unwinding ribbon of tarmac rising through the foothills ahead of him, illuminated in the glow of his headlights. He had turned north at the earliest opportunity and the road was cutting into the heart of the Serrania de Ronda. It was only just beginning to dawn on him that he had made it clear. By killing Angelito, Gorman had effectively removed any chance of pursuit. Now all that was needed was for Jack to put sufficient miles between himself and *chez* Gorman.

He felt relief settling through him like a tranquilizing drug and he began to realize how close he had come to death back there. At the time, there had been no opportunity to consider it. Everything had sped by in an adrenalin rush of unreality. Even with Angelito's gun pressed to the back of his head, even hearing the ugly metallic click of the hammer, Jack had refused to believe that his number was really up.

Now he saw that only luck had intervened, coming to his aid when he most needed it. Angelito had received the bullet with Jack's name on it. Thinking of that made him feel curiously light-headed and he was suddenly aware of an acute tingling sensation in every part of his body. He was alive, at a time when life had never seemed so precious.

He glanced at Lisa, but she seemed preoccupied with her own thoughts. Perhaps she too was contemplating her narrow escape . . . or maybe she was simply planning how she would spend the money in the case.

Jack smiled. Something else he had forgotten about in all the excitement. Lisa had promised him half of whatever they got. Two million . . . could there really be that much? And diamonds, she'd said something about diamonds . . .

He glanced in his rear-view mirror as headlights came looming out of the darkness behind him. They were on full beam and after a few moments, it was difficult to look in the mirror any more. The vehicle was accelerating. It settled into position, a few feet from his rear bumper and Jack gave a tut of annoyance. He waited for the car to overtake, but it didn't, it hung right in there, as though the other driver was content to follow.

Jack frowned. He pressed down on the accelerator and got up to sixty miles an hour. The other car accelerated too, maintaining that dangerously short distance from the jeep's bumper.

A nagging doubt assailed Jack. Perhaps Gorman had found a reserve driver. Perhaps he had already discovered the deception and had set off in hot pursuit . . . He tried to persuade himself that he was being overimaginative. All that was behind him was a road-hog. And yet, if that was the case, why didn't he overtake?

Ahead of him, Jack spotted a signpost, a junction coming up a short distance ahead on his right. *OK*, he thought, *let's put it to the test* . . .

When he came to the junction, he didn't bother to indicate, just slewed the jeep hard to the right and went around in a tight, reckless skid, fighting with the wheel to keep the vehicle from sliding out of control. He found himself on a lesser road, little more than a dirt track, leading upwards at a steady incline. The jeep's rear wheels kicked up clouds of dust, which broiled restlessly in the glow of the tail lights. Jack peered hopefully into the rear-view mirror and grunted as the other car's headlights stabbed through the intervening screen.

Lisa was staring at Jack, a little shaken by the unexpected manoeuvre. 'What's the matter?' she demanded.

'Someone following us,' he said quietly. 'Maybe Tony had second thoughts about letting us go.'

Lisa frowned. 'Could be they've discovered the money's gone.' She glanced in the rear-view mirror. 'I don't recognize that car – it's not one of ours.'

'Police, then? Christ, I hope not. That money's going to take some explaining away. Would Tony have been crazy enough to put them on our tail?'

'I doubt it. He'd have some explaining of his own to do . . . besides, he hates the police, he's absolutely paranoid about them.' She was twisting around in her seat now, craning her neck to get a better view of the vehicle. 'Doesn't look like a police car,' she told Jack.

'OK, so maybe Tony phoned one of his crooked friends to come after us.'

Lisa shook her head. 'How could they have found us so quickly? And who'd ever dream of looking for us out on these roads . . .?'

'Well it has to be *somebody!*' snarled Jack. 'Unless . . .' His eyes widened in realization. Suddenly, he knew who was in that car, knew it as surely as he had known that he would achieve that fateful Full House back at Leo's card game. He knew the calm grey eyes that watched him from the following vehicle. He knew the big, powerful hands with the long spatulate fingers. Jack had crushed four of those fingers beneath the heel of his shoe, not so very long ago. He remembered Eddie Mulryan's bruised and battered face, staring at him as he walked through passport control, the way the eyes had promised him that it wasn't over yet, not by a long chalk. Fear jolted through him now but he tried to retain an outward show of calm for Lisa's benefit.

'Fasten your seatbelt,' he said quietly.

She did as she was told and helped him steady the wheel, while he secured his own belt. The road ahead was rising more steeply now. He punched in the four-wheel drive, thinking that it might give him an edge on the other vehicle. He urged the jeep up to seventy and it bucked and shuddered on the uneven surface of the road. The other car hung on his tail, as though secured by a length of invisible rope.

'You know who's back there, don't you?' asked Lisa fearfully.

'Yes.'

'The man you told me about? From England?'

Jack nodded grimly. He threw the jeep into a bend and the tyres shrieked in protest. The road was still rising and for an instant, the headlights picked out a steep rocky descent to their right. Now the other car was moving closer, trying to nose alongside. Jack swore viciously and put his foot down to the floor. The jeep crested a hump in the road and momentarily lost contact with the ground. It came down again with a bone jarring crash but they'd gained a little on the other car. It dropped back behind them again. The speedometer brushed eighty miles an hour, perilously fast on a road like this, but the route was straight now, rising higher in the darkness ahead. To Jack's right, only the occasional twinkling light against deep black. To his left, the land rose into rolling hills, jagged outcrops of granite, stark white in the headlights.

If he kept his head, he told himself, maybe he could outrun his pursuers. He glanced at Lisa. She sat grim-faced and silent, bracing herself against the juddering of the jeep, her gaze fixed resolutely on the road ahead. In the glow of the dashboard, the bruises on her face looked doubly shocking. The scab on Jack's right palm itched maddeningly where it touched the steering wheel. He thought back to the night he had acquired the wound. It had been what, eight days ago? A lifetime seemed to have passed by since then, but Mulryan had somehow tracked him down. If he caught Jack now, he wouldn't be content with just maiming him . . .

The road dropped away with heart stopping abruptness and he saw the narrow stone bridge over the stream, just as the jeep left the road in a long, stomach churning leap. He grappled ineffectually with the wheel, the tyres spinning on empty air and he heard Lisa gasp. Then the chassis came down with a thud, rubber squealed against gravel and the jeep veered sideways. It entered the bridge at the wrong angle. Jack wrenched the wheel back to the left and there was a grinding roar as the chassis glanced off the stone parapet, flinging up rubble and a shower of sparks. Somehow he kept the bonnet pointed straight ahead and they were through the gap and powering upwards again. He glanced hopefully in the mirror, but the little convertible had negotiated the bridge with ease and was gaining again.

'You'll kill us both if you go on like this!' cried Lisa. Jack didn't answer. He was aware of the other car moving up on his left again. Now he could see the big, hunched figure in the passenger seat, the face partially obscured by a broad-brimmed straw hat. He felt a jolt of hatred punch into him and almost instinctively, he eased back on the accelerator. As the car moved up alongside, he turned the wheel to the left, slamming the wing of the jeep hard against the Polo, trying to shunt it off the road against the rocky incline. It moved away a few feet, then swung back, sideswiping the jeep with a grinding crash. The jeep swung out to the verge of the road, wheels kicking gravel over the edge of what was fast becoming a sheer drop. Jack cursed, moved the jeep back to the centre of the road. The other car edged out to meet it and the two vehicles locked together with a dull clang and went screeching onwards, both drivers wrestling for supremacy.

'Jack, for Christ's sake!' Lisa was sitting bolt upright, staring straight ahead, her face frozen into a mask of fear. Up ahead, something was hurtling towards them, two headlights blazing out of the darkness. The headlights were too high up to be a car. It was an articulated lorry, thundering down the incline, its horn wailing.

'Pull out,' whispered Lisa. 'Drop back for God's sake!'

Jack shook his head grimly. 'Let *them* drop back,' he snarled. He kept his foot down to the floor, glancing left, he could see Mulryan gazing calmly straight ahead, his ruined face illuminated now in the glare of the oncoming juggernaut. A woman sat beside him in the driving seat, an expression of sheer terror on her face. The lorry was close now. Jack could make out the driver, his eyes bulging, his mouth working around a string of Spanish curses. The blast of the horn filled Jack's head.

Suddenly, the Polo was gone, dropping away with a scrape of metal on metal. The lorry thundered past, a great, brutish colossus, filling the interior of the jeep with a blaze of light. Then it was no more than a set of red tail lights sweeping on down the hillside. Jack studied his rear-view mirror hopefully but his hopes were instantly dashed. There were the other car's headlights swinging out to overtake him once more.

Jack groaned, thumped his left fist down hard on the dashboard, sending ripples of pain jolting through his hand.

451

The road angled steeply upwards again and he stamped down on the accelerator, coaxing the jeep back up to top speed. There was a sheer rock wall to his left now and it melted to an insubstantial grey blur as the speedometer crept back up to eighty. He noted with satisfaction that he was lengthening his lead now, the other driver no doubt intimidated by the near miss back there. If he could just increase that lead, maybe he could lose them at the next turn off.

He glanced in the mirror again. The car was dropping further back, maybe they had engine trouble . . .

'Jack!' The one word, spoken fearfully, snapped his attention back to the road. He registered the scatter of fallen rock, noted the large boulder that rested on the right-hand verge. He attempted to take evasive action but he hadn't reckoned on the jeep's speed. The rocks were shooting towards him in a mind-numbing blur and his chance was lost in the split second gap between forming the intention and acting upon it. The jeep's right front wheel hit the largest boulder and flipped upwards. There was a horrible instant when the world seemed to invert and a shocking moment of deep silence as the jeep left the ground and went turning through the air.

We're dead, thought Jack with a calmness that surprised him.

The jeep came down on its left side with an impact that slammed the breath out of him. He was dimly aware of Lisa screaming somewhere and then the jeep was skidding down the road on its side, with a noise that sounded like worlds colliding. Jack kept his hands on the wheel, bracing himself as best he could and the jeep was still turning. It rolled over on to its back and Jack felt the seat belt bite into his shoulder. Flying glass peppered his face with liquid fire. Blackness spilled in through the shattered windshield to engulf him and then, for a time, there was nothing.

Chapter Thirty-Two

Jack woke in chaos, in a dark up-turned world of pain and petrol fumes. He hung there for a moment, trying to collect his scattered senses. His mind was smoke.

'Jack!' Lisa's voice brought him into focus. Perhaps she had been speaking to him for some time. He shook off the last shreds of unconsciousness with a groan. He knew exactly where he was now and the knowledge brought him no comfort at all.

'Lisa? You OK?'

'Think so. Uh . . . not sure . . . you?'

He grunted, felt around for his seatbelt release, but it wasn't where it should be. He tried to stay rational, reminded himself he was upside down. His hand found metal and he tugged at it desperately. There was a click and he fell on to the roof in a sprawl of arms and legs.

'Gotta get out,' he told the darkness. 'The petrol . . .'

He heard a metallic click beside him, knew that Lisa had released her own belt. He twisted around awkwardly, straining muscles, tearing his jacket on fragments of broken glass. His hands found the door handle and he lost precious moments pulling on it the wrong way. Then he had the presence of mind to push and the door unlatched but wouldn't open more than a chink, as it ground against the surface of the road. The stink of petrol engulfed him and he fought his rising panic. He scrambled back around and pounded the door frame with his feet. It gave a little each time. Beside him, Lisa groaned.

'Hang on,' he urged her. 'Nearly there . . .'

The gap was wide enough to crawl through. He reached back, grabbed a handful of her clothing, pulled her after him. He pushed his head and shoulders out into the real world and crawled free of the wreckage, cutting his hands and knees on the broken glass that littered the road. Free, he turned back and pulled Lisa after him. Her face twisted in a grimace of pain.

'My leg . . .' she whispered.

He ignored her, continued to pull her free. He got her out on to the road which was swimming with spilled petrol. He gathered her in his arms and helped her to her feet. Now he could see the inverted wreck from which they had just escaped, the roof crushed flat, petrol pouring from the ruptured tank in a steady stream. It was a wonder they weren't dead.

'Come on,' he told her. They limped, stumbled, staggered downhill from the ruined jeep.

'The case!' groaned Lisa. 'The money . . .'

He shook his head.

'Keep moving,' he told her. 'It could blow!'

But she was pulling stubbornly against him. He swore,

turned to look back at the jeep, saw that the rear doors were hanging open and that a jumble of luggage was strewn for yards along the surface of the road.

'Not there,' he assured her. 'Now for Christ's sake, will you come on?'

He threw an arm around her waist and propelled her onwards, keeping her on her feet until they had put a reasonably safe distance between themselves and the jeep. Then he released his hold and she sank to the ground exhausted. Jack slumped down beside her. Now they were out of immediate danger, he felt exhaustion settle around him like a cloak and he became aware of pain – a sharp stabbing sensation where he had gashed his forehead, a dull ache in his right shoulder. Lisa had suffered a nasty cut on one knee and blood was pulsing through the fabric of her jeans. Jack fished a handkerchief from his pocket and tied it tight around the wound.

As he did so, he scanned their surroundings, searching for a potential escape route but he knew instantly that there was no hope. Neither he nor Lisa had the strength to try and run. Impossible to scale the steep heights to their left nor scramble down the stony decline to their right. All they could do now was sit and wait as the red car came slowly up the road towards them, its headlights illuminating the area where Jack and Lisa were sprawled.

'I don't suppose you're carrying a gun?' Jack asked Lisa.

There was no reply. He looked closer and saw that she had passed out on him.

'It was just a thought,' he said glumly.

The car came to a halt. There was a long silence and Jack imagined Mulryan sitting there watching, probably savouring this moment, imprinting it on to his mind, a mental snapshot to keep as a souvenir.

The car doors opened and two people got out. Mulryan looked different, he looked somehow uncomfortable in the unfamiliar clothes, the Bermuda shirt and straw fedora. Jack could see the woman properly now, a big-boned woman with teased up hair, she must be the one the hotel clerk had mentioned. Where in hell had Mulryan recruited her? They began to walk slowly across the intervening space, strolling, no need to hurry now that the chase was over.

Jack glanced nervously up the road, praying to see headlights approaching, his only hope of salvation. But nothing came. The road was deserted. Now he became aware of the deep silence that hung over the area. He slipped an arm protectively around Lisa and she moaned softly. Jack told himself that Mulryan might spare her. After all, she had done nothing to harm him.

He waited. Mulryan was close now, illuminated by the glow of his car's headlamps. He was smiling, showing those perfect teeth. Like an old friend greeting him in this strange place.

Mulryan came to a halt a few feet away. He nodded politely.

'Mr Doyle,' he said. 'So I've caught up with you at last.'

Jack bowed his head in defeat.

'You're a hard man to shake off,' he said. He lifted his gaze and looked at the woman. 'And you're quite a driver,' he observed.

The woman was looking at him with avid interest, as though anticipating some sport. She glanced at Mulryan. 'You going to kill him?' she asked.

Mulryan nodded. 'Oh yes, sweetie. I think so. You might want to take a little walk or something. This won't be pleasant.'

'I'll stay and watch,' she said calmly. 'If it's all the same to you.'

Mulryan shrugged. He reached to the back of his shirt with his left hand and brought out a big, jag-bladed knife. He held it out so Jack could see it.

'Like it?' he asked. 'A present from a friend, Toledo steel.'

Jack nodded. 'It's charming,' he muttered. He felt a coldness permeating his bones. So this was how it was going to end, here in this godforsaken, lonely place. Lisa moaned in her sleep, as though aware of what was about to happen. He reached out a hand to stroke her hair. Mulryan hesitated, glanced down at her, as though noticing her for the first time.

'Who's she?' he asked.

'Her name's Lisa.'

'Nice name.' His eyes narrowed suspiciously. 'She's familiar from some place . . .'

'Listen, Eddie, you don't have to hurt her, OK? It's between you and me, right? Just the two of us.'

Mulryan looked doubtful.

'We're all judged by the company we keep, Mr Doyle. Rotten old world, isn't it?'

Jack licked his lips.

'Come on, Eddie, you know she's no threat to you . . .'

'But I don't know that, do I? How do I know you haven't given her my name? I'm sorry, Mr Doyle, but . . .'

'Listen! Supposing I offered to *buy* her life?'

Mulryan frowned. 'I'm listening,' he said.

'Somewhere in that wreckage, there's a case. It's got two million dollars in it.'

Mulryan and his woman exchanged glances. The woman's eyes flashed with excitement.

'Go on with you,' said Mulryan.

'I swear I'm telling you the truth! We ripped it off Lisa's husband. You . . . you could just take that money and forget you ever saw us.'

Mulryan chuckled, shook his head. 'Maybe I could forget that I saw *her*,' he said. 'But you, Mr Doyle, no amount of money could buy *you* out of trouble.'

'I'll go and see if it's there,' said the woman breathlessly. She started back up the hill, wobbling precariously in her sling-back shoes.

'Be careful,' Mulryan shouted after her. He turned back and hefted the knife experimentally. The blade flashed in the moonlight. 'Still haven't got used to using this left-handed,' he told Jack. 'That's all down to you, Mr Doyle. Put me in a right mess, didn't you?'

'What did you expect, you were going to kill me, weren't you? Just because a scumbag like Lou Winters gave you the nod.'

'Don't you speak ill of Mr Winters. He's dead now.'

'So I heard. Leo King told me. And I suspect you were responsible for it.'

'That was unfortunate . . .'

'Oh, go on Eddie, next you'll be telling me you didn't enjoy doing it! That's what you always say, isn't it? You don't enjoy it. But the truth is of course, that you love what you do. And like every psychopath, you make excuses for it.'

'And what was your excuse, Mr Doyle? I take it Tam McGiver didn't drown without some assistance?'

'I didn't think you knew him. He claimed not to know you, just before he died. And by the way, it was self-defence. He was trying to cut my throat at the time.'

Mulryan shook his head. 'I should have known. A man without honour, that one. Not like us, eh, Mr Doyle?'

'Us? Don't kid yourself, Eddie, we've got nothing in common. Anyway, what are you waiting for? Let's get it over with. Why all this talk?'

Mulryan spread his hands in a gesture of appeasement.

'Oh, come now, Mr Doyle, I've travelled a long way to find you. You surely don't begrudge me having a friendly little chat, do you?'

'Some chat!' growled Jack. 'You just like to gloat, that's all. So why don't you just finish it? Then you and the Bride of Frankenstein there can be on your way!'

Mulryan's eyes narrowed. He glanced back at Rosie and then scowled at Jack.

'There's no need to be insultin',' he said.

Jack sensed an opening and took it, not caring now what happened. At the back of his mind was that if he could make Mulryan angry, it might put him off guard.

'Well, let's face it, Eddie, she's no oil painting, is she? Where did you pick her up, *Exchange & Mart*?'

Anger flashed across Mulryan's face. He dropped into a half crouch and Jack steeled himself to meet the impact; but then Mulryan hesitated, smiled. He straightened up again.

'Oh, I know what you're tryin' to do. Get me rattled, isn't that it? But it shan't work, Mr Doyle, I'm wise to your little tricks. I'm going to take you in my own sweet time. I'm going to pop you as cool as a cucumber.'

'Sure, whatever you say. But listen, I want to make this deal with you . . .'

Mulryan tilted back his head and laughed.

'You're not in a position to make deals, Mr Doyle.'

'OK, not for me. For Lisa here. I'm giving you that money, on the understanding that you'll let her go. Grant me this one favour, Eddie and at least you'll be proving that you've still got an ounce of humanity left in you. That you still have a choice.'

Mulryan shook his head.

'Oh, now isn't that a pretty speech? Such a good talker. I admire that, Mr Doyle. I've always admired that in you. I reckon you could talk your way out of just about anything, if you put your mind to it. But how clever are you really? What are you like with riddles?'

Jack gazed at him for a moment. 'Riddles? What are you talking about?'

'I've got a riddle for you. If you get the answer right, then maybe . . . just maybe I'll let your lady friend go.'

' "Maybe" isn't good enough. How about a promise?'

'I might break a promise.'

'No, I don't believe you would. You promised you'd

come after me and you did. I think, if nothing else, you are a man of your word.'

Mulryan considered this. Then he smiled.

'All right,' he said. 'It's a promise. I won't kill her, not if you get it right.'

'OK, let's hear the riddle.' Jack shifted his position, leaned back on one hand. His fingers went into a warm wetness and a smell came to him, the powerful stink of petrol. He made an effort to keep his face impassive, but his mind evaluated the situation. He sneaked a glance towards the wreckage of the jeep and saw the long trail of petrol, running downhill across the parched dirt surface of the road. The woman had just reached the jeep. She was leaning in the open doors, hunting through the jumble of litter in the back.

'As I was going to St Ives . . .'

Jack snapped back to look at Mulryan.

'Sorry, I didn't catch that!'

'Pay attention, Mr Doyle. You're a gambling man and this will be the last flutter you ever have!'

'Sorry, go on . . .'

'As I was going to St Ives, I met a man with seven wives . . .'

Jack nodded. He slipped a hand nonchalantly into his jacket pocket and Mulryan leapt forward, holding the blade of the knife against Jack's throat.

'Steady,' whispered Jack. He drew his hand slowly out again to show that he was holding a packet of cigarettes. 'Need to concentrate,' he said.

Mulryan glared at him. 'That was very stupid, Mr

Doyle. Maybe we shan't bother with the riddle after all.'

'No, go on, I'm fascinated,' croaked Jack.

Mulryan frowned. He pulled the knife away and stepped back. He continued. 'Every wife had seven sacks. Every sack had seven cats . . .'

Jack extracted a cigarette and put it between his lips.

'Every cat had seven kits. Kits, cats, sacks and wives. How many were going to St Ives?'

Jack slid a hand slowly into his trouser pocket. The Zippo was there where it always was. He drew it out, flicked back the top. He struck the flint. It sparked, but didn't light.

Mulryan was watching him expectantly.

'Well?' he asked.

'Run it by me again,' suggested Jack. He struck the flint. Only a spark. Godamned thing must be low on fuel.

'You've heard the riddle,' Mulryan told him. 'Now give me an answer!'

'Well, let me see now. Kits, cats, sacks and wives . . .' He struck the flint a third time. A faint spark. The wick glowed redly, fizzed and died. 'So that's seven, times seven, times seven . . .'

Mulryan smiled confidently.

'Plus the husband and the man telling the story . . .' Jack gave a tut of irritation. 'Eddie, you wouldn't have a light, would you? I can't think straight without a fag.'

Mulryan shook his head. 'Oh, I don't think I should be encouraging you to smoke. It's bad for your health!' He threw back his head and guffawed with laughter.

'Come on, Eddie, I know you've got a lighter!'

Mulryan chuckled. 'You're not catching me with that trick again!' he said. 'To put my good hand in my pocket, I'd have to put down the knife, wouldn't I? Do I honestly look that stupid?'

'Yes, as a matter of fact, but that's got nothing to do with it.' Jack offered up a silent prayer and gave the flint a last, desperate flick. The damn thing lit, the flame burning strong and bright. It surprised him so much, he almost dropped it. He leaned forward and lit his cigarette. He took a deep drag on it and thought that a cigarette had never tasted so good in his entire life.

'So, let me see now,' he murmured. 'Kits, cats, sacks and wives.' He paused, then looked Mulryan straight in the eye. He smiled. 'One,' he said. 'The answer is *one*. Sorry Eddie, but I learned that at school.'

Mulryan stared at him in dismay. 'You ... you knew it all along? But that's not fair!'

'Who said life had to be fair, Eddie?'

Mulryan's eyes narrowed. He'd heard those words somewhere before, a very long time ago. And he'd had plenty of time to prepare the answer. 'Nobody,' he whispered. 'But don't worry, I'll keep my promise. I won't kill the girl.' He grinned. 'That'll be Rosie's job.' He raised the knife and took a step closer.

'Just before we get down to the nitty gritty,' said Jack. 'I've got a little riddle for you. How fast can fire travel in a straight line?'

Mulryan stopped and glared at him.

'What?' he cried.

Jack leaned backwards and dropped the lighter into

the petrol. The effect was dramatic. Fire leapt upwards in both directions, one of them climbing the hillside in a whoosh of bright yellow flame.

Mulryan's jaw dropped open. He glanced towards the jeep, saw Rosie still rummaging in the back of it.

'Rosie!' he screamed. And then he was running towards her, moving with surprising speed for a big man, his sandalled feet slapping in the dust. Rosie had glanced up at his shout and now she saw the flame speeding towards her. She stood there mesmerized, her mouth open and Eddie was trying to race the flame, as it darted across the last few yards of intervening space. And now Rosie was turning her head, her gaze tracing the trickle of petrol back to its source and she finally got her legs into motion, but instead of running, she was trying to stamp out the flame before it could reach the jeep and it was almost comical, because the flame just danced across her foot and moved on. Then Eddie reached her, his big arms outstretched to embrace her, to try and pull her away.

Jack covered Lisa with his body but couldn't take his eyes off the couple by the jeep, silhouetted by the flame as it flickered up the side of the vehicle, reached the rupture in the petrol tank – and then seemed to go out.

'Oh shit,' said Jack. There was a moment of deep silence, deeper than anything he had ever heard before.

Then the jeep exploded quite suddenly, erupting into a great orange blaze that belched outwards, engulfing the two figures beside it. For an instant, Jack glimpsed them deep in the flames, embracing like lovers. They seemed to be waltzing, their hair blazing like torches, their clothes blackening like old paper. Then they were sucked into the inferno and the shockwave hit Jack and Lisa, flattening them to the ground. Even at that distance, Jack could feel the scorching heat on his face. The noise of the explosion erupted in their ears and passed on over their heads. Chunks of metal debris crashed down on the road around them, raising plumes of dust. Then there was just the blazing wreckage up there on the hillside, illuminating the whole area for hundreds of yards.

'Jesus,' whispered Lisa. Jack glanced at her in surprise and realized that the noise of the explosion had shaken her from her slumber. She lay there, looking at the conflagration, her mouth open. 'What . . . what happened?' she whispered.

Jack shrugged. 'He didn't run fast enough,' he said. He got painfully to his feet and began to limp closer to the wreckage, aware of the terrible heat on his face, but wanting to be sure . . .

He got as close as he could, so close that the very air he breathed seemed to burn in his lungs. He stared into the blazing orange depths of the fire, hoping for a glimpse of the bodies. Something shifted in the hellish depths, something solid that seemed to displace the flames. Jack narrowed his eyes, lifted a hand to shield them. He made a small sound of disbelief.

Something came stumbling out of the fire. It was man-shaped, but there was little left to identify it as a man. No clothes, no hair, no features to speak of, just a shambling

upright column of sizzling meat. It was cradling something in what had once been its arms. Something much
like itself, but something that was clearly dead. The man-
thing staggered to the edge of the flames and stood there
swaying like a drunk. The blackened eyes clearly had no
sight left in them. The ragged maw of a mouth opened,
noisily trying to draw a tortured breath, revealing the
one remaining source of identification. The false teeth,
grinning perfectly from their charred surroundings. As
Jack watched, horrified, the burned lips collapsed and
the teeth fell down the thing's chin and on to the ground.

Mulryan shuddered, gave a last, wheezing groan. Then
he stooped, twisted, fell heavily into the dust, still cradling Rosie tightly in his smouldering arms. There was the
sudden overpowering stink of roasting meat. Jack turned
away in revulsion, feeling the sting of tears welling in
his eyes.

He walked quickly back to Lisa and helped her to her
feet. He slipped an arm around her and led her away a
short distance. Then they turned back again, to look at
the wreckage, blazing like a funeral pyre under the great
dome of heaven. It would go on burning far into the
night.

Epilogue

Jack woke to a mass of aches and pains. He lay in the unfamiliar bed, in the unfamiliar room and reminded himself that it was over. He turned his head to look at Lisa. She slept the sleep of total exhaustion, her hair tousled on the pillow, her face displaying the cuts and bruises of last night's misadventures. Jack reached out a hand to stroke her hair. She stirred, muttered something but didn't wake.

He turned over, gritted his teeth and sat up with an effort. He moved aside the sheet and got out of bed, then limped over to the window and peered out through the wooden shutters. It was a fine, clear morning. Across the road, people moved in and out through the entrance of a post office. Cars moved up and down the street. He didn't even know the name of this town, it was just a place they had reached in the early hours of the morning, when he could drive Mulryan's car no further. They had chosen a small hotel, somewhere that wouldn't baulk at their grubby, dishevelled appearances. They hadn't had much in the way of luggage, just a few things they had salvaged from the jumble of baggage littered along the road.

He turned back from the window and walked across to the chest of drawers. The attaché case rested on top of it. They had found it after a brief search, still tucked away inside Lisa's suitcase, amongst the other debris littering the roadside. The diamonds, too, were still safe inside the case.

Jack unlatched it and looked at the wads of neatly stacked money inside. He reached out a hand and traced an index finger experimentally across the ranks of printed paper. Touching a fortune didn't feel any different than touching a folded newspaper.

He glanced at Lisa, but she was still in deep sleep. He found his clothes and dressed quickly. Then he took a thick wad of notes and put them into the inside pocket of his jacket. He went out of the room, closing the door gently behind him.

Lisa woke to the sound of a siren. She sat bolt upright in bed, listening intently but the wail of the police car was moving on down the street. She closed her eyes, let out a gasp of relief. Then she realized that she was alone in the room. Her gaze fell on the open attaché case and she noted the gap where some of the money had been removed. Her eyes narrowed and she flung aside the sheets, clambered out of bed. She limped over to the case. She couldn't tell how much was gone, no more than a few thousand dollars, she supposed.

She went to the window and peered out, fighting a

sense of rising panic. They had parked the car some distance away from the hotel and she didn't know if he had taken it or not. Confused, she went and found a packet of cigarettes, then remembered that she had nothing to light them with. She threw them aside and paced the room, wondering what in the hell she was supposed to do now.

The door opened and she turned in surprise to see Jack standing sheepishly in the doorway. He was carrying a paper sack.

'Good morning,' he said.

She went to him, threw her arms around his neck, almost crying with relief.

'You bastard!' she said. 'Why didn't you tell me you were going out. I thought you'd run out on me!'

He shook his head.

'I just went to get us some breakfast,' he told her.

'Breakfast?' She stepped back and looked at him inquiringly.

'I've got freshly made doughnuts and some coffee. I didn't want to wake you.' He nodded at the attaché case. 'I had no money so I took some from there. I hope that was OK.'

She shrugged. 'Half of the money's yours,' she said. 'That was the deal, remember? It's up to you what you do with it.'

He walked across to the table and set down the bag beside the attaché case. He looked at the contents for a moment, then shook his head. 'I can hardly believe we made it,' he said. 'For a while back there . . .'

He left the sentence hanging. Lisa moved to the bed and sat down with a sigh. 'I feel I could sleep for a month,' she said.

'Me too.' He followed her, sat beside her on the bed. 'But we'd best not hang around, just in case Tony has second thoughts.'

Lisa shook her head. 'He won't. I think he probably admired the way we stood up to him. And if he's stupid enough to call the police, I know enough to have him put away for life.' She lay down, easing her aching body on to the mattress. 'So, what now?' she asked him.

'Well, breakfast first. Then maybe a little shopping. We'll need some new clothes. And a good car. After that, we can think about moving on. Head for Madrid and catch a plane somewhere.'

'Where shall we go?'

He thought for a moment. 'I have this vision in my mind. Had it for some time, now. A small tropical island. Palm trees, white sand, clear coral waters. Not much to do other than lie around in the sun, eat, drink, make love. Know anywhere like that?'

She nodded.

'I did a photo shoot once in a place called Tioman. It's a coral island off the east coast of Malaysia. It's about the most beautiful place I've ever seen.'

'Sounds perfect.'

'Or maybe we should go to civilization first. New York. There's a lot of old friends I'd like to catch up with. There's theatres, cinemas, art galleries . . .'

He looked doubtful for a moment, then shrugged his shoulders.

'Well, either way, I don't mind. You decide.'

'No, you!'

He chuckled. 'Looks like we've got a problem,' he observed. 'Tell you what . . .' He reached in his pocket, extracted a coin. 'Heads, Tioman. Tails, New York. What do you say?'

'I say, what the hell?'

He tossed the coin. It span briefly in the air and he caught it, slapped it down on to the back of his hand. 'Heads,' he announced. He extended his hand to show her the coin.

'Hmm.' She glanced at him suspiciously. 'Sure you didn't cheat?'

He laughed, shook his head. 'I should have warned you,' he said. 'I'm lucky like that.'

A selection of bestsellers from Headline

NIGHT OF THE DEAD	Mike Bond	£4.99 ☐
SPEAK NO EVIL	Philip Caveney	£4.99 ☐
GONE	Kit Craig	£4.99 ☐
INADMISSIBLE EVIDENCE	Philip Friedman	£5.99 ☐
QUILLER SOLITAIRE	Adam Hall	£4.99 ☐
HORSES OF VENGEANCE	Michael Hartmann	£4.99 ☐
CIRCUMSTANCES UNKNOWN	Jonellen Heckler	£4.99 ☐
THE ASCENT	Jeff Long	£4.99 ☐
BRING ME CHILDREN	David Martin	£4.99 ☐
THE SIMEON CHAMBER	Steve Martini	£4.99 ☐
A CALCULATED RISK	Katherine Neville	£4.99 ☐
STATE V. JUSTICE	Gallatin Warfield	£5.99 ☐

All Headline books are available at your local bookshop or newsagent, or can be ordered direct from the publisher. Just tick the titles you want and fill in the form below. Prices and availability subject to change without notice.

Headline Book Publishing PLC, Cash Sales Department, Bookpoint, 39 Milton Park, Abingdon, OXON, OX14 4TD, UK. If you have a credit card you may order by telephone – 0235 831700.

Please enclose a cheque or postal order made payable to Bookpoint Ltd to the value of the cover price and allow the following for postage and packing:
UK & BFPO: £1.00 for the first book, 50p for the second book and 30p for each additional book ordered up to a maximum charge of £3.00.
OVERSEAS & EIRE: £2.00 for the first book, £1.00 for the second book and 50p for each additional book.

Name ....

Address ....

....

....

If you would prefer to pay by credit card, please complete:
Please debit my Visa/Access/Diner's Card/American Express (delete as applicable) card no:

Signature .... Expiry Date ....